THE CASE OF THE
RED-HANDED RHESUS

THE CASE OF THE
RED-HANDED RHESUS

A RUE AND LAKELAND MYSTERY

THE CASE OF THE RED-HANDED RHESUS

JESSIE BISHOP POWELL

FIVE STAR
A part of Gale, Cengage Learning

GALE
CENGAGE Learning·

Farmington Hills, Mich • San Francisco • New York • Waterville, Maine
Meriden, Conn • Mason, Ohio • Chicago

GALE
CENGAGE Learning®

LIBRARY OF CONGRESS CATALOGING-IN-PUBLICATION DATA

Powell, Jessie Bishop.
   The case of the red-handed rhesus / Jessie Bishop Powell. —
First edition.
     pages cm — (A Rue and Lakeland mystery)
     ISBN 978-1-4328-3144-8 (hardcover) — ISBN 1-4328-3144-5
(hardcover) — ISBN 978-1-4328-3154-7 (ebook) — ISBN 1-4328-
3154-2 (ebook)
     1. Animal sanctuaries—Fiction. 2. Murder—Investigation—
Fiction. 3. Human animal relationships—Fiction. I. Title.
PS3616.O8797C37 2015
813'.6—dc23   2015022053

First Edition. First Printing: February 2016
Find us on Facebook– https://www.facebook.com/FiveStarCengage
Visit our website– http://www.gale.cengage.com/fivestar/
Contact Five Star™ Publishing at FiveStar@cengage.com

Printed in the United States of America
1 2 3 4 5 6 7 20 19 18 17 16

To all the families, teachers, and staff at Churchill Academy in Montgomery, Alabama.
Every day, you prove that autism has many faces.
You will never be puzzle pieces.

ACKNOWLEDGMENTS

This is a work of fiction, set in a fictitious town, with fictitious characters. All of them live only in my mind, but they wouldn't be there at all if I didn't have help from some monumentally awesome people. Writing is a collaborative effort, even when only one person creates a world. Support systems, first readers, editors, and subject experts are all essential components of any work such as this.

First, I must once again thank my husband Scott for not only taking over most of the childcare and housework so I could complete this book, but for also being my first editor. He is also an amazing writer. Second, I must thank my children for failing to mutiny when I was a less-than-present mother and for acting impressed when told that Mom is an author. Caroline, Sam, even if you're faking it, I appreciate the support. Everyone in our extended family has cheered me on. They shore me up when the inevitable self-doubts creep in.

And *oh* the self-doubt. I am grateful beyond words to Deni Dietz, senior editor at Five Star, who has supported my writing from the first time we met. When she accepted the first book in this series, *The Marriage at the Rue Morgue*, for publication, she gave me validation I'd wanted since I was ten years old. Everyone at Five Star, in fact, was amazing in putting *Rue Morgue* together. The book would not have happened without Tiffany Schofield, Nivette Jackaway, and Diane Piron-Gelman, to name only three. As I send this second title out, I know I am extending my hopes to a highly qualified team.

I have been able to maintain my connection to Detective John K. Schadle, who is now the Chief Deputy of the Adams County, Ohio, Sheriff's Office, and through him to a network of experts. Rural law enforcement is different from work in the city, though I'm sure there are many commonalities. I may have grown up rural, but I've lived in cities for sixteen years now. I need his perspective to help me grasp some things that never made sense and learn others I didn't know.

Lisa Harvey, a fellow writer and social worker, taught me a bit about the foster care system, though I have taken a few creative liberties. Lisa was also the primary voice behind the Trifecta writing challenge. Although the website she created is no longer active, the friendships and communities it has fostered are long-lasting.

Natasha's poem "Soulful Eyes" is really by my friend K. Donovan, to whom I owe a debt of gratitude. I am not a good poet. I don't have the mastery of metaphor that poetry requires, and the piece she created for my character is so perfect.

For my knowledge of primatology, I must thank at least two people. Melanie Bond of the Center for Great Apes in Florida has given me ideas and guidance from the start. Although I pretend my fictitious sanctuary can house orangutans, the Center for Great Apes is really the only great ape sanctuary for orangutans in the United States. Zoos we have several, sanctuaries but one. Her knowledge of these fascinating creatures is combined with a keen editing eye, and I am grateful to have her friendship.

She also connected me with Bob Ingersoll, who (among many other roles) once held the title of president at Mindy's Memory, a primate sanctuary in Oklahoma. He is known for his work with the chimpanzee Nim Chimpsky and his adamant stance against primates as research tools. My imaginary sanctuary is dedicated to studying those animals currently in captivity in order to better understand them and meet their needs. I do not want my novels to promote unethical treatment of primates in any way. Bob helped me understand rhesus macaques and their care. More than that, he gave me a sense of what it feels like to be on the front lines of animal activism, and I am enormously grateful for his time and insights.

After Scott, my first readers for this book were DL Bass Kemp, Melanie Bond, Linda Myers, Kirsten Piccini, and Detective Schadle. I don't expect them to find all my errors, and I have boundless gratitude for their corrections and honesty. First readers don't merely exist to shore up a sagging ego. They are also meant to save me from myself as much as can be done, and they do.

The two children introduced in the book, William and Sara, have Asperger's syndrome, and I also need to thank my personal autism community for ideas and support. Both of my children have Asperger's syndrome, and my psychiatrist assures me I have a "touch of it" as well. This knowledge came as such a relief to me, since I grew up bullied, unable to understand other kids or make sense of their behaviors. I didn't fit in with any group until I was in college. I did *not* recreate my kids or myself in the children in this book. They are drastically different. Instead, I considered my characters first and foremost as characters. Autism was only one aspect of the personalities they developed.

My friend Dawn Beronilla was hugely informative on the topic of receptive language delays. I understand what they are in principle, and I've seen them in action. But receptive language problems are essential to William's role in the book. I needed to know its practicalities, and Dawn gave me some wonderful hardwiring in this area. It is thanks to her that I know what a "cheese-light" is.

My knowledge of autism and Asperger's in particular is formed by personal experience. Asperger's syndrome often gets stereotyped, both in literature and in real life, even though it has technically been lumped under the general heading of "autism spectrum disorder" in the United States. Plenty of nations still acknowledge it as a distinct diagnosis.

I tried to avoid the stereotypes about autism and Asperger's. Not everyone with Asperger's is literal-minded; some speak in fluid metaphors. Although I was a terribly literal-minded child, I got the hang of figurative language early on. Savant syndrome is not the same as Asperger's syndrome. I am not brilliant in anything, and neither are my kids, though we're all pretty good at most things. Asperger's does not mean a lack of empathy. As it happens, that's something I've always suffered from an overabundance of. Asperger's doesn't mean speaking in an uninflected robot voice. My kids and I have always had a full vocal range. Indeed, when my daughter *was* working through some speech issues, she was always easy to understand because her tone of voice was usually clear. Asperger's doesn't always mean an avoidance of eye contact, or a lack of enjoyment of social activities, or a too-quiet conversational style. You get the picture. These are traits that appear *sometimes* in *some* people, and when they are present, they vary in degree.

I have seen extremely well-written books featuring autistic characters who run the personality and intelligence gamut just like everyone else. I have also seen some horrible literary presentations of autism that rely on stereotype and assumption. I hope my characters fall into the former category, rather than the latter.

Finally, while many details of the book are fictitious, some children on the spectrum do wander, sometimes with tragic results. Autism affects communication. A nonverbal individual can easily wander away from a group, distracted. Children do this anyway, but when the ability to call for help is in any way hampered, the wanderer's danger is greater.

William is a wanderer. He wears a tracking device made available by a group called Project Lifesaver International. The device and company are real, and I am grateful to CEO Gene Saunders for permitting me to use the real thing rather than having to make something up. The commendable work of the group allows rescue parties to rapidly hone in on a person's location, saving precious minutes. Moreover, there are grants to fund it, and costs to individual families are typically low to nonexistent.

Finally, thanks to you, reader, for picking up my book and giving me a whirl. I'd love to know your thoughts, and you can always find me at http://jesterqueen.com.

CHAPTER 1

Natasha's cell vibrated on the counter, but I ignored it. She often forgot to turn it off when she surrendered it to my care at ten p.m. It was well past midnight now, and I was busy unpacking. The move into Ironweed had been sudden, though anything but impulsive, and my husband and I were busy with the kitchen boxes tonight.

Tasha's phone stopped buzzing as Lance lifted a stack of plates and set them on the counter. "I hate all this waste," he complained, unwrapping the dishes and putting them in the cabinet above the sink. "Will you be able to reach these if I put them on the lowest shelf, Noel?"

"Try not to think about the waste." I sliced open a box, revealing our stemware, then walked to the sink and stretched my arms into the cabinet. Since I top out at five feet, most kitchen shelves have to be accessed with a step stool. Day-to-day items are best stored in easy reach. "As long as the plates are in front, I should be okay."

The phone buzzed again. Lance groaned. Natasha's grandparents, Gert and Stan, had only recently adopted her, and now they were both hospitalized for the long term. Since she had come to live with us, our fifteen-year-old foster daughter had blossomed socially. So much so that we found it necessary to place limits on everything from the Internet, to outings with friends, to the aforementioned cell.

We had also been forced to adapt our views of what it meant

13

to be a teen, which had heretofore been shaped by our contact with my sister's children. Natasha was nothing like the college-bound Rachel or Rachel's fifteen-year-old sister, Brenda. For that matter, I doubted Tasha would have much resembled ten-year-old Poppy at the same age. Perhaps when she was eight. Maybe when she was my nephew Bryce's age, she had seemed like a child. But right now, she was more like a badly confused adult in an underage body.

In fact, Natasha was a large part of the reason for this move. Lance and I used to pride ourselves on our economical lives in our small house, but that home had what Natasha called "one *bedroom* and one *room with a bed.*" It was all we could afford while trying to run the financially strapped Midwest Primate Sanctuary that was our passion as well as our profession.

Stan, a wealthy man who donated to all of Ironweed's foundations, made three bedside calls and purchased the home behind our backs. Then he sold it to us for a dollar. When I told him, "You can't buy us a house like that, Stan!" he smiled and went mute, as if the pneumonia he had developed in the hospital had suddenly stolen his vocal cords.

What I wanted to tell him, "You can't buy back Natasha's mental health," didn't need to be spoken. He knew it. And it hurt him as badly as the broken bones that had put him in the hospital.

His realtor was sitting across the bed from us with a pinched look. Nurses stopped by regularly to count us (we technically numbered entirely too many for this wing of the hospital) and shoot glowers reminding the patient he needed to stop doing business when he should be healing. Our refusal to accept the sale was delaying him.

Lance looked as frustrated as I felt, but we had experience in arguing with Stan. It was pointless. He had been known to forge signatures to achieve his philanthropic goals, while judges in our small Ohio county pretended not to see. The fact that he was in a Columbus hospital coated in casts, tubes, and wires made no difference. The officials would come to him if he could not get out.

If he wanted to buy us a house, then we could either live in it or rent it to someone else. Mostly, we could be grateful he was a kind man, because money bought things in Muscogen County, and it would have done so regardless of Stan's intent.

On the way home from the hospital, Natasha wept, "This is my fault. I told him I got scared at night out there."

"None of this is your fault, Tasha," I told her. "He's assuaging guilt. He also blames himself for Art's death and everything you've been through." It didn't matter to Stan that until he and Gert finalized her adoption, Stan had been her step-grandfather. Natasha was his only grandchild, and he and Gert were her only grandparents. She was the most precious thing in their worlds. Art was our good friend who founded the Midwest Primate Sanctuary and headed it until his death. He had also been dear to Stan.

Gary, who had hurt Natasha and killed Art, was technically Gert's nephew, but Stan had paved the man's path in Muscogen County. It certainly didn't affect Stan's position that he himself had nearly died at Gary's hands; he still felt at fault. The fact that we had *all* failed to grasp how dangerous Gary was did nothing to ease Stan's mind. Gary was determined to come to Muscogen County with or without Stan. He manipulated his way into the invitation to hide his illegal activities. Art simply got in his way.

We *all* got in his way. If Chuck, an orangutan abandoned on the sanctuary's grounds, had not interrupted Gary's encounter with Stan, Stan would have been dead before rescue workers could find him in the Ohio woods. As it was, he was preserved by his cell phone's GPS.

Although his survival was now certain, his departure date from the hospital was far less so. Gary's mother, a participating member of the pornography ring her son operated, had poisoned her own twin sister. Gert was alive, but her health was far less stable.

Natasha was the only one with any idea of what Gary was capable of at that time. And he'd terrified her into silence. She had spent four, nearly five years trapped by him, not even completely escaping when her mother's death from a drug overdose allowed her grandparents to adopt her over the protests of her mother's boyfriend, who turned out not to be her father at all. With Gary dead and the majority of the people who had hurt her in federal custody, Tash had finally developed a sense of empowerment in our care. She recognized and was willing to identify many of the guilty parties.

But that, too, took a toll. Because she was a minor, she would be providing taped testimony for several trials, not taking the stand. But she had not yet done so, making it even more difficult for her to move beyond the things that terrorized her. She took a veritable pharmacy of anti-anxiety medications to get through each day. And our old backyard had too many dark shadows.

When we realized how badly injured Gert and Stan were, and that Natasha had nowhere to go with her grandparents disabled, we impulsively invited her to stay with us. I thought Lance was motivated purely by sympathy. But it was more personal for me. I knew a little more about what she had been through, once having been sucked into an abusive relationship myself, and I hoped I could reach her where another might not be able to do so.

After Stan bought us the house, we didn't do anything at all for two days, as our workload at the sanctuary, where Lance and I shared management duties, was heavy this time of year.

We didn't have summer interns from Ironweed University, like we did the rest of the year, and many of our long-term volunteers were vacationing. Natasha provided a highly useful pair of hands. We all left for work early in the morning and came home exhausted each night, making a perfect excuse to avoid talking about Stan's latest purchase.

But on the third morning, when the sound of a tree branch scraping against the house had kept Natasha up most of the previous night, the topic became unavoidable. "We should consider going," I told Lance. "For now, anyway. I'm afraid out here at night, too, these days." After all, I wouldn't have known Natasha was awake and frightened if the same noise that troubled her hadn't also pulled me from a deep sleep to check all the doors and windows. I hated not feeling safe in the country, but I couldn't deny the pervasive unease I experienced when the sun set each evening.

We rented a truck, packed up our things, and moved into the town of Ironweed. However, now that we had done it and were preparing to rent out the old place, I felt less sure of the decision. I wanted my small home back.

As we placed the last of the plates and silverware, the phone once again ceased to rattle. Lance picked up another box. "That thing makes the whole counter shake."

"It doesn't." I started working on the pots and pans.

When we invited Natasha into our home, we hadn't realized Gert would suffer a disabling stroke as a result of the poison her sister had administered. We hadn't realized Stan's broken pelvis alone would have left him in the hospital and rehab for a long time, and this didn't begin to address the other bones Gary had smashed in his uncle's body.

Yet again, the cell on the counter vibrated. "Gah! If that thing goes off again, I'm turning it *off.*" Lance banged the spice box too hard, and I was momentarily grateful for the wasted paper and overpacking.

"If it rings again, I'm answering it. These kids can't keep calling here at all hours." In fact, I was delighted to have those kids calling late at night. Not that I was planning to let Natasha stay on the phone after ten, but it meant she had friends to call.

When she came to us in June, she was friendless. Partially, this was because she was still grieving for her mother. Partially, it was because she had finally passed the seventh grade the day after her fifteenth birthday. Schoolwork was simply not a priority for her mother and the other criminals who had provided most of what passed for her care. But much of Natasha's condition resulted from her inability to accept that she was a victim rather than a perpetrator. She still apologized out loud to her grandparents in her sleep and took responsibility for everything that went wrong in her vicinity.

Her therapist had been helping to ease her fears of socialization with amazing speed. She *wanted* friends, after all, and her sweet personality made it easy for her to keep them. But she hadn't known how to make them.

Her other problems were taking more time to deal with. When she was in the ring, she had gone to extreme lengths to dull the pain of exploitation. She had come to Gert and Stan the year before with a cigarette addiction and an unhealthy taste for whiskey. They had cured her of the cigarettes, and they thought they had rescued her from the alcohol. But Lance and I quickly figured out otherwise. She was still self-medicating.

After she'd watched me throw away a cabinet full of perfectly good liquor, Natasha complained, "I only drank a finger! I needed something to stop spazzing out so bad." Her "finger" was nearly half the bottle of whiskey. "I want to go home so hard I could throw up, and every time I see Gram's face half frozen, I feel so *guilty.*"

"Gert and Stan don't blame you for what happened to them.

This isn't your fault."

"Your saying that doesn't make it true." That was when we took up her psychiatrist's refrain and pressured her into trusting the anti-anxiety meds over her nonpharmaceutical varieties. We also emptied the house of liquor to ensure the behavior's cessation.

Until she moved in with us, Natasha had been largely a stranger. We knew her grandparents better. Gary had passed easily for an uptight graduate student with a few decision-making problems to work out of his research plans. Only after he murdered Art and nearly killed all the rest of us did we learn Gary was harming not only Natasha, but also the apes and monkeys at our primate center by putting them in his pornographic photos and films.

Again, the phone stopped. "Dr. Rue," Lance said to me, "I believe we are moved in."

"Dr. Lakeland, I think you're right." Other than the detritus of boxes scattered around the living room and the trash can full of pizza boxes and paper plates, we had now unpacked everything. It helped to live so economically.

"A celebration!" He reached for the stemware I'd so recently put away and I went for the bottle of champagne that was the only alcohol in the house.

"A toast!" I held up my glass and looked around our new home, with its four bedrooms and basement of unseemly proportions. "To excess and holding down two jobs to achieve the American Dream." Not that we were technically carrying a mortgage for the house, but we had agreed between ourselves to set aside money as if we were, so we could argue appropriateness with Stan at a more suitable time. If we were going to live here, we were going to offer at least something like market value.

"Indeed. May our return to teaching this semester be as

simple as hiring graduate students to move our boxes proved to be." We toasted and drank, but didn't get to enjoy so much as an entire glass of the bubbly.

On the counter, the phone buzzed again. "Really?" I sipped my champagne and picked up the offending device.

"Turn it off." Lance flopped on the couch with an arm crooked for me to sit in. "Her friends need to learn to call at reasonable hours."

No name displayed with the number on the caller ID panel. "It's not in her contacts list. And it's a Columbus number. Six-one-four area code."

Lance sat up and lowered his arm. Columbus could mean bad things for Tasha's grandparents or bad things from her past. If it were the grandparents, someone would have been trying to reach *us*, not her. Which meant this might be the other.

"Hello?" I used my "Dr. Rue" voice, the one I had been practicing to use on undergraduates. The one I used setting limits with my foster teen.

"I thought I was calling Natasha Oeschle." It was a woman on the other end of the line. An adult, not a kid, and she sounded breathless.

I kept my tone professorial. "Who's calling, please?"

"You must be her foster mother. I'm Nelly Penobscott. Tasha fostered with me when she was twelve, and we've always kept in touch."

"I see." When she was twelve, Natasha had been making skin flicks for two years. Her mother's drug issues meant she *had* briefly been in the care of the state, but I didn't trust this caller. Lance had moved to stand behind me, and I twisted the phone so he could hear, too.

"Yes. I don't have much time. I know what she's been through, and I'm glad you're protective of her. I have a message, and you can deliver it or not."

"And what message is that?" I had dropped from professor to ice queen.

"When she was here, there were these twins, Sara and William. They went to live with an aunt and uncle in Muscogen County about the same time as Tasha went to her grandparents out there. Only now they're back in care, and the little boy's gone missing. They're mounting a house-to-house search, and I thought maybe Tasha would want to help. They've bumped into her a couple of times. William knows her, and maybe he'd come out for her. If he's only hiding. He's *got to be* only hiding." Her voice shook, as if she was begging me to make this missing child be a hidden one, not something worse. "You can call the sheriff's department if you think I'm lying."

I didn't speak. Not initially. My recent experience with liars and deception was too raw to accept her words at face value. And yet, the conversation was punctuated by bursts of another voice in the background, like she was being hurried along to come help with something. Her urgency seemed so real. "I'll talk to Natasha," I finally said, "and I'll call the sheriff's department. *They* will be able to tell us where to meet." *If this is real. If you aren't calling from some rented phone trying to lure my foster daughter into danger herself, under the pretext of a rescue mission. If June isn't about to come back around and bite us in August.*

I hung up the phone. "What do you want to do?" I asked Lance.

"You wake up Natasha," he said. "I'll wake up Officer Carmichael."

Over the course of the investigation in June, we had become friends with a deputy, a junior detective, at the county sheriff's office, and he could be trusted to give us honest information, even if we dragged him out of bed from a sound sleep.

Lance got out his own phone and started dialing while I walked down to Natasha's room. I knocked. She didn't answer.

"Natasha?" I knocked again.

"G'way, Gram. I'm sleeping."

"It's Noel. I need to talk to you about something."

A pause, then, "Yeah, I think I'm up."

Natasha's meds knocked her out soundly and fast. Although she was allowed to stay up until midnight on these last few summer nights before school began, she was often in bed by ten-thirty or eleven. As soon as she surrendered her phone, she powered down. Right now, it was going on toward one in the morning.

As soon as I said Nelly Penobscott's name, though, she leapt out of bed and started pacing. "Why didn't you let me talk to her?"

"For all I know, she's one of those crazy people." I didn't finish the thought. I didn't need to. Lance and I had been lured by Gert's murderous twin Gretchen to try to find and rescue Natasha at the primate center. Gretchen showed up at our wedding, looking enough like Gert, and projecting sufficient distress, so we played right into her hands, rushing in where we should have maintained caution.

"Let me see the number. She's in my book."

I handed Natasha the phone. "This one came up without a name."

Natasha studied her call history. "If it's really Mrs. P," she finally said, "she's calling from someone else's house."

"Agreed."

"But she knew so *much*! I saw Will and Sara at the pizza place yesterday and again earlier this afternoon. Sara was the little girl talking my ear off while we waited in line. You might have noticed her, but Will's quiet. He doesn't talk much. He'll wander off where nobody can find him. Wait! Did Mrs. P. say kindergarten? Anywhere in the conversation, did she use that word?"

"No-o-o, why?"

"It's our safe word. So I'll know it's her. But if she was upset, and confused because you answered, she might not have remembered."

Lance poked his head into the room. "Be right back," he said.

"Why? Where are you going?"

"Drew says it's all legit. I want to check out the place where the volunteers are gathering."

"Don't go." Natasha, who had blazed at me for withholding her phone call, sounded frightened. "Let me call Mrs. P back first."

"If it's not . . ."

"She didn't say kindergarten. If it's her, *somebody* is going to answer at either this number or the one in my book. And then we'll know at least one thing."

Natasha's wariness since June was equivalent to that of a jealous spouse. While she would go places with her friends and stay out past her curfew if not monitored, she made Lance or I check all destinations first. Her friends grumbled when their own parents wanted to speak to a new pal's mother before allowing more than a casual gathering. Natasha begged us to pretend we were doing the same thing against her will, when in reality she was the one who wanted her new acquaintances checked out. She told them a limited amount about her situation and had established safe words with *all* of them. I had packed the list somewhere in the pile of boxes from the office. It had accidentally gotten lumped in with something nonessential and gone missing. Natasha knew them all, but I certainly couldn't keep track of them. And she was right. A call to a trusted number could at least establish some things.

"Use the number in your contacts first," I advised her.

Our arrangement worked out well, since it meant we had an

honest kid. Her social worker, the same one who had been with her in the months leading up to being adopted by her grandparents, had warned us to expect problems with lying at the same time as she congratulated us for clearing all the system's hurdles in a mere two months. I had no doubt that even from what had nearly been his deathbed, Natasha's grandfather had eased those to speed the process. Somehow, the home study was already in progress while we completed the six weeks of parenting classes, even though the classes should have come first.

Thus, what should have been a three- to six-month delay to formalize Natasha's durability as our guest wound up only taking eight weeks. We might not have needed to go through the formality at all if our connection to Stan and Gert hadn't been so tangential or if Natasha's former situation hadn't been so dire. In the height of absurdity, we'd started receiving checks from the state to support her care, even though Stan had ordered us to use his credit cards and buy her anything she needed.

She shifted the phone from hand to hand after she dialed. From the look on her face at the answer, something was wrong. Natasha handed me her handset and buried her head in her pillow. "This is all my *fault!*"

"I . . . uh . . . kindergarten . . . ," I blurted out.

The woman who answered had obviously been asleep. "Natasha? Honey, it's the middle of the night," she said.

"I'd better call Drew back," Lance said. "I'm going to bet that kid didn't wander off." He snorted. "It's like one of those problems in your mother's advice column. 'Dear Nora: Stalkers keep trying to lure my teen into danger. Please help or send thread."

I appreciated my husband's stab at humor, but I doubted we would be seeing my mother tackle this issue in "What's Next

Nora?". I briefly outlined the situation for the real Nelly Penob-scott, but hurried her off the phone. I needed to make another call, this one to a federal agent. And I needed to see about get-ting Natasha a new cell phone, one with a better protected number.

CHAPTER 2

Dear Nora:

I have the worst trouble with houseguests. It seems like they're always dropping by uninvited. What can I do?

Teeming in the Country

Dear Teeming: Lock the doors. Pretend you aren't home. If that fails, leave.

Nora

The next morning brought Trudy Jackson and her partner, Darnell Marshall, who worked for the feds. Technically, the agents had come and gone once already, but they only popped in for a few minutes in the middle of the night before leaving to contribute what they could to the search for the boy. None of us slept well. We were worried about the missing child, but we weren't stupid enough to go rushing out after our last similar experience. Other people could hunt for now.

At first light, I opened the back door and waved to Trudy's beat-up sedan, the same one she used to pose as a sanctuary volunteer. "Come on in, Trudy," I called reluctantly. "Where's Darnell?"

"Talking to our people down the block." Trudy joined me on my front stoop. For a moment, I hesitated to step aside and let her in. I didn't trust her. Not any longer. When she was merely a volunteer technically in my employ, I had held her in great esteem. I still felt conflicted about her role in the federal operation ongoing when Art was killed. If she and Darnell had broken their silence to let at least Lance and me know a little, could our friend have been saved?

She waited outside the door, not answering my confrontational stance. I didn't mean to be so judgmental, not when my own decisions also contributed to Art's death. If Lance and I hadn't been dashing around with last-minute wedding preparations, we would have been there to keep him from going out back looking for the abandoned orangutan that would ultimately save Stan, Lance, Natasha, and me. It tried to save Art when he crossed Gary's path out there. I drew a deep breath and moved out of the way.

Once inside, Trudy gave Natasha back her phone. She had taken it when she pulled up in the middle of the night. By the time she and Darnell arrived then, they had already researched the number Natasha got the call from. Their clothing had been neat, but Trudy's hair pointed out in several directions, as if a mere hairbrush had been inadequate to tame it when she rose from slumber. Darnell had motioned to us, and Lance followed him outside, while I stayed with Tasha and Trudy in the doorway.

Trudy had told Natasha, "The phone number belongs to somebody named Ivy Dearborn. Mean anything?"

"Dearborn does, not Ivy."

At the time, Tasha had simply handed the phone to Trudy, who didn't elaborate. Now, however, Trudy said, "Tell me what you know."

Natasha sat at the kitchen table, her back rigid, clasping and unclasping her hands. Then she sagged. "About Ivy Dearborn? Nothing."

"About the missing boy, his sister, how you know them, and who would know you saw them since you came here." Trudy's voice was clipped and professional. She needed information, and she needed it fast. A national alert had been released hours before the alarming call Natasha received, but most people wouldn't see it until they got up in the morning. Right now, the authorities' best chance of finding the boy lay in talking to the people who knew him.

"Okay." Natasha swallowed. She rested her head in one hand. "I guess Mrs. P . . . Nelly Penobscott . . . could tell you more *about* them than I could . . ."

"We have someone interviewing her now. What do *you* know?"

"Not much. I mean, I guess more than you. I'm not sure." I wondered if Natasha's mood was addled by more than her meds. I didn't smell alcohol on her, but there wasn't any way to surreptitiously look at the champagne bottle, and I didn't want to outright ask in front of Trudy if she'd taken a sip.

Instead, I got her a soda pop and told my part, about the phone call itself, first. By the time I finished speaking, Natasha had gathered her wits. "Here's what I think," she said.

"Is that different from what you know?" Trudy had a tablet computer out, ready to take notes.

"A little. I know you didn't pick up *any* of the other kids they were using in the ring, even though you got most of the adults."

Natasha had already provided a list of names and descriptions; the best she could, anyway. She was often drunk when she was acting, and even many of the children she knew well had been kept on a first-name-only basis. "We all came from out in the sticks, and if we didn't, our folks did, especially the moms." This was information she had already given back in June. "Will and Sara—the missing boy and his sister—they weren't in the ring." To me, Natasha explained, "We didn't age in until we were ten. Gary and Aunt Gretchen had the idea it was all okay after that, but you were too young before. But the twins' mom was in. She and my mom used to do . . . scenes together." Natasha shuddered. This was hard. "They got picked up together in the drug bust."

"The one leading to your placement with Mrs. Penobscott?" Trudy tapped her screen and scribbled with a stylus.

Natasha nodded. "The twins weren't quite two, and they didn't know what was going on. There was another girl named Layla whose dad got picked up with the twins' mom and mine. But he was a gang-banger . . . I mean, he was T-Bow Orrice. You know him, right?"

Trudy stopped writing to stare at Natasha. Yes, she knew T-Bow Orrice. We *all* knew T-Bow Orrice, currently serving concurrent life sentences for murder. He was a major player accidentally caught when agents believed they were only breaking up a pimping ring. "*I* know," she said. "I didn't know *you* knew. Why haven't you talked about Layla before? Did you know she was living out here?"

"T-Bow was only connected to Gary and them tangentially, and Layla wasn't ever in Gary's ring, as far as I know. T-Bow had custody of Layla, because her mom was adamant about getting his name on the birth certificate in the hospital, but ultimately took off and ran back to her parents out here. I guess she spent a year getting clean. It pissed T-Bow off, her ditching him with the kid. He doesn't like his women and kids to get hooks in him. He wants the kids, but he doesn't want anything to do with them. He . . ." Natasha trailed into silence.

"Tasha?" Trudy finally prompted.

"Sorry. It was a memory, but it went away. Anyway, once he *had* Layla, T-Bow wouldn't give her up to her mom for anything. He was punishing this woman by holding onto Layla, but his arrest changed everything around. In the end, Layla got out with her mom. He hated that. He didn't approve of the mom."

I couldn't stop myself from interjecting. "A gang-banger didn't approve of an ex-porn star?"

"He's weird. He's real protective of all his kids. The ones he

29

acknowledges, anyway. Plus, the mom, Shannon, she got out."

Trudy steered the conversation back to its original focus. "Out. You've used that word twice. Out how?"

"Out. *Out* out. Home free, no films, no drugs. Layla went to her mom, and T-Bow promised to leave them alone if Shannon didn't tell what she knew about T-Bow and his gang. The rest of us were supposed to pretend Layla never existed."

"She went away and you stopped talking about her?"

"We all knew what would happen if we talked."

"Not pleasant," Trudy agreed. Clearly, she and Natasha had already discussed the finer points of life inside Gary's ring.

Natasha sank her head into her arms, which were crossed on the table. "What does it matter anymore?"

"Natasha?" Trudy placed a hand on Natasha's arm. "We don't know what matters or what doesn't until we know what it *is.*"

I sat on Natasha's other side and scooted in close to her. Sitting up straighter, she nonetheless moved away from me. I felt the most helpless as her guardian at these moments. I had to call on my own painful memories to connect with and help her.

And what had I felt in those first couple of years after Alex Lakeland tried to beat me to death with my telephone? I moved away. If I could keep another body at arm's length, then it would be harder to reach and hit me. But at the same time, I craved softness. Lance and I had known each other for a long time but only moved beyond friendship after I realized how diametrically different he was from his brother, and how much more I wanted his gentle personality than Alex's cocky cowboy attitude. I would sit near Lance, simultaneously yearning for him to lightly rest an arm on me and grateful when he didn't.

I scooted back a pace from Natasha and she immediately turned in my direction again. "Hang on a minute." I got an afghan and tossed it over her shoulders before resuming my seat.

Natasha muttered, "Thanks." She shifted in the chair, wrapping herself in the throw. I sent a mental thank-you note to my grandmother for crocheting us a new one every Christmas. Finally, Tasha flipped her hands palm up and threw her arms out toward Trudy, as if the unpleasantness was obvious. This time, I couldn't help it. I put my arm across her shoulders. Her mother had, after all, most likely been killed by Gary's people, even though the death was formally ruled an accidental overdose.

"Don't." Natasha shook me off.

I pulled my hand back.

"*Did* anybody talk about this Layla?" Trudy was writing again. I could see a little of her reasoning. She wanted to know Layla's last name, her age, and her physical description. I couldn't remember what names Natasha had given in June, but I was willing to bet Layla had *not* been one of them.

Tasha shook her head. "I don't even know what happened to her after she got out."

"What has this got to do with the missing boy?" I said. Was it necessary to put Natasha through this?

"I'm getting there," Trudy said. I met her eyes across the table until she leaned away from her tablet and at least pretended to ease off.

"I know where she's going," Natasha said. "Layla's last name is Dearborn. But I thought her mom was Shannon, not Ivy. Was *she* the one who called me?"

"Bingo," said Trudy.

"I wondered about her when you said the last name before."

"You should trust your instincts."

"But it's been so long, and we weren't friends. Not at all. We were all with Mrs. P for a while before they decided Shannon was clean enough for Layla to go home. She's my age, maybe a year younger, but she sounds older. Her voice was always grown

31

up. I still don't get why she'd call *me*. She was always jealous because Granddad bought me things. I didn't know she knew I lived around here. I guess she lives around here, too, then. She *could* have seen me *and* the twins *and* known we were *all* here. If she knew anything about something happening to Will, maybe she'd have tried to call me and used Mrs. P's name."

"You got it in one, kiddo."

"But who gave her my *number*?"

"Mutual acquaintance," Trudy said. From her briefcase, she produced two eight-by-ten glossy photographs. She could have been a talent agent pulling out her model client's head shots. She pointed to the first picture. "Layla?"

Natasha ran her fingers over the features of the girl in the picture. "I even know when it was *taken*," she muttered. "T-Bow didn't know about the kid side of things, or he'd have never even sold Gary and them drugs. Like I said, he was funny about his kids. Layla ran with us, but she never knew everything. She thought she did. She thought it was a talent agency and we were all famous models. Gary let her 'try out' and took cute kid pics."

Trudy indicated the other shot, an obvious school picture. "What about her?"

Natasha shook her head. "I think she's some girl over at the public school . . . ohhh." She sat at the table, looking back and forth now, from one picture to the other and back again. "She doesn't look the same at *all.*"

"You recognize her."

"Yeah. Now that you put the pictures together, I do. I guess I *have* seen her at parties and things. I had no idea who she was."

"Ivy Dearborn is her aunt. Layla figured you wouldn't answer anything from her, and when Noel answered, she had already decided to be someone else."

"She used Mrs. P's name."

"Right."

My mind was racing ahead of theirs. "So everything's okay? Nobody was trying to harm Tasha?"

"I wouldn't say 'okay,' " Trudy said. "We've still got a missing little boy who's been gone since seven o'clock yesterday evening."

"But we can help look for him now? He knows me. He might come to me!" Natasha was already out of her seat.

"I don't see why not." Trudy rose to join Natasha.

"Sorry for the panic." I went to the basement door and leaned in. "Hey, everything's cool. Let's go help."

"It's been useful to us," Trudy said. "We had no idea there was another former child member of the ring who we could talk to."

Natasha groaned. "She wasn't ever *in.* She's going to be so pissed at me."

Trudy and Natasha continued to talk while Trudy gathered her things. I explained the situation to Lance, and he came up the steps carrying a computer cord. He'd been setting up our wi-fi. Neither of us liked being without a connection to search engines. Social media sites, which were the primary Internet access we could use with our particular smartphones, were not helpful at all in the event of a need to do real research. Technically, we could use the Net from our cells. In reality, we hunted, pecked, and committed more autocorrect errors than nearly all the other people we knew.

I hated the phone, but it had become an ingrained part of my life since June. With my oldest niece going away to college, I was forced to admit my weekly phone calls with her would no longer be a practical means of communication. Using Stan's money, she, her younger sister, and Natasha had conspired to set Lance and me up in what they termed the modern world right after our wedding. They called it a spontaneous gift. I called it a spontaneous hassle.

Seeing Lance with the hookup paraphernalia reminded me I needed to check my text messages. They tended to accrue before I remembered to open the folder. Indeed, I had seven now, all from my grandmother. The girls, in their enthusiasm, had also brought my parents and grandmother into the twenty-first century. Actually, Mama had owned a smartphone before the teenaged conspiracy, and got upgraded considerably. She now liked to say she had a genius phone and it was too bad her IQ was only average. Nana, though she hadn't quite gotten the hang of texting, adapted better than the rest of us. Nana's only real issue was she thought if she didn't get an immediate reply to a text, her note hadn't gone through. So she sent it again. And again. All seven messages said: *No el. Restaurateur youre tacking me to colobus for med apt Weds.*

Translated, she was reminding me I was driving her to Columbus for a doctor's appointment tomorrow. However, the combination of the small screen, random text corrections, and her generally bad eyesight led to a message suggesting she might know something about a wedding involving colobus monkeys. Nana still tooled around town on her own steam, but she didn't drive on the highways any longer, and she relied on us to ferry her as far as the big city. I would also be bringing Natasha to visit her grandparents and do a little school shopping at the same time. I hadn't done that last since I was in grad school. I planned to take a book, and Tasha could get what she needed while I waited and Nana napped in the car.

I set aside my thoughts about tomorrow in favor of today's concerns. Lance said, "They're dispatching all the volunteers from the foster parents' home on East Clover, and we're doing a fingertip-to-fingertip, house-to-house search."

"Can we do something first?" Natasha, who had been so eager to go once she realized there was no immediate threat to herself, suddenly seemed hesitant.

"What?" We were climbing into the primate-mobile, the beat-up truck that was our only real means of transportation these days, and I paused with one leg hanging out of the vehicle.

"Can we run by The Submarine Pizza?"

"It's on the other end of town. Why do you want to go there?" Lance looked at his watch and tapped its face as if to remind us all how important this trip could be. "If we're going to be any help, we need to get into the search."

Natasha pulled her door shut, and I finished mounting the running board and did the same. "He's been gone twelve hours now," she said quietly. "They won't find him."

"They may."

"The longer he's gone, the less likely he'll turn up. I promise I'll be quick. Can we *please* go to the pizza place?"

"Why?" But Lance was already turning left rather than right to accede to Natasha's request.

"He might be there," she mumbled into her shirt.

"He might . . ." Lance applied the brakes, slowing the truck well ahead of the stop sign at the end of our road. "Natasha, what part of 'the other end of town' isn't computing here? How would he even get so far from East Clover?"

"It's not *that* far. And it's where I saw them yesterday. Autistic kids sometimes go a long way, and faster than anybody would expect. And it's the last place anybody knows where he was for sure, right?"

"Did his foster mother lie about where she saw him last?" The woman insisted he came home with her.

"Trudy told me to trust my instincts, didn't she, Noel?"

"She did. Maybe the foster mother *convinced* herself she saw him in the car." I *did* think Natasha's theory was worth looking into.

Lance made a final stab. "Don't you think they've looked

there already?"

"He likes to climb up into small places. If they were looking outside and after dark, and he was inside or crawled up under something, maybe they didn't see him."

"Text the detective, then. Tell him why we're running late. He knows you know the kid, and he's looking to get your ideas over at the foster mother's place." He tossed his cell to Natasha so she could send a message to Deputy Carmichael.

We drove fast, Lance darting through the early stages of what passed for Ironweed's morning rush hour. "Let's let Lance go around the block and talk to the owners, and you and I look around outside," I said once we reached the Marine (as Submarine Pizza was fondly known all over Ironweed).

Natasha nodded. She was still clutching Lance's phone with the deputy's reply. It said, *Good idea. Gibsons live a block over. Sending Greene to meet you there. Tell them you're searching again. They should open up to let you look around.*

As she and I climbed out, Tasha passed the device back to my husband. "He said it was a good idea!" She sounded like an infatuated schoolgirl, and it took me a minute to realize she was responding to the praise about her thought process. Her fragile self-confidence had been bumped up a notch. Points to Deputy Andrew Carmichael.

We started around front, peering under hedges and in bushes. I took a quick glance around the Marine's stylized sign, where a wooden scuba diver resolutely held a pepperoni pizza out in offering to the world. Reluctantly, we concluded the boy would have had a hard time putting himself in the blue mailbox (and someone with a key would have to confirm this), then we moved around the building to one side, both softly calling William's name.

Out back, the Dumpster smell permeated everything. Without discussion, we went to examine it first, even though it meant we bypassed a parked delivery truck and broke up our otherwise methodical examination of the property. A police siren whooped to a halt up front, and Natasha spared it a dirty look. "Turn that thing off," she grumbled. "You'll scare him away if he's here."

She was dressed fashionably, in high-cut shorts and a pair of tank tops that had probably cost more individually than every shirt in my wardrobe combined. Still, she dropped to the pavement without hesitation to look underneath the looming garbage bin. "Noel!" she hissed as I lay down beside her.

She didn't need to say my name. I saw the same thing she did. An oblong object connected to a distorted shape. A child's shape.

"How did he get under there? William?" Natasha burst into sudden tears and forgot to whisper. "Will?" she shouted. She gasped for breath and I suddenly realized I'd left her inhaler in the car. The little torso jerked, and the head thumped against the bottom of the Dumpster, but he didn't cry out. It seemed he'd been asleep. His head swiveled around and he reached for Natasha. She quickly mastered her own emotions. "How did you get . . . never mind. Scoot over to me, and let's get you out."

William kept reaching, but he didn't move. Footsteps clattered around the corner out of our sightline. I pointed to William's hips, wedged between the Dumpster and the asphalt. "I think he's stuck." He lay mostly on his stomach, and he retained a full range of motion, even if he wasn't getting anywhere.

"Is he there? Did you find him?" That was Deputy Greene, whose face appeared cattycorner to ours under the Dumpster.

William began to keen, a wordless howling wail that punctuated the morning more loudly than the police siren. "It's all right!" Natasha had reined in her voice and was whispering again. "It's all right. We'll get you out." She inched forward until her fingertips brushed Will's.

Deputy Greene was up again, and from the sounds of it, he was talking on his radio. "Clear the channel. Clear the channel. Cut the chatter. Deputy C, do you copy? Over."

After a pause, Andrew Carmichael's voice replied, "Copy. What's the noise? Over."

"We found the boy. Copy? Repeat, we found the boy. But he's stuck, and I need a dozen guys here ASAP to get him out from under this Dumpster."

CHAPTER 3

Dear Nora:

I can't find bras that fit anymore. I think I'm a J or K cup. I never knew they got that big! It's like I'm constantly being crushed by a tendril.

Done In

Dear Done:

I think you mean anvil, and I'm assuming there was a question in that list of statements. I'm somewhat under-endowed myself, but those things will smother you. I'm sending my plastic surgeon's number. I see her for plenty of other complaints, and you'll love her. I want to hear back in a week telling me you made an appointment and purchased a dictionary.

Nora

"One, two, three, heave!" Strategically positioned people hoisted the Dumpster high in the air.

"Go! Go! Get it clear." Deputy Greene led the staggering charge away from Will like a man guiding a battering ram. There had been a discussion of using car jacks to hoist the thing, but it would have taken longer to get those than it did for the half-panicked rookie deputy to run door-to-door and roust neighbors out of four houses. Clearly, he was posted at this edge of the search because it was where William was *least* likely to be found.

In all this time, the child had not stopped screaming, though he only bumped his head once more before the hastily assembled team lifted the weight off his hip. His piercing cries intensified as sunlight struck him.

"Easy." Natasha's voice was barely audible. "Easy, I've got you Will."

Deputy Greene called, "Natasha, don't move him. We don't know how he got there. He may have broken bones."

Natasha looked up long enough to glare at him. Her eyes carried a level of sarcasm her voice alone couldn't have conveyed. "I'd *never* have thought of that. Would you stop shouting? You're making it worse." We could barely hear her over Will's wails.

She disentangled her fingers from his long enough to scramble to him on all fours. When her body's shadow fell over him, partially blocking the bright light, he suddenly fell silent and looked up. He saw her, then flipped from his stomach onto his back and seized her shirt, nearly pulling her down on top of him.

"I'm thinking his bones are fine," I said.

"Careful, buddy." In the absence of Will's cries, Natasha sounded loud. I crawled over to them and pried his fingers free from her shirt so she could sit down. At once, he sprang up and tackled her in a hug that would have sent her sprawling backward if I hadn't caught her. As it was, I tumbled and scraped an elbow landing.

His poor foster mother arrived. "I could have sworn he was with us. I *know* I saw him in the car," she sobbed. Will wouldn't go to her and remained wrapped around Natasha.

"He's hungry," his foster mother said. He couldn't eat until X-rays confirmed his hip had only been wedged in his crawl under the Dumpster and he didn't need surgery of any kind.

A few cuts stood out red on his black skin, and his wild tangle of hair had picked up debris. Tasha tried to pick it out while she held him, but it seemed firmly twisted in. "You're safe," Natasha said, rocking him.

Finally, he looked up, as if seeing us all for the first time. He found his foster mother and launched fluidly into her legs. She sat and held him. He wrapped one of Natasha's hands in a death grip.

And then he saw me. His eyes lingered. "Hey there." I gave him a small wave.

At once, he grabbed my hand so that he held me captive along with Natasha. It seemed like an afterthought to him. Something necessary because hands were for holding. But for me, that moment was life changing. In the instant that his fingers clasped around mine, I felt myself rent by a gulf of loneliness. I wanted to clasp him and Natasha both and never let go.

It didn't feel like much time had passed, though my phone swore it was nine in the morning, before William was swept away for a medical evaluation. Will remained spastic and disoriented, repeatedly blatting, "no more circle dots" every time a new police car arrived. I couldn't say why, but when he and his foster mother climbed into the ambulance for a potentially unnecessary ride to Ironweed General, I wanted to take her place with him, never mind that I had never met him before.

I reminded myself he was safe, a thought that made me smile in spite of the empty feeling. I caught Lance's gaze for a moment and saw the most peculiar expression on his face. "What's that?" I asked.

"Talk later," he told me.

With the departure of their star subject, reporters crowded around hoping to talk to Natasha and me. Tasha had been identified only as an anonymous victim in all the June scandal. Her name and face had been kept out of the news, and, given that she was already well known through her grandparents, she preferred it. I wasn't surprised when she waved off the microphones shoved in her direction. The reporters persisted and, although they were on one side of a crime-scene tape and we were on the other, their cameras all followed Tasha.

I put myself between her and them, but I'm shorter than she is, so it didn't have much effect. Then Lance got in the way, hiding us both, and I let out my breath in a long sigh.

"Come on." Detective Carmichael beckoned us through the Marine's back door.

"Thanks, Detective," I said.

"Call me Drew," he reminded me. That was far easier to do when we saw him socially and he wasn't in uniform.

He and Lance shook hands, Drew's chocolate skin highlighting the sunburn Lance perpetually sported by this point in the summer. They and Natasha sat down so she could give her statement and Lance his. I joined Deputy Greene for the same purpose.

As I signed the form, a woman I hadn't noticed coming in said, "If it isn't the fastest home study in the Midwest."

I froze in the middle of handing back the deputy's pen. I liked Natasha's social worker, a smiling woman with wrinkles around her eyes and at the edges of her mouth. Jane Hurtz's concern for Tasha was evident in every one of our interactions. This woman was not Natasha's social worker. This was Merry Frasier, whose mouth turned perpetually down at the corners. She spoke every sentence like it was a question, but somehow made each of those questions into a command. Also, she stood with a slight stoop and dangling arms that had led Lance to dub her "the Orangutan Lady." As in, "Look busy, Noel, here comes the Orangutan Lady," followed by nudging and giggling equal to any grade school kid.

Merry was one of the bevvy of people we had met during the whirlwind of classes and home-study meetings. Never mind we had only ever considered the process a formality necessary to keep Natasha, she had visions of us housing half the county in our tiny house. She never seemed to realize this was the home with one bedroom and one room with a bed. Every time she saw us, she turned her baggy eyes on Lance with a covetous expression that said, "stable father figure." At a guess, she was in her mid-sixties, and surely she used the same hairdresser as my mother, because their hair was dyed the same horrible shade of bright yellow I called way-off-canary.

"Ma'am." Deputy Greene plucked the pen from my fingers, tipped his hat, and departed.

"Not a chance," I said, even as Merry poured herself arms first into the seat opposite me. From the kitchen, pizza odors began wafting out. It seemed the Gibsons were planning to open as usual in a couple of hours. "You aren't going to fob some kid off on me. This has always been about Natasha." Merry had never failed to present me with a list of Ohio's waiting children when we met.

"You listen to me." Instead of domineering through questions, Merry spoke in a flat voice. She leaned across the table and exhaled a stench of garlic and onions. She appeared unaware I had eased backward. "That woman is overwhelmed."

"Who?"

"Natalie Forrester. His foster mother. She's got too many children to keep track of a kid like that, and she knows it. She took him on a provisional basis, and she's not going to keep him after this. He needs a house with few or no other young children . . ."

Not going to keep him? I tried to quell an irrational jolt of hope. Hope for what? "Doesn't he have a sister?"

"It's why Natalie took them. Sister's fine. She's not going to have a problem there. But they're going to have to be split up . . ."

No! "I thought the foster care system tried to keep sibling

43

groups together."

"Except in extreme circumstances. And I have to say, these are some pretty extreme circumstances. You ought to see her house. Red stop signs everywhere and alarms on all the doors, and she still lost him because she took her eyes off him for a split second at the pizza parlor. There will be an investigation, and in the end, all we'll determine is her house isn't suitable for a child who needs constant supervision like that one. She didn't do anything *wrong*. I'll guarantee it. It's so easy to lose a kid like that."

Right. Easy to lose. Settle down here. I'm just reacting to a stressful morning. I can't save the world. I'm hardly ready to mother a young child, let alone one with autism. Autism! What do I know about that? And what about Lance! He's never wanted children. Fostering him is out. Right. Out. I tried to still my spinning mind and the jumble of answering emotions in my chest.

"Like *William*," Natasha said. "I take it *you're* his social worker?"

Merry hadn't seen Natasha coming up behind her, and now she jumped as the girl who *was* in my care leaned forward so her hair brushed lightly against Merry's face. Natasha carried a tray of sodas, which she managed to keep upright. She held the pose a moment too long before standing up again and setting the tray down. "His name is William."

Merry flushed and fumbled with her top, as if its scoop neck might somehow reveal too much cleavage. She didn't know Natasha's history and so didn't know what had happened to her, but her discomfort was evident.

"Why can't he and his sister be sent somewhere together?" I asked in the ensuing silence. *Stop. Be quiet. Stop. Don't do this.*

Natasha eased into the seat beside me, the sexual body language evaporating as if she had never displayed it. "Nobody wants kids like them," she said.

"Pretty much," Merry agreed. The sodas manifested in front of us. Merry squnched her considerable eyebrows together and viewed hers with suspicion.

"I hope you don't mind." Natasha sipped long from her own straw. "I took the liberty of ordering for our table." She cocked her head and tapped her tongue to her top lip.

I wanted to laugh, but knew better. It was easier to shoot her my own raised eyebrow in a *cut-it-out* gesture, knowing what it felt like when she turned those carefully widened eyes on me or how badly Lance squirmed when she pulled the tongue-tap trick while he was looking. Natasha didn't always do this deliberately, and it was her default response to new or uncomfortable situations. She, Lance, her therapist, and I had held a few tense meetings on the subject of appropriate behavior and boundaries when she first came to us.

But right now, her actions were utterly over the top. She wasn't acting this way by accident, but because she agreed with Lance and me about the Orangutan Lady and considered her fair game. She nettled people like Merry on purpose.

Before Natasha could come up with some way to obey my unspoken order to the letter without doing so in spirit, Lance loped over and nudged Merry further into the booth so he could perch on the end beside her. Surely he and Natasha had planned this, but it didn't seem to be having the effect of rescuing me from Madame Long Arms. Rather, she and I were now both sitting on the inside of our respective seats, more effectively trapped into conversation than before.

"Let's have a hypothetical conversation," Lance said without preamble. He stared in a pointed semi-circle at the collection of police officers in the room and then back toward the kitchen, where the wafting pizza smells were reminding me I hadn't had breakfast.

"Why," I asked, "would we want to?"

"Because Drew Carmichael said he loves hypothetical conversations, especially when all of the speakers have good intentions." He directed his gaze at the woman on his right, not at me.

Merry had been blushing bright at Natasha's suggestive behavior, but Lance's stare brought her face to a deep purple. To keep from snickering, I raised my eyes as if rolling them. "Hypothetically, what does the detective suggest we discuss?"

"Let's assume there was a childless couple in Muscogen County. One who had previously expressed an interest in foster care but who had, for their own reasons, ultimately only decided to foster one teen girl. Why would they, who had never been put in charge of children at *all*, be an appropriate placement for a little boy who requires constant eyes-on supervision?"

Lance, what are you doing? Don't let me break my heart over this kid!

Merry said, too quickly, "Oh, other than wandering, he's easy to care for. Other than a little bit of autism. Hypothetically."

"Has he learned how to talk, this imaginary kid?" asked Natasha. "Other than randomly repeating stuff?" The eyes she turned on Merry were suddenly narrowed like Lance's, and she folded her hands around her drink and leaned into the table. "Does he eat more than three foods? Has he stopped having night terrors? Hitting? Biting?"

"Wait a minute." Lance laid a hand on Natasha's arm, and she jerked it away. "Sorry." He meant the arm. "I thought *you* were the one who wanted to have this conversation in the first place."

Stop! Oh, stop! Oh, won't you all please stop!

"Didn't you say Drew . . ." I began.

"I *am*. I *do*." Natasha appealed to Lance with her eyes before she turned to me. "And the detective was backing me up. But there's a difference between being hypothetical and spouting lies." She did *not* look at Merry.

Merry flinched. "It seems obvious . . . you would . . . this hypothetical couple . . . be perfect . . . well, because they already work with monkeys all day!"

We all recoiled. Pizza arrived. Natasha had ordered something meaty with a thick crust, something I normally wouldn't have taken even a bite of. We stared at Mr. Gibson as he deposited the hot pan in our midst. "It's on the house!" he said. "We're celebrating because we could be mourning, right? Chase away the bad with the good." He backed away from the table as if the daggers we were staring were aimed at him.

"Autistic kids are a bunch of *monkeys*?" I didn't shout, only because Natasha had latched onto my shoulder. She was pushing down on it, like she could hold my voice down by pressing on my body.

She leaned close to my ear, but before I could get on her case about inappropriate sexuality, she murmured, "You *do* call *her* the Orangutan Lady." *Touché Tash, touché.*

"I don't know much about autism, but your analogy sounds pretty inaccurate to me." I snatched a slice of pizza too soon and scalded my fingers, then crammed it in my mouth—beef, pork, and all—and burned my tongue.

"No . . . of course not . . . but they . . . he . . . *this particular* hypothetical autistic child needs constant supervision. Who better than researchers? You're behavior specialists. You spend all *day* supervising creatu—"

"Stop." Lance had engaged in a similar murder of his fingertips, but he stopped short of killing his taste buds. "Pull back. Are there classes this couple could take to . . . prepare to make such a decision, maybe with a more realistic understanding of the situation?"

A Grinch-worthy smile blossomed on Merry's face. "Hypothetically," she said, "they already have. You have my business card. Now if you'll excuse me, I should meet William and his *current* foster mother at the hospital." She pushed past Lance and left without eating any of the pizza, suddenly far less interested in talking to us.

Lance tried to continue the conversation in her absence, but I shut him down. "Later. I'm still completely overwhelmed, and I'm not thinking rationally."

"You're right," he said. "I'm probably not either."

I brooded over his words on and off for the next several hours. Was he experiencing the same things I was, or exactly the opposite?

We hid out longer than anyone else, and by the time the Marine opened as usual at eleven, most of the press had given up trying to get a glimpse of Natasha and me, but one persistent Columbus reporter met the three of us sneaking out the back. He had a camera, but no video recorder. Lance shuttled Natasha to the truck. I gave a short statement and let him take a single picture of me so he would go away quickly.

Stan Oeschle's granddaughter had already been identified from today's news coverage, but I refused to discuss her presence with this man. She was too easily recognized in this part of the state. There was another reporter I *would* talk to, but he wasn't hanging around. He knew how to find me later, and he doubtless already had his photos.

"Where to?" Lance asked.

My stomach rumbled a complaint about a late breakfast of meat pizza and soda. "Someplace to get me antacids."

Ten minutes and one drugstore visit later, Lance dropped Natasha and me off at Ironweed University and drove toward the primate sanctuary himself. I needed to finish and print my syllabi before the semester started, not to mention get them turned in for copying. Lance needed the same things, but he planned to wing it when classes started next Tuesday.

Tasha could have opted to spend time with friends, but by the way she alternately yawned every few minutes and flinched away from small noises, I suspected she preferred to curl up on the couch in the department secretary's office and sleep nestled in the certainty of being watched and safe. She could have crashed in my office, but it had been Art's, and the sofa in *there* was legendary. The secretary rushed to greet us as we stepped out of the elevator in the Biological Sciences building. "I saw you on the *news*, and I was so *worried*!"

"Thanks, Travis," I greeted him as Natasha made straight for his couch. "We're doing fine."

"What about the little boy? How did you ever find him?"

"I think he'll be fine, too." *If his social worker doesn't get him killed from ineptitude.* "How are you settling in here?"

"One day at a time," he said. "One *long* day at a time." He patted my arm as he moved away toward his office.

Travis was the new secretary. The old one had retired in the wake of Art's death. Travis was, like Lance and me, still getting used to the department. We shared regular stories of bewilderment about policies and the locations of things. Lance and I had always taught part time at Ironweed U, but our one class each per academic year was an upper-level course taught out at the primate sanctuary. The school didn't even maintain office space for us.

When Art was murdered in June, only Lance and I could teach the classes his students had already registered for at the end of spring term. Cancelling them would have created havoc. Lance and I had been cordially invited to fill the gap. In other words, the department chair called us up and told us our new schedule in the middle of July.

I hated the man, but we needed the money. We didn't argue. Where Natasha's name had largely been shielded from the news of the pornography ring, the sanctuary's had not. A few pictures of our monkeys in lewd shots had been leaked. We lost funders almost daily for the month of June, and when things stabilized in July, we had to make some hard decisions. We already only employed three people besides Lance and myself. Everybody else was a volunteer. We needed to cut one salary. Rather than let go any of the hands we desperately needed, I fired myself.

For the present, I was formally a volunteer. It made no practical difference to day-to-day operations. Lance and I were both still in charge. But it was a slice to our personal finances, and those university courses were something of a godsend.

And there was something else. I didn't think the sanctuary would ever recover to the point of being able to pay me again. Lance and I needed to *keep* the added income. Ironweed U was advertising Art's position for the following fall. Once someone was hired to replace him, the need for part-time faculty to teach his courses would evaporate. If the wrong person got hired, someone with a different pet project, the university's desire to fund the sanctuary might also evaporate, and besides Stan Oeschle and his personal fortune, Ironweed U was our largest source of money.

The solution seemed simple to me. I loved to teach. I wanted Art's job. But Lance and I had long ago agreed we were field researchers, not teachers to be trapped into semester schedules. I didn't think he would like it when he found out I was applying.

CHAPTER 4

Dear Nora:

Why am I the only person who can do anything around here? My husband and kids will hardly lift a finger. Help!

Worked to the Bone

Dear Worked:

Hire an expensive housekeeper and present the bill to your family. Then take yourself for a spa weekend. Repeat as necessary.

Nora

Half an hour later, I jerked at a knock on my open door.

"Sorry." Bryan, Travis's partner, shifted from foot to foot in the hall.

"No, *I'm* sorry. I'm jittery and distracted. Here, come in. I didn't expect to see you so quickly." I shifted some books encroaching on the couch. Because it had been here longer than the current doorway, that particular upholstered nightmare would only be coming out in pieces. It had automatic priority over my need for space. Natasha's complete unwillingness to sleep on it was testament to its age and condition. If I got Art's job, my first official act would be to evict both the sofa and my current officemate, even if the former had to be removed one axed-up piece at a time and the latter bribed with gourmet coffee.

Bryan didn't answer my implied question. Instead, he began reshelving titles. "Lance can't keep those things in order, can he?"

"I guess I've already made room for you one too many times. You know where all of them go." Lance's and my shared office at the old house worked because it was at least four times this size. Even at our old house, the room had been twice as big as this cramped hole in the university wall. But we were part-timers, and it was something of a coup to score Art's old office, which was considered large by departmental standards. Techni-cally, we were not entitled to the bigger spaces afforded our full-time colleagues, but nobody else wanted to clean up Art's mess or deal with his files. The tradeoff was Lance and me having to share *everything* here, even the desk, like a couple of teaching assistants. Still, there were certain tasks best accomplished at school, and completing syllabi and writing out assignments seemed to be among these, since paper was at a premium at the center and the department offered free printing in exchange for timely submission.

I hated to come in after Lance had been here. He was untidy at best, downright sloppy at worst, and the desk brimmed with his stacks of papers and inexplicable notes. I always swore half the reason he and Art had gotten along so well was their mutual disregard for anything resembling organization. I'm hardly a neat freak myself, but I can keep a desk cleared. I can put away my books when I'm through using them.

Bryan finished his work as my personal librarian. "Saw you on the news." He didn't quite manage to keep the curiosity out of his voice. "Pretty freaky stuff." He sat.

"And now the kid's social worker wants to place the kid with *us*, but you may *not* print that." *And why won't that idea leave me alone?* Bryan was one of the two editors of the *Muscogen Free Press*, and the only reporter I would even consider talking to about this morning's adventure. He had done wonders to keep the sanctuary's name held in high regard, at least in the county.

"With you and Lance?" His question held personal, not professional, interest.

I resumed my work at the keyboard. "What is she *thinking*?" *And what am I thinking?*

"A couple of people she knew nothing about would be perfect for the kid because you happened to find him, naturally."

"She knows about us. Knows too *much* about us. She's the one who wouldn't leave us alone when we were taking classes for Natasha."

"The *Orangutan Lady*?"

Bryan and Travis had listened to me rant about Merry for most of the summer. They were interested in our progress through social services because they were considering an adoption from foster care themselves. They had been working with a private agency for nearly three years and were no closer now to parenthood than when they started out. The foster care system was looking better and better to them.

But even within the system, there was a delay for a couple hoping to adopt an infant, as they were, and they had already been through a home study with the private agency. Our rapid and tumultuous experience with Natasha hadn't given them much confidence in the system. For the present, they were planning to stay the course and keep waiting.

"What did she say?"

"You don't want to know. It was racist, now I think about it, though at the time, all I noticed was how offensive it was about the little boy's mind."

"You going to report her?"

"I'm going to talk to somebody once I've calmed down. Officer Carmichael heard the remark too, and I want to get his take." I hit enter three times and typed my name into my document. "You have a minute to proofread something?" Bryan's sharp editor's eyes were exactly what I needed now.

"Sure. Travis is going to be embroiled with the department chair for at least the next thousand years." He glanced at his watch. "At this rate, our lunch date is going to be tomorrow." It was already one o'clock, and the biology chair was notorious for last-minute demands, making lunches nigh on impossible for his employees. One of Travis's chief complaints since taking the job was his schedule as a salaried employee. He'd been hourly at his former jobs, and the lack of guaranteed breaks irked him.

I hit print and retrieved my sheets. Art's personal printer was another advantage of the university office. "Thanks for the help." While he read and red-lined, I checked on Natasha. Travis had left her in the care of a graduate assistant, another semi-friendly face who didn't seem to care one way or the other that the sleeping girl behind her was tossing and talking. "Don't," Natasha said. "She's only sleeping."

"Tasha," I called.

She twisted, but didn't wake. *"No! . . ."*

"Natasha." I patted her arm.

"Get off of me!" She jumped to her feet, then jerked her head from side to side, her arms held in a defensive pose. As quickly, she collapsed to her seat, gasping for breath like she'd been running. "It's you," she said. "Thank God, it's only you." She lowered her forehead to her palms.

"Are you all right?"

"I saw the EMT . . . when Mom died . . . purple . . ." She shook her head, clearing it, and said, "Yeah. Can I lock myself in the conference room and call Trudy? I remembered something."

Natasha never wanted to talk to me about the things she remembered. Stan said she never talked to him, either. Perhaps she confided in Gert, but I don't think so. The memories came to her jaggedly, in nightmares and waking flashbacks. When she volunteered at the primate center, I often heard her talking in a low voice to Chuck, our resident male orangutan, who we had captured after he saved us all in June. I wondered if she was telling him about the things that made her shudder and cry out in her sleep, and clam up and pull away while waking. Without fail, if she felt something was significant, she rang the FBI agent.

"Let me make sure it's not where the chair has Travis cornered. If it is, you can use my office. Otherwise, it should be fine." The conference room was empty when I looked in, but the stink of rotting food emanating from the departmental fridge and its unofficial pantry in the cabinet to one side made both of us gag. "Trash can."

Shirts pulled over our noses, we dashed in with the can from the hall and emptied both the pantry *and* the fridge. I nearly pitched the fresh lunch Travis would probably not be enjoying, but Tasha swiped it back at the last second. Lacking anything to scrub with or any cleaning liquids to employ in such a project, I was prepared to unplug the fridge and leave the door open to let it air to the room. But Natasha saw a can of disinfectant spray on the top shelf. "Help me push the big table over there, and I'll reach that," she said.

In fact, the top shelf was so high above her head she ultimately fumbled around until the can fell out, bounced on the table, then landed on the carpet, its trigger depressed, and noxious lemon scent spewing straight up. "I got it! I got it!" I aimed it in the pantry and fridge. I jammed the nozzle, but it went on spraying. "Now what do I do with it?"

"Get rid of it before it smells as bad as the food!" Natasha jumped down.

"Where?" I threw it in the sink.

"Not there!" She grabbed it back. "Get it out of the room." She popped it in the garbage still fizzing. "Help me out, Noel!"

We tied off the bag to a hissing chorus. "Shouldn't it run out soon?"

Natasha grabbed the brimming trash can on the far side and dragged it backward across the carpet. "I don't know. It felt almost full."

I shoved with her. As we forced the lid down atop the overfull bag, the chair's voice drifted down the hall. "Get the ad out there," he grumbled, doubtless hassling Travis. "I want to interview for this position on the conference circuit this January." Their footsteps echoed down the hall, headed for us and our smelly mess. Here he was talking about the job I wanted and about to come upon me manhandling a fetid, whooshing container that probably, now I considered the problem, contained his lunch.

Natasha seemed to have reached a similar conclusion. "What do we do?" she mouthed to me.

"Run! Hide!"

"Where?"

"My office."

We scurried around the corner as the chair asked, "What in thunder is that *smell?*" By the time he demanded, "What's wrong with the trash can, Travis?" we were scooting in my door. Bryan perched on the couch arm, one of my red grading pens in one hand, my CV and cover letter attached to a clipboard on his lap.

He didn't look up. "What's the commotion?"

Natasha leaned into the door, clicking it gently shut. I snatched up my phone and dialed the desk. When Travis picked up, I said, "The noise in the trash is an overzealous can of lemon spray. It may overwhelm the other smells. Your lunch is the only one I didn't pitch." Then I hung up. "I guess you'll need to use my office," I told Natasha. "I'm thinking the conference room is out."

"Is Travis free?" Bryan handed over my papers. "I bled all over these. All the mistakes are nitpicky stuff, but a letter-perfect document will stand out. You have no idea how many reporter applications the *Press* gets from people who can't spell or put a sentence in the right order."

"Maybe you could do a series about it."

"I don't want to mock . . . but Nora could! Get your mother to call me later, will you?"

"What's Next, Nora?" was one of the *Free Press*'s most popular columns. It had started as a series of sewing tips years ago, when Bryan's parents ran the paper. Back then, it was called "Tell Me More, Lenore," and questions traditionally ended with, "Please help or send thread." Over the years, it had blossomed into a more general column as people started to send in a broader range of questions. Now, it seemed nothing was off limits. Hence, the updated name. Mom responded to queries about everything from sex to lawn maintenance. Muscogen County had a love for the outré, and Lenore Rue's column was one of the first sections people turned to when the paper hit their doorsteps once a week.

Occasionally, Mom stepped out of her assigned role to editorialize or satirize something. "It does sound right up her alley." I followed Bryan out of the office and shut the door behind us to give Natasha privacy. "I can imagine Nora would have *tons* to say on the topic." Although she was a seamstress by trade, Mom had grown up the child of a single mother in the 1950s, and she and my Nana had lived under the community's constant scrutiny. She might be making up for her straight-laced childhood in other ways, like badly dyed hair, living in a house that used to be a funeral home, and writing a sometimes racy advice column, but Mom had the diction and grammar of an English teacher. She would enjoy a chance to take aim at some of her pet peeves.

"I do want to talk to you about this morning," Bryan said more quietly. "But I don't want to print anything that could make trouble." Although he appeared to be the least aggressive reporter in the business, Bryan had a way of putting people off guard and extracting far more information than speakers ever meant to give him. But he was also ethical, and on our side here, and not only because Stan was one of the newspaper's major funders.

"You don't go to press for a few days, right?"

He nodded.

"Give us another day to get moved in, and we'll have you guys over for dinner with the detective. I'm not promising gourmet fare; we'll probably order in pizza from the Marine, but it would give you a chance to talk to all of us at once."

"Noel, I love you!" He planted a big kiss on my cheek right as Travis came out of the office.

"Honey! Cheating on me!" Travis said in mock horror.

"It's not what you think. I mean, I love her, but I don't *love* love her. I don't. . . ." He paused, then untangled his verbal web by kissing Travis on the lips. "See? Cheeks are for friends, lips are for families. Let's go to lunch."

"You know I can't. I've got a dozen syllabi to make fifty copies each of, and . . ."

"Of course you can!" Bryan interrupted Travis's spiel. "You're salaried. Nobody is watching you punch the clock."

"The chair is watching everything I *do*. Besides, I brought my lunch."

"Technically, I did, too. Let's go anyway. If you want, we can sashay past his office arm in arm . . ." Travis and Bryan were about the least sashaying couple I knew.

"I'd like to, but I'd rather get home on time tonight, and he wants me to revise his ad for Dr. Hooper's position. He wants somebody with a different specialty to bring new ideas to the department."

My heart sank. Travis rolled his eyes. Bryan patted my back. Travis had known I was applying for the job ever since it came open, and if Bryan hadn't already, editing my cover letter had surely clued him in. "Don't worry about *him*," Travis said. "The rest of the committee won't go along with it. They like the ad exactly as it's written. I have to compose something for them to reject to humor him. Come *on*! Half of them expect you or Lance or both of you to apply for it. You're a *shoo-in*."

"I wish I felt so sure. Listen, Lance doesn't know . . ."

"You haven't told him? What if he wants to apply, too?"

"You know something I don't?"

"No . . . no, but it seems . . ."

"Noel!" Natasha came pelting down the hall. "Where's your cell phone?"

"In my pocket, why?"

"Call Lance back. He's been trying to get hold of you ever since he got to the sanctuary." I pulled out the phone. Predictably, I had it silenced. I had missed ten calls. "He rang the office," she went on. "And he wants to know if we can get a ride out to the sanctuary."

"What? Why?" I fumbled in my haste to dial. Naturally, Lance didn't answer. "Is something wrong?"

"I think so. He sounded rushed. He said something about catching the little termites before they got into more mischief."

"The what? Bryan, can you . . . ?"

"You bet, but I want an exclusive on whatever it is . . . as long as it won't mess you guys up." He turned briefly to Travis. "You. Me. Tomorrow. Lunch," he said. "And the chair can go to hell if he tries to interrupt."

CHAPTER 5

Dear Nora:

My neighbor's cat gets out of his house and uses my yard as a litterbox. The neighbor refuses to believe this is happening, even when confronted with direct evidence. What can I do?

Pooped

Dear Pooped:

Get a dog.

Nora

"Don't open that!" Lance slammed the barn door as I tried to come in through the back.

"Hey! You nearly mashed my fingers."

"Should have warned you." He opened the door a crack and rapidly ushered Bryan, Natasha, and I through.

"Good thing we're all thin. What's the . . ." Something brown shot by my ankles and connected with the door as Lance threw himself backward once more. It ran back the way it had come, brushing me again on its way past.

Natasha screamed and jumped as it latched onto her.

"What was *that*?" Bryan demanded.

"A monkey," I said. "A rhesus macaque. The more relevant question is, what's it doing in here?"

Natasha screamed again. The monkey shimmied up her body and sat on her head, yanking her long brown hair as it chittered insults at Lance. "Ow!" The barn rose in a symphony of answering simian screeches and screams.

"I'll get it." Lance reached over me, but the monkey used his arm as a launching board to make a bid for the wall above the door. As it grabbed for purchase, I looked up to find the source of the other voices. Our rafters were littered with macaques. They stared down at us with interest writ large on their human-esque faces.

"Lance, what's going on?"

"I guess I forgot to lock the enclosure after head count last night. Jen said it was wide open this morning when she got here to do breakfast. They were hanging out all over the other enclosures."

"We weren't here yesterday. We were moving."

"I was. I ran by between loads to check in around dinnertime." He meant primate dinnertime, not ours. "The volunteers were all scrambling to keep up, so I pitched in for half an hour or so. I was distracted the whole time, and I couldn't stay long. But I did the rhesus enclosure. I must have forgotten to lock it up.

"Jen lured them into the barn with food when she found them earlier. She was trying to call me the whole time we were finding that kid. If we'd transferred the landline to the new house or had our cell phones on this morning, we'd have known about it sooner."

"Wow." Bryan looked around the ceiling. "You have a regular barrel of monkeys, don't you? How can you be sure you get all of them?"

"Head count."

"But what are you going to do now?"

"Catch them and return them to the enclosure."

"Which enclosure?" Natasha asked. A recent change in Ohio's exotic animal ownership laws had resulted in an amnesty period inviting people to give up wild "pets" without penalty before they had to obtain permits. This included certain types of monkeys. A record number of several varieties had been surrendered to the sanctuary in the month and a half since Art's death.

Although rhesus macaques were one of the most popular monkeys to find their way into private hands, ownership of that specific primate was not affected. This was unfortunate since, as they got bigger and developed a tendency to bite and destroy furniture, their owners often removed teeth and claws and neglected them. Even so, we had received more of them than any other.

Few sanctuaries are even set up to handle rhesus macaques. They're mischievous and stubborn, and they are extra territorial. Plus, they don't carry the same cachet as apes. An ape sanctuary gets more donations. People look at apes and see hairy humans. They imagine their own ancestries and ask themselves what-if. They look at monkeys and they see dogs, cats, and birds. Pets, in other words. All of our chimps had several adoptive "parents" who funded a portion of their care in exchange for a photograph, a thank-you letter, and a tax deduction. Even Chuck already had several extra mothers and fathers.

But few people wanted to invest in monkeys, which they often considered better fodder for zoos and research laboratories. And even though it was driving us to outrageous lengths, our fears of the owners donating the animals to facilities engaged in less ethical research than ours, which was focused on studying the behaviors of primates in captivity, led us to keep adding space for more macaques.

Merle, the volunteer in charge of the area, had recently presented us with ten new intakes and the apology, "They all came from the same pet store. It was getting late, and I was the only one here, and I didn't know what else to do." What he should have done was call Lance or me or one of the three actual employees to complete the intake. By accepting them, he had put us close to our capacity for housing. But I doubted any of us would have turned them away in his place.

The general public also lived under the illusion that the state would euthanize animals given to a state holding facility, when in fact the facility was designed with the goal of finding appropriate placements for exotic pets across the nation. By and large, people contacted zoos and rescue centers like ours privately. Most zoos won't take hand-reared animals, and sanctuaries were filling up fast.

We were nearly overfull ourselves, but our mission, Art's mission, had always been to protect unwanted primates from inappropriate public scrutiny. In the wake of his death, our friend Christian Baker, an ape-keeper at the nearby Ohio Zoo, had banded together a group of keepers to donate materials in Art's honor for several new enclosures, including a second spider monkey area and a second rhesus macaque enclosure. Art's nephew Rick, a builder who maintained ties to Midwest Primates even after his uncle's death, assembled the structures, doubling our available housing for several species. If necessary, we could take on up to 150 rhesus macaques in particular. We were running dangerously close to the line.

"The new one," Lance answered Natasha. It wasn't actually a new construct, merely the newest of our acquisitions. We had purchased it at auction from the same defunct zoo that once housed our orangutan. Enclosures aren't typically mobile, but one of the less savory aspects of the unlicensed facility were its enclosures, which were entirely too easy to disassemble.

We hadn't initially been interested, but here again Christian helped us out. "The materials are fine," he said. "Lance ought to come up with me and see if there's anything you can use."

Lance took Rick, who also approved. The structure he built

us was as solid as anything he had made with newer materials. But it was smaller. "Good," Natasha said. "Fewer to catch. How does this work?"

Natasha had learned our procedures quickly, and she had proven adaptable to our constantly changing needs. "Anybody got soft fruit candy?" I called. In all the time I had been with the center, I had only ever known something like this to happen one other time. Then, someone had noticed the open door right away. Only a couple of monkeys had escaped, and they were quickly captured. But we were all trained for this kind of problem in theory.

"Candy?" Natasha knew our enrichment foods didn't typically include sweets. "Aren't those bad for them?"

"Not half as bad as staying out." The macaques had been swooping down from the rafters stealing things all morning. Lance typically wore a ball cap this time of year, to protect his balding scalp from summer sun. He was not wearing it now, and its pieces drifted down from the ceiling. Jen, who was quite nearsighted, had the bad luck to have been wearing her glasses instead of her contacts this morning. The glasses were now somewhere high overhead, and she was squinting her way through the day.

"I guess I'm grateful I can be sure it was my mistake," Lance said. "We can spare the volunteers a lecture."

"How do we get them back?" Natasha persisted.

"The same way we acquired them in the first place," Lance said. "One at a time."

Three hours later, all of us were sweat-soaked and covered in scratches. Only I had been bitten, the others having the common sense to get their hands out of the way before sharp things happened. We had dodged countless bombs, as the monkeys let their bowels loose wherever they happened to be, without much care for who might be standing underneath. Actual shit slinging was more of a capuchin problem. Only one of our rhesus macaques had suffered from the kind of neglect causing that particular stereotypical behavior, but he had not lost his skill since moving in back in June. He possessed uncanny accuracy.

Our basic tactic was to lay out a couple of candies and wait for an interested party to come close enough. Mostly, the monkeys swiped the first offering and escaped with ease but got snagged on their attempts for a second or sometimes a third treat.

At last, Lance said, "We've only got twenty-four. I've counted four times." We were standing in a sweaty huddle around the enclosure.

"There." Natasha pointed. The final rhesus macaque was hanging out on the spider monkey enclosure chittering away like a neighbor popping over to talk across the fence. Two more candies got him back into the right place. We counted twice more and went back in the barn.

"Why *did* they stick around, Noel?" Bryan asked. "If *my* cage was unlocked all night, I'd be off like a shot." The rest of us all had extra clothing stashed in lockers, and we had changed out. Bryan wasn't a regular volunteer, and Lance was tossing through some of Art's old things to find at least a shirt not covered in monkey hair.

"What would you do if you locked yourself out of your apartment, though?"

"I'd try to get back in!"

"Right. And what if you got lost in the middle of nowhere?"

"I'd want to go home."

"Exactly. These guys associate us with meals and safety. I'm sure more of them were visiting pals before Jen and the breakfast crew showed up, but most of them came up to the place with the food as soon as it was available."

Jen confirmed my thinking. "They explored around the

grounds pretty thoroughly, but they didn't go far. They rushed the barn when I opened the back door." While we talked, a pair of volunteers went out back with a delayed dinner delivery for the other animals, all of whom were still worked into a frenzy. The primates keyed off of our emotions and each other's so acutely. They picked up on our tension and excitement, and reflected it in their behaviors.

It would be late tonight before the security guards got any peace in this part of the county. Which reminded me, "Why didn't the deputies notice we had an empty enclosure overnight? They're supposed to do visual patrols." In the wake of Art's death, we had been forced to abandon our old security company. Rather than find a new one, we had started hiring off-duty police officers to keep an eye on things overnight. Rural cops don't get paid much, and all of them, especially the rookies, needed the extra income.

"I think Lance talked to them," said Jen. After that, she let herself into Lance's and my office to call and let our network know the "termites" had been returned to their enclosures.

Later, as Lance, Natasha, and I rode back home in the battered primate-mobile, I posed the question to Lance. "Deputy Greene swears they were all full when they swept the place at four," he said.

Of all the members of the force who cared for our property when we were absent, Greene was both the most detail-oriented and the most likely to err on the side of over- rather than under-zealousness. If he believed the cages were full, then he had done everything short of a head count. "Must not have noticed they had an exit option until closer to sunrise."

Lance started to berate himself for leaving the cage open as we rounded the corner on our street, but he dribbled to a halt as we all realized we had a welcoming committee of one sitting on our front porch.

"Crap, that's William's sister," Natasha said.

"I was afraid you'd say that," I told her. I *did* recognize her from the pizza shop the day before. "Remind me her name?"

"Sara. She's Sara." The little girl sat on the step, elbows propped on her knees, chin cupped in her hands. Frowsy black hair framed her face, and she stared into space without turning her head, even after we pulled into the driveway.

"Let me out, Lance."

As soon as Sara saw Tasha, her lassitude evaporated. "Hi, hi, hi, hi, hi, hi, hi!" She threw her arms around Natasha's middle.

"Hi, Sara." Natasha wiggled loose and took Sara's shoulders. "Tell me . . ." she began.

"*You'll* tell me!" Sara's excitement vanished in an instant. She looked up with wide, entreating eyes. "Everybody else acts like I'm a baby, and they won't say a thing, but *you'll* say."

"Say what?"

"Is William okay? The TV doesn't make any sense, and nobody wants me to know anything."

"The last time I saw him, he was fine." Natasha smoothed Sara's hair.

"Then why won't they *tell me*? They all act like he's *dead.*"

Natasha shook her head. "He was pretty shaken up, and I guess he was sore, but he was alive at the Marine this morning."

"Thank *God.*" Sara didn't sound like she was six. She sounded like she was a hundred. She collapsed against Natasha and began to sob. "I thought he was *dead.* I was for sure somebody had killed him."

"Sara, listen." Natasha seemed to have regained some of her original purpose. "I need *you* to tell me something. Does anybody know where you are?" In the time we'd been talking, no adult had manifested.

Sara blinked and sniffled, hiccupping like she'd been crying for much longer than she actually had. "Y-yes," she wavered.

"Who?" Natasha said. "Who knows where you are?"

"*You* do," Sara said, as if this should have been obvious.

Natasha groaned. Sara burst into tears again. Natasha hugged her more tightly, but the look she cast in my direction was a helpless one. It begged for an established protocol for escaped foster children matching the one for escaped rhesus macaques.

Behind me, Lance muttered as he scrolled through his phone contacts. "Detective . . . Drew?" he finally asked, "is the girl missing now? The sister of the boy we found this morning?" I couldn't hear Detective Carmichael's response, but I knew what it was when Lance's groan mirrored Natasha's earlier one. "You can cancel the alert. She's here. At our place. We got home from work and she was out front. I don't know how she arrived. Okay. We're not going anyplace."

Lance put his phone back in his pocket. Sara had amped up from a sob to a wail. "I thought he was *d-d-dead*!" she bawled. We all tried to talk to her, but nothing could shake her from her screaming dismay.

"Noel, I have to pee, and she's *crushing* me."

"Sara, honey, you have to let go," I said. I peeled her off of Natasha, and she latched instead onto me. Tasha buzzed toward the door, and I lifted the little girl. It was at once the most natural and unnatural thing in the world. I had cuddled my nieces and nephew through many hurts and temper tantrums, but I had never simply picked up a strange child. I had never whispered soothing things to a person who clearly couldn't hear me. The lonely feeling that had come over me while holding William's hand swallowed me once more.

I tried to gauge Sara's weight as I swayed from leg to leg. She felt too light. It seemed like my sister's children had weighed more than this when they were six. I knew I hadn't been able to lift them so easily by this age. It was like holding a much younger girl.

Lance joined us and wrapped an arm around me. Natasha returned and picked up a handful of papers off the porch. Wordlessly, she passed them to Lance.

The top sheet proved to be a computer-printed map with nearly two and a half miles of walking directions. Then came two envelopes, addressed to "Sweet Sara" and "Wonderful William," respectively. The return addresses were circled on both cards. "They collect cards." Natasha shouted to be heard over Sara. "As soon as I started seeing them around here, I got their address from Natalie so I could write."

"How'd Sara even know to come here, though?"

"Saw . . . saw . . . saw Natasha on TV," Sara blubbered from my shoulder. Her sobbing finally started to taper off.

"And so you . . . what, dug up your card . . ." Lance probed.

"It wasn't *buried*! I don't put things underground."

"Okay, Miss Literal-minded, you . . . found your card . . ."

"And William's!"

"So you went online . . ."

"And printed out a map like Natty does when we have to go into Columbus!"

"That's . . . impressive," my husband marveled.

"Miss Becky will be so *proud* of me!" Sara veered from one form of hysteria to another with fluidity. "I . . . I remembered left, and right, and before, and after, and even *then* all afternoon."

"Have you had anything at all to drink? It's ninety degrees out here!" Her little body felt sweaty, and she didn't seem overheated, but I suddenly feared heat stroke.

"I'll get her some water." Natasha turned to go back in.

"I *hate* water."

"Sara, you're dehydrated," I said. "You need to drink something . . ."

"No! No. No. No. No. NO!" Perhaps this was an improvement from the implacable fit about her brother. At least now, she was engaging with me. With us. But she needed to replenish her system.

"Okay, no water," Natasha said. "What *will* you drink?"

"Lemonate. I only drink lemonate." Sara enunciated her mispronunciation.

Where the hell am I going to get that? Ah! I now live in a neighborhood. There are benefits. "Tasha, I saw kids playing out front two houses down when we were unloading yesterday. Will you see if they have anything even resembling lemonade?"

Natasha returned with an entire pitcher, and Sara guzzled it. She had resumed the hiccuppy breathing that came with hysterical weeping, and I had an idea this was only a short gap before she launched into another crying jag. Instead, she dropped the paper cup Tasha had brought and clutched her crotch with one hand and my arm with the other. "Now I have to *go!*"

"Come on, I'll show you the bathroom." Natasha guided her away from us and toward the house. Sara tripped going up the porch stairs and would have fallen if Tasha hadn't been holding her by the shoulder. While we waited for her to come back out, Drew arrived in a squad car. "She in there?" He pointed to the house.

We showed him inside, where we found Natasha standing outside the bathroom. "But you *have* to come out," she said.

"I want William," Sara bawled.

Tasha turned to us. "She locked herself in. She won't come out without her brother."

"If we have to, the fire department can take the door out with axes," Drew said in a low voice.

"I can probably pick it if you give me five minutes," Lance offered.

"Less traumatic for her."

"Not to mention our house."

While we waited for Lance to root through my hairpins, I said, "How come the junior detective drew two high-profile problems in one day?" Typically, Drew backed up investigations led by the senior detective. "Boss on vacation?"

"Right now, I am *the* detective. Hugh Marsland's supposed to be at a conference in DC, but nobody can get ahold of him. His wife's about out of her mind."

I whistled my dismay. "What's going on?"

Drew shook his head, unwilling to say more. Sara went on caterwauling while Lance began to probe the lock, which proved to be sticky, drawing what should have been a two-minute operation into ten. Sara didn't seem to notice we had stopped rattling the handle and had, instead, started loosening it. Bit by bit, she quieted down, and by the time Lance finally got the door to open, she had been entirely silent for some time.

He twisted the handle and pushed gently on the frame, prepared to use his weight against the door to nudge a resisting body out of his way. Instead, the door opened freely. Sara was curled into a sleeping ball on the bathmat. She was sucking on four fingers of her right hand.

I bypassed the others to crouch beside her. "Come on, Sara. I'm sure your foster mother is worried to death about you."

Sara rolled over and curled tighter around her own knees. "I want William," she mumbled around her hand. She did not wake.

"Say what?" asked Drew.

"Same thing she's been saying all along," I told him.

"I'll take your word for it. All I heard was slobber."

"Let her sleep," Lance said. "I'd imagine she's gotten little enough since last night."

"She can't stay on our bathmat." I slid my arms under the child and lifted her, marveling again at how little she weighed.

"I'll take her." Lance reached for the girl. A jolt of static electricity sparked between us when I handed Sara over. She twitched, and Lance grabbed her with reflexive tightness.

I glanced up at him and saw a disproportionate level of shock in his eyes. "Day catching up to you?"

"Must be. She hardly weighs anything, Noel."

Lance's face closed as quickly as it had opened. But in the moment I stared at him, I remembered he had spent a portion of his own childhood in foster care. No wonder he had reacted so oddly to William earlier and to Sara now. For all the time I had known him, Lance had only told me this after our wedding, and then only under duress. He had not spoken of it since, but I now wondered what happened to him in that year, and what could possibly have been worse than the insanity his mother was perpetuating at home.

The front doorbell rang, then the door popped open. "Yoo-hoo! Hello the house!" called an all-too-familiar voice.

"I'm going to hide in my room now," Natasha whispered.

"Too bad I can't go with you," I told her. To our new guest, I called, "We'll be right out, Merry."

I let Drew greet the newcomer and went with Lance to settle Sara in on the couch, covering her with the afghan we kept draped over its back. We sat with her for a few minutes in silence. I gathered my thoughts and stroked her forehead.

I started to get up, but Lance laid a shaky hand on my arm. The look I had seen in the hall had returned. I settled back down and he pulled me in. For several long minutes, we sat in silence, listening to Drew bustle around our kitchen making coffee like he lived here. Perhaps he, too, had seen Lance's open, wounded expression. Or maybe he knew we hated the Orangutan Lady and expected us to delay a second meeting with her.

Finally, Lance found his voice. "Noel, we have to talk," he

said. "We've needed to for a long time, but especially since this morning. I owe you some explanations."

CHAPTER 6

Dear Nora:
  How can I make people believe me when I speak my mind?
                                                    Fed Up

Dear Fed,
  Stop acting and start doing.

                                                    Nora

"You're sure?" Lance held my face in his large palms, looking into my eyes as if he expected uncertainty.

I nodded, sorrow and guilt in my heart stopping my voice at the throat.

"Then let's go talk to Merry." We rose, and he embraced me. "Thank you," he said. "Thank you for believing in me. Thank you for trusting me. Thank you for . . . everything."

"Easy," I murmured, patting his back. "We still have to deal with the Orangutan Lady." Why was it so difficult not to cry?

Sara's foster father arrived, the mother being still wrapped up at the hospital with William. He checked on the little girl but opted not to wake her, since there were forms to complete and conversations to hold before he could take her anyway. Besides, as we had suspected, she had not slept at all last night.

"I've barely talked to Nat since she went to William this morning," he explained. "It seemed impossible to me he could be fine, especially when they've kept him at the hospital so long.

74

I kept watching the news, looking for some proof he wasn't all right. I think Sara picked up my worry. And then I fell asleep with the TV on, and when I woke up, Sara was gone. None of the other kids saw her leave, but then they wouldn't. None of the others have much to do with the twins. But I never thought she'd . . . she's not my wanderer! That's Will! I had no idea she could use the computer like that, and I . . . I . . . I can't do this anymore. Those children need to be in a home without other children . . . they need . . ."

"There," said Merry, using Adam Forrester's discomfiture to transition seamlessly into her earlier harangue of Lance and me, adding William's sister to our imaginary foster tribe as if she hadn't had the two of them all but broken up before. "This would be the perfect foster environment for William and Sara. There's only one other child, and she's a teen who . . ."

"Stop!" Lance's voice sounded unnaturally harsh, but he repeated, more gently, "Please, stop. You can't keep doing this to me. To us."

"Merry, we don't want to foster those two children," I said.

"But if you . . ."

"Would you shut up long enough for me to finish a sentence?" I'm not normally so rude, even to people I can't stand, but my recent conversation with Lance had left me more rattled than I could have expected. It was the first time he had ever spoken to me of his mother's mental illness, another thing I had only learned about recently. It was her instability that led to his and his brother's placement in foster care in the first place.

On the couch, he had told me, "Mom was always so . . . angry, Noel, and we never knew why. We never knew what to expect. She used to yaw between exhilaration and fury. One hour, we'd be on a shopping spree, drinking milkshakes in the mall while she bought pairs and pairs of shoes. Then, on the car ride home, she'd be screeching at us about school, and our grades, anything at all.

"It was one of those trips . . . I won't go into depth about it, Noel. I can't. But I was a ten-year-old kid, and I couldn't take any more of her ranting. I told her . . . and I waited for her to take a break and get quiet before I said it, so I could sound calm to prove she couldn't make *me* lose my temper . . . I told her she was the worst mother on the planet. And she looked back at me . . . I'll never forget the hatred on her face. She didn't say anything else, but she took off her seatbelt, twisted the steering wheel and plowed the car across two lanes of traffic into the opposite embankment.

"She rode out from the accident scene in one ambulance and Alex and I rode out in two others. I had a broken collarbone and a compound fracture on my arm. Alex had whiplash so bad he couldn't move his head; he was convinced he had broken his neck. And she was thrown from the car and landed in a blackberry bush. I could barely think over my own pain, but she was screaming, "Look at your little brother, Lance Lakeland. Look at him. He's probably going to die, and it is *all your fault.*"

"Do you blame yourself?" I asked him. I hadn't meant to interrupt whatever he had to say, but his cheeks were etched with remembered pain, and it seemed so important to know.

"Not anymore. But I did then. It was a long time before I stopped holding myself accountable for her actions. It was a long time before I realized I probably had the worst injuries of anybody in the vehicle.

"She wouldn't consent to inpatient psychiatric treatment, and Dad wouldn't abandon her while she went through an intensive outpatient program. Alex and I were removed from the home and placed with a family. We saw Dad once a week and Mom hardly at all."

"It sounds awful."

"It was *wonderful*. It was the best year of my childhood. It was . . . there were two other kids in the house, one of them Alex's age, the other a year older than me. We were instant best friends. Every day after school Angelina made us a snack, and we did homework at the kitchen table. And when I was a sassy little jerk, she called me out on it. She'd say, 'I'm sorry you feel that way, Lance. You should go upstairs to your room and think about things until you feel better.' Then she'd come up and talk me through it.

"She had to take away slumber parties, field trips, all kinds of things. I did everything I could think of to make her mad, but she never lost her temper. She always said the same thing. 'I'm sorry you feel that way. You should go upstairs to your room and think about things until you feel better.'

"And Noel, if I have any patience myself now, it's because she was patient with me. She let me rage and get my anger into the world, then. Alex repressed everything. The anger came to him later, and by then . . . you know." I did know. I had been engaged to Lance's younger brother for a short, violent period a long time ago, and I saw Alex in Lance's descriptions of their mother.

"If I am a scientist," he went on, "it's because she let me cut up her nature magazines and glue them to poster board with pages I copied directly from the encyclopedia. It's because she told me I could go to Africa if I was resourceful and brave enough. I owe so much to her, Noel, and at the end of the year, when my mother's course of treatment was over, Alex and I were taken away from her. We had to go back home, and Mom tried to kill herself again almost immediately. She finally went inpatient, and Alex and I were stuck with Dad, who didn't know anything about little boys. He went back and forth to work and watched sports on TV and did the bare minimum to keep us from being taken by the state again. I never had the kind of stability Angelina gave us again until I was an adult, and I could make my own peace."

Lance didn't explain any of these things to the group at the table now, but he laid his hand over mine and looked straight at Merry Frasier. "My mother was mentally ill," he said. "You must know that." Part of our home study had included an extensive background check. She probably did know it, but Drew clearly didn't. He jerked in surprise. "My brother and I spent a year or so in foster care when she was in treatment. We had all of our foster mother's stability taken away when we had to go home. It was devastating to enjoy certainty and safety only to have it snatched back right when I got comfortable with it.

"Foster care is meant to be temporary, Merry. I will not, I *cannot* do that to a child. Natasha's situation is wholly different. When her grandparents get better, she'll go home to them. To their *safe, stable* home. Who knows where these two would go next. Any foster kid is apt to get shuffled around in the system when one thing works and another doesn't. Look at where William and Sara have already been. From family, to foster care, back to family, *back* to foster care. I can't be part of that cycle. The only child we can foster is Natasha." Lance steepled his hands under his mouth as if in prayer.

Adam studied his own folded hands on the table like a guilty child. "They're good kids," he mumbled.

Merry's coffee cup was halfway to her lips. "Yes, good," she backed Adam up. "They simply need an environment . . ."

"Did you not hear a word Lance said?" I demanded. "We *do not want to foster* William and Sara."

Before Merry could interrupt with more protestations, Lance returned one of his hands to its place on top of mine. "We *can't* foster them," he said. "We *want* to adopt them."

"You wha . . ." Merry dropped her mug. It bounced off the table's edge and shattered on the floor. "I'm so sorry, I . . . but

. . . you . . . have you got any paper towels?"

I was already halfway across the kitchen for a broom and dustpan. "I'll clean it up."

"But I thought . . ." she continued to stammer, her gaze never straying from Lance. "You keep telling me you're childless by choice," she finally finished.

"And we are." His voice was steady, pressuring. "I never wanted to have children. I know my genetic makeup. The probability of making somebody exactly like my mother or brother was too high. But it doesn't mean I dislike kids. This is the first summer in I don't know how long we haven't had one of Noel's nieces or her nephew staying with us. We do okay with them."

"A summer visit is hardly the same as an adoption," Merry warned.

"We know." I slopped shards into the dustpan. "But before all the brouhaha around our wedding, we were talking about how empty the house felt without kids in it."

"And it was one *tiny* house." Nobody had heard Natasha coming in, but now she was standing in the hall, leaning against the wall with an *I told you so* smile making me wonder whether we were caring for her or the other way around.

"But you can't announce out of the blue . . . you don't . . . you have to *meet* them first, for heaven's sake!"

"We met them already," said Lance. "We met them today."

"That absolutely does not count." Merry had regained some of her control. "We have to schedule a *formal* meeting, and you have to be approved, and . . . there are *steps* to be followed. Adoption is a process!" Since Lance wasn't giving any ground, she turned her appeal to me.

"Start following them," I said. "We aren't exactly all set here anyway."

"Precisely!" She leapt onto my statement. "Beds. You have to have beds for . . ."

"We have beds," Lance cut in. The bunk beds from the infamous room with a bed had followed us, along with a new double bed we had purchased for Natasha.

"There are lots of things you still need. Call me tomorrow at my office if you're still interested." Merry abruptly rose and huffed out of the kitchen, then let herself out of the house entirely.

"Don't expect her to be helpful." We had all nearly forgotten about Adam, still staring down at the table. "She'll want you to do all the work."

Lance whistled. "You don't say."

"She keeps looking for a permanent place to park them where she can drop in from time to time like a benevolent dictator. Natty and I have been fostering kids for ten years now. We've adopted twice. I have never met a social worker as unhelpful as Meredith Frasier.

"Natty thinks half the reason William got away from her last night was because Merry accosted her in the parking lot of the Marine, and she got stuck talking while she was trying to get everybody buckled in. She forgot to do a head count—when you have a house full of kids, you *always* do a head count. One of the big kids was supposed to buckle William. He swears he did, but I doubt it. Normally Sara would have noticed something as big as her brother not being in the car; they sit right by each other. But Sara was arguing with our thirteen-year-old the whole way home. All the kids insist they saw William get out of the car at home, but I think they're covering for each other. Natty and I are beginning to think he never got *in* it in the first place, poor kid.

"Anyway," Adam sighed heavily and finally looked up from his hands, "am I free to take her home?" He nodded toward our living room and looked at Drew. "I'd like her to wake up somewhere familiar."

Drew had been waiting in silence for some time. "Yeah. We've got everything we need for now." The two men rose together, leaving only Lance sitting at the table, and he made no move to follow when they departed.

I left what remained of the coffee mess and watched Adam collect Sara. When he tried to disentangle her from our afghan, she knotted her fingers through its holes without waking. "Let her keep it," I said.

"Are you sure?" But he was already picking her up without trying to further unswaddle her.

"Yes," said Lance. I hadn't heard him come up behind me, but now I leaned automatically into his warm chest. "She'll be bringing it home soon enough anyway."

CHAPTER 7

Dear Nora:

My crazy family is driving me out of my mind. Every time I turn around, my parents and uncle are going off on extravagant vacations and trying dangerous stunts. My mother jumped out of an airplane! Now, my grandmother wants to run smack into buildings and climb up the sides because Parkour is big in Europe. What can I do?

Appalled

Dear Appalled:

Stop living their lives and live your own instead. Also, the Parkour club jams on the Ironweed U campus Saturdays, and we try to be flexible. You aren't required to scale the buildings if you don't want to. We could always use new blood.

Nora

"Are you out of your minds?" My mother was washing the dinner pans in her lavishly oversized sink while Natasha loaded them one by one into a dishwasher so large you could lose a small country in it. "I think your friend's death has given you a case of the crazies."

"Or is this some kind of belated April Fool's joke?" My father puttered by with his rose shears, ready to do some serious pruning out back.

Lance stopped wiping down the counter and met Dad's eyes.

82

"It's not a joke."

"And," I added, "I think we're finally *in* our right minds." I did not stop cleaning the table, but instead continued wiping overlapping ovals of wet onto its surface.

"You *never* wanted children!" said Mama.

"*I* never wanted children," Lance corrected her. "I'm pretty sure Noel's always wanted them."

I heard a question in the silence following this statement. I wasn't sure how to answer. Although Lance and I had only married back in June, we had lived together for nearly a decade, and been a couple since we finished grad school. When we first got serious about each other, Lance had warned me, "You should know I don't want to have kids. It's not something you can change, and if it isn't something you can live with, we should probably stop teasing each other along."

In those early days, most of our discretionary funds went toward primate research in rescue centers and wild areas around the globe. Although it made me sad to set aside the desire for children, I knew by then that Lance and I were a good fit, and I would be left freer in my research without small encumbrances to check with my luggage at the airport.

Never, not once in the intervening years, had it occurred to me that when Lance said he didn't want kids, he meant he didn't want to add to the gene pool. I had not known how volatile his mother is, and I hadn't realized how adamantly he feared bringing a child into the world to struggle with the same insurmountable obstacles she faced.

Maybe if I had known, I would have argued the point more heavily. I might have pointed out the leaps in which mental healthcare has grown in the decades since we were children ourselves, never mind when *she* was young. It's impossible to say.

Instead, I contented myself with science and the delight we

both took in hosting my nieces and nephew for portions of every summer. But the kids came less and less as they grew up. Rachel had graduated high school the previous spring. She was getting ready to head west to a college in Arizona that would put her about as far away from her mother as she could get. (I understood the sentiment. My sister can be overbearing, to put it lightly.) Brenda had aged into summer sports camps, and Poppy had outgrown month-long stays away from her own friends. And the primate center had never fascinated Bryce the way it did his sisters, so he spent most of his time with us bored, and he had quietly turned down our offer to stay after the wedding with a mumble and a blush.

Sometimes, watching Lance play with them, I wondered about his attitude. But I also knew when he said a thing in a certain way while looking at me eye to eye, which wasn't easy considering our height difference, he meant it completely. I set aside my hopeful "maybes" as impossible "what-ifs."

But when we sat on our couch with Sara sleeping beside us, when he said we needed to talk and completed for me the picture of his childhood, I finally understood what he meant. It was not at all shocking when he had finished his story by telling me this was why he didn't feel right about fostering the twins.

But I was rendered speechless when he added, "I've always wanted to be a daddy. Would you consider adopting them?" There were other things, how he thought we could handle their special needs and why he felt so connected to them. He hadn't needed to tell me those things at all, because I felt them myself.

Clutching William's hand in the Marine's parking lot, holding Sara while she was screaming in our yard, and lifting her off the bathroom rug had reawakened the same primal urge in me. And this time, it wasn't some vague desire to have children triggered by playing with somebody else's babies. This time, it was something utterly different, alien. I didn't merely want to be a parent to some child, I wanted to be a parent to *this* child, to *these* children.

I admired their tenacity. Whatever propelled William into the Marine's back lot in the first place, he had exhibited the sense to crawl under the Dumpster, a safe, confined area that was nonetheless sure to be visited by human feet sooner or later. And Sara's bravery in looking up an address and printing directions bespoke the kind of kindred soul who would study and analyze a situation, then take appropriate action. Her method needed some ironing out. For instance, she needed to add a step where she told an adult *before* she acted, not after. But this was a girl who wouldn't be bored growing up with a pair of researchers.

I'd finally had to interrupt Lance to say, "Yes!" so we could go talk to the pair drinking coffee in our kitchen.

I could understand my parents' reactions. Everyone, including ourselves, accepted Lance and me for the perpetual aunt and uncle, always available to pick up the slack in summer and help out in a crisis. Nonetheless, I didn't want Mama and Daddy to weasel out of the conversation with their astonishment. "Aren't you going to congratulate us?"

Every one of Marguerite's pregnancies had been greeted with joy so overwhelming that my sister had never once gotten to tell me herself she was expecting. It was always Mom calling to breathlessly proclaim, "Noel, I'm going to be a grammy!" as if each child was the first.

"Yes, dear, of course we're happy for you," Mama said. But she added, "If you're sure that's what you want. It's an awful lot for me to digest at once."

"I hope you know what you're getting yourselves into," Daddy said, and he stomped on by to the garden.

We didn't manage to communicate our own enthusiasm to anyone until the next day, when we took Natasha to see her grandparents in Columbus. "You are?" Stan demanded from his hospital bed. "Hot-diggety, you finally did it. Art's going to be so damned proud." There was a long silence while Stan remembered Art, his best friend and our mentor, had been dead since June. "Art would have been proud," he said more softly. "He'd have been so happy for you two. Now tell me everything. Lay it all out for me. I want to know all the details."

It was gratifying to find someone finally willing to listen. We told him the whole story, ending with my parents' barely unspoken disapproval.

"They'll get over it," said Stan. "You gotta remember, your Nana raised your mom alone back when girls who got themselves in the family way were shipped off to homes. If your Nana didn't have a spine tougher than the rod they've got jammed down my back and her own mother wasn't exactly the same way, your mama might have been somebody else's baby. And your dad . . . when did he ever take sudden news well?"

"Never," I had to admit. He had greeted Mama's ghastly new hair color by practically moving into the garden shed for a month.

"There you go. Now listen, this social worker sounds like a real number. There's bad ones, and there's good ones, and she sounds like she's a category all her own. Even the foster dad says this won't be easy."

In fact, while we helped Adam buckle Sara into her car seat, he had told us, "You're going to need an advocate. It's a free service, but you have to go down to Columbus. Merry's liable to squirrel everything around. If you're serious about this, you'll have to keep setting her straight."

"True enough," I told Stan.

"Here's what you do," he began, "this is our lawyer from when that son-of-a-bitch . . . what was his name, sweetie?"

"Terry." Natasha stared out the window as she spoke. "Terry Dalton."

"Yes. That Terry fellow tried to claim he was Tasha's father, and we had to get DNA tests before we could prove he didn't even have the legal right to be visiting her. It was my man Jacob Alston got everything taken care of quick. You go down and see Jacob, and tell him I sent you. Have him send all his bills to me . . ."

"This is getting out of hand, Stan," said Lance. "We shouldn't need a lawyer. You bought us a house, and we're still trying to figure out how to pay you for it. You can't go around and buy—"

"Yes I can, and I will!" It was as close to heated as Stan had become for the entire visit. "Art set so much stock by the two of you. You have got no idea . . . *no idea* what it means to Gert and me to know Tasha's with you all when she's not with us. This little baby is all we've got left, and knowing she's safe, *completely* safe, when Gert and I can't even get to see each other . . . *that's* what I can't buy. I know you didn't take her in expecting things out of me, and I know it because I know how much Art loved you.

"The first thing I said . . . tried to say . . . when I came around in the hospital with my jaw wired shut, the first thing I wanted to know was, 'Did Tasha get away? Did I at least buy her time enough to pick the padlock?' And when the nurse told me she was with you, I said, 'Thank God, because they're the only people on the planet Art would have trusted right now.' Of course, I didn't make any sense to her because she didn't know Art at all, and I was all woozy and muddleheaded, and I couldn't open my mouth to talk, so she didn't give it much stock anyway. It was the next day when I actually saw you all three together before I realized if she was with you, something must have happened to my Gertie.

"Art *always* wanted you to have babies. He wouldn't have

cared a whit how you got them. He's up in heaven right now dancing with the angels and throwing you a big old shower. Your folks will come around, Noel. Not everybody in our generation is as adaptable to change as this old geezer." He swung a finger toward his bed stand to indicate the host of electronic devices technically prohibited by hospital policy, but overlooked by the staff because about the only people Stan couldn't bully into giving him his own way were his doctors.

"And I'm telling you," he went on, "a bad social worker can throw the whole thing off if she wants to."

"But she's so eager to get these kids a home," Lance protested. "Surely she wouldn't do anything to impact it."

"Not on purpose," said Natasha. "But she's awful. Aw. Ful. Granddad's right. She'll mess everything up by accident and make it out to be your fault."

"There's my girl!" said Stan.

CHAPTER 8

Dear Nora:
   I can't stop lying. It's compulsive. What should I do?
                              Dishonest in the Big City

Dear Dishonest:
   Tell me the truth.

                                        Nora

Stan and Adam were both right. Merry did cause problems simply by being herself. But we didn't need a lawyer. With guidance from a state advocate, we were soon cleared to formally meet the twins.

We all agreed that their unique circumstances required a slow transition. But even Ann, our advocate, was disappointed in us for setting our hearts on these particular kids when there was no way to be sure they would come to us.

"This isn't how it works, folks," she said. "You're supposed to evaluate possibilities while the state determines appropriate placements."

"I think we've already gotten to do more evaluating than most parents, and rumor has it that these two will be hard to place."

"You're right. Please don't mistake me. I'm elated to have a pair of parents willing to adopt two special needs children. But

I need to evaluate their specific needs and your ability to meet them."

"We'll learn," he said. "We aren't expecting easy."

"You have absolutely no idea how hard it's going to get."

"Please," I told her. "We're willing. Let us try."

"The first meeting date is set," she said. "We can see how things go and move forward from there."

It was a nonsensical sham of a meeting, held in the artificial setting of the social services office. Natasha was also with us, and all the twins had been told was that she was worried about their adventures and wanted to spend some time with them to make sure they were all right.

"This is stupid," said Sara, as soon as we came together in the playroom chosen for the gathering. Lance and I had seated ourselves in child-sized chairs around a child-sized table. Natalie Forrester sat on the floor with Natasha. Merry and Ann stood by the door, apparently guarding it should one of the children attempt to bolt.

"Sara," said Natalie. "Be polite."

"I'd love to know why it's stupid," Merry said. The door was outfitted with Plexi-glass on top, and the sun shone in the windows of the corridor beyond. Our advocate's summer tan looked deep and golden in this light. Merry, in contrast, looked more sallow and put-upon than usual.

Sara, don't give her ammunition. This was supposed to be a casual get-together between them and Natasha where we adults merely happened to be present. We were not, in Merry's words, "to raise their hopes unnecessarily." Like Ann, she still feared we would back out.

Sara sighed loudly. She and William had retreated as far from the adults as they could get, but we were still all crowded together. The room was not large. "Fourth of all," she said, "Playdates happen in houses. Ninth, we come here to get ditched. Every time. And *seventh,* we all . . . *all know* Natty and Adam are trying to get rid of us. Who knows where we'll go? We probably won't ever see Tasha again, so we're here to say goodbye."

A babble of adult voices rose in protestation, but none of them even began to answer the challenge Sara had issued. She didn't speak in the monotone her folder would have led me to expect, and her cross-armed posture showed body language wasn't totally alien to her. Obviously, her folder wasn't fully descriptive. I decided to take its contents with a grain of salt. Aside from its recitation of obvious facts, such as the twins being biracial and Sara being talkative, it seemed to be made largely of Merry's random observations anyhow. The parts from Natalie Forrester were much more likely to be helpful.

We adults dribbled into silence as quickly as we had started talking. It was Natasha who finally took up Sara's gauntlet. "You've got it wrong," she said.

"But they *are* getting rid of us, Tasha," Sara wailed. Suddenly, she was only six again, six and scared. "And so are you!"

"I know they are." Natasha looked only at Sara, or she would have seen Natalie blushing. But Sara was right. Whatever else happened, Sara and William *would* be leaving Natalie and Adam's house soon. And the child deserved the truth. "But I'm not. I've missed you for too long. I'll *always* find you from now until forever. Pinkie swear." Warily, Sara met Natasha's outstretched pinkie with her own. "I also know," Natasha went on, "that you're right about this being the weirdest playdate ever. You know I'll always tell you the truth, right? And I absolutely promise you we're here to play, and you'll see me again soon."

"How soon?"

"Later this month." Natasha stared at Sara. "Maybe even at Natty and Adam's house. I was worried about you the other day, and so were Lance and Noel here. It's upsetting when a child is missing . . ."

"Yes, because I know all about stranger-danger, and I didn't talk to anybody at all when I—"

Sara would have gone on longer in this vein, but Natasha cut her off. The folder had this right, then. It said she was easily distracted and would hone in on unexpected portions of a conversation as if those things were central to the discussion. Natasha repeated the first part of her statement. "I was worried about you," she said, "and so were Lance and Noel here. Do you understand what I'm telling you?"

Sara's nose started twitching like a rabbit's, and she creased her brow and poked her tongue out of her mouth, deep in thought. "Maybe you'll see us at Natty and Adam's, and maybe . . . somewhere else?" she guessed.

"Right," said Tasha, before the adults could shush her.

Suddenly, Sara's expression lifted, the furrowed brow smoothed, and the eyes grew wide. "Oh!" she said, looking straight at Natasha now. "Okay. Got it. Let's play."

The folder warned she struggled to understand cause-and-effect relationships, had trouble connecting the dots between points A and B in any given conversation. But I thought I had seen quite a few dots light up on her face right then. She wasn't all the way to point C yet. She hadn't figured out we wanted to adopt them, but she knew we planned to foster them if this meeting went well. And that was enough.

Sara grabbed her brother's shoulders. "Do you got it?" she asked.

"You got trucks," William said. *His* folder had identified him as practically nonverbal. It sounded like he had a few more words than Meredith Frasier was letting on. Also, he was stating a fact. While the rest of us had been so focused on Sara, he had emptied two small backpacks onto the floor. He and Sara both had cars and trucks he had stretched end to end in a small line of traffic between the table and a wall. The vehicles were arranged largest to smallest, with like colors together. Each time he picked up a new one from the pile, he adjusted the line to place the newcomer in the right spot.

"Noel," Lance breathed. "Look. He's *classifying*." His tone said, *See? Our little scientist,* as if he and I had somehow had a hand in William's skill with putting trucks in a row. "Hey, buddy, I love the way you've got these organized." Lance sat down beside William. "Can I maybe try a few?"

William went on picking up and placing. He did not answer.

Natalie warned, "Nobody is allowed to touch William's trucks."

Before the sentence was half out of her mouth, though, Lance had plucked a car out of the pile William was drawing from. William looked up sharply and watched Lance, but he didn't say anything or take the vehicle back.

"Let's see. This one is yellow, and it's kind of little. I'm going to put it here." Lance moved two other cars to place his in the line.

"No!" William flicked Lance's out to the side, then sat back and watched.

"Okay, sorry."

"He does them by number of doors, too," Sara explained. "That one's got four and the rest of those have two. It should have gone all the way in back of the yellows."

"Ah." Slowly Lance picked the rejected car up again and scooted it to a different place in line.

"Yes," said William.

"Can I try another?"

William didn't answer, but he allowed Lance to choose and place again, and when it had been scooted to his satisfaction, he nodded and said, "Yes."

"Now there's something," said Natalie. "He's never let Adam and me play with them. But then, I don't think either of us figured out his method."

"Duh." Sara hadn't moved. "Half those are mine," she told her brother.

"Be polite," Natalie reminded her again.

"What do you want to play?" Natasha indicated the other toys in the room, which seemed designed for younger children.

Sara was evading even her friend's eyes now. She didn't say anything.

"Sara, would you like to play trucks?" Natalie asked.

"Yeah, trucks," she mumbled. She seized half of William's pile. He ignored her. Where William's game consisted entirely of lining the cars up, Sara handed Natasha and I each a car, deliberately walked past Natalie and Merry, then offered a car to Ann. "Now," she told us, "they go in a big circle." Her play was repetitive. While she seemed to enjoy it tremendously, I couldn't help feeling a bit bored.

Still, the first meeting was successful, and when we left, Ann said, "You're obviously interested. I'll be in touch."

"We do want to take this slowly," Lance reminded her. "We know this is going to be hard on them."

"You don't have forever," Merry warned us. "They have to be moved out of the Forresters' for good, and soon."

They followed Natalie and the twins outside, and we took Natasha back to school to meet her math tutor, who would bring the girl back to us at the center later in the day. "I don't understand Merry's hurry," I told Lance.

"I don't understand Merry's anything," he replied.

The Friday before Labor Day, I went out to dinner with my friend Hannah while Lance got the center shut down for the evening. Two other friends, Liz and Mina, couldn't come but sent us good luck in the form of toy store gift certificates. "Who *are* you?" Hannah asked me. "Married a couple of months, and you're already lying to your husband and nesting at the same time. Art's dying's got you rattled. Why don't you at least tell Lance you've applied for the job? It makes sense one of you should take it."

"Because we agreed not to. We're field researchers. The teaching has always been a sideline. And I don't want to start a fight about money. He doesn't worry about it like I do."

"What are you going to say when they hire you?"

"*If* they hire me, Hannah. I graduated from Ironweed, I'd be a teacher whose style closely imitates the person they're replacing, and I've only ever taught part time. All of those are strikes against me."

"*When* they hire you," she repeated, "what are you going to tell your husband?"

"Individual health insurance is too expensive for four people." Ironweed might bill itself as the only social justice–oriented science university in the nation, but the attitude didn't extend to part-time instructors' health care. And the center couldn't afford to offer such an extravagance. Lance and I had always carried our own policies. When the twins came to us, they would initially be covered by the government. But the day the adoption became final, we had to have them on *our* plan.

"I guess that's one angle." Our entrees came then, and we devoted ourselves to food in uncomfortable silence. Hannah had never been the sort to keep her opinions private. Her outspoken enthusiasm for Ironweed's historic downtown area had served as a springboard not only for her own business, Hannah's Rags, but for a total revitalization of the area. In an area with a largely white population, she was a successful black woman who thrived on a large personality.

But she sure wasn't saying what I wanted to hear today. "Are you with my mom that we've lost our minds wanting to adopt these kids?"

"Now there's a whole different story. I've *always* thought you and Lance would make cute parents. It was one of those things I kind of wondered about but never asked. I mean, I'd heard you say 'childless-by-choice' but I know it can mean many things. I think it's all good. It's this secrecy thing bugging me. Him not telling you . . . you've been together ten years, and he never mentioned his mother was a stark raving lunatic."

"She's mentally ill . . ."

"Noel, there's a difference between 'mentally ill' and 'completely whacko'."

"And the difference is?"

"She blew up your car." I couldn't argue with Hannah's logic. We were down to one car right now because my mother-in-law had set my car on fire the day before the wedding. "And you telling him one thing and then doing the exact opposite," she went on. "You're a good couple, Noel, but you'll screw yourselves over. Every one of my ex-husbands would say the same."

I started to tell Hannah she only had one ex, but my phone buzzed in my purse, the ringtone Natasha had programmed into it for her own number. "Speaking of kids . . . what's up, Tasha?"

"Can you come home *now*, Noel?" Natasha's school had scheduled a teacher in-service to correspond with the holiday, so she had been out at the center for much of the day. Lance had dropped her home on his way in to Ironweed University to grade quizzes. Now, she was there alone, waiting for a ride with friends to go to what she swore was a poetry slam later in the evening. I was personally skeptical about the number of teen poetry slams being offered in Muscogen County, but we had the same agreement Natasha had forged with all of her family and closest friends: always the truth, no matter what. I had agreed to extend trust until I saw evidence to the contrary. Even when I confronted her about the alcohol back in June when we hardly knew her, she had stuck to her own policy.

"What's wrong?" My mind flew immediately to the sight of her half-dressed in a borrowed shirt, trapped with us in an empty enclosure on our property. Her life had been in danger then, and so had ours. "Do you need the police?"

"It's not so bad. It's *awful.*"

"Tasha, calm down, which is it?"

"It's . . . I'm in the kitchen and everything is horrible. Fine. Really. Dreadful." *Kitchen* was her paranoid code for "It's okay, nobody's forcing me to say this." If she'd said she wanted to go lie in her bed, I'd have known to call the cops, and the feds, and probably also her grandparents. Though it was possible I would have left them for last, since there wasn't a thing they could do but worry.

"Okay. I'm coming, honey."

Her first couple of weeks with us had been hysterical ones, and this sounded like a return to the girl who had wakened sobbing quietly every night. I hoped she also hadn't returned to self-medicating in my absence.

Ironweed is a small town, and I was home within ten minutes. But it felt like a thousand years. Natasha was no calmer when I walked in the front door, but I didn't see any conspicuous bottles, and I couldn't smell any booze.

"Tasha, what?"

I sat beside her on the couch while she tried to tell me something coherent. I had to keep reminding myself she would get prickly if I got too maternal. She related to me because I had been a victim myself for some time. I tried not to treat her like a kid when she was struggling with her past, but sometimes, like right now, when her face was buried in her hands and soaked-through tissues littered the floor around her feet, I wanted nothing more than to hold and rock her. I laid a hand on her shoulder, but no more. It was about all the human contact she could handle at times like these. She didn't shake it off immediately, so I knew I'd done right.

Finally, she hiccupped to enough of a stop that I could understand her. She said, "I guess Layla . . . I guess she got in big trouble for imitating Mrs. P."

"I can see why!"

"She blames *me* for it. It's not *my* fault, Noel. Is it?"

"Of course not!"

"But it doesn't matter because she put it around at school I used to do *sex tapes.*" Now she shuddered away from even my hand on her shoulder. "The public school hasn't gone back yet, and she's got nothing better to do than sit around and make trouble for me. I can't ever go to school again. I'll die of shame."

Naturally, Stan and Gert had enrolled Tasha in the only private school in the vicinity, a parochial school with conservative attitudes. I understood Natasha's worry about the other kids. Her mother had never put her education at a high priority level, and at fifteen, she was only starting her eighth-grade year. All of the friends she had made over the summer were freshmen at the least. Most were sophomores. She had already spent the last week and a half trapped in classes with the same kids she had dealt with the year before and without a friend at her side.

"Natasha, that's horrible!"

"It gets *worse,*" she wailed.

"Worse how?"

"She got her hands on a copy of my *first* film, when I was ten, and high, and . . . Noel, I don't even *remember what happens in it.*" She wheeled around and seized my shoulders. "It could have anything. And I found out because Emily went to Christina's birthday party last night, and these guys Ryan and Eric were there, and they brought a copy, and Emily tried to get the disc, but she couldn't, and now *everybody knows*. I nearly *went* to that party. What if I'd *been* there? And sooner or later Trudy and Darnell are going to find out, and then I'll have to testify about it, and I'll have to *watch it to remember what it has.*"

"Easy, easy. One thing at a time. I've been going back and forth with the high school headmaster about whether you ought to be promoted to be a freshman. It's time to get your grand-dad involved there. Then you'll be up with your friends, and they can shield you."

"But it's my friends who found out! And Gram and Grand-dad don't *know*! I mean, they *know*, but they don't *know* know . . ."

"And we don't have to tell them. I'm going to tell Stan the same thing I've been telling the headmaster for the last two weeks. You're smart; you'll catch up; we'll get you more tutoring if you need it; and if your friends are good ones, it won't matter what they know. How did Emily act when you talked to her?"

Natasha gulped. "Worried," she finally admitted.

"Not judgmental? Even a little?"

She shook her head.

"See? I've met a couple of your friends. They'll stick with you. You need to be with them where you'll feel safe at school. It will give Stan something he can do for you, honey."

"Yeah, okay, but I'll probably be expelled for violating the moral code once this gets around." She exploded into another crying fit.

"I wouldn't put it past them, but I'll leave it to Stan." I patted her back. "How many copies of this thing do you think there are?"

"I don't know. At least two. Layla had to have copied it."

"I need to talk to her mother, and to Ryan or Eric's . . . both, I suppose. What about Christina?"

"You *can't*. Then I'll never live it down."

"Tasha, it sounds like Layla is in enough hot water already. If I offer her mother the chance to keep from having charges added, don't you think she'd listen? And if Ryan and Eric's parents understand what their sons are facing—if you want to talk about who is in violation of the school's moral code, I think you should start there—I'd have to imagine they'd cooperate. I assume they go to school with you, don't they? What about Christina, honey? Is she in on this or not?"

"Emily says Christina was in another room. She was pissed when she found out. What good could it do? How could it change anything? It's already out there, Noel!"

"It's out there, but on a limited scale. Possibly it will turn up over the course of the trial anyway. Possibly Trudy and Darnell already have a copy and haven't asked you about it. We won't bring it up with them until they ask. And it makes a difference because I'm going to tell Layla and those boys if every copy they know of isn't in my hands by tomorrow afternoon, all three of them will be charged as part of a federal investigation. Believe me, it will carry some weight."

"You'd . . . you'd blackmail them for me?"

"Absolutely, honey." I tried not to think about what I was agreeing to. Trudy and Darnell were too intense with Natasha. They had plenty of information in their investigation. She didn't need to be pushed on any other points. "We'll get this taken care of, and things will be fine. Trust me, okay? I'm right, and I'm telling you the truth."

CHAPTER 9

Dear Nora:

I tried what you suggested. I got a dog. But it won't chase the cat, and now they're both dropping dung in my yard. Now what?

Pooped

Dear Pooped,

In that case, stay inside lest you become the next member of the family who needs to cop a squat in the great outdoors.

Nora

It was midday before I got to the primate center the next day. Lance had snagged a ride with one of our volunteers so I could have the truck. I had to first find Natasha's high school headmaster at home on a Saturday, then finagle him into a helpless position sure to make Stan proud when he finished the job by phone later in the afternoon. Then I needed to negotiate with Eric and Ryan's parents and meet them at their homes to soundly humiliate their sons and get back the offending material. Against my own better judgment, I followed this up by taking Natasha along with me to meet Layla's mother.

It turned out to be Layla's Aunt Ivy who met us, along with Layla herself. "Do you have any idea how much *trouble* I'm in?" Layla demanded, her voice sounding nothing like a fourteen-year-old girl and everything like a thirty-year-old woman. I no longer had trouble believing this was the person I spoke with when William vanished. "And I was only trying to *help.*"

"Why did you pretend to be somebody else?" Natasha refused to come in until I tugged her arm. Ivy led us to an L-shaped couch.

Layla studied her shoes. "I didn't figure you'd want to talk to me."

"You'd have been right, but I'd have taken the call, idiot."

"No name-calling," I said to Natasha between gritted teeth.

She brushed me off with a wave. "Do you know how hard my granddad has worked to keep everybody from knowing about me and those films? It's about the only thing holding me together. It's . . ."

"Lucky you." Ivy had her arm around Layla's shoulders. "Layla never even showed in one, and she can't get into that school because everyone knows about her mother."

"Ohhh." Understanding settled on Natasha's face. "That's . . . I'm so sorry."

"Not all of our grandparents can own the whole county," Layla added. "You know that's why those girls hang out with you, don't you? Because Stan Oeschle has more money than God."

I was afraid this would unsettle Natasha, who had spent the morning running through a list of people who she couldn't possibly face. But she said, after only a beat of silence, "Yeah? Then why weren't they my friends last year when I was stuck in seventh grade? Everybody knew who my granddad was then, but they all thought I was some kind of stoner and stayed away from me."

I wanted to steer the conversation back on track before the quarrel could get any worse, but Layla's face suddenly reddened, and she jumped up. "You get everything you want because nobody knows the truth."

"Do you want to know the truth?" Natasha was up too, right in Layla's face.

"Easy, Tasha." I stood up and took one of Natasha's arms, but she shook me off.

"*My* mom's dead. How's that for truth? I take four kinds of anti-anxiety medication, and I have nightmares anyway. I can't talk to anybody on the phone without making sure, *double-sure,* they're who they say they are. I can't go anyplace Lance and Noel don't check out first because I'm so afraid of my great-aunt sending somebody after me. My cousin tried to *kill* me in June, Layla. Granddad nearly got killed trying to save me. And Aunt Gretchen poisoned my grandmother so bad she's still having muscle problems. She may never get out of the nursing home. Still jealous?"

"Girls!" Ivy maneuvered between Natasha and Layla, and she shoved them in opposite directions. "Sit down. Both of you. You asked to come here for a reason, Natasha. Layla, would you *please* get her that disc so she can *leave*?"

Layla, who had thrown herself down onto a couch when ordered to sit, did not initially stand. "Yeah. Okay." She finally slouched off toward her room.

When she had gone, her aunt turned to me. "Look Mrs. . . . Dr. Rue," she said. I had been pulling the professor card all morning to get people's attention. There are times when it pays to have a title in front of my name. "I know we aren't in a position to ask any favors, but Layla is in a horrible spot right now because of what she did. She's a good kid. We've been trying to shield her for the last five and a half years, and she's gotten nothing but bullied. She doesn't think through her actions all the time, and it . . ."

"If she's so nice, where did she get a copy of that thing in the first place?" Natasha demanded.

"Your stupid cousin." Layla tossed a CD case into Natasha's

lap. From the cover, I would have guessed it held useless health and exercise tips. It was generic green and showed a woman in a warm-up suit. The title *Physical Education 101* was printed across her middle. It was the kind of box liable to hold a weight loss video. It had the look of something a college professor might assign.

"He gave it to me about a year ago when he figured out I lived here. He wanted me to put it around then, but I wouldn't do it. But I kept it because . . . I don't know . . . I guess I wanted ammunition if you ever did something to me." Layla flopped back on the couch, her passion deflated.

"Why would *I* do something to *you*?"

Layla flipped her hair and rolled her eyes. "As if you didn't know."

"I *don't* know," said Natasha. "Obviously."

"Your mom's dead," Layla taunted. "Why not live with your dad? Why not go to the—"

"This conversation is pointless." I interrupted them before their argument could devolve into violence. "Tasha, we have what we came for, and Layla's aunt has given us her word nothing like it will ever come out of this house again. We need to—"

"Wait. Please, sit down." Ivy beckoned to the couch again. She was perched on the edge of an armchair. Layla started to say something. "Layla, hush a minute, child." She turned, not to me, as I had expected, but to Natasha. "We aren't in a position to ask you favors," she repeated. "And Layla's attitude probably doesn't make you want to, but I think it would help us out an awful lot if you would tell those federal agents Layla didn't mean any harm. She didn't, you know . . . not with the phone call, anyway. She's . . ."

"Yeah," Natasha interrupted. "I can. For what good it will do. Mostly, she ought to tell them everything she knows about everyone she *knew* when we were kids. It's probably why they're pressuring her anyway." She stopped talking to Ivy and looked directly at Layla. "I left your name out of my list for a *reason* when they were asking me what other victims I knew. I figured you didn't want to be having to explain your whole life to a bunch of people you'd never met. And for your information, I don't even know who my dad *is*."

Layla seemed ready to speak, but Ivy was glaring daggers, and the girl kept silent.

We rode out in moody silence, the disc from Layla and the one ultimately recovered from Eric's dresser tucked in my glove box. On my way to the center, I settled Natasha in with Emily and Christina (who was horrified the whole thing had happened at *her* sixteenth birthday party) to figure out what kind of damage control they could do as a group.

It was eleven o'clock before I got to Midwest Primates, and I opted for the back gate rather than the front. I hadn't been down to see our resident orangutan, Chuck, in what felt like ages, and, since he was directly responsible for saving Natasha's life when Gary tried to kill her, he was on my mind this morning.

"Morning, Ms. Noel!" Drew Carmichael's brother Ace was the volunteer who worked most closely with Chuck. He was, in fact, the man who had dumped the orangutan on our doorstep back in June in deplorable health. Although he had a poor relationship with his brother and a deep suspicion of officers of the law in general, Lance and I liked him.

Frankly, Chuck needed Ace. He had rescued the animal from the same mismanaged Michigan zoo whose enclosures we bought at auction. The zoo had been closed when two disaffected zoo employees released all of the animals into the wild, where Michigan and Ohio police had killed most of them to protect human populations. Ace thought his options were to hide the big orangutans or place them in mortal danger. He had meant well by Chuck and that zoo's other orangutan, Lucy, but he had lacked both the resources to care for the animals and the common sense to hand them over to those who could help until it was almost too late.

Now, he spent at least part of every day with Chuck. Lucy, who had become pregnant in Ace's care, was still in the Ohio Zoo with our friend Christian Baker. She was hand-raised herself, and had no idea how to parent, but she watched her infant with a surrogate each day and allowed her keepers to pump milk for its bottles through the enclosure's mesh. Christian had hopes of reuniting mother and child, though those hopes waned every day Lucy showed no interest in the baby.

For his part, Chuck was thriving in our care, though I worried about loneliness. Orangutans don't typically live in large groups in the wild, but they don't eschew all contact with others of their species, either. Still, Chuck loved Ace and associated the keeper with forbidden treats and good music. He was allowing Ace to slowly cut off the fecally encrusted dreadlocks hanging over his entire lower half.

I tucked my keys into my pocket. "How's everything in this part of the world?" Because Art had added the orangutan enclosure as a surprise wedding gift to Lance and me (one that we had promptly donated to the sanctuary, as I'm sure Art intended us to do), it was separated from the rest of the enclosures by a large swath of forest. There was an unoccupied mall in the adjoining site. Stan had gifted it to Art, who had given it to us along with the orangutan enclosure. We had no idea what to do with it.

"It's all good down here. *Now.*" To my surprise, it was Lance who answered.

"Hey, thought you were up at main," I told him.

"I came down to get some stuff done and wait for Rick."

When Art added the orangutan enclosure, he also put in a

much-needed administration building. Lance and I maintained an office in the barn, but we had shifted most of our actual paperwork to this part of the sanctuary. "Why are you waiting for Rick? What do you mean, anyway, that everything is okay down here *now*? Was it less than okay before? Is everything not okay someplace else?"

"Noel, the monkeys were out again this morning."

"What? Why didn't you call me?"

"You had enough on your plate." Lance's right hand had worked its way up to the top of his scalp, where it was tracing whorls in a bald spot I knew well. His left hand drummed on the handheld radio clipped to his belt. He looked like nothing so much as a giant ape himself. I wanted to kiss him.

I focused instead on what he had said. "What do you mean the monkeys were out? The rhesus macaques?"

"The same."

"Surely you didn't forget the lock twice." Things had been hectic between meeting Natasha's needs and preparing our house for the twins' hopeful arrival, but Lance was methodical, and he had been feeding the rhesus at bedtime ever since their last foray into the barn. By putting himself personally in charge of the headcount, he felt like he could compensate for his earlier error.

"I don't think I even forgot it once," he replied. "Deputy Parks said the primates all went bonkers around three or four o'clock, but when he went around back, nothing seemed amiss. He mentioned it to me when I got here at five, and stuck around to make sure everything was fine while I got set up."

"And when I opened up the back door, the whole second cage of macaques came spilling out toward the barn. The deputy stayed around to help me round everybody up. And after we'd caught them all, we had a look around the perimeter and found some suspicious footprints."

"How could you tell the suspicious footprints from the unsuspicious ones after you'd all trampled back and forth a million times taking the monkeys back?"

"Because these particular footprints had a rotated toe, and they were about twelve inches across. It looked like the walker used the outside edge of—"

"Stop." I told him. "We do *not* have a *third* orangutan loose on the property."

Lance shot a look at Ace, whose back was turned. "That hasn't been ruled out," he said. "Not completely. But I have a feeling what we have is a problem with the current resident."

"What about a chimp? Lector is a pretty big fellow . . ."

Lance shook his head. "It's good and muddy all down in there, and there aren't any footprints around the chimps' enclosure. Besides, I don't think even Lector's feet are quite this big. Rick is on his way down to study the enclosure and see if he can find anything Chuck could be exploiting to get out."

"And then . . . what? Put himself back in after he's busted out some of his buddies? If he's letting them out, why isn't there evidence of damage to the rhesus cages?"

Lance shrugged broadly. "No idea. None. Drew's coming with Rick, and we'll all try to brainstorm. In the meantime, I've put a plain old padlock on the macaque cage so if somebody has a key and . . . I don't know . . . orangutan boots or something, they'll at least have to use bolt cutters next time. You, Jen, and I are the only ones who ever open up in the morning, and Jen has one key, and you and I have the other."

"It's been a long day."

"And," Ace added, "here it is not even noon."

Half an hour later, Rick and Drew arrived. Lance and I had thrown ourselves into working on several of our grant proposals all needing similar data. "Hello, hello!" called Drew, and for one moment the familiar greeting, in a rhythm so like Art's but a voice so different from his, pulled my dead friend to mind so strongly that I rose half expecting to see him in our hall. But no, it was another friend, one we wouldn't have made if Art hadn't died, and one whose eyes looked tired in spite of his jovial grin.

"Welcome, gentlemen." Lance got up with me and we left our papers behind. "Coffee? This is a brand new machine. It lacks the overused office aroma necessary for all workplaces, and we need to break it in."

"Thanks, no," said Rick. "I've already got my caffeine for the day." He jumped up and clicked his heels together Tin Man style.

Drew laughed. "Me too," he said. "Been up and going since early, and I think I've had a dozen or so cups." Drew did not click his heels. "Rick and I had a look around out there before we came inside."

"Chuck's getting out, all right," said Rick. "We found those Sasquatch footprints you described overlapping each other coming and going from his enclosure, but I'm buggered if I can figure out how he's doing it."

Before we went any further, I left a message on Christian Baker's voice mail. "I think I need another favor. Call me." Then we all went outside.

"See, the prints start about here . . ."

"Wait," Lance said. "The area directly around his enclosure isn't disturbed at all?"

Rick shook his head.

"Then we can't be sure he's getting out. What if we *do* have . . . er . . . company?" Lance scratched madly at his scalp.

"He might be exploiting the tree," I suggested. At Art's behest, Rick had constructed the enclosure so its domed center encircled a huge old oak. The tree actually grew up beyond the mesh, its trunk protected by a steel circlet designed to prevent the orangutans from climbing directly up and out.

"Might be," said Rick. "Do you want me to take it down at the top of the mesh? I could close off the dome.

"I hate to if it isn't called for. Art wanted this tree."

"I know," said Rick. "I know."

My phone shrilled in my pocket. "Christian, hi!"

"What were you needing, Noel?" he asked in his faintly Scottish accent. "I don't mean to rush you, but we're shorthanded."

"Oh, dear. Have you got room to babysit an orangutan? We think Chuck may be getting out of his enclosure at night, but we aren't sure how."

"Normally, I'd say I'm on my way to get him, but today, with us being shorthanded as we are, I don't know how I can."

"We could provide transportation."

"See, four of our volunteers got in a nasty wreck last night carpooling back to the zoo after we all had dinner out."

"I'm so sorry to hear it."

"Not as sorry as them. They'll be fine in the long run, but one of them came in nearly every day and *all* of them were scheduled for this morning. Right now, I barely have enough hands to deal with what I've got. I've had to pull in the other keepers, and you know how it can go."

I did know. Working outside your own specialty in a zoo was a daunting task. It might look like zookeepers knew everything, but they were as specialized as the employees in any other field. Pulling from another area was the rough equivalent of asking the HR department in a firm to bounce on over and write a marketing report. "Do you have any ideas for us? What *can* we do?"

"If you can hang on until tomorrow, I'll be back on track here. I've got almost all my slots filled, and I can set up our quarantine area for Chuck so you can study the enclosure. I'm assuming *your* quarantine zone is all full of macaques again?"

"And four other kinds of newcomer. Four! We can leave him in his night enclosure to *study* the thing, but I don't know how long it will take us to *fix* it."

"I see the problem. One day inside won't hurt the big guy, so . . ."

"Oh! . . ." I suddenly realized the flaw in my thinking. "He's getting out at night *already. That's* the area he's exploiting. No wonder the outdoor enclosure doesn't have footprints directly around it. We may not be in such a bad spot after all. Art built the downstairs with room for several separate containment areas. They're all ape-centric. Couldn't keep a monkey in if we tried. And believe me, we would have tried if we could! Maybe we can shift him to one of the unused ones."

I hung up with Christian feeling much relieved only to have the phone ring again before I could put it away. "Hi, Noel," Ann said when I answered. "I hope I'm not catching you at a bad time. Do you have a minute to talk?"

Uh-oh. "Sure." I held the phone up with one hand and clutched Lance's arm with the other. From the serious tone of her voice, I knew at once Merry had fouled it all up. We wouldn't be parents after all.

"Thanks. I appreciate your taking the time."

I tried not to let my thoughts spiral as she spoke, but it was next to impossible. She had a long-winded description of the custody process we had already memorized ten times over, and I knew how it was going to end. *Hurry up so I can go cry.*

". . . Sunday afternoon?"

"What?" I'd gotten lost in my own mind and missed her actual words. Was there a chance to argue our case? Could there be an authority to appeal to about Merry's idiocy? On a *Sunday*?

"I asked if you are able to take custody Sunday afternoon."

"What? Tomorrow?" I repeated, feeling slow and stupid, like the kid who arrives late to a birthday party without a gift for the guest of honor.

"Noel, you heard the woman." Lance pried himself free of me. "Give me that thing." He took the phone. "Yes," he said. "We're absolutely ready. We can't wait. What? Noel's fine. I think you stunned her into silence."

"They're coming?" I couldn't escape my daze to process the information. Dizzy joy enveloped me, and I sat down hard.

"Hey, watch out!" Drew offered me a hand up, but I didn't stand.

"They're *coming*? To our house? To live forever?"

Lance beamed and nodded, then went on answering the advocate's questions. The dizzy feeling still hadn't left me, so I tucked up my knees and buried my head between them. I heard Lance's goodbyes, and then he sat next to me and slung an arm around my shoulder. "They're coming," he reassured me.

The dizziness finally lifted enough for me to look up at my husband. "Lance," I said. "We have to go buy a car. Right now!"

CHAPTER 10

Dear Nora:

I work in a cubicle, and a coworker eavesdrops on my conversations, even personal ones! My boss shrugs it off!

Muzzled

Dear Nora:

My company is a cubicle maze. One coworker places personal calls all day long and shouts across the room, broadcasting "juicy" tidbits. The boss doesn't care! Help!

Overheard in the Office Pool

Dear Nora:

My employees are crowded together in cubicles. Two of my best workers constantly report on each other over trivial concerns. Short of replacing them, what can I do?

Bossed Into a Corner

Dear Muzzled: Stop gossiping.

Dear Overheard: Put on some headphones and mind your own beeswax.

Dear Bossed: You're welcome.

Nora

We had met the twins several more times in the three weeks since our first gathering, in a variety of different venues, each time with Ann, along with Merry and either Natalie or Adam present. We had watched them clamber out of high-backed booster seats at a restaurant and a mall. The restaurant was more popular with the children because of its play zone, so we had chosen this for our most recent meeting. However, for the first time, we arrived without Natasha, and Will pitched himself under the table screaming, "Tasheeeeeeeee!"

"What's wrong with him?" I asked Natalie.

"Welcome to autism," she told me. Lance reached for the flailing boy, but Natalie held him back. "He hates being touched when he's melting down." Her voice was slightly raised, but her body language was relaxed. She did not seem to notice the other diners, many of whom were openly gaping at us. A woman standing near the play area muttered something I couldn't hear and led her own child away with rolled eyes. Never in my adult life had I felt so exposed.

"Can I go slide?" Sara didn't seem to be any more perturbed than Natalie. Merry and Ann had vanished. I craned my neck and saw them outside walking beside the cars.

"What do we do?"

Natalie shrugged. "Depends on what set him off. In this case, since you won't be producing Natasha, we wait it out."

"How do we . . ." Natalie turned away before I finished the question. She didn't answer me. I suddenly realized she and Adam were not in agreement about relinquishing this pair of difficult foster children. She wanted to keep them, and my questions were showing her how incapable a replacement I would be.

The restaurant manager made his way around the end of the counter and began maneuvering toward us. Natalie plunged a hand into her purse and produced a handful of business cards. She handed them to me and walked away. "I'm going to keep an eye on Sara." I doubted Sara needed many eyes right now.

Where the hell did Lance go? I found my husband crammed under the table with the screaming child, his knees curled up at a painful angle and his arms tucked in close by his sides so he was not actually touching the boy. He was talking, though I couldn't hear him.

"Excuse me, ma'am," said the manager. "You'll need to quiet him down."

I started to retaliate, but then realized I didn't need to. I handed him one of the cards Natalie had passed me instead. They had Will's picture on one side, and the other bore the text, "Hi, I'm William, and I have autism. I don't talk a whole lot, and sometimes I can be a little loud, but if you give me a few minutes, things will be fine. I'm sorry if my words don't make much sense to you, but they're the only words I've got, and if you learn how to listen, I bet we can be good friends." Cheesy, but effective.

The manager took the card. He looked from it to me and back again. I thought he would hassle us further, but he shook his head and walked away. Screaming kids were in his purview, but autism, it seemed, was above his pay grade.

I sat on the floor in front of my husband. There wasn't room for three under there. It was the first time I had been forced to face the things Will struggled with every day. Until then, he had been an adorable curiosity, too small for his age, short on words, large on trucks, bounces, and smiles. Now, he was rocking back and forth, his knees tucked under his chin. Every time he rocked back, he came within centimeters of smacking his head against the chair. Every time he rocked forward, he seemed ready to topple onto his face.

I could hear Lance. ". . . Tasha said to tell you 'hi' from her, though, and she'll see you soon. She's trying to get some makeup work done for school."

Natasha's consistent academic progress was my biggest gun

in the battle against the headmaster. As soon as the school year started, she had gotten a friend to "borrow" her freshman textbooks in the classes she wanted to take. She got the assignments through her friends' grapevine, and, while she largely blew off the eighth-grade homework, she completed everything assigned to the freshmen and sent it in to the baffled teachers for grading.

Lance went on chatting to William about Natasha and school, as if the boy could possibly hear him. "Adam said you're a straight-A student. Natasha has a little trouble in school, and now she has to catch up, and a friend is helping her study for a big test." Close enough.

Possibly, Will's shrill screeching was dropping in volume. It was hard to tell. I doubted he heard a word Lance said, though the soothing tone might have been coming through. Mostly, I thought Lance was talking for the benefit of the other people in the restaurant, the ones whose eyes I could still feel. They couldn't hear him. I laid a hand on Lance's arm and shook my head.

When I told my younger sister we were adopting six-year-old twins, she squealed with delight. Unlike my parents, Marguerite was not ambivalent in the least. Her four children had all spent summers with Lance and me when they were younger, and she had spent a few years begging me for nieces and nephews for *her* to spoil.

When I told her the twins were autistic, the other end of the line grew quiet. I bit my lower lip and waited for her to say something unkind. Margie wasn't known for having a warm, open mind. Instead, she said, "I'll give you one piece of advice, then I'll shut my mouth. My friend Shelby has a thirteen-year-old autistic son. She spends too much time justifying her parenting to complete strangers, because they can't understand some behavior. Don't you act like that. Don't let people you've never met parent for you. They probably won't *ever* understand, and you'll make yourself miserable if you take them seriously."

For once, my sister and I were in complete agreement. "We better get used to this now," I told Lance. "I think we're going to be sitting under a lot of tables in the next few months, and not only with William." As we had seen when we first met her, Sara was perfectly capable of a full-scale nuclear collapse of her own. "Those people can't matter."

Lance fell silent, and we sat instead in helpless observation while William's meltdown ran its course. Though it felt like hours later, my watch swore only ten minutes passed before Will's "Tasheeee"s dropped in volume and his rocking slowed.

The rocking didn't stop altogether. Will's rocking almost never stopped. He needed constant propulsion. He turned his head to one side and regarded Lance without blinking. "William," the little boy said, "are you sure you want to go live with those people? They don't even have TV!" Then he pushed past Lance and darted for the door.

He would have gotten away from us. His words had stolen my breath, and Lance and I were staring at each other in shocked silence. It was the most he had ever said at one time in our hearing, and he was clearly parroting some adult. We didn't expect him to bolt, and we didn't react quickly enough when he did.

But he ran straight into Natalie's legs as she returned. "Other way." She steered him back toward the giant structure full of slides and germs. He didn't go but stood, instead shifting his weight back and forth, lifting one foot off the ground every step. Back and forth, back and forth, a mesmerizing dance that drew all of us to look at his feet. Lance and I rose, and he watched us closely for a minute before returning to his toes.

I finally broke away from Will's hypnotic rocking and looked at Natalie. Her wide eyes showed me plainly she had overheard

Will's speech. "You know Adam and I wouldn't say something like that, don't you?" Her face entreated me to believe. "Kids pass into and out of our care all the time. We'd never say something so damaging . . ."

In fact, I did tend to think she was telling the truth. I knew exactly who *would* have said such a thing, never thinking of the harm she was bound to cause. I glanced out the door, where Merry and our advocate stood, glaring daggers at one another between two cars. Natalie nodded slightly, accepting the shift in blame, silently sharing agreement about the twins' social worker.

"William." I got down on my knees and back on the hard tile floor. "Can you look at me? With your eyes?" I accepted a miniscule uptilt of his chin as the best I was going to get. "We do so own a television. We even have cable, since we live in town. You don't have to worry about missing your shows."

I knew from Natalie that Will had two favorite programs, and we could expect massive upsets whenever he missed them. After a painfully long minute, his chin dipped and rose, possibly acknowledging my words. It was impossible to tell whether he believed me. Then he trotted toward the play area, where he bounded past Sara, who was stationed on the third step from the bottom of the structure, not sliding at all, but staring all around as the other children flowed around her going up and down.

When Will had clambered past his sister, not paralyzed by the same fear of heights that had gripped her, I finally let myself relax a little. Natalie, though, looked away from Lance and me, staring instead at her own feet, much like Will had been doing. Finally, she said, "It's hard, letting these two go. I've never had to give up a child under circumstances like these. They've gone to families, they've gone back home, and they've aged out of the system, but I've never had one leave me for something I did wrong. You can't help every child you foster, and you're bound to screw up sooner or later. But I was so sure I could make a difference for them. I have. A little. But mostly, I failed them.

"I forgot him. I *forgot* him. I still can't believe I forgot him. You have to watch for him taking off when he's upset. And he was stressed at the pizza parlor. Something set him off in there, and he nearly melted. He got it together, though, and we didn't have to stop everything. And yet I let myself lose track of him." She crossed her arms and went on staring down. Finally, she repeated, "It's so hard to let them go. I can't escape the feeling there's something I need to do for those kids. Some outstanding debt to them and I'm the only one who can pay it back."

What could I tell her? *We're going to do a good job?* Saying so would feel like telling her we could do *better* than she could, a laughable idea at best. "We've been lucky," I finally said, still groping for words. "We've gotten to meet them several times, where most adopting families only get one or two chances to gauge the emotional temperature. We know their first foster mother, Nelly Penobscott, and she still remembers a lot about them. And I know we're going to be calling you for advice."

Natalie smiled a little then. "I know," she said. "It's not *you* I'm worried about. It's me. It's *them.* They've been failed so many times now. I thought I could be the one who *didn't* fail, who gave them stability."

"Were you thinking about adopting them yourself?"

"Adam's too afraid of the dad." The twins' file was spotty on the topic of paternity, and the father was simply listed as "unknown." But Natalie, Merry, and Adam all thought they knew who he was, and they were pretty sure he was serving a life sentence for murder. "Whether they go to you or somebody else, they're leaving us. Losing Will was a last straw. But I thought I could give them some security, let them see how a real mom acts."

The twins' mother still lived in Columbus, but the children

had been emancipated from her. They had stayed with Nelly Penobscott for almost two years. The mother hadn't been able to keep them six whole months after they finally returned to her. Neighbors in their apartment complex used to find Will shambling filthy and naked down the hall, and be unable to locate an adult to take care of him. Sara nearly got run over when she took off across the street after a stray cat. When she hit her head on the curb and got a ride in an ambulance, social services couldn't reach her mother at all. The children were taken the second time for neglect, rather than outright abuse. Then, her drug issues and failures to appear at hearings and supervised visits had ultimately led to the termination of her parental rights.

That was when the children came to live with their uncle and his wife in Muscogen County. But they were no better than the mother, in the long run, though it took two years of back and forth to figure it out. Then they had come to be in Natalie and Adam's care. "They've fallen through the cracks so many times," she said.

"I follow," said Lance. "Especially the part about wanting them to see a real mother. I think they got some from Nelly. I *know* they got a lot from you. A year can make more difference than you might think. I don't talk about this often . . . I've only recently started talking about it at all, but I spent a year in foster care growing up." He went on to give her an abbreviated version of his time with Angelina.

"She sounds wonderful," Natalie said.

"You remind me of her."

"Okay, then tell me something." Natalie turned to watch the twins rather than look at us any longer. "Why don't you want to foster them? Why are you so quick to want to adopt a pair of kids you barely know who have a condition that's nearly impossible to explain?"

"Because after I left Angelina, I nearly fell right back through the cracks, just like they've already done twice. I skidded home to a mother with severe mental illness, a father who didn't know how to parent, and a group of friends who were already heading down the wrong path. I'd have never climbed out of that hole if my grandparents hadn't kited through the year I was fourteen.

"These were Dad's parents, and they didn't have anything to do with my folks, probably because of Mom. But they figured out what was going on with me, got me a passport, and dragged me off to Kenya with them. They were jet-setters. Conservationists. They were visiting a sanctuary over there, and they tagged me on because they couldn't figure out how else to help.

"I don't know if my brother was too young, or if they thought he was already someone they couldn't reach. He was never a nice kid. Not that they carried any warm fuzzies themselves. I hated my grandparents. They were cold, distant, and strict. But Kenya! Africa! They didn't save me. Africa did. It was my dream come true. Here I was, this white kid in a sea of black. It was the first time in my life I stood out because of my skin color. But the people at the sanctuary didn't treat me differently. I remembered the things I'd dreamed about the year I lived with Angelina, and I came home determined to get back there on my own someday.

"But it was all coincidental. *If* my grandmother hadn't suddenly decided we were worthy of her time. *If* Mom hadn't been back in an institution. *If* I hadn't been failing so badly in school. I didn't get lost after I left Angelina because I got lucky.

"I can't do what you and Nelly do. I can't bring a child into my home only to lose track and never know what happened. I admire what you do, but I can't be that. I *can* make the long-term commitment.

"It took me nearly ten years to get Noel to say she'd marry

me. I've got the patience. And I loved her from the first time we met. I know it's possible to have love come suddenly and stay forever. You haven't failed these kids. You've given them solid ground, and Noel and I can build on it."

"Pretty words, but wait until you deal with Sara's night terrors." In spite of her sarcastic reply, Natalie seemed more relaxed for the rest of the visit, like she thought we might after all be a fit for children she considered her own.

As we were leaving, I realized the vehicle crisis had come to a head. When Lance's mother burned my car up back in June, she created a manageable transportation hassle. We could drive each other places and swap rides with our volunteers. Natasha could ride in the back of the primate-mobile when we all three travelled, and, rust and rumbling aside, the truck was in decent condition for a vehicle of its age.

But when I buckled Sara into her high-backed booster seat in Natalie's car and contemplated its width in our little truck, my mind locked. There was no puzzle solution leaving us room to fit two of those chairs *and* Natasha. We needed to replace my car before the children came to our home, and we needed to do it with a vehicle wider than the current one. We needed a minivan.

CHAPTER 11

Dear Nora:

What is the proper etiquette for returning inappropriate gifts?
Overwhelmed by Generosity

Dear Overwhelmed,

The proper etiquette is to write a thank-you note. The proper action is to place the item in full view the first time the giver comes over, then promptly hand it off to a friend in another country or state, someplace you won't get caught re-gifting.

Nora

Or for God's sake, Noel, you could just be grateful and enjoy it.

Love,
Mom

"Sedan." Lance glared at the road and gripped the steering wheel harder.

"Is Natasha riding on the roof?"

"We'll put one of the twins in the middle. Tasha can have a door."

"I am *not* jamming my hand down in between two hard plastic pincers every time we need to buckle one of those kids in."

"They can buckle themselves."

"Will can. Sara still needs help. And before you say it, there isn't going to be room for his hand between those seats either."

We had left Rick and Drew to attempt to reconstruct Chuck's full route and Ace to find a way to keep the big ape from exploiting his indoor area. And now, driving to the dealership, we were still engaged in the quarrel that had filled our house ever since our last meeting with the twins.

Back at the restaurant, I had accepted the practical reality of owning an outsized fuel hog without question. The money would have to sort itself for once. Our choices were clearly a minivan or large SUV, and as far as I could tell, the former far outstripped the latter.

But Lance lived under the illusion we were shopping for a sedan. "Minivans are so *expensive*," he protested. "And the big SUVs are worse."

"And you have researched this by, what . . . gazing lustfully at sports cars?"

"*One* sports vehicle, and I was *not* seriously considering it. We need a four-door sedan with a reasonable-sized back seat."

"And how will it make Natasha feel? I don't want to turn her into some kind of fifth wheel."

"Noel, do you want to be making car payments for the rest of our lives?"

"If you weren't so obsessed with buying new, we could get something a couple of years old in great condition and . . ."

". . . and get five or six fewer years out of it."

"Nonsense."

We were still squabbling as we entered the dealership, and when the salesman asked us, "How can I help you?" Lance and I replied simultaneously: "We need a car." "We need a minivan."

"Would you tell him three children, two in booster seats and one a teenager, will not fit in a sedan for long?"

"Would you tell *her* how much minivans *cost*?"

The nonplussed salesman opened his mouth to speak but

didn't say anything. Clearly, he couldn't decide who to answer first, or whether he should be speaking to either of us at all. His manager saved him. "Hey, folks!" said the manager. "You must be the Rue-Lakeland family. Or is it the Lakeland-Rues?"

I stepped to the right, suddenly needing Lance nearby. "How did you know our names?"

"Mr. Oeschle said you'd probably be by sometime this week. We've got everything ready to go for you. All we need is some signatures, and you'll be on your way."

Lance groaned. "He *can't*. Stan *cannot* buy us a car."

"Don't worry," said the manager, "he bought you a minivan *and* a car, seeing as how you couldn't decide between them."

"How did he *know*?" I demanded.

Lance answered. "Natasha."

As if he needed to tell me. How else would Stan have known we had narrowed things down to one dealership? "It's like living with the world's most loving spy! What are we supposed to do?"

"Write nice thank-you notes," the manager advised. "Because these are some of the best vehicles on my lot."

"Let's see what we've gotten ourselves into."

He made us sign forms first, page after page of material with significant lines of data, like models and price tags, covered over with sticky notes. Then he led us out back with the pomp of a graduation. It was like getting married all over again, except this time I got to clutch Lance's hand throughout the whole ceremony.

"There you go folks. What do you think?"

"I think I may pass out." It wasn't the minivan that jellied my legs. That was a nice vehicle, no doubt. Seafoam green, just like half our wedding party had worn in June, it stretched under the dealership's overhang like a land-bound boat. No, it was the convertible that made my head swim and my knees wobble. "He *can't*," I protested. "He *can't*! He can't, he can't, he *can't*!"

"Yup. He knew you'd say as much. It's why he told me to make you sign blind."

Lance had abandoned me. "So *sleek*. What aerodynamics!"

"Baby blue." I joined him at the car. "I can't believe she gave him our wedding colors."

"Natasha didn't do this alone," Lance said. "I doubt she even *knew* our wedding colors. The color coordination has Marguerite's handwriting all over it."

"And look at those side-view mirrors. The driver can adjust them in two places."

"Is that a satellite radio antenna?" Lance pointed to a tiny shark fin on the vehicle's tail.

"Yup." It looked like half the sales force was outside to watch this exchange.

"You can barely see where the roof folds in." I traced the outline of the small compartment.

"Fully automatic, and fastest on the market," said the manager.

"Are these leather seats? The options I saw were canvas and vinyl." Lance was inside the car now, stroking the seats as he discussed them.

"Fully custom. You don't think we can put whatever we want in a car like this?" The manager held the keys out to my husband.

Lance hesitated. "We don't do leather." Living in rural Ohio, we've made some compromises. A vegetarian lifestyle is possible, but it would be hard to maintain. We ate chicken when it was ethically farmed. More rarely, we ate beef. But by and large we avoided animal by-products.

The manager chuckled. "It's called pleather. No cows were harmed in the customizing of this vehicle." His manner was calm, and only his eyes gave away his sudden worry at Lance's hesitation.

"Until I read otherwise, pleather is fine." I opened the passenger door and slid in beside my husband. "It's every bit as low-slung as the ad made it sound."

Lance's arm paused on its way to plug the key into the ignition. "*Which* one of us was doing research by lusting after sports cars?" he asked me.

"I never said I didn't bring up a couple on the Internet, too," I protested. "But I did a little more looking into what I thought we might actually be *buying* than you did."

Lance slid the key home and turned it. The car sprang to life in an instant, where, even on a good day, the primate-mobile had to turn over a couple of times before it rumbled on. "Listen to her purr." Lance stroked the dash.

Getting the cars home turned into something of a three-ring circus. I drove the minivan back to the house willingly enough, then rode with the top down beside Lance to return for our truck. Back at the dealership, he seemed to think he got the convertible again, even though I hadn't had a turn at all behind the wheel.

"Share and share alike." I told him. "Move."

He stayed put, but I refused to get out of the car on my own side. We might have remained that way for much longer, but we had forgotten the spare keys to both new cars, and as the dealer lured us out to get them, I snatched the convertible fob out of Lance's hand and popped myself behind its wheel.

"Hey!" Lance protested.

I turned on the engine, rolled up the windows, and put up the top. Lance stood helpless outside the vehicle, trying to pop the locks with the spare keys. However, as I had learned the time I locked myself out of my previous car while warming it up one morning, those key fob beepers don't work once the engine is actually running. I beamed at my fuming husband as I adjusted my seat and the mirrors, then I made a great show of smoothing down my hair and blew him a kiss. I rolled down one window as I drove past. "See you at the house after I grab Tasha," I said. "Remember, we've got to put those beds together today."

I put down the top once more as I exited the lot. Behind me, Lance was shouting, "Damn it, Noel," but the rest of whatever he wanted to tell me was lost to the roar of the wind in my ears as I hugged the road on the drive to Christina's.

Natasha flew out her friend's front door. "You went! You went! You went! I didn't think you were *ever* going to go. Do you know how hard it's been to keep it secret? And how did you get your hands on the convertible? I thought Lance would hide the keys for sure."

"He may yet, so we better enjoy our ride."

"Ha! You can hide this set first." She bounded around the car once, inspecting it before she jumped in. "Note. Pleather interior. You are totally *not* to take small people in your gorgeous car and get it all junked up. That's what the minivan's for."

"If you think I'm junking up *any* cars, you don't know me. I kept my last car so clean I wouldn't let Lance in unless he took off his shoes or put down paper first."

"Noel," Natasha said with mock solemnity, "you have *tons* to learn about parenting."

What a difference this was from the young woman who had come to live with us a couple of months ago. "Did you figure out a disaster management plan?"

"Yup."

"And it is?"

"Close ranks."

"Meaning what exactly?"

"Meaning since now all my friends know, I don't have to hide it from *them* anymore, and if anybody else tries to bring it up, we band together and ignore them."

"Not a bad plan." Three months ago, she hadn't *had* any friends. "You seem to have bounced back pretty well. I was worried about you this morning.

"If it had happened in June, I'd have still been trying to hide from everybody. And that was my initial reaction. I wanted to crawl under a rock. But it makes such a difference not having any secrets. Gary used to harp on about how I liked it, and how bad it would make my grandparents feel to find out. But once they found out, all any of us cared about was the other ones being alive." Suddenly, her joy at the car diminished. "I want to go *home*, Noel. You have no idea how much I want to go home. I want to go back in time and erase June completely.

"But not all of it. I want to take away all the bad stuff and hang on to the part when it was all over, where Gran said, 'Honey, I knew something was going on. I thought it was drugs, maybe Stan and I were taking on somebody who had a habit we couldn't touch.' She found out I was a child porn star, and all she said was, 'Thank God it wasn't drugs.' And Stan was the same way.

"I feel bad for Layla. I want to help her if I can. It's kind of stupid, but if she hadn't done what she did . . . keeping my friends in the dark was the last wall. I wouldn't have told them. Not in a million years. They've only *been* my friends for a month or two, and only because of the slam thing." *Slam thing . . . yes. The poetry group.* I still wasn't sure I believed in that completely. "And I felt the same way as I used to about Gran and Granddad, afraid of what they'd say when they found out. I mean, they barely know me, too.

"But instead of messing everything up, it made us all closer. It made me feel like one of them. It made me . . . don't freak out, okay, but this morning was the first time I didn't wake up and wonder, even for a few minutes, where you hid the wine in the new house. And that was before I got the disc back."

"I'm glad, Tasha." I didn't want to say too much. Natasha was rarely this open. However, when she had been silent for several miles, I deemed it time for a change of subject. "But you *can't* keep reporting our every want to your grandfather! It's getting outrageous the things he's doing for us."

Natasha smothered laughter in one arm. "I'm sorry. I shouldn't. But it's so funny. Was Lance pissed? Did his face turn purple?"

"Yeah. Right up until the second he saw this car."

"Ha!" she crowed. "I knew it! I knew he wanted the convertible."

"Didn't everyone? My point is, your granddad is generous, but he doesn't have to *buy* our friendship. He hears everything you tell him as something else to shop for."

"Would you *relax*?" said Natasha.

"You of the four anxiety medications."

"I *know*. I'm a total spaz, too. And anyway, I'm not guilty here. Or mostly not, anyway."

"What do you mean?"

"After you told your sister you were adopting, she called *me* up and asked if you were still . . . how'd she put it? 'Rattling around in that heap of a truck.' It sent me into a major panic attack, because I *don't* have a safe word with her, and she *didn't* want me to tell you a thing, and I had to hang up and call your mom and make *her* call your sister to make *sure* it was for real, because it was *such* a good idea, and she knows you better than I do."

"Wait, back up," I said, when I could get a word in edgewise. "Marguerite wanted you to get your grandfather to buy us a sports car?"

"No, no, no. She wanted you to have the minivan. The convertible was your dad's idea."

"My *dad's* idea? Natasha, how much of my family is in on

this? They know how uncomfortable Stan's gifts make us feel."

"Yeah, but see, they knew you and Lance would wind up getting the sedan, and Marguerite knew the sedan was stupid. And your dad felt bad for not being more excited. Plus, everyone is still bummed *your* car burned up, and *everybody* has heard Lance talk about this car."

"It's more like salivate. But Natasha . . ."

"Chill *out*, Noel. Listen, this is how it's going to go. While I'm with you, you're right there in the front of Granddad's mind. And he has got almost *nothing* to do in the hospital. He can't send clowns and teddy bears to the children's wing every day, and you *know* he totally would, right? Anyway, when he gets home, he'll have all his stuff to keep him busy again, and I'll be back at home. It's not like he'll love you any less. I think he's kind of substituted you for your friend Art in his heart, and once that wears off, he'll have found a new place for you to fit. But he won't be thinking of you all the time, and then he won't dump houses, and cars, and . . . I should probably warn you there's a treehouse kit coming from Columbus . . ."

"A what?"

"Yeah. For Sara and Will if they ever get there."

"They'll get here, Natasha," I told her as we turned down our street. "They're coming tomorrow."

"*What?*" With the top down, I felt pretty sure the whole neighborhood could hear Natasha shriek.

"As long as our assembled friends and family don't have something drastic to tell us."

"Who?"

I pointed to the front of our house. Besides the new minivan and the primate-mobile, Trudy Jackson's beat-up sedan was parked on one side of the street, and my parents' car was on the other. I couldn't have told you who I wanted to see less.

"They *could* have heard the good news and be stopping by

with congratulations."

"And scientists *might* have found life on Mars and be getting ready to hold a big news conference at our place. Come on, let's see what's up."

I parked my new car and closed the roof, my euphoric mood dampened by our guests' arrival.

CHAPTER 12

"Mama, it's fine." I passed my mother a mug of the coffee Lance had been brewing in my absence. I ticked gourmet coffee beans off the list of things I could expect not to afford in the near future. Lance and I have always lived on a budget, but we were about to develop economy in untold quantities.

"It's not fine, and you know it." She collected my sugar bowl and resumed her seat beside Trudy. They had the same stylish pixie haircut, Mama's in her appalling shade of yellow, Trudy's in a more sedate brown. Although Trudy looked much younger, in reality she was, like me, fighting the gray one bottle of dye at a time. Mama had long since given over the battle and gone, if not punk, then at least neo-grandma.

My father, who already had his cup but hadn't bothered to sit down, patted my shoulder. "I think what it boils down to is this. You've never made a quick decision in your life. You analyze and think things through. Marguerite's always been our impulsive daughter."

"I don't think Margie has done a single impulsive thing since she and Dag eloped." In fact, I had been one of the few attendants at her courthouse ceremony some twenty-two years ago. She had taken her own relative lack of a proper wedding as license to fully plan Lance's and mine this past June. Good thing, too, or it probably wouldn't have happened.

Still, I understood my father's point. I was briefly engaged to Lance's brother. After that ghastly relationship ended, I moved on reluctantly to dating Lance. Then, Lance and I were a couple for some time before we got an apartment, let alone a house together. It was hard to believe we would soon be putting it on the market. Even when Natasha went home, we would never have room in our old place again. Now, not two full months after a wedding ten years in the making, we were becoming parents. It *was* a lot to process.

"Noel, can you give us a hand down here?" Lance called from the basement, where we had stored the things we weren't yet ready to unpack. He and Darnell were down looking for our table leaf. In its current arrangement, the table barely seated four. It would be crowded with seven today, even when we added the extra two feet. Starting tomorrow, we would be seating five regularly. The leaf wouldn't be coming out anytime soon after we got it in.

"What do you need?" I was already halfway down the stairs.

"This thing is completely buried."

I joined my husband and realized Darnell wasn't helping him at all but was, in fact, standing in another empty room of the basement murmuring on his cell. By the time tonight was over, our office would be there, and we would have taken down the bunk bed and transformed it into twin beds, one in Lance's and one in my former office. Part of me hoped to get Art's job purely because it *was* nice to have my own space.

I cocked my head and shot a wordless glance between my husband and our agent friend. And Darnell was a friend. Trudy, too, as frustrated as I might be with them right now. They had volunteered undercover at our sanctuary for a long time, and we considered them more than acquaintances.

The table leaf was not buried at all. It was leaning neatly against the wall. Before I could ask what was going on, Lance said, "Trudy and Darnell want to tell us something, and since your folks are here, they'd like to tell them too. Only . . ."

"Only we can't pass wind without getting official clearance." Darnell joined us. "Yeah, it's okay. Let's move this thing."

"Does this have something to do with Natasha? Because the less my mother knows about her, the better." Mama already pitied and babied Tasha entirely too much. The girl would never get any peace from my parents if they knew the full extent of what she had been through.

Darnell shook his head. "It's your kids," he said. "We've been waiting to find out they would be coming here before we moved forward."

"With what?" I was surprised by the edge in my voice and the accompanying protective clutch in my chest.

"It won't make sense out of context." Since neither Lance nor I had picked up the leaf, Darnell hoisted it himself. As we mounted the stairs behind him, Mama's voice drifted down to me. ". . . and I realized I was rejecting my own grandchildren!"

"Mama, it's *fine*." I collected her cup and the sugar bowl so the leaf could be put in.

"It's not fine," Mama continued. Daddy set his mug on the counter and crawled under the table to open the hinges for the leaf. "We're both so sorry, loves. Here you are bringing me people still young enough to appreciate my sewing, and I'm acting like your sister did when she found out Rachel is a lesbian!" Everyone except Marguerite had welcomed her oldest daughter's coming out. Margie still acted like it might be a bad dream she would wake from.

"If it's the sewing that brought you around, I'm all in favor." Lance joined my father, and they each pushed a different rusty hinge, both of which remained indifferent to their efforts.

"Yes! And common sense. Have you seen this week's column?"

In truth, I had not. I usually scooped up the *Free Press* straight off the step to see what new advice Mama had to dispense, and which absurd questions she'd been mailed. But this week I had been so busy the newspaper sat neglected on the counter, where it had been moved in an effort to clear the overcrowded table to make room for everyone.

"You should," Dad grunted from under the table. "Do you have anything to lubricate these?"

"Garage," Lance said.

Both men came out from under the table, but neither left. Everyone seemed to be waiting for me to pick up the newspaper. It was out of its wrapper, and I realized belatedly Lance had read the column already, and Mama had known I had not when she asked. Instead of its usual polite square, "What's Next Nora" was the headline story. *Slow news week?*

Dear Readers,

I have plenty of questions that want for answering, but all of them will have to wait. For once, I need your advice. I've gone and tripped on my own tongue, and I don't know how to put it back in my mouth, so to speak. Recently, my middle-aged daughter and her husband told me they were adopting two children from the foster care system.

I should have been overjoyed! I've spent a great deal of time not *harping on this particular child to give me grandbabies. Instead of cheering for such a wonderful revelation, I reacted as if the news they had brought me was* bad.

There isn't any excuse for my behavior. I've been dreaming imaginary children for some time now, yet when they turned real, I reacted from a combination of gut fear and unreasonable prejudice. It was a full two days before my daughter's words sank in. She was bringing me grandchildren.

My other daughter has children as well, but only two of them aren't already teens. Here are little people, a pair of six-year-old twins, giving me back something I thought had almost passed forever. How could I not want them?

Yet that was exactly how I behaved. If my daughter had come to me pregnant, I'd have whooped and started planning the shower. But since she was adopting older children with special needs, I asked if she was out of her mind. Was it because these twins were six and not newborn? Because both children have autism? Was I asking such things because the children are biracial? Was I so prejudiced?

I don't know why it took me so long to wrap my mind around that concept, but once I did, I felt like I'd swallowed a brick! I've broken my daughter's heart, readers, and I need to know how to mend it. I've said words I want to swallow back. Please, help me make amends. Send your words to the usual address, but put the word "ADVICE" on the envelope.

Yours, Nora

By the time I finished, I had blown my nose at least three times on the tissue Lance provided. He was rereading over my shoulder with an arm around my waist. I didn't cry, but it was largely because we had an audience. "Mama, has Margie been after you?"

"Yes. Her and my own conscience."

"And don't forget your Nana," my father added.

Nana had been delighted by our news, and as she and Mama squabbled almost constantly anyway, I could imagine the sorts of things she would have said. "Then I guess I owe you an apology, too," I said, "since I'm the one who accidentally sicced them both on you."

"We deserved it," said Daddy. "We both feel dreadful. We want to make it up to you."

"You already have," said Lance. "And I do *not* mean those cars."

Daddy gave Lance a half-smile. "Let's go get your oil. Your

137

friends have something to tell us, and while you were reading they asked your mama and I to stay and hear."

Once the table was enlarged, Trudy said, "This is classified information. It's not for public consumption. But it's the kind of thing no parent should go without knowing."

"We already know the dad is serving life."

"Not that. We're reasonably certain of their paternity, but this doesn't have anything to do with him. As far as I know, he's only ever evidenced any interest in a couple of his children, though he has several. This has to do with the incident in late July. Sit."

"The Dumpster," said Natasha.

Trudy nodded. "In spite of what Natalie Forrester has convinced herself, she did *not* forget William at the pizza parlor."

"What?"

"We believe William was lost only moments before she noticed he was missing."

"Did he wander? Impossible! It's a *long* way from her house to the Marine. When Sara walked here, she had worked it out by map."

Trudy gave a wordless shake of the head. "He has wandered before, yes," she said. "And far. But Noel, he was taken. Natasha found him under the Dumpster because he got away."

"Excuse me?"

"Let me show you a video and tell you what we think. William can't tell us. He's tried, but the more stress he feels, the fewer words he says." Darnell plugged a flash drive into Trudy's ever-present tablet. He and Trudy remained behind the machine, and the rest of us scooted our chairs around to squint at the monitor like preschoolers at story time.

First, they showed us footage from the Marine on the day Will vanished. Trudy pointed him out for us, and we tracked his progress in a cobbled-together video including data from two or three cameras. He started in the dining room, rocking with his hands over his ears. Then he wandered into the kitchen while Natalie paid for her pizza. He returned about the time she jerked her head around and noticed the absence in the first place.

The footage shifted to the kitchen at the point in time when he entered it. Something startled him and he ran out the back door, where he could be seen dashing up the open ramp of a delivery truck. An employee emerged carrying him a few seconds later. Then he either set Will down or the boy wiggled loose and darted back through the kitchen. Tony Gibson came out of his office and followed Will as far as the door to the dining room. Then he shook his head and walked away.

The scene changed again, and split into two images. Trudy walked us through what we were watching. "Point one." Trudy used a small laser to indicate the screen. "This is the synchronized security footage in back of the Marine for the period between when William went missing and when Natasha found him. Mr. Gibson has two cameras because he's had a couple of break-ins. You can't see the Dumpster because it's on the other side of the delivery truck. What you *can* see here is the approach to both sides of the building." She fast-forwarded through several hours of film in a few minutes. "Tell me what you saw."

"Nothing," said Mama. "Not going so fast."

I tended to agree with her. "It looks like they finished unloading the truck and wheeled a few cases around the side of the building before shutting it down. Then Mrs. Gibson took a couple of bags of trash out the back door before the place closed for the night, then nothing until we blip by in the primate-mobile. So if he'd been under there, Mrs. Gibson would have noticed, you think?"

"Yes, point one," Trudy agreed. "She might have. But she didn't, and he might have been there but keeping quiet. Point two. The cameras are situated with one aimed at either corner of the building. Mr. Gibson wants his truck parked there when it's not in use to force would-be thieves to approach those cameras close enough that they can be identified. What *don't* you see?"

"Anything," Mama reiterated.

"Exactly." This clearly had significance for Darnell.

"If Natalie had forgotten him and he had gone straight around back, we would, at some point, see him here." Trudy pointed to one corner of the building, "Or here," she indicated the other. "But we don't."

"And if she had forgotten him, and he wandered away from the Marine and then returned from the back, so the cameras couldn't pick him up, there's a high probability someone would have noticed. It's a largely residential area, and Natalie was there near enough to rush hour that the people coming back from work in Columbus would have likely noticed him alone.

"Even if they thought he was a neighborhood child out playing without a parent, *someone* would have marked him. The way he walks, with that rocking gait, is distinctive. It draws the eye. But nobody recalls seeing him."

"But he didn't teleport under there," said Lance.

"No," Darnell agreed. "And so we can't convince Natalie she didn't forget him. She's sure he walked around out of camera view or the neighbors didn't notice him. But here's point three." He reached back into his briefcase and pulled out a watch without any hands.

"What's that?"

Darnell handed it to me. "You can handle it. It's not evidence. It's a tracking device from a group called Project Lifesaver. William has one like it. It contains a radio tracking device that should allow us to find him instantly. As soon as Natalie reported him missing, the locals tracked the device. It was in a sewer grate near the Forresters' house."

"But doesn't that suggest he took it off and walked back to the Marine?"

"It's hard to get off. He's capable of doing it. And he *could* walk there. But he *loves* his bracelet. That lifeline saved him at least once, in Columbus, when he had wandered several miles in an incredibly short period then. Natalie is certainly convinced he slipped out of it, or maybe one of the other kids wrestled it off him and threw it out her open back window on the way out to the pizza parlor. The twins drive her oldest foster children nuts, and the big kids torment them in return sometimes.

"It *is* possible, but again, that's a long hike for a little kid. And he has *never*, not before, and not since, exhibited a desire to take it off. When Detective Carmichael gave him a new one, he got hysterical because he wanted the old one back."

Trudy waited until Lance had also studied the device and given it back before she picked up Darnell's thread. "Here's what we think happened. An unknown individual was watching the Marine, maybe waiting for a group like Natalie's, a single parent with a group of children to keep track of. This individual then followed the Forrester minivan home. The individual may have planned to wait for an unsupervised child to come outside, or perhaps he or she zeroed in on William when William walked away from the group a couple of times at the pizzeria.

"In any case, William certainly became the target nearly immediately once the family got home, probably because he *did* wander a slight distance. The individual lured William to his car. These types of predators are almost always men. William struggled, and the individual tore off the watch and threw it out the window.

"The individual then took the boy home. William showed no signs of sexual assault, but he had oddly placed bruises on his back and arms, and he was absolutely concussed as if he had been struck. After holding him in one location several hours, the kidnapper tried to move the boy and drove past the Marine.

"William's a smart kid. He may not be able to tell us how it happened, but he's good in a crisis. He was one of the people who called 911 when Sara nearly got hit and hurt her head, when he was very young and almost completely nonverbal. He had to hand the phone to an adult after someone answered. But he let himself into a woman's apartment and placed the call.

"We think he knew he was in trouble, and we know he can operate a car door. He waited for the car to slow down, and he jumped out. He had abrasions on his hands and knees consistent with that story. He scrambled to his feet and ran. Knowing the person pursuing him was larger, almost certainly faster, and highly motivated to catch him, he looked for shelter.

"*That* is when he ran up behind the Marine on the other side of the truck, out of sight of the cameras, and crawled under the Dumpster."

"And then the kidnapper walked away and left him there?" I shared the skepticism I heard in my father's voice.

"Hardly. This would have been early in the morning, and news of the disappearance would have been everywhere. As I said, the kidnapper was *highly* motivated to get the child back. Something happened to *force* him to go away."

"What? What happened?" Mama's eyes were wide.

"It's hard to be sure. But your truck has a loud engine, and it would have been easy to hear you coming."

"You're not saying when we drove up there was somebody . . . he seemed to be asleep, though, until Natasha woke him up."

"Perhaps," Darnell said. "Maybe he'd been stuck for a while. But I don't think so. I think he was hiding as quietly as he could. It's possible if you had not arrived precisely when you did . . ."

"Stop it!" bawled Natasha. "Stop!" Nobody had been paying

attention to her, but she was shaking and in tears, every bit as volatile as she had been in June. "Don't you dare tell me my baby brother nearly got killed."

CHAPTER 13

Dear Nora:
Now the dog has fleas.

Pooped

Dear Pooped:
Better it than you.

Nora

Lance smacked his forehead. "*That's* why you've been so adamant about this from the minute Merry suggested we foster William."

"What?" I passed Natasha the box of tissues Lance had given me earlier. Layla's taunt, her asking Tasha why she lived with her grandparents instead of her father, must have triggered something. But I would have put this low on my list of expected responses. I tried to conceal my shock to keep from upsetting my foster daughter further. She still had a poetry slam to get ready for, after all.

"No," she said. "Or not on purpose. I only remembered it now, when Darnell was talking." She dabbed her dripping mascara, hiccupped, and blew her nose. "We have . . . the same Dad . . . and *God* I remember why I hate Layla so much." She snatched the tissues.

"I wondered if you knew," Trudy said. "It seemed like a large thing to omit, but you never discussed it, and it didn't hurt anything for you to keep his name to yourself if you wished."

"Whose name?" said Mama.

"T-Bow Orrice," said Natasha. "Layla's my sister. The twins are our siblings, and I can't believe I forgot!"

"It's a protective shield," I reminded her, masking my own amazement by talking. "I couldn't bear to face certain things about my relationship with Alex, so I stopped knowing them for the longest time." *Also, in my case, there was head trauma.* "You have more to face than I did. Be patient with yourself." Of Trudy, I asked, "You knew the twins are her siblings?"

"Are *probably* her siblings. Nobody has put the thing to a DNA test, but we have no reason to discount it. He has numerous children, few of whom share a mother."

I turned to Lance. "What did you mean about her being adamant since we found William?"

"Back at the Marine, when I let Merry pigeonhole us about fostering the twins, it was because Tasha said, 'Please, listen to her.' And since *she* hates the Orangutan Lady as much as we do, I went along with it. Then Drew said, 'He could do worse than you for parents,' and by then I was already feeling protective. What he said really set me to thinking. By the time Sara turned up, Tasha had been after me two more times during the monkey chase, and my mind was going in four different directions."

"I'm confused about something here," said Mama. "And I've never minded putting my foot in my mouth, so I'll just say it. T-Bow Orrice is black. Natasha's as white as *I* am."

"I'm not." Natasha blew her nose. "Biracial doesn't always mean looking like somebody poured cream in the coffee. I mean, I thought I was too, but I've got plenty of friends whose looks favor one parent or the other. I'm not half so pale as Mom was, but I've still got a fair complexion, and I have her hair. I need the truck key." Lance tilted his head quizzically, and she added, "Relax. I'm not going anywhere. There's something

I need out of the dash."

"Goodness but I have a lot to learn!" Mama said.

"I didn't know it either until we all wound up at Mrs. P's. And now . . . I remembered so much all at once. It's all running together. See, I always thought my dad was Terry Dalton. Give me a minute." She left to go to the truck.

She returned with the DVDs we had spent the morning so carefully gathering to protect from federal discovery. "I don't think you've got this one," she said.

Trudy studied the case of the DVD we had gotten from Layla and the unlabelled silver disc we had recovered from the young men involved. "Same format as the others," she noted. To the rest of us, she explained, "The material was distributed as physical fitness videos, video games, and straightforward perfectly legal porn."

"This was my first one." Natasha resumed her seat. "It was before half the operation got busted for drugs with T-Bow's people and all the kids got pulled for a while. I'd forgotten, blocked, what was on it." Natasha was about to cover ground I had been trying to keep Mama from finding out about. Didn't the girl know the torrent of mothering she was about to unleash?

"When you were ten, Gary and his crew threw a big party, got you drunk and high, and . . . and . . ."

"You don't have to say it, honey." Mama's fingers curled on the table. I was proud of her for respecting Natasha's need for distance. It was hard to balance the urge to protect against the need to listen.

Tasha shrugged. "And they filmed it," she finished. "And that was your first tape." She went on to explain how this one had come into her possession. "Layla said I ought to know why we hated each other so much, but I didn't. When you were talking about William like he'd come close to dying, I was thinking about Mrs. P's and things started rushing in. Everybody knew who the twins' dad was, but he didn't claim them. He only claimed Layla because her mom pulled a runner. But when the state put the twins in with the rest of us, Layla said we were *all* siblings."

"She didn't figure I'd be with them in foster care long, and she was jealous. Gary was about the only one who didn't get nailed for something. He was my squeaky clean cousin. Layla figured he'd find a way to get Mom off so I could go home with her or that Granddad would buy me free.

"Layla and I didn't much like each other anyway, and she was jealous because I'd aged in and would *get* to go back. She should have aged in, but Gary didn't want trouble with T-Bow, so he kept her out. She didn't understand why I was all of a sudden so desperate to get out."

The more she spoke, the more Natasha's points jumbled together, much as her memories must have been doing. Trudy's fingers flew on her screen. She was taking notes as fast as Natasha could talk, and I had no doubt the machine was also recording every word Tasha said.

"Gran and Granddad were looking into getting custody of me. They knew Mom was a prostitute, but none of us talked about the films to people on the outside, especially not relatives. We knew better. When social services picked me up, I had to be pretty much detoxed. I don't know . . .

"Anyway. Layla. She told me the boy who . . . who . . . aged me in," she shook her whole torso like an animal rinsing away water. "Layla said I was her sister and he was our brother and not even T-Bow knew it. And that just set me on fire. I grabbed her hair and smashed her face into Mrs. P's mailbox. Crunched her front teeth in pretty good and busted her nose.

"I was labelled violent, and Gran and Granddad pulled back. And it caused social services to have to listen to Layla's mom, because she was raising Cain about her kid getting injured so badly in the system.

"All of a sudden, our roles were reversed. I went back to Mom, and Layla got out. I got what she wanted, and she got what I wanted. And Shannon never cared much for my mom or knew the tapes were more than straightforward porn. When we were little, we all thought our mothers were famous actresses. They even showed us some of the cleaner stuff on the films. Shannon was a big star, because she was petite and soft-spoken. She looked so fragile and easy to break. That kind of thing is popular. She got special treatment, and I doubt she knew how bad life was for everybody else.

"When she went clean, it was about a year before she started fighting to get Layla. Then after T-Bow got arrested, she used her insider knowledge for leverage. And I'm willing to bet she knew some devastating stuff.

"At Mrs. P's, I had time to fall in love with the twins. I mean, they were practically babies. I felt responsible. I cared about them even when I couldn't remember why. I've tried to keep up with them ever since. I forget so much, though, and my memories come back slowly. When Layla told me I was their sister, all I heard was what she said about the guy who was supposedly our brother. I don't think he was, by the way. I think she said it to get me going. I *hated* her so much. I guess I didn't want to remember why.

"Before Mom died, I remember asking if T-Bow was my dad and her saying, 'Probably, but I wouldn't put it around. As far as everyone is concerned these days, Terry Dalton is your father, and that's the story you stick to.' "

"Layla remembered *me*, though. Easy to do when you aren't stoned all the time. And the only thing we *ever* agreed about was the twins are awesome. I think that's why she called me when William went missing and why she didn't think I'd talk to her as herself. It's why it matters so much to get the twins here.

I'm tired of saying goodbye to them. Even when Gran and Granddad come home, I'll still live close. They won't be far away anymore."

Trudy tapped the case. "Why did Layla have this? How did you get it from her?"

Natasha refocused herself. "Layla is . . ." Natasha pursed her lips and clicked her tongue against the roof of her mouth, thinking. ". . . scared, for one thing. She's in trouble over the phone call, when she meant well doing it. But she's still jealous of me. She gave me the film to give you, even though she said the opposite. I think it was kind of a dual challenge. She never got to be a part of things, and they tried to keep her in the dark. But she thought she knew what it was, and she wanted in. We all thought we were going to be famous actresses like our mothers until it happened. I guess she finally found out for real when she saw this. And I think she had to admit her mom wasn't who she wanted her to be.

"She wanted me to have to deal with something she knew, or thought she knew, I had kept hidden, because Gary gave her these over a year ago and she hung onto them out of fear I'd do something to her."

"And she gave them to you now, why exactly?" Darnell pressed.

The longer Natasha talked, the more dead her voice sounded. "Because her mom made her? To get you off her back?"

"Interesting. I've never met her mother. I've only ever seen her with her aunt," said Trudy.

Tasha shrugged. "I'm pretty sure these are the only copies of this video. Gary kept all the first films for his personal pleasure. His ring was falling apart when he pulled out of Columbus and went to hide up in Michigan, then followed me here to the sticks. He knew sooner or later I'd break and tell. I was always his weak link. I was scared. I wouldn't go anywhere with him.

But he came by every week to 'check in.'

"My grandparents had no idea how closely affiliated he and Mom had been. They thought he felt sorry for me because my mother died. It didn't occur to them he all but murdered her."

"That explains one." Trudy tapped the case. "What about the other?" She tapped the disc.

"Layla made a copy. She gave it to a couple of classmates to cause me trouble. They gave it back to me as soon as they realized what was on it. It's how I knew to get the original back from her. And no, before you ask, they don't have *anything* to do with this." Natasha was skirting the edges of honesty to protect a couple of guys who I honestly found pretty creepy. But they had clearly come by the CD the way they claimed, and I wasn't sure I'd wish federal questioning on *any* kid about this issue.

"Hm." Clearly, Trudy didn't entirely believe Tasha, but she let it pass. "Then it's good we were already here."

"Listen to me," Natasha snapped. "Layla's an idiot. But she's in a bad place. When the college isn't in session, this is a small town. *Everyone* knows her mom used to be a prostitute, and it's not hard to get a copy and see Shannon in *Jolly Roger: Booty Call*. She can't get into my school because of something her mom did years ago. She's not one of the bad guys. But I'm scared now that whoever took William might be."

"I won't lie to you, Natasha," said Trudy. "They might. It might also be a random attacker. The news has issued a regional warning, in case you hadn't noticed."

"Oh."

"We've been a little busy," I pointed out.

"Police have gone door to door warning parents in Natalie's neighborhood, the neighborhood behind the Marine, and now *this* neighborhood. While we don't want to induce unnecessary panic, nobody wants to be responsible for some child getting kidnapped.

"But we've been giving a generic warning. You're the only ones, aside from the people who are looking for him, who know William may have been targeted before. If so, he might be targeted again, because this time, he will also remember his assailant."

"What do we do?" I asked. "We can't live like hermits. The semester is going to be busy, and we're already trying to figure out childcare for the nights we both teach."

"Officially?" said Trudy. "Nothing. Stay alert. Call the police if anything at all seems out of place. Unofficially? Darnell and I are only accomplishing a little down here no matter how hard we look. He can do most of our job alone."

"I don't follow," said Lance.

"Congratulations," said Trudy. "You're looking at your new nanny."

CHAPTER 14

"I got a day pass, and I'm by God using it!" If Stan Oeschle wasn't suffering pneumonia any longer, he certainly was still in no shape to be out of rehab. But it hadn't stopped him from arriving at our annual fundraiser gala via ambulance. He rode in a wheelchair, pushed by a beaming Natasha, his leg sticking straight out in a cast. I doubted the pants he had ruined to accommodate the cast were inexpensive, and I did not tell him his neck brace cheapened the look of the entire outfit, though he would have found it funny. He probably also would have taken off the brace.

This was the one occasion a year I regularly wore a dress anymore, and I kept smoothing the skirt as it crept up my stockings, even though I knew it revealed nothing. Lance looked natty in his suit and tie, and the evening was going well. We circulated among our guests, encouraging them to bid on the items donated for our silent auction, grateful for the space Art had provided for this activity in our new administration building. I wished he could have been alive to see us finally hosting this away from a university conference room or barn. There are some places that simply cannot be made swanky. "Rigid Academic" and "Country Chic" were the best we had ever achieved.

Our volunteers, Trudy and Darnell among them, delivered a variety of wines. The agents briefly introduced us to two of their superior officers, a woman who looked to be in her thirties, and a man who was perhaps in his sixties. I was unsure whether these two had come in their official capacities or because we had extended a social invitation to their office.

William and Sara were at home with my parents. A rapid conference between the agents had determined it was better for Trudy to act as a nanny tonight. A rapid conference with my mother had determined she would be hurt if I didn't let her have a chance to grandparent. Mom won.

"You have to watch Will," I warned her. "He vanishes so quickly, and he barely knows you."

"But he's seen me nearly every day for a month!"

"He's *lived with* me every single day for a month, and I'm not sure how well he knows me. Let him play video games, put him to bed on time, make sure they both take their night meds, and it should be fine. But watch him."

Mama sighed when I handed her the pill minders. "Are these really necessary?"

Did she not remember the screaming panic that consumed William the day I forgot his evening and morning meds back-to-back? Lance assured me this attitude was generational, but I felt judgment in her reluctance. Mama wondered why we were taking these kids on if we had to drug them to control their behaviors. She didn't understand we weren't "drugging" them at all. The medications made it possible for Will to function and for Sara to slow down long enough to enjoy the world.

"Yes. Make sure they get them," was all I told her.

I had already called in twice to check. The third time, Mama didn't answer and replied with a text. "Cut it out. We're fine."

I tried to pay attention to the party, an event I normally enjoyed enormously. The volunteer servers were encouraged to share out libations freely among the guests. We didn't want them drunk, but we wanted them to open their pocketbooks wide, and alcohol always paved the road more smoothly than lemonade.

I saw Natasha lingering too close to the bar early in the evening and headed her off. "If he needs a drink, one of us will get it," I said. "I don't even want you on this side of the room." That Stan wasn't supposed to be drinking went unspoken. He was enjoying his "day-pass" to its fullest capacity.

I thought she might appeal to her grandfather to arbitrate, so I was a little surprised when she said instead, "Okay. Message received. Thanks," without a note of sarcasm in her voice.

"How many people are there?" I asked Lance in a rare moment together.

"It looks like a good crowd."

A stir at the door caught my attention. "This is an invitation-only event!" said Jen. The gala was half over; we were going to start shutting down portions of the silent auction soon. We were twenty minutes out from the beginning of the live auction.

"But my dear," purred a silky, feminine voice, "I have a donation."

One by one, people fell silent as a sumptuously dressed woman paraded into the crowd. She looked like something out of a fifties movie with her blonde up-do, net-veil hat, and black and white polka-dot dress. She led a capuchin monkey on a leash.

The animal was obviously edgy. It first resisted her pull, then shot ahead and jerked her arm. It danced from one leg to the other, its performance anything but endearing. Then it darted into the crowd, yanking the leash entirely loose. The woman stood gaping as her pet shot away. She gave chase. "Come back here!"

The upsets started nearly immediately.

"Hey, give me that!"

"It took my glasses!"

"Gah! That bracelet cost a fortune!"

"My wallet!"

The owner tripped as many people as her pet, stumbling through the crowd, clutching arms and waists to keep herself upright. If the capuchin's leash hadn't been clipped to a harness, the animal might have been uncatchable. It moved so quickly and had so many feet to tangle up its pursuers. Additionally, it was vicious. Though it spun its own way through the room, anytime someone made a move to catch it, it bared its teeth in an evil grin and hissed menacingly. Finally, Lance stomped on the leash and pulled. The capuchin ran up and bit his hand. Lance flinched, but stood his ground as blood welled.

He seized the animal by its harness. "We don't normally accept animal surrenders during the center's nonworking hours. But I believe we'll make an exception in this case."

"Oh, no, you don't understand. He's not a surrender. He's a donation. For the live auction. He's well trained."

This was exactly the impression we *didn't* want to give our donors. I doubt the woman had seen me sidle up to her. I'm short, and she wasn't. Plus, she had on stiletto heels. "We're a sanctuary, not a pet store," I told her in a low voice. "In case you hadn't noticed, you have a short time to register or hand over that animal under the new law. Were you planning to get a permit?"

"My lord, no! Have you seen what those cost? If you won't accept the donation, I'll take him back."

From the way the monkey was thrashing in Lance's grasp, I thought it was ready to escape, biting as many people as it could on its way to the door. "We'll be happy to accept your *surrender*. But we're not a clearinghouse. Our animals are here for life."

"Poor things. Those are the ones you can't socialize." Her voice dripped with equal parts honey and battery acid.

"We don't socialize *any* of our animals. Not in the way you're thinking. We socialize them to each other. Not people. Primates aren't pets, ma'am. Now if you'll kindly accompany me so we can complete the necessary paperwork, we'll transfer this fellow to our quarantine facility." We had exactly one open.

It took nearly half an hour and a great deal of cajoling to part the woman from her monkey without so much as a donation letter for her taxes. But when she left, she did so without even looking in on the animal, which was huddled in a corner of the quarantine cell chewing on its organ grinder vest. Though he got bitten again for his efforts, Lance did retrieve the valuable bracelet. The monkey had dropped the glasses in the heat of the chase.

"I didn't think she was going to sign," he muttered after we had escorted her to her car and watched her drive away down the lane.

"I was going to call the deputy at the gate to come arrest her if she hadn't." When we *did* call, said deputy told us she had flashed a piece of paper. He assumed she was an invited guest arriving late because of her vehicle and demeanor. He hadn't noticed the monkey.

By the time Lance and I had dressed his wounds and

returned, the live auction should have been in full swing. Instead, someone had given Stan the microphone, and he was holding forth. "That's why you need monkey sanctuaries," he was explaining. *He's turning a disaster into a success. Only Stan. Or Art . . . Art could have done that.* For a moment my heart ached. "It takes special training to know how to handle these primates. Apes get more attention, but they aren't the only animals in need of safe havens. The public service Midwest Primates provides is vital to the state of Ohio."

I glanced around and found Natasha near the stage, all too casually sipping. From a distance, I couldn't tell if the beverage was the wrong color, though color wouldn't have shown if she used vodka. I thought it unusual enough for her to be away from her grandfather that I poured her a fresh glass myself and wordlessly held it out in exchange. She accepted with rolled eyes, and I threw the other one away without checking the contents. After all, maybe it hadn't contained alcohol.

Once I had retrieved the mic and set off the rest of the evening's festivities, I hid away and called my mother one last time. "We're *fine*," she insisted, though I could tell from the strain in her voice they were not. "I read to the kids and tucked them in together half an hour ago. Sara's only been up twice since then."

"And their meds?"

"*Yes*, Noel. I gave the children their medications." There was a long silence. Finally, she sighed. "Don't ask questions about the food all over your kitchen ceiling, all right?"

CHAPTER 15

Dear Nora:

My husband's run off with the housekeeper. Thanks for nothing.

Worked to the Bone

Dear Worked:

Good riddance to bad rubbish. Be sure you get a fair shake in court. I'm sending my attorney's name. You'll love him. I want to hear by next week that you've called.

Nora

Natalie Forrester nursed the last of my gourmet coffee. The shambles of my kitchen surrounding us included an oatmeal mountain, all of my pans, and something gloppy and brown that dripped onto Natalie's hand from the ceiling. "Pudding." She licked her finger idly clean.

Typically, a pair of foster parents wouldn't have had this much contact after a child was transferred, but there was nothing typical about our adoption of the twins. The Forresters had made themselves unconditionally available to us early in the process, and two and a half months in, we were still taking them at their word. Natasha was visiting her grandparents in the respite home for the day, and we needed their help.

In the living room, her foster children were vying for control of the video game console with William and Sara. "Take turns,"

Lance told them for the umpteenth time.

"Or it's the dungeons and salt mines for all of you," Adam added.

"Dungeons!" shrieked Sara, setting up a general hue and cry of "Dungeons, dungeons, dungeons."

"Come on, Lance. I haven't got enough arms to carry all of them. You take those two." Adam swept by with Sara and another girl (Macy? I had already forgotten her name) under one arm and a little boy under the other. Lance followed with William and the Forresters' third child (whose name also escaped me). They all trumped down to the basement.

"Why are they so *happy* when you're here and so miserable when you're not?" I drank my own coffee, the first cup of the second pot, made from an inferior brand. The compulsion to clean was nearly uncontrollable. *Look! They're out of the room! I can pick it up.* It was hard to make myself remain still, sipping away like Natalie was an old friend dropping by for brunch, not the rescue train rolling in to save Lance and me from ourselves for the fourth time in as many days. It didn't matter she was nearly a full decade younger than I. Natalie was the wiser party here.

"I have to be honest. You and Lance aren't equipped for this."

"I noticed, Natalie, but I'm not giving up. I need help, not . . ."

"Relax. I'm not criticizing. People aren't always willing to admit it when something is falling apart, and I need to make sure you and I are on the same page. I'm *glad* you noticed. Keep in mind, families weren't lining up to adopt those two, Adam and I included. You're all they've got. But you need to learn how to parent them, and you've got to do it fast, or you're going to join the list of people who have failed them."

"Do you know anybody giving out speed parenting lessons?"

A dish in the overloaded sink shifted, a belated response to the thunder of two men and five children crashing down to the basement.

"I am, actually. I teach a six-week series of parenting classes, and you and Lance are going to sign up. But you don't have six weeks to get this under control." She waved at the room. "Natalie and Adam Forrester's School of Mom and Dad is now in session. Here's how it will work. After school every day from now until the next session of my class starts, either you or Lance or both of you together will come to my house with your kids. We'll do everything together and ease their separation from us a little bit more. They don't deal well with change, and that's part of your problem here.

"At least once in the next week, you and Lance will still shadow me with my younger ones during the day, while your kids are at school. And take advantage of the help you've got! I'm glad to see your mom around so much."

"But she's as much underfoot as the children. She's trying to do all our cooking and housework, and half the time, we have to come along behind her and redo it."

"Quit."

"But she's doing it like she's at her house."

"Show her how it works here if you must, but frankly, I'd say get out of her way and let the woman help you." Natalie stared at me until I looked away. "You also had the sense to hire the student volunteer from your center to help you out here while you get started."

We didn't even know Natalie in June, and she had never met Trudy in the debacle following William's kidnapping. Drew's people had been the ones warning parents of a child predator, not Trudy and Darnell. Natalie only knew the agent in the context of her semi-undercover job, which included posing as a university student who interned at the sanctuary.

"But . . . what's her name, Trudy? She needs an education, too. I can see how frustrated she gets dealing with them, and there's simply no point. She's got to come along too, whenever her school schedule will allow. She doesn't seem experienced with kids."

"I know."

"I mean, she *knows* she can't give a chimpanzee a time-out, right?"

"*I* know."

"So why does she think she can clicker-train a child into obedience?"

"I had a conversation with her about that." Trudy had muttered swear words when I told her to stop reinforcing the children's behaviors with the noisy little tool we used with our apes. She couldn't understand why I found it offensive. In any case, Sara loved the clicker game, but William glowered and sat with crossed arms and legs when she pulled the device out.

For my part, I was beginning to see why even Drew had been so willing to let pass Merry's obviously inappropriate comparison between the twins and monkeys. It seemed to be a prevailing attitude among even some who worked closely with them that kids with autism were, at some level, lesser, not full, humans. These children were *hard* to understand. Even though we, too, struggled to communicate with them, especially William, Lance and I instinctively knew better, reinforcing my belief that we were their parents. But in the weeks since they had come to live with us forever, we had learned we didn't know much else.

The worst part wasn't merely the unpleasant surprises, though there were many. Like William's sudden incontinence when faced with long-term stress. And Sara's stubborn unwillingness to eat anything but processed macaroni and cheese and greasy tater tots. And their twin insistence upon sleeping curled up together in William's bed, rather than in their own rooms.

It wasn't only the horrific number of *things* we suddenly owned, though there were many. I honestly don't remember what I had expected. I'd heard foster kids rarely had much of their own. Perhaps I had imagined the twins would arrive with a lone suitcase stretched between their tiny hands. If so, the sight of the children spilling out of Merry's car with Ann and a trail of objects behind them set me quickly straight. Not only did these children come with those high-backed boosters, they also each had an armada of toys and clothes. Natalie had spent a year ensuring they *did* have personal possessions. They had overstuffed suitcases and a shared gaming system that had travelled with them from home to home since their mother gave it to them, along with hundreds of CD-based games. Lance spent two hours attempting to hook the system up to our older television before he gave up and called Adam for instructions.

It wasn't our complete ignorance about the education system. The twins brought school bags lovingly packed by Natalie, who correctly assumed Lance and I had no idea what to send with first graders. She included highlighted copies of the Individual Education Programs detailing what services each child could receive because of their autism diagnoses. She called these forms by their initials, instructing us, "Start with the IEP whenever you're unsure if the kids are being treated inappropriately." She also included a calendar from each child's school. And no, they didn't attend the same one as I had expected. Sara was, to use Natalie's word, "stuck" in East Ironweed Public, while William had won the magnet program's lottery and been placed in the charter school for gifted children across town.

The worst thing wasn't even the lack of sleep, though we stayed awake almost nonstop for the first fourteen days and slept in shifts after. Between Sara's combination of insomnia and night terrors, William's overnight incontinence, and our own brooding insecurities, we became heavily dependent on coffee early in our tenure as parents. The worst part wasn't even all of these things together.

Lance put it best when he told Natalie, "They want to go back with you, and at the exact same time, they don't ever want to leave Natasha. *We* don't figure anywhere into their plan."

"Not yet," Natalie told him. "You will. I've had kids with attachment disorders who couldn't bond with caregivers. That's not these two. Change comes hard for them, and they've faced too much of it."

Now, she was extending an extraordinary gift that might help us support the twins through that change and convince them we were their parents. I had no idea why the state had ever allowed the twins to be moved into our care from hers. Surely if she had spoken one word against us, the twins would still live in her home.

She seemed to read my mind. "They belong here," she reassured me. "It's hard to explain, Noel. But there's a click, a moment of certainty, of 'this one is mine.' You felt it with the twins. I can see it. We've clicked with a couple of our kids, but mostly, the kids who come to us belong to other people. And that's better for them. To go home.

"Adam says it's complete nonsense, that I make my mind up for things to go a certain way and then exert my will on the world to shape events to my liking. But I think I'm pretty good at picking out families for my kids. What did you feel when you found William under the Marine's Dumpster?"

"Relieved, obviously. But until I saw him, I was worried in a more distant way. Then when he was under there, where he shouldn't have been able to fit, I suddenly felt like a weight was lifted, one I hadn't known was all on me. Then . . ." How to explain that emptiness, that sense of loss when he got in the ambulance. I didn't have the words. "It was all action, reaction, and reaction again."

"Do you remember how hysterical I was?"

"Who wouldn't have been?"

"You. You weren't. You, Lance, and Natasha. You were calm in that maelstrom. Me? I was making it worse for poor Will, but I couldn't get my own emotions under control. I thought they were going to have to sedate me; I did. I remember how much worry I saw in you. You were every bit as distressed as I was. But you were calm. I remember thinking, 'She might be his mother.' I may have said it out loud. I don't know. If I did, I'm probably the one who accidentally set Merry on you. What about Sara? What was your first knee-jerk impression of her?"

"I knew who she was right away, even though she and William don't look all that much alike. And I knew she was alone."

"Yeah, but what did you feel?"

"I felt like crying. I . . . Lance was the one who always said he didn't want kids. I went along with him, and I only minded every once in a while. But when I saw her on our porch, I felt like the Gulf of Mexico was stretched between Lance and me, because . . . because I knew she was mine, and I was so sure he wouldn't feel the same."

"Exactly," said Natalie. "That's what I've seen in both of you all along. That protective energy they need so much. Don't worry. These kids belong to you. Did you make the decision to adopt them too quickly? Without question, yes. You didn't take the time to learn about autism or young children at all. But your speed isn't the same as I've seen in some others. I've seen couples so desperate to have a child, *any* child, they scoop up the first one available without pausing to find that connection. They hope love can cause bonding. And it can. Sometimes. But sometimes even love isn't enough.

"You and Lance were excited, and Merry pushed to go too

fast, but you weren't child hungry. You don't want *a* child or *any* children. You want *these* children. And really, you had a narrow window of opportunity before Merry spirited them off in her hurry to find them placement."

"Why *was* she in such a hurry? Wouldn't it be worse to have an interrupted adoption than to take her time and be sure?"

"I don't know," said Natalie. "But she was pushing hard. And they *are* yours, Noel. Now, you have to learn to all live together."

"And you think you can teach us that?"

"Of course I can. Now let's tackle this mess while the guys have a captive audience downstairs."

She *could* teach us. And I fervently hoped we could learn. We restored some order to our kitchen before lunch, and the Forresters taught us a couple of tricks to curb the rather immediate problem of our children refusing to do anything we said.

After lunch, I asked Sara, "Do you want to take your plate to the sink for me?"

"No." The child didn't sound defiant, but it was clear she didn't intend to follow my instruction.

Immediately, Natalie said, "Sara, please take your plate to the sink."

"Okay," Sara chirped, and she took not only the plate, but her cup and silverware as well.

I turned to Natalie. "Why did that work for you when it had just totally failed for me? Is it because she knows you better?"

"Maybe a little. But mostly it's because you asked her and I told her. You asked if she wanted to take her plate to the sink. Of course she doesn't! I mean, do *you* want to take *your* plate to the sink? No! But you know why it needs to be done. She doesn't. You can bore her with the reason—only some of which will stick, and that's true of any kid—or you can assert your authority. Gently.

"As far as she's concerned, you asked for her opinion. Any

time you *need* the twins to do something, you can't ask it. It's fine to ask about the optionals, but when you do, be prepared to accept 'no,' especially from Sara."

She also steered us away from some behavior methods frequently used with autistic kids, many of which we'd never heard of. "Do *not* under any circumstances tell William to have 'quiet hands.' "

"Quiet hands?"

"It's a way to remind him not to flap and touch everything in sight. I guess that works for some people. But his uncle took it as license to strap down his arms. He will *bite* you if you tell him to keep them quiet. Personally, Adam and I let him flap and touch as long as he isn't hurting anything, and if he is, we redirect him to do it elsewhere."

"Tie them *down*?"

"That's what Will told me, and I don't have any reason to disbelieve him."

"How could you understand what he said? He hardly talks, and everything he says sounds like a question. I can engage in back and forth with Sara, but Will . . . he hardly seems to hear me." Circular, unusual, often unintentionally hilarious back and forth, but at least my new daughter was having conversations.

"He clams up in new places. Be patient. Plus, nobody had worked with him much before he came to us. With the receptive language delay, you have to help him to understand new words and ideas using words and concepts he's already got. He's obsessed with categories. If you can categorize something, you can help him understand it."

"Meaning?"

"Okay. To teach him about garden squash, I had to start with generic categories, 'yellow foods' and 'curved foods,' and narrow from there. Lemons are yellow. Butter is yellow. *Squash* is yellow. I can eat lemons. I can eat butter. I can eat squash.

Bananas are curved. I can eat bananas. Squash is curved. I can eat squash. He eventually caught on, but he called it 'lemon-banana.' "

"He's been telling me 'William has a lemon-nanner' all week!"

"There you go. Get him some squash. And when you do, keep substituting the correct name. Eventually, it will stick."

Actually, I liked "lemon-nanner," now that I knew what it was. I thought squash in our house might have a permanent new identity. "But how does it help me understand what he's already saying? How can I get him to work it backward for me?"

"You can't. But I know most of them. Give me a for-instance."

"Cheese-light. Is it a kind of cheese? A refrigerator?" He spent a good portion yesterday night begging us, "William, do you want a cheese-light?" Of course, none of our offers of food had been sufficient.

Natalie laughed. "It's a camera. He's a little ham."

"I get it. You say 'cheese' and a light flashes."

"Exactly."

"What about circle-dot cars?"

"That one's recent. It showed up after he vanished. I think it's rescue vehicles, but I'm not sure. When Detective Carmichael comes out to change the battery in his wristband, he's fine. He's excited to see *that* cruiser, but it's the only one. He covers his ears and makes siren noises when he hears an ambulance or fire truck now, when he never used to do that. It may have to do with context, or it may be something else entirely. Be patient. You'll learn how to listen to him."

She hugged us as she left, and I snagged the convertible keys to go get Natasha. I didn't care if it was November and I had to drive with the top up. The car was sexy, and I'd never felt less like an antique frump. "I guess I'll get some of this laundry started," said Lance. But his eyes followed me out the door. Tasha was right. I needed to hide myself a set of those keys before Lance thought to lay claim to them.

CHAPTER 16

Dear Nora:

My teen has more drama than a soap opera! Every time I turn around, she's having the end of the world again. Help or send thread.

Seeking Peace

Dear Seeking:

Take her to see Hamlet *or* Macbeth. *Not* Romeo and Juliet. *Something good and gory to remind her she doesn't have it half so bad as anybody in a Shakespearean tragedy. Keep her away from long swords for a week or so after, just to be on the safe side.*

Nora

P.S. I'm sending thread and a nice cross-stitch pattern I found online. It will cheer you up even if it doesn't do her any good.

"Natasha, stop crying and tell me what's wrong." Tasha was slumped over her lap sobbing in the respite home's white lobby, her face streaked purple with mascara.

"It was supposed to be a big . . . big family reunion," she wailed. "Because they're both out of the hospital and over here, and Granddad can visit Gram's room if she had a good day. I snuck in cookies and *everything*." Tasha collapsed in tears again, and I tried to ignore the nurses sending me dirty glowers. In addition to leaving a minor alone on the premises, I was now letting her continue to make entirely too much noise upon my return. And I couldn't touch her to offer comfort without being instantly shaken off.

"What happened?" I prompted her.

"I'm afraid we gave her some rather bad news and didn't do a good job cushioning the blow." I hadn't heard Stan enter, as he arrived on smooth wheels, one leg still braced straight out in front of him.

"Noel!" Natasha, who had shoved my arm off her for the third time only moments before, suddenly clamped onto my hand. "Gran isn't ever . . . she isn't . . . she won't be home again!"

"Yes, she *will*!" Stan explained. He appealed to me, "What am I going to do with these *women*?" as if I didn't share Natasha and Gert's gender.

I was the only one standing, hunched at an awkward angle because Natasha was dragging on my arm. Clearly, we wouldn't be leaving right away. I eased in a hard wooden chair. This was no state-run facility of the variety where we had visited my paternal grandfather in his final years. This was a swanky private home where Gert and Stan's rooms, though in separate wings, were more like hotel suites than nursing home beds. We had been lucky enough to get Nana placed here in one of the two Medicare beds when she broke her hip last year.

Natasha accepted a handkerchief from Stan. Though legally her father, he was not her biological grandfather, and her round face had never looked more different than his narrow oval one than it did right now. Nonetheless, they shared a closeness I couldn't achieve. He stretched a hand out and stroked the weeping girl's hair. She didn't shove him away. "It's going to be fine, darling," he assured her.

"How can you *say* that?" Natasha scrubbed her face. "She

170

has multiple sclerosis, Noel. She's going to deteriorate and deteriorate and *die*. And there's nothing you can buy that will change her back to how she was before Aunt Gretchen poisoned her."

Stan ignored the jibe about money. "Natasha, it's a regressing and remitting variety. She should stabilize. Honey, she was hiding things from both of us long before. She told me she'd fallen a couple of times getting out of the tub when she hadn't slipped. Lucky she never broke anything. She was having muscle spasms. Gretchen merely put her in a position where she couldn't deny it any longer."

"It doesn't matter. You can't buy her better."

"No," Stan said. "I can't. I can throw money into research. I can give her access to cutting-edge medications. I know the research won't likely pay off in her lifetime, and even the best meds on the market won't cure her.

"But I *can* bring her home, Natasha. Your grandmother's problem is as much depression as it is anything else. She always knew Gretchen and Gary were a little cold-hearted. But she never knew what they had done to Linda. What they were doing to you. It doesn't matter how your mother died right now, all Gert can think about is how she *lived*.

"We had to shut your mother out a long time before she died, honey, even though it meant separating ourselves from you as well. And now Gert's blaming herself for things completely out of her control. We've all been doing that lately."

"Wait." Natasha's hysteria was gone. Although she was still swiping off her ruined makeup with the handkerchief, the girl looking up at Stan was totally focused. "I thought you separated from me because I busted Layla's teeth in."

Stan's face registered shock. "You were a kid in a horrible situation. Why would we have cut off a child? Your mother blocked us. The first thing we had to do after she died was prove that Terry creature couldn't possibly be your father."

"How did you know he *wasn't*?"

"She didn't even meet him until you were two, dear. We didn't know she was passing him off as your actual father until after her death. We were lucky enough to have your real birth certificate, or his forgery might have passed muster, and then it would have been hard to get you when she died."

"Why'd he forge it? Why not adopt me? They all had money for that kind of thing."

"Your biological father would have killed him. He wanted that side of the page blank. But a forgery? Something unlikely to be checked against formal records as long as your mother was alive? It was a measured risk to keep control of you and her."

They stared back and forth, grandfather to grandchild, until Natasha said, "*Is* T-Bow Orrice my dad?"

"I thought your mother would have at least told you that."

"She did in a roundabout way, but . . . you know Mom. It was hard to tell whether she was telling the truth or lying. But if he *is* my dad and everybody *does* know it, why wasn't he on my birth certificate?" She sounded like she already knew the answer.

"He doesn't want his name on *any* of his children's birth certificates. It would have given you, and more importantly, your mother, a claim to him."

"Then how come you're so sure?"

"Your mother told us. Then, after Linda died, I asked him. The only chance your grandmother and I had to get our hands on you was to prove you weren't Terry's daughter. You were so strung out you could barely put two sentences together, and you were rightfully angry with all of us. You seemed to think that bastard . . . excuse me . . . that Mr. Dalton *was* your father."

"*Yes.* I forgot I knew different until the day I came home with you."

"Your original birth certificate was on file with the state, and once we got a lawyer involved, the forgery became evident. But it still took DNA testing to prove they hadn't altered the document to reflect a fact. On paper, at least, he was effectively your stepfather for all that your mother never married him. Your mother was the one with the drug problems. It took a long time to prove he was supplying *your* drugs.

"In the meantime, I contacted T-Bow and asked him for the truth of the matter. He gave me the truth because he knew I didn't want a connection to him. He's vain, but he isn't naive. And he wanted to be clear of the Daltons. T-Bow thinks *he* pushed me into adopting you. Between having me as your father and Terry Dalton, he preferred me by far, especially as everyone would *know* you're adopted."

"You didn't buy him?" Natasha made no effort to mask her skepticism.

"My dear, there is nothing I can offer T-Bow Orrice. He's already in jail. He runs his gang from the inside, and I'm sure he has more money than I'll ever see."

"When Terry died? Was it a coincidence?"

"I have to hope so, Tasha, but we'll never know. Orrice doesn't like his women to have their claws in him, but he's extremely protective of his children. And I assure you, he knows who all of them are, even when he denies it. T-Bow Orrice is all about control. He really does think I adopted you on his say-so, dear." Stan sounded so offhanded about something that seemed to me like it had obviously been a murder. He seemed perfectly comfortable trading Natasha's life for that of this Terry person.

"But back when I was with Mrs. P you didn't stop coming to see me because I pounded on Layla?"

"No. Your mother and Terry showed up for a hearing, and then for a visitation, and she stopped testing positive for drugs. Once she got you back, she took out a restraining order. And

Gert and I had to accept we almost surely couldn't win in court against a mother who seemed to have it together. But we knew better. And Gert couldn't stand to get her heart broken anymore. We pulled away completely, and we never had a chance to tell you why, or how sorry we were.

"We thought we'd put a stop to it when we finally brought you home. But we hadn't. And Gert feels like she failed your mother and you both . . ."

"But she didn't . . . she couldn't . . ."

"I know," said Stan. "I know. But I feel the same way. It's a lot for her, and it's slowing down her recovery. We'll all be home before you know it."

"And I can come here for Thanksgiving with you guys?" Natasha's voice wavered again. She took hold of Stan's hand, which was cradling her cheek now.

"Absolutely. We'll spend Thanksgiving together here, and Christmas, too, if we have to."

Merging onto the freeway half an hour later, I mulled the levels of secrecy and deception in Natasha's history. The day had turned rainy, and I was wishing I'd brought the minivan to navigate traffic. Travis called when we were halfway between Columbus and Ironweed. Besides teaching me to text since she had come to stay with us, Natasha had programmed my phone and Lance's both into the car's audio system. I still hated texting, but I did it when necessary, and I rather enjoyed thumbing my steering wheel to answer a call.

"Hey," said Travis. "Did you ever tell Lance you applied for Art's old job?"

"Mmmno." I flashed a look at Natasha, and she rolled her eyes at me. She couldn't understand this complete failure to communicate on my part.

"Then you better make sure he's no place near in the next twenty minutes or so. The chair's going to be calling you."

Natasha barely had time to get into her anxiety-ridden lecture about the things she feared would happen to our marriage and relationship when the phone rang again. "Shush," I said. She rolled her eyes once more.

"Noel," the chair's voice boomed. Winfred Prescott *always* boomed. Natasha turned down the volume. "We've determined a short list of initial candidates to interview up at the Biological Research Organization Convention in January. Of course, you won't be there, so the committee has agreed to make an exception for you and interview you on campus." He didn't sound happy about this. "We're expecting to take under an hour, and it's scheduled for the Wednesday after Thanksgiving at two."

What? The other candidates get two months, and I get a little over a week? He hung up before I could say a word. "I thought I was a long shot," I wailed.

"I told you Lance needs to know. Travis has said all along . . ."

"What does he know? He's only worked here a few months."

"*Plenty,* obviously."

"Wednesday after Thanksgiving . . . okay. Lance will be at the center."

"You have to promise to tell Lance after the interview. I don't see what the big deal is, anyway. Why *weren't* you two supposed to apply for this thing?"

"We're field researchers, Tasha. If we're married to a university schedule, we'll never be out in the field again. We'll get tied to classrooms, and labs, and . . . why are you shaking your head?"

"How are you going to take the twins on field research? Me, I'm temporary. Gran and Granddad come home, and I go with them. Sara and William aren't going anyplace."

"Of course not! We'll have to adjust our schedules to accommodate theirs, of course, but we'll travel in the summers."

"You'll travel in the summers. You'll take William with you in the summer?"

"*Yes.* He's a smart little boy, Natasha. He already loves the sanctuary. They'll both get so much . . ."

"Trudy isn't going to play nanny forever, you know. Eventually, they'll find her an actual job instead of leaving her to follow up on a practically closed case. She won't have free time to play around with your kids then. How are you going to get any research done keeping track of a kid who follows bugs off into the brush?"

"I haven't worked it all out in my head, but we'll *manage.* But if I'm stuck teaching a summer class, or if there's a unique research opportunity one of us could take *during* the school year, what then? We can't both go, of course, because the kids will be in school, but if I'm at the university, the only one who can go is Lance. I won't have any kind of clout to take sabbaticals like Art used to do."

"It sounds to me like you've got it all worked out *not* to take the job if you *do* get it."

"No, but . . . I'm buying trouble. I probably won't get hired. But one of us has to do *something.* We can't raise two children on Lance's sanctuary income and what a few adjunct classes can bring in."

"Have you and Lance talked about this at all?"

I shook my head. Mama was right. Adopting the twins was the most impulsive decision we'd ever made in our lives. I didn't regret it for a moment. But I wished we'd spent a little more time getting ready to be parents.

The phone rang again. "Wow. Three calls in one ride. You're getting to be quite the twenty-first-century gal," Natasha teased.

It was Lance. "Yeah, what's up?"

"Honey, are you almost home?"

"Ten minutes out. What's up?"

"Drive faster. I've got the Forresters coming back, and Drew swears . . ."

"Go back, what's wrong?"

"I can't find William! Drew swears his Project Lifesaver bracelet is in the house, but what if it isn't attached to his arm anymore? Trudy's almost here. I've looked everywhere. I can't find the damned thing. I can't *find him.* Sara's sitting on the couch, and her eyes are huge, and I can see she's reliving the last time he got lost."

"I'm coming. Calm down. I'll be there. Nobody broke into our house and took him. And he didn't go out either, if you didn't hear the alarm. If Drew says the bracelet's inside, then it's inside *on William.* Sit down and make a list of all the places you've already looked, and when I get there, we'll start all over and go room to room methodically."

"But honey, what if we've lost him forever?"

My heart wanted to panic, but my voice locked into calm. "He's fine, Lance. We need to find him, but he's okay." This was almost always how I acted in a crisis. As long as there was action to be taken, I asserted control, analyzed, and organized. It was only when completely helpless that I fell apart. In contrast, when we couldn't do anything at all in a bad situation, Lance drew himself together and asserted calm. When Gary murdered Art, all I could do was cry. But Lance started dealing with it right away.

At this moment, there was plenty we could do. And Lance's hysterics were surely making Sara's fears worse. I needed to get home to her as much as him. I urged the car forward above the speed limit, only to see blue lights in my rearview mirror as I exited the bypass.

"Not right *now,*" I muttered, aiming my car for the side of the road.

The cop car blasted its horn when I slowed down, and I

glanced in my rearview mirror. It was Drew, and he was waving me ahead, not pulling me over. I was getting a police escort home to find my kid.

CHAPTER 17

Dear Nora:

I can't ever find my car keys. Please don't tell me to hang them on a hook by the door. I can never remember which one I used last. And please don't tell me to have one certain bowl or something, because I've tried that, and I could never remember where I put it.

Lost in the Sticks

Dear Lost,
  Get a bike.

Nora

After several hours of searching, I was all out of actions, reduced to a weeping puddle on the couch while Lance directed traffic and assured me, "We're going to find him honey. The device is in the house. The kid is in the house. He's going to be fine." Our roles had utterly reversed.

"We've looked everywhere," I groaned.

"Twice," Sara added, because that was how I had phrased the statement the last time I said it. She was curled between Natalie and me, sucking her hand, then wiping it dry on my pants.

"Obviously, we're missing something." Lance paced out to the kitchen, where Mama had brewed a pot of the new stuff that everyone agreed tasted like road tar or battery acid.

"Think about your house," Adam advised me. "I know you haven't lived here long, but imagine its layout, and try to picture the tiny spaces. What would appeal to a child who likes to squeeze down little and hide?"

"We've looked under beds, in the tops of closets, and even in the attic, though I've got no idea how he would have gotten there. I've emptied every cupboard and cabinet, and he won't come out. The only thing left is inside one of those packing boxes in . . ."

"I think we've got something down here!" my father called from the basement.

Lance scooped up Sara and pounded down the stairs ahead of me. Daddy and Drew had muscled our few remaining moving boxes out from the wall, checking each as they went. Reaching them without stepping on our belongings was hazardous going. And they had to shush the crowd of us twice so we could hear what they had found.

Although the basement is finished, it had clearly been in need of some repair since before Stan bought us the house. Our boxes served to cover over a couple of small gaps between pieces of drywall. Daddy thought he had seen something behind one of these gaps, so he tapped gently. Nearly at once, his tap was echoed. Once we fell silent, he continued rapping back and forth for a few moments, until Lance burst out, "William, is that you?"

"Are you stuck, William?" I asked at the same time.

An aching silence, nothing, then three more taps. Drew turned his light into the crack. "I still can't see a thing. If it is him, I'll be damned if I know how he got in."

"Of course it's him! Our walls don't have an echo. Let's get him *out*," said Lance. He set Sara down and reached for the crack. "I'll pull this whole wall down if I have to." He gave a mighty heave, but instead of breaking off a portion of drywall, he caused a creaking rip running the length of the wall. "Look at that."

Drew shone his light along the length of the tear, which ran smoothly to the other chink in the drywall we had been concealing with boxes. Lance yanked again, and a whole panel peeled free and flopped open, revealing, alongside several nests of spiders, one William, curled into a ball. "Somebody had themselves a regular little hidey hole, didn't they?"

While Drew followed the tiny tunnel to see where it originated, my father fingered the rusty inner hinges Lance had folded down. Even with the panel lowered, William was still trapped behind a lip of real drywall. He knocked again, with the back of one hand. "William," he said in a conversational, if muffled voice, "is that you? William, are you stuck?" Then, he went on to add, "William, would you like some help there, buddy? We don't want to be playing in the salt mines all day."

"Looks like it goes into the furnace closet, like it was originally supposed to be part of the ducts but never got hooked to the central system," Drew called. "There's a grate pushed out onto the floor behind the furnace itself. That hole is *tiny*! How did he get *in* there?"

Lance didn't answer him. "Let's see what we can do." Lance grabbed some of the real drywall and pulled. A handful came away in crumbling clumps. He repeated the maneuver with similar results. The going was made slower because William was pressed right up against both sides of the wall, making it hard to keep from grabbing *him* as well or else suffocating him with plaster dust. Eventually, though, he popped free, and Sara threw herself on top of him as soon as he rolled out.

He seemed unhurt, if somewhat dazed by his adventure, and when he got tired of Sara's clinging, he pulled away and darted upstairs calling, "I bet she's hungry. Would he like a little dinner?" William frequently mixed up gender pronouns in this way, treating them interchangeably.

Lance chased after him, but I remained on the floor, stroking Sara's back while she sobbed the tears she had held in all afternoon.

"His Project Lifesaver band saved his life," I said. "I want to kiss whoever put it on him in the first place."

"Nelly Penobscott, of course," said Natalie. "His mother and uncle took horrible care of the equipment, though, and he was with us a little while before we got it functioning in our house. I didn't sleep until we did. You can see why."

"We wouldn't have known where to look! We would have been sure he was gone. We would have . . ."

". . . found him for you by the middle of the night if we had to tear your house down one piece at a time," Drew said. "But it would have been hours from now, and he might have hurt himself getting free. Those little bands save people. I don't know why more places don't use them. If you all will excuse me, I've got a report to fill out and Hugh Marsland's wife probably still in my office to deal with."

"Nothing good there?"

"Ah, poor thing, I shouldn't sound so callous. We're all worried about him. She got a nasty letter. Supposedly photographic evidence he left her. He's standing on the beach with some trophy girl. It's an obvious digital creation. She doesn't understand there's not a thing I can do I'm not already doing. I put the picture in a baggie and labeled it, then looked at it through a magnifying glass to make her feel better before I sent it off as evidence."

"He's missing?"

"The whole thing is weird, Noel. I sent the picture down the pipe, but I doubt it will do any good. Maybe somebody can trace the postmark."

"Can I ask a weird question?" We hadn't been paying attention to Natasha, the only other one who lingered to comfort Sara with me after Mama and Daddy followed Lance up the stairs.

"Ask away. I may not answer, but you can *always* ask," Drew told her.

"What's the beach babe look like?"

"Hugh's digital girlfriend?"

"Yeah."

"You know. Typical specimen. Blonde, fake tan, red bikini."

"Heart tattoo on her hip? Is she turned away from the camera looking back over her shoulder?"

"Y-e-s-s." Drew turned a one-syllable word into three. "How did *you* know?"

"Definitely digitally altered. You should get a copy to the feds. Stay put. I'll get you the original."

"You'll what?"

Upstairs, Trudy called a greeting to the house along with, "It looks like I missed all the fun! I'm so glad you found him safe."

"I'll get you the original," said Natasha. "But you have to promise not to shred it to pieces and at least try to get it back to me."

"Natasha, I'm not following you," Drew said.

"Do I have to spell it out? The woman in the picture is my *mother*, and it was originally Terry Dalton with her. It was another one of those weird things Gary's guys used to do. When somebody was a danger to the organization, they killed him, then put a photo of his head on the picture in place of Terry's and glued the new picture to his face when they buried him, so he'd have a cute piece of tail to look at while he rotted."

Drew whistled. "Why in the hell did *you* hang onto it? If you don't mind my asking."

"Because I took it in the first place. It's one of my last decent pictures of her on the only vacation we ever took together."

Drew accepted the photograph when she gave it to him. He gave her a receipt, but said, "I don't know when, or if, it's coming home."

Tasha nodded. From her complacent manner, I guessed this wasn't her only copy.

When she had left the room, I said, "Drew, I don't think William is the one in real danger. I think he was only ever a lure to draw out Natasha. She's the one I'm scared for."

Drew nodded. "So am I. More and more, so am I."

Later, Merry arrived, looking wan and thin. *You've certainly lost weight!* "You look wonderful," I said. *You look like hell.* Her face was pale and pinched, like weight loss didn't sit any better with her than being overweight had done.

She half-smiled at me. "Wonderful," she echoed.

She didn't say anything else, not even when she looked in on William, and she left soon after. "She could have waited until morning," Drew remarked.

Later still, after Drew and even Trudy had gone, all five of us sat squeezed together on the couch, William still shedding dust onto everything he touched. He needed a bath but had rejected the idea of taking one, and we were loath to force the issue, since he had endured the entire episode without wetting himself, largely convinced this was another round of Adam's dungeons and salt mines game, which seemed to be an elaborate form of hide and seek requiring each person to perform a chore when found.

"I thought they had him again," Natasha said. "If I hadn't already spent all afternoon so frantic for Gran, I'd have had an anxiety attack."

"I'm glad you didn't." Lance went on stroking William's hair, brushing dust out with his fingers.

"Yeah. Would have slowed everybody down," she agreed.

"That's *not* what I meant."

184

Sara wiped her hand on my pants again, as she had been doing all afternoon. "I think I need a question?" she informed me.
Like William, most of Sara's sentences ended in the same lilt-
ing, questioning tone.

"Okay," said Lance. "Shoot."

"Shoot a doodle," Sara echoed.

When she didn't say anything else, Lance face-palmed himself
for accidentally derailing her. "I meant ask your question," he
clarified.

"Yeah. Okay. Here's the thing? You guys are great at bringing
William back to me and stuff?" She stopped again and put her
hand back in her mouth.

"Is that the question?" I finally asked. *And is the answer,
"You're welcome"?*

She nodded and went on slurping her fingers. "And," she
suddenly added, "We like you because you make good macaroni." Clearly her nod was meant to be a shake. This time, we
waited her out, and I resisted the urge to prod. "But we kind of
already have a mom? And she's a famous actress? I'm a little
worried we'll go home to her when you get rid of us and maybe
get to keep Lance but not Noel?" *Ah. The question at last.*

When Sara said "famous actress," Natasha sagged into the
back of the couch. When Sara said our names, Lance and I
flinched. The twins were supposed to call us Mom and Dad.
But so far, the closest either could come was, "Person-who-is-
not-my-mom, please I need a macaroni?" It wasn't discourtesy
keeping the twins from using the titles. In their minds, we simply
weren't their parents. Although they clearly didn't know what to
do with us, neither of them resisted our company.

William and Lance had developed a game with the trucks
where they took turns creating and changing arrangement pat-
terns. Sara's play was mercilessly repetitious, but she had
discovered the small store of children's books we had rescued

from the box they got relegated to when my nephew outgrew them. She wanted them read to her over and over. And, although I was sick of hopping on pop and wearing the fox's socks, I loved Sara's head nestled against me, her slobbery little hand in her mouth.

But I couldn't tell. *Was* she worried they wouldn't be able to keep me, or was she hopeful? She often mixed up opposites. "You know how you and William are a package deal?" said Lance. "Noel and I are the same. You get both of us or neither, not only one."

Sara slurped a little harder while she contemplated this. "When Mom finishes her movie, we have to go home without either of you?"

"*This* is home now," said Lance.

"You're like me," said Natasha. "You've been emancipated. Your mom isn't allowed to come take you away."

"No," Sara countered. "Your mom is *dead*. And dead people *can't* come take you away."

"Tasha's basic point is right, though," said Lance quickly. "Your mom can't come get you, even though she's alive. The law says she can't even know where you are."

Sara wedged herself further against me. "Not ever?" Worried, then. Not hopeful. Sara *wanted* to stay here. I squeezed her more tightly.

"Not ever." Lance leaned out so he could meet her eyes. She held his gaze without looking away, but William rocked and looked everyplace but my husband's face.

Sara took her hand out of her mouth. "Then what *does* happen when you want to get rid of us?"

Not if. When. "We're not . . ." I stopped short. Natalie had warned me to think my answers through with Sara. She had so many questions it could be easy to miss the big ones. And *most* of them were big.

"Mom got rid of us, Uncle Ugly got rid of us, and Natty and Adam got rid of us. I think I need to know where's next, so I don't have to worry." Her voice betrayed no hint of sorrow, but the questioning tone was gone. Possibly she was asserting her bluntness to mask fear, and possibly she was simply planning for the future. "Also, what about if *we* want to get rid of you? William and I wanted to get rid of Uncle Ugly for a long time before he was ready to get rid of us. I think we need some options here."

"Was that one question or six?" Lance was rubbing his temples.

Sara didn't reply. *I* certainly didn't know what to say. "It's more complicated," Natasha said.

"Is not." Sara's hand had come out of her mouth for most of the previous speech, but now it was back in place, making her words hard to understand.

Before Natasha could get trapped into an "is too" loop, I said, "Let's look at it this way. Your mom had a hard time taking care of you."

"Yup. She was too busy acting. And it left her tired all day." At least I think that's what Sara said. Her hand was lodged between those lips.

"It sounds like you didn't want to be at your uncle's any more than he wanted you to be there," I continued. Sara shook her head. "And Natalie and Adam were a foster family. You were only *supposed* to stay there for a little while. Natasha's our foster daughter."

"Her grandparents are sick," Lance added. "When they get better and come home, she'll go back to them. But we're *adopting* you. Forever."

"He thought Uncle Ugly kept us forever." Surprisingly, this came from William, who had barely spoken since we rescued him from the wall.

"I know," Lance said. "But that was an awful mistake. We're not a mistake. And we're not going away. You can trust us."

But could they? After this evening, I wasn't at all sure about my ability to keep them safe.

CHAPTER 18

Dear Nora:

My husband likes to shop out on the bypass, but I prefer to shop downtown. What's your take?

Trying to Keep it Local

Dear Trying,

The marriage sounds hopeless. Get a divorce. I'm sending my attorney's name. You'll love him. His office is right downtown. In case you're determined to beat a dead horse and save the relationship, I'm including my therapist's name as well. You won't love her, but she'll get the job done. I want to hear back in a week that you've contacted one or the other. (And I'm telling you, those men who shop out on the bypass aren't worth a dime.)

Nora

"I know it's a lot to ask." Natasha stood on the kitchen table flicking a wet dishtowel at the ceiling. Bit by bit, she was divesting it of the new pudding William had shot up this morning. I caught him before he flung his own breakfast, but hadn't thought to put the larger bowl out of his reach in the fridge. He'd gotten himself a tasty refill to pitch around while I tried to wash dishes. Lost in thought about my upcoming interview, I hadn't been aware he got in the fridge, let alone climbed on the table. But when the bowl cracked against the ceiling, I sure noticed!

After the nightmarish experience of losing William, I knew I couldn't possibly interview the Wednesday after Thanksgiving. I had gone into school and twisted the chair's arm about the amount of warning I was receiving in comparison to the other candidates. Reluctantly, he moved the date to early December, but he once again put me on a Wednesday, the only day every member of the committee was present. It meant scheduling a sub to run my final lab of the term, but it meant I had enjoyed Thanksgiving in relative peace, and I had been able to react without panic about lost preparation time when Natasha asked me to come to her post-Thanksgiving poetry slam tonight.

"Honey, it's not. If you want me there, I'll make it." I was back on dish duty, and Lance was sweeping up the remains of the bowl. Even plastic snaps in multiple places if hurled with enough force.

"Thanks. It means the world." She flicked the dishtowel again, then handed it to William. "Rinse it out again, Bud," she instructed. If it wasn't safe for him to collect the sharp-edged plastic, and he was too short to wash the ceiling, Will could at least help Natasha. William *had* been required to wipe the table clear of what had landed around his seat, but he didn't seem to view this as much of a consequence. He had installed himself as the chief table wiper at our house on day one. Helping to clean the ceiling, though, was clearly a chore, and he kept drifting away from the table. He did so once more now, only to find himself redirected wordlessly by Lance. With William, nonverbal communication was sometimes best.

The only one not in the kitchen was Sara. We tried to assign her chores, as Natalie had suggested, but she found subtle ways of resisting them. She agreed readily to whatever was asked of her, but then completely failed to perform most tasks, or did them slowly enough to make the frustration of supervising her not worth the supposed lesson in responsibility. Lance and I had landed at the compromise position of picking our battles.

When the issue was scattered toys and games (as it would be in a scant few minutes, the twins having devastated all of the hard work of a day before in two hours of morning play), we worked as a family. Sara was then more apt to comply. But when each of us had a separate task to perform, we let her off the hook.

Because Natalie was also the one who taught us to let some things go. "You'll lose your minds if you don't," she had explained bluntly, after watching us argue fruitlessly with Will about taking himself to the bathroom right away in the morning instead of holding it for three hours and wetting himself again.

He complied willingly with pull-ups at bedtime, particularly as Sara, who slept tangled up with him, insisted. But during the day, he forcefully insisted, "William is a *big boy*. Day-diapers hold babies."

"I know it smells bad," Natalie had told us, "but you have a rug and upholstery cleaner, and you've *got* to pick your battles. This is a stress thing with him, and he'll get over it faster if you let him help with the clean-up and otherwise pretend it didn't happen."

Allowing Sara to skip individual chores fell into this category. "You can screw up adoptive parenting as easily as you can screw up biological parenting," was the mantra Natalie had programmed in us. "And as long as everybody is happy about the mistakes most of the time, then you're no worse off than any other mom and dad out there." At the moment, Sara was installed in the wreck of a living room, playing video games, while the rest of us cleaned up from breakfast.

"Hey, Will," she called. "I'm bored without you."

"Will's busy," Natasha said. "You could come help us."

"Boring." After a few minutes, she tried again. "Hey! I know. Let's watch Mom's movie! We haven't done that since we moved."

"What?" The skillet I had been wiping sank out of my hand and back into the suds. "Tasha . . ."

"Right," she said.

By the time we reached the living room, Sara had located the disc. "That's mine!" she said when I took it.

"Honey, we'll try to find you . . . this isn't . . ."

She sighed explosively. "I don't know what the big deal is about her being naked! I had to steal it back from Uncle Ugly twelve million thousand times before we moved." Sara's mother was not a minor, so her movies were not hidden except, as this one had been, in plain sight. *Jolly Roger: Booty Call* appeared to have more swashing and unbuckling than actual seamanship. All the women on the disc cover had hats, eye patches, and virtually no clothes. The heart on one woman's hind end suggested Natasha's mother was also in the video.

"Older one," Natasha remarked. "Do you want me to go through the rest?"

"We'll let Trudy."

Natasha returned to cleaning the ceiling. "Come on, Will. Help me out," she said.

I was about to dial the federal agent when the doorbell rang. "For heaven's sake. Hannah knows she doesn't have to stand on ceremony with us." I had been expecting my friend, but I'd hoped to get things a little cleaner before she arrived. Trudy had not been present much lately. As time passed and no threat to Will emerged, she saw less and less need to front as our hired child-minder. Also, Tasha was right. Her responsibilities in Columbus were increasing.

"Oops. I'll get it. Forgot to tell you," said Lance. "Ann called this morning. Merry resigned. The twins have a new social worker."

"Lance, you can't . . ." But he was gone, and I didn't see any way around letting the social worker see our mess in any case. It wasn't as though we could stand around on the front porch chatting him or her up, hoping to keep the door closed. Random spot-checks were part of the landscape of adopting from the foster care system. Or they were supposed to be. This was our first. "Wait . . . what about Merry?"

"Merry, Merry, quite contrary," Sara chanted.

"Hush!"

At the last second, as Lance led the woman into the room, I remembered to hide the offensive video in my waistband. I was wearing yesterday's sweatpants and a stained sanctuary shirt, and I hadn't showered since the day before yesterday. My hair wanted for cutting, and I had pulled it back into a raggedy ponytail. I was *not* ready to meet a new authority figure.

The new social worker preceded Lance from the kitchen into the living room, her crisp blazer and skirt a vast contrast to my own disheveled state. Rather than introducing herself, she stared at Natasha. "What's she doing on the table?"

"Spider detail," Tasha lied easily, hopping down and guiding William to the sink to empty the water bowl. In spite of her history of lying, Natasha rarely dropped any bald-faced untruths into conversation these days. And when she did, she often felt she had good reason. I never knew when to call her on it.

In this case, William darted from the sink to the social worker and began a chorus of "The Itsy Bitsy Spider." Pick your battles, then. "Thanks, hon," I said to Tasha.

"I'm Chandra Evans." The woman extended her hand in a four-fingered shake, forcing us to only touch fingertips rather than actually gripping.

"Noel Rue."

She and Lance began a discussion I barely heard. I was having problems with my wardrobe, as the disc slid down instead of remaining stuck to my skin. I had pulled these pants on in an exhausted stupor. I only realized there was something wadded up in the crotch when I sat down to breakfast. I hadn't had time to deal with it, and yanking out my waistband long enough to cram in the disc had shoved the bulge ever so slightly. Now, I regretted not dealing with the problem immediately. But there was little I could do. Yesterday's panties were slowly, and in accordance with the laws of gravity, sliding down my leg. The porn disc was all set to follow them.

"William!" I said suddenly, and in my brightest voice. "You haven't been potty yet this morning!" I clamped my hands against my backside to halt the disc from further descent. The underpants were a lost cause, but the disc needed to stay hidden.

"Noel, I thought we weren't . . ." Lance began.

I trammeled along as if I hadn't heard him. "Let's have a race to see who can get to the bathroom first!" I darted out of the room, not caring whether William met me or not.

To my surprise, he *did* come, barreling past me in the hall, and darting into the toilet with his shorts already halfway to his knees. He flipped up the toilet seat and let out a stream of urine so pent up I heard it hit the water from three rooms away while I rapidly changed into slacks.

Sara followed, too, begging me to return the disc, which I disappeared under my bed in the band of the sweats. Natasha saved me. "Sara! Check this out! I downloaded your princess song on my phone!" I blew her a kiss over the little girl's head.

Hannah arrived as Chandra was leaving, and they passed in the living room doorway. Though we typically used the back door for entrances and the front door only for departures, Hannah *always* came to the front. Chandra glowered at Hannah like she was a criminal we were letting into our home. "I'll be back to check on your housekeeping." The social worker gave a final look around our house as she swept out front.

"Lovely lady," Hannah muttered.

"You're not kidding. She'll be back to check on our *housekeeping*?" Yes, the living room was a mess, but it had been thoroughly cleaned only a day before, and Lance and I had kicked a path through the toys before breakfast. It wasn't like she was stepping on any of the kids' plastic bricks or trucks.

"Mmm mmm mmm." Hannah watched Chandra climb into her car and drive away. "You do know how to pick them, Noel."

"We don't get a choice."

"The Orangutan Lady was *better*." Lance shut the door behind my friend, and with her inside, he set the door alarm and fastened the latch so William would have a harder time getting out. We had learned the doors and windows were all we needed to keep armed to prevent Will from leaving without our knowledge. Although Will hadn't met a lock he couldn't pick, we still got plenty of warning to stop him when he periodically decided to explore.

"How'd you get this one, instead?" Hannah asked.

Lance and I both shrugged. "Beats me," I said. "We saw her the other day when Will vanished."

"Merry resigned," Lance explained. "Ann said something about her health."

The image of her sallow face back when we lost Will flashed into my mind. "I hope it's not serious." I felt a rush of guilt for all my nasty thoughts about the woman.

"It *sounds* serious," said Hannah. "I'll make sure I key this one's car next time she shows up in my shop looking for those neckerchiefs she keeps tucked in her front."

"You will *not!*"

"But if you do, call me up so I can see!" said Natasha, rejoining us.

"*What* was the deal with the spider?" I asked her.

"She got assigned to me when Jane was out on maternity leave. Gran and Granddad had a couple of run-ins with her. We all called her the Iron Lady. She's got a real thing about cleanliness and bugs. I figured she didn't need to know we store food on the ceiling around here. And I wanted to creep her out with the spider."

Hannah snickered. "All right," she said. "I hear there's a young lady here who wants twists."

Sara, who had seemed to be playing her game, completely oblivious to us, leapt up to stand on the couch. "Yes!"

"Did you get the supplies, Noel?"

"Everything on your list." And it had certainly cost a pretty sum. Among the many things I hadn't anticipated when adopting our children was the significant difference in their hair texture.

Natalie hadn't saved me from myself there; Hannah had. All Natalie had advised was "Their hair's dry. You wash it every day, and you'll give them a good case of dandruff. Once a week is plenty. Less maybe." I liked this solution because the twins hated showers and only enjoyed baths when nothing got dumped on them from above and they weren't required to lie back and dunk themselves. Natalie had given us scalp moisturizers and instructions on their importance, but she'd never had time to style the twins' hair herself, especially since neither of them could hold still for more than a few minutes, and both hated to have their hair pulled. I had already discovered the only way to get soap in or out of their hair was to brush it in and out again, but the process was long and tedious; they were a pair of tender-scalps.

When Hannah met them, with their unruly mops and hopeless tangles, she said, "No, honey. No. You are not *even* going to start out this way. You leave their hair wild much longer, and people will start thinking you don't love your kids. You need to cut his short if he won't let you style it, and *she* needs braids."

"Why would people think I didn't love my kids because they have curly hair?"

"White people might not notice," she said, "but the black ones sure will. Hair *matters* to us, and you need to learn how to do it up front."

But William ran screaming at the mere mention of clippers, and Sara clamped her hands over her head and put on her most stubborn expression when Hannah told her about braids. Here, I thought, was one of those situations my sister had mentioned, where I was going to have to carve my own path instead of letting someone else parent for me. Hannah, who kept her own hair braided tight against her scalp and wore extensions down her back, might know about black hair and culture, but she didn't know squat about autism.

"Fine," I told her. "You convince *them* it needs doing, and we'll get it done. But I'll tell *you* up front their uncle shaved Will nearly bald right before he gave up custody, and he left the kid's scalp all nicked up. He'd barely started letting Natalie comb it without a fight when we came along."

"Okay. Then we start with Sara."

Hannah was patient, coming over to sit on the couch and pretending to browse a hair magazine several Saturdays in a row. It showed a variety of different braids. It bothered her to know I was putting my little girl on the bus every morning with wild hair. Sara didn't say anything about the magazine, but I saw her darting glances at it from time to time while Hannah ostentatiously thumbed through it.

Then, one day, Hannah "forgot" the magazine, and Sara picked it up for herself in my friend's absence. She turned the pages thoughtfully, touching each one as if the smooth paper might hold a texture she could stroke. At bedtime, she announced without any segue, "See, here's the thing. I know what you guys are up to in there." I couldn't tell what she meant or if she was echoing. It sounded like she might have been repeating some past scolding she had received. "But I guess it's okay if you don't pull." Then, she trotted out, retrieved the magazine, and informed me, "I want this one." By a miracle, it looked like something simple, something I might be able to master without paying to have it done weekly by someone else.

"Braids, braids, braids," she chanted now.

"It's a twist," Hannah said, as Sara jumped on the couch and squealed.

"How come you know so much about hair?" the little girl asked.

"I learned on my little sister and kept up my skills on her kids."

"You know how to do it without pulling?"

"Scout's honor."

How was Sara to know Hannah and I dropped out of scouts together as kids? Still, Hannah didn't pull, and she showed me how to hold the hair in one hand and comb with the other, so I was never yanking on Sara's scalp as I detangled, a process she had hitherto resisted, and how to part and twist the hair.

The only hitch came when William plopped down beside his sister on the couch and proclaimed, "William's turn is next, and next is now."

Though I had grown accustomed to watching him out of the corner of my eye, and I had a rather close eye on him this morning after the pudding adventure, I had not noticed he was flipping through the catalog, rather than playing trucks on the floor by Sara's feet. "Those are cornrows, buddy," said Hannah. "Those are going to take longer than twists." *Longer?* We were only halfway through Sara's head, and it had already been two hours.

Lance popped in on his way out to the center. He had finally returned the rhesus enclosure to the volunteer who was normally responsible for it, but we both still liked it best if one of us could be around to make things flow during the day and be sure the locks clicked at night. Chuck might later break himself out and undo all our hard work, but it was comforting to know we'd done everything in our power to prevent him. "You need anything before I go?" he asked.

"Nope. But remember I'm doing the poetry thing with Tasha tonight, so you need to be home right after you close things down." After he had gone, I said, "There is no way I can learn to do cornrows."

"Of course you can."

"Hannah, this two-twist thing . . ."

"Isn't as simple as you thought it was going to be, right? You'll get the hang of it."

"I don't know . . ."

"Listen, Noel. When I moved out for college, I was within a deuce of never coming back. You want to know what I hated *worst* about being the only black family in town?" She didn't wait for me to answer. "It was having to go to school with *white* hair. We straightened, chemicalled, and otherwise destroyed my head so I could fit in with every other kid. I came back when I realized Ironweed U had *finally* started bringing us some real diversity, and I could be part of a real black community in the town where I grew up. Now I am not, and I mean *not*, going to sit here while my best friend adopts a couple of biracial kids and let her act like they've got white hair when they don't."

"Cornrows," said William. "Grow some cornrows!"

"Okay. Cornrows, then." *Pick your battles.*

"It's a name for a type of braid, not a food," Hannah warned.

William flapped and squealed, "Grow some eating cornrows!"

Understanding clicked into place. I placed a quick call to Lance. "Honey, pick up some frozen corn on the way home. I think we may have found another vegetable William will eat." Unless he had to have it on the cob. Then, he'd probably have to wait until next summer, when his permanent teeth filled in the gap at the front of his mouth.

"You finish up over there with her, and I'll get him started," Hannah instructed, though thanks to Sara's squirminess and my general ineptitude, she wound up doing his whole head.

Of course, Sara couldn't sit still for an instant, even when Natasha came through taunting, "I got my mother's hair; it's so much easier to style," and popped a nice safe cartoon into the DVD player.

"Yeah, but it doesn't look half so pretty," Hannah shot back. She and Tasha had developed a teasing relationship both of them seemed to enjoy. I worried one day one of them would launch a barb the other couldn't laugh off, but so far, my fears had been unfounded. "Now if you can do two things at once, Noel, keep twisting and watch what I'm doing over here. See, I part the hair and detangle it. His hair is thinner than hers, by the way."

"I noticed when I was washing it. It looks like it's thick because it's so curly."

"It means this won't take as long as doing the same thing on Sara might." She seemed unperturbed by the way Will kept rocking while she worked. "See, watch. I start at the front, and then it's nothing more than a tiny French braid." *Great. A tiny French braid. Maybe she can teach it to Margie and Margie can come down from Cleveland once a week to do her nephew's hair.*

"How often does it need fixing?"

"Depends on the kid. Usually about once a month. With

them, I'd say wait maybe three weeks, then fix a little each night."

"Could be worse."

We worked side by side, taking breaks as the children demanded it. Finally, she said, "All right, Señor Wigglebutt, you're duded out."

William hooted laughter. "Wigglebutt. Wigglegut." He cackled. *Thanks, Hannah.*

Then she turned to Sarah to help me finish the twists that should have been the easier job. Nonetheless, by the time Lance got home, and I threw my purse over my shoulder, we had two well-groomed children.

"You ready, Tasha?" I called. We had a little extra time tonight, since I wouldn't be dropping her off to ride with friends, but would be taking her myself. But I didn't want to be hunting for this place after dark, and I wanted to know what kind of place she thought she could pass off as a poetry bash to invite me so easily.

"On my way." *Make it three well-groomed children.* Natasha, who normally let her dark hair hang loose around her shoulders, had pulled it back in two braids along either side of her head that met in a glossy ponytail. "Let me borrow your phone." She rooted in my purse before I could grant or deny permission, then she took a selfie with the twins. *Ha,* she texted Hannah. *I'll show you half so pretty.*

Sara darted back to the living room and her video game as soon as she'd seen the picture. But William took Natasha's hand and led her to the door like a boy headed out on a date. "Natasha," he said, "is ready to grow duded cornrows with William."

I met Natasha's eyes over his head, and I could read her frustration. She wanted to get going. She wanted me to come. She wanted family around her. But she didn't want Will there causing disruption.

"William," I said, "We aren't growing cornrows. We're . . . reading poetry." He didn't move.

Natasha gave it a shot. "We're pretty . . . stark," she said.

William still didn't move.

"Boring," I suggested.

He crossed his arms.

"I had to get special permission from the group for Noel to come, Bud," she tried. "I didn't ask them about any little brothers."

Neither cajoling nor bribery could coax William from her side. Ultimately, it came down to a question of whether this was worth a meltdown, and we left that answer up to Natasha. Finally, she said, "Okay, but don't say I didn't warn you." I grabbed the headphones he often wore to cancel out noise and a handheld electronic game before we left.

Hannah texted back. I didn't bother to read it, but passed over the phone to my foster daughter as we got in the minivan. (We *had* hoped to take the convertible.) Natasha snorted. "She says, 'Pretty is as pretty does.' "

Leave it to Hannah to get the last word in with a teen.

CHAPTER 19

Dear Nora:
  My life is a torn page.

                                                    Ripped

Dear Ripped:
  I suggest tape.

                                                      Nora

As I had suspected she would, Natasha directed me to a place on campus. Not a bar, where I would have called foul on the whole operation, but to the large central building housing the college bookstore, a food court, and half a dozen conference-style classrooms. I was a little worried when she led us around back, because there was a student pub in the basement, Ironweed having dodged the "dry campus" trend by banning all fraternities and sororities instead. But our destination turned out to be the closed bookstore.

When Natasha knocked on the employee entrance, the door opened immediately, and we joined a group of teens at a series of beanbags and folding chairs arranged around a microphone. It was Tasha's therapy group, convened in a location other than the rather sterile psych building. It made sense now. This was the closest thing the group could get to a social setting without going off campus, and yes, these were kids who might *well* do poetry.

Technically, this psychologist was a graduate student who worked under the supervision of a licensed professional, and it gave Tasha access to some of the newest therapy techniques available. It helped dramatically with her anxiety. Plus, it was how she had connected so quickly with others her age after June left her in such a bad position.

The therapist welcomed the visitors (William and me) and explained the rules, largely for our benefit. These were high school students using poetry and storytelling to exorcise their strongest demons. The emphasis was *not* on factuality, but on emotional depth. Everything shared was private and not to be repeated elsewhere. I wondered how it would play out with William's echolalia but nodded my agreement so they could begin.

The students went around the circle sharing painful stories of abuse and mental illness. There was poetry of the teen angst variety, only these teens had more cause for anguish than some of their other age peers. The poems followed a similar pattern, with a lot of rhyming and verb–noun juxtaposition. I've never been much for poems and stories, so I concentrated on the words' importance to avoid seeming bored.

When Natasha's turn came, she dug a piece of paper out of my purse. Most of the poems had been presented from memory, but a few of the teens, especially the storytellers, read from pre-prepared manuscripts. Natasha held her paper up in front of her face and picked up the microphone. Generally, this had been an unnecessary addition, as the circle was small, and most of us could hear the central speaker well.

But Tasha was soft-spoken, unusually so as she began to read.

"Soulful Eyes"

Soulful eyes
Let them say what
they will they know not your heart

Strong arms are a safe haven
from an emotionally troubling world
Your soulful eyes breathe life into me
when I look at you, I see a savior
one that thought more of me than I did of myself
Capture this breath with the wind
and toss it back to me with your carefree smile
Dance with a devil-may-care freedom
It matters not that they do not understand
The world fades into melodic blur when you take my hand
Walk with me down this path
My "person of the forest"

By the time she sat back down beside me on the uncomfortable beanbag chair where William roosted in my lap, her whole body was shaking.

"Are you all right, Natasha?" the psychologist asked.

Some of the students had explained their stories afterward and gotten ideas and coping strategies from the group and its leader. "Yeah. I'm okay. I'll be fine. I don't want to talk about it, though." Tasha leaned into me, and for the first time ever let me wrap an arm around her and rub warmth back into her shoulders. "Thanks for being my friend," she all but whispered.

"Thank you for being mine."

William wiggled over into her lap. He had been listening raptly the whole time, rocking gently. Unlike me, he hadn't needed to force interest in everyone else's words. I doubted he could have done so. At the end of the session, the psychologist joined us. "Are you sure you're okay?" he asked Natasha.

"I'm good. I'm . . ."

The microphone gave a squelch of feedback and the stand crashed. "It is William's turn next," a small voice informed us, "and next is now."

"I'm so sorry." In the seconds we had been speaking, William had scurried into the center of the ring and captured the mic, which the last speaker had left turned on.

The exiting people stopped and turned around to look at the tiny six-year-old and his cornrows. I was suddenly grateful for Hannah's braids. Even as oblivious as I could be about appearances, I knew I would have felt even more self-conscious if he had looked in the least bedraggled under so many gazes.

"It's fine," the psychologist assured me. "He isn't hurting a thing." To William, he offered the same introduction he had given to the other members of the group. "What would you like to share?"

William tapped the microphone against his chin and rocked on the balls of his feet. Finally, he looked straight at me, through me really, and said, "William is home-hungry." Then he dropped the mic, flopped on his stomach, and bawled.

December came, and with it, the twins' birthday. Two days before my interview, Sara bounded around the kitchen singing, "It's my birthday, it's my birthday, it's my bi-irthday. Gonna get lots of presents to open for me-e-e." She tapped her spoon on her cereal bowl when she sat at all, and Natasha nearly tripped over her twice trying to get her own breakfast together.

William joined us in the kitchen late, since his morning ritual always included a rinse in the tub. "It's my birthday, too, Dummyhead," he greeted his sister.

His outburst stopped everyone on the spot.

He didn't ride the bus like Sara did. I drove him. The first school day he was my son, I picked him up at carpool. His teacher, Mr. Bender, met me at the curb. I'd been afraid of trouble, having already spoken with Sara's principal on the phone over her behaviors. But Mr. Bender had been all smiles and concern. "We loved the Forresters," he told me. "But we're so excited for William. He's talked about your husband nonstop today." *Really? Sara's my talker.* "But we're going to need your help with a couple of things." *Here it comes, then.* "By the end of last year, he could use 'I,' 'me,' and 'my,' and I noticed he's reverted to referring to himself in the third person. He also needs help remembering to use the number fifteen on his way to counting to a hundred."

"Five-teen!" William announced from the back.

"Fiff-teen" his teacher and I corrected together.

"*Five*-teen," William insisted. And I could tell from the following laughter that we would be fighting the battle of five-teen for some time to come.

"Anyway, we'll get all that sorted out. We've already seen improvement since the beginning of the term. Our kids are *nothing* if not inconsistent. I wanted to introduce myself and say hello. You have a wonderful little boy."

It was the most stunning moment of parenting, to hear William referred to as mine, to find out he had spoken positively of Lance, to hear him argue with us about the number five-teen. And now, not four months later here he was using those personal pronouns precisely as Mr. Bender had assured me he could do, and in a perfectly grammatical sentence no less.

"Good job, William!" I praised him.

"But your sister is *not* a dummyhead," Lance added, joining us after draining William's tub.

Sara looked hard at her brother, then resumed her tapping song. "It's *our* birthday, it's *our* birthday, it's our biiirth-birth-day. Gonna get lots of presents to open for me-e-e."

A step in the right direction.

We had worked it out; Lance would take after-lunch cupcakes to William's school; I would do the same for Sara's. Since he got the more desirable location, I got the more desirable car. Also, I had missed my convertible ride with Natasha on Saturday when William had once again insisted upon attending her poetry slam. The group had adopted him as a sort of mascot, and he got the benefit of a couple of hours spent in the company of those who seemed to understand him whether he used his words correctly or not.

"He's a poet," one girl assured me. "Listen to his metaphors, and he makes perfect sense." Great for those who grasped metaphors intrinsically, I supposed. Not so great for Lance and me.

I was much too smart to bake thirty-five cupcakes for Sara's class and another fifteen for William's myself, but Mama was outdoing herself in her efforts to make up for what amounted to her initial shock. She implemented every idea her readers sent in and a few she came up with herself. We had endured all-girl shopping-lunches, received randomly delivered packages, and been bombarded with a barrage of "special-day" cards. The birthday itself had brought bicycles from her and Daddy.

Thus, the box riding in its own seatbelt on the way to school contained nothing from the grocery store or even the local bakery, but forty of Mama's pink-and-white iced chocolate and yellow dream cupcakes. The ones Lance was porting to William's school were sports themed.

After I signed in at the office, I had a few minutes to wait with Sara's teacher before the class came back from lunch. Between the few terse e-mails and several phone calls we had received from her and the principal, I was braced for an unpleasant meeting. "You're Sara's new foster mother," she said.

"We're adopting her, you know."

The teacher shrugged. "I'll tell you something, if you haven't already figured it out for yourself. That girl is lazy."

My gut clenched. I wanted to throw a cupcake at the woman. I pictured Sara at the kitchen table the previous Thursday begging, "But I don't *want* to go to school. The kids are all mean, and Mrs. Grim never lets me have recess."

"Honey, we'll talk about this later," I had told her, herding her out to the bus. "Everybody has to deal with frustrations at work and school." But the conversation had never come. I regretted that now.

"I've *seen* children with autism. I know what it looks like, and she's not it. I taught her last year. If she hadn't come to me with the educational diagnosis, I can assure you she would never have been assigned it here. I—"

"You will need to discuss this with my husband and me at Sara's next IEP meeting. Today, I'm here to *celebrate* her birthday." Natalie had cued me into the hazards of the Individual Education Planning meetings controlling what accommodations the school would have to make for our daughter. Sara's IEP bought her extra time on tests, a quiet testing location, away from the classroom, and visits with the district occupational and speech therapists, but little else. As Natalie had ruefully told me, "She's too high functioning. The system won't help her like Will."

In fact, William's placement at the charter school was a result of his IEP as much as any lottery. He had good grades, but the district had few mainstream classes able to meet his unique needs, and fewer still teachers willing to look deep enough to help him achieve his potential. Perhaps because it was smaller, the charter school was completely onboard with the process of working with him so he could perform to his best.

In contrast, Natalie had warned me, I would have to fight for every little thing Sara required. She had been sorry to see Sara assigned to this teacher a second year in a row, thinking they had left the woman behind in kindergarten. The teacher's real name was Mrs. Grisby, but she had always been Mrs. Grim in our house. Mrs. Grim had been promoted to first grade along with her students, and she had nearly exactly the same class all over again. Natalie's efforts to have Sara's class changed had fallen flat with the principal.

The children returned from lunch before Mrs. Grim could launch another attack. We had exactly ten minutes for this ritual, and I suspected she would hold us rigidly to her schedule. "Everyone sing happy birthday to Sara," she commanded in a weary voice as they sat down.

The chorus greeting her instruction was halfhearted at best. Sara didn't notice. She stood beside me beaming, humming her own birthday present song from the morning while the other kids almost chanted through the more traditional version. "Now," the teacher went on. "Who wants to help her pass out cupcakes?"

Nobody raised a hand.

The knot in my stomach tightened and twisted. In my day, birthday cupcakes were a *big deal*. Surely school hadn't changed so much that nobody cared about an influx of lesson-delaying sugar. "Never mind," I chirped. "More fun for Sara and me, right honey?" But Sara's bright smile faltered.

"I'll help," one little girl said. I couldn't tell if the hesitation I heard in her voice was shyness or something else.

"Thanks!" I called out before she could add "I guess" or anything at all to suggest unwillingness. It was enough. Sara's lips turned up again, and she began her deliveries.

I don't know how the trouble started. I asked those who wanted yellow cake to raise their hands and sent Sara and her half-willing assistant to deliver them. Then we moved on to chocolate. The treats had nearly all been distributed when a scuffle erupted at the back of the classroom. I turned in time to see Sara smash a chocolate and a yellow cupcake together, then cream them down the front of a boy's shirt. "I guess that makes you a floop-de-dooping dummyhead," she shouted.

"That," Mrs. Grim's bellow was almost triumphant, "is exactly what I'm talking about. That kind of attitude is *exactly* what holds you back, young lady. As soon as Mrs. Robinson can get down here from the library, I'm taking you to the principal's office."

"But he said I . . ." Sara opened and closed her pink-and-white frosted fingers.

"I don't care what he said. You do *not* swear in my classroom, and you are not entitled to ruin other people's clothes."

"She didn't swear," I protested. "She said . . . dummyhead and floop-de-doop. The one is an insult, and the other I'm pretty sure she made up."

"You should not encourage her behavior."

"You know what? You're right. I shouldn't. Sara, come with me. We're leaving before someone gets hurt."

"But he . . ." The smile was gone completely, and Sara was smearing the icing on her face as she swiped away tears.

I tucked the cupcake box under one arm and swept Sara along with the other. Damned if I was giving that woman Mama's chocolate dreams. "Mrs. Sara's Mom!" Sara's assistant was suddenly all afire. She grabbed my elbow on the way past, and I nearly dropped the box. "He said she has *lice* and she smells like poop all the time. But he's the one who had . . ."

"Right. Got it, sweetie. Thanks, gotta go." I hauled Sara out the door behind me.

She wailed, "We have to sign out!" She had gotten icing all over both of our shirts by then, and the chocolate dreams were significantly squashed under my arm. I didn't get her coat, and I skipped signing out on my way past the office. By a tiny margin, I resisted the urge to flip the principal a bird. I wasn't sure I could un-ruin my daughter's day, and I wasn't even sure how to try.

But at the car, she gasped, the tears replaced by wide-eyed amazement. "I get to ride in the *convertible*?"

Oops. Natasha was supposed to be the only kid who got in

there. Aside from the twins being roving disasters, it was a two-seater. No back bench for small boosters. And speaking of boosters, I didn't even have hers packed along. *Double oops. So much for clean seats and child safety.*

"Absolutely. You ought to get *something* out of today."

"But I thought I was in trouble."

Where to draw the line? "Sweetie, we'll deal with it later. If I argue well, they'll give you an out-of-school suspension and buy me time to think. You shouldn't have mushed the cupcakes all over your classmate's shirt, and it probably would be good to ask an adult for help next time something like that crops up. But it's your birthday, I'm not angry, and . . ." I cut myself short.

"Mrs. Grim is another *dummyhead.*" Sara finished for me.

I had been thinking "big meanie," but it amounted to the same thing. I scraped a portion of the icing off both of us so only a minimum got on the seats. "I've still got to teach today, but I don't have to be there for another forty-five minutes. What do you say we get some ice cream? And I want you to tell me again how mean your classmates are. This time, I promise to listen."

CHAPTER 20

Dear Nora:

I put groomer's dye in the spot where the cat poops. Of course, my dog got blue feet, too, walking through it, but I caught the cat in the act! And I filmed it! My neighbor was not home to confront. However, the next day, my beloved dog went missing for several hours. When it mysteriously returned to my yard, it had been groomed with a rival team's football colors! Please Nora, I need some real advice here!

Pooped

Dear Pooped,

Have you considered a different hobby? You seem to have exhausted all the possibilities this one has to offer.

Nora

Monday never improved above its cupcake-smashing baseline. Travis arrived at the ice cream shop right after Sara and I sat down. He dropped a newspaper over my shoulder with a scribbled note attached to it. The note said, "Chair, six o'clock." The newspaper said, "Cancer claims social worker."

It took me a moment too long to realize the note and paper were unconnected, and I wasted several seconds trying to figure out how I was supposed to meet the chair at six, why I should desire to do so, and how it related to my sudden need to flip over every copy of the *Free Press* floating around the shop.

Thus, in spite of Travis's warning, Sara still surprised me with her cry of, "Hey, there's your boss-guy. Hi boss-guy!" Sara and William had met Dr. Prescott exactly once, and it had gone badly, as he continuously tried to engage William in conversations and William only stared harder at the ground. *Chair at six.* He meant I should look straight ahead to see Dr. Prescott at the six o'clock position on my personal clock.

"Hello Noel, and . . . Mara, is it?"

"No, I'm Sara. Mara is somebody else, and I've never actually met her before, or come to think of it even heard of her, so I don't think we probably even look alike."

"Mmm."

I set down the paper long enough to crumple Travis's note, and Sara saw the article. "Oh my *gosh!*" she said. "Miss Merry Quite Contrary is *dead.*"

Thereafter, I juggled the conversation between her and the chair, answering questions that weren't questions from both of them at once.

"We're certainly looking forward to your presentation."

No you aren't. "Thank you, sir."

"*Wow,* it says she had terminal cancer. I didn't know there was a special cancer you catch in airplane terminals."

"In this case, terminal means final, fatal, Sara." *No wonder she was in such a hurry. Did she rush to place all her kids, or only these two? I didn't wish this when I wished she'd go away. And I certainly didn't wish for the Iron Lady in her place!*

"A pipe broke in the bathroom above the room we wanted to use. The ceiling's still dripping. We've had to relocate you to the conference room." *And when were you planning to let me know this?*

"Then I guess I'm glad we ran into you. Thanks for telling me." *Now go away.*

"*That's* how we wound up with the Iron Lady! It makes *so*

much more sense now. I thought Merry had ditched us, too, but it turns out, she ditched *everybody.*"

"Cancer's not the same thing as ditching." *And will you hurry up and finish your cone.* As if on cue, Sara jumped up and pitched forward. The cone flew over to splat at the chair's feet, coming within centimeters of decorating his wingtips.

"I'm *sorry!*" she wailed.

"You know what? Let's get half a gallon and take it home so William can have some too after school."

"And can we get a box of waffle cones? I love waffle cones."

"Yes, absolutely. Waffle cones." The shop sold them six to an overpriced plastic box. I cut in line ahead of the chair to get Sara out before the inevitable tears began. We were due for a meltdown after this morning, and I didn't want it to happen right there.

In fact, she twitched but held steady until we got home after my class, even when we had to store the ice cream in the smelly department freezer. Then she finally went off because we hadn't thrown a formal birthday party. She forgot we had discussed this and agreed a family trip in lieu of a party might be more fun anyway. She hadn't gotten to enjoy her cupcakes with her classmates, and I couldn't give her the alternative she wanted.

I had barely convinced her to settle down in front of a video game when the phone rang. I spent much of what remained of the afternoon negotiating with her principal. He wanted to shame Sara with an in-school suspension, masking his desire with concern, saying she didn't want a *real* suspension on her permanent record. I said, "Yes, she does," at least forty-five times, and he gave up.

"Fine. It's five days. She can come back next Tuesday; you have to sign off on it; she has to do all her work, but she isn't eligible for any credit." I hung up before he could make the list longer. I suspected the sentence length was connected as much to my bad attitude as Sara's. I had bought my time to think, but I had no idea what it would do for me. I couldn't see why a child this young wouldn't be let off the hook with detention or some other, less intense punishment. He had labelled her behavior "bullying" to justify Mrs. Grim's overreaction, but I had expected no less.

I had been prepared for him to try the in-school suspension tactic, which Natalie said had been used twice the previous year. Those were worse for Sara than even sitting in an overloud class, because everything she did was observed and criticized, and even her usual restless wiggling got her in disproportionate trouble. The kid needed a break. I hoped I hadn't purchased her one in exchange for an entire school year. I could absolutely imagine Mrs. Grim flunking Sara out of first grade over this.

The next morning was one of our days to open the center, a duty we had been juggling with Jen, as our actual employees were usually responsible for closing. Lance sometimes did it alone, but Natasha liked to help, and the only way we could manage to give her the chance before school (without inciting a twin riot) was to travel as a family and let the kids change clothes after they carried around food.

Natasha took the duty seriously, and her favorite part was after we had finished with the rest of the primates and we could drive over to the other end of the property and give her a few minutes with Chuck. Ace saw to most of the orangutan's needs, especially now that he'd practically moved in to help identify and quell the roving problem. But the big ape shared a special bond with Natasha. He offered her a safe outlet for her pent-up emotions. Days when she saw Chuck in the morning, Natasha had fewer anxieties.

But when we arrived at the center, we were greeted by a full-blown crisis. We knew something was up from the din being raised out back.

"Surely to *God* those macaques aren't out again." Lance hurried ahead while I coaxed the twins out of the van. They disliked the frosty ground, and though William refused to put his coat on, he stood shivering while we opened the barn's big double doors. Inside, I paused to let my eyes adjust. Something looked wrong, but I couldn't pinpoint what, and the deputies hadn't flagged us down from their cruiser, as they tended to do if there was anything to report. I let William bring up the buzz of overhead lights while Lance jogged to the stubborn back door. He never remembers to handle it gently, and he curses it regularly. I was surprised to see it swing open at once. His "Oh shit," followed by cacophonous chatter could only mean one thing.

"But how did Chuck get out?" I demanded before the host of rhesus macaques swarmed in, hunting for breakfast and fun. This was a huge invasion. There were too many monkeys. This wasn't one enclosure's worth. This was *all* of them.

"*Monkeys!*" Sara and William shrieked in unison. They leapt around as the animals poured in the door. Neither child understood the "look but don't touch" injunction all the animals carried, and they wanted to stroke, hold, and otherwise cuddle the inhabitants.

It didn't seem to bother William that these were his least favorite variety. He didn't melt down as he had the first day we brought him to the center. That day, he had been happy until he saw the rhesus macaques. Then, he dashed back inside and sat in the middle of the barn, rocking, muttering, "No cages, no cages, no cages" to himself. He clearly didn't buy my distinction between a cage and an enclosure, and he still watched those particular enclosures with suspicion at feeding time or whenever else I approached them. Now, he hollered, "Free, free, get *freed*," as the monkeys scattered through the door and up into the rafters, leaving a trail of little red footprints in their wake.

"Lance, what are we painting? Who left a can of open . . ."

"Shit," Lance said again. "Shit, shit, shit, shit, shit. Noel, get the kids in the office and lock the door. Then stay put."

"What's with the . . ." I pointed to the smeared path.

"Don't ask. Don't ask. Do *not* ask. Get the kids in the office and *don't leave*." He practically shouted the last, which was completely out of character for him.

"This is going to be such a pain," I grumbled. "We're out of candy!"

"Forget the candy. Go!"

Natasha was as rattled as the twins were enchanted. "What's going on?" she demanded, her voice unreasonably terror-stricken.

"It's going to be fine, Tasha," Lance said, physically herding us all along. Then he dashed out into the barn, and slammed both our front double doors and the back door the monkeys had so lately rushed.

Back in the office with us, he placed a call. "Drew," he said. "Listen carefully, because I'm talking above my kids' heads. Tasha, be cool."

But Natasha was rooting through my desk for one of her inhalers. We had learned early on to keep them handy for the times when panic stole her breath. I found it, and she took two big puffs. She was pale and shaking, and she sat on the floor. The twins clambered over the desk chasing the sole monkey who had followed us into the office.

"Kids, quit it. That's a wild animal, not a pet, it's . . . Lord, Lance, *what* did we paint? It's getting *everywhere*." The monkey scrambled over piles of paper, scraped its claws against the window to the barn, climbed on William's back, and skittered under the desk, leaving a trail of red behind it. Sara and Will shrieked and gave chase, scattering even more paper than their primate pal.

Natasha blocked them at the desk, separating them from the monkey with one leg. "Quit it. It's not a pet. It's going to bite you."

"Who would leave a can of paint . . ."

"Noel, that's not *paint*," Natasha snapped. "We aren't *painting* anything."

"But . . . I . . ." I dropped beside her on the ground. "Are you sure? What else could it possibly be?"

"Didn't you get a look through the door?"

"All I saw was monkeys." *And my kids trying to catch them.*

"Noel, Chuck . . . he . . ."

"Hang on, Drew," said Lance. "Not Chuck, okay, Tasha. Not Chuck. I had a clear view. Absolutely. Not. Chuck."

"You swear?"

"Yes. Please. Be tough."

Frankly, I still feared hysterics, but she sat up straighter. "Yeah. Okay. Not Chuck."

"You listening, Drew? These kids are too smart. They'll pick up if I have to repeat myself. There is an . . . overtly deceased individual at the primate center . . . I can tell because the individual in question has been relieved of a scalp carrying appendage."

"No." *Not paint. Not paint.* The red footprints up William's back caught my eye. *Not paint.* Belatedly, I smelled iron. Suddenly, I thought Natasha had been highly rational to panic. I looked to her for confirmation, and she sliced a finger across her throat. *There wasn't anybody at the gate when we pulled in.* "The deputies . . ."

Lance nodded his understanding. "You need to check in with the deputies who were doing security here overnight. We didn't see them when we pulled in. We're good. We're locked in the barn office with a monkey and the kids."

Then the sanctuary exploded into life of all the wrong sort. I wound up being grateful for our blood-spattered little primates because the twins saw *none* of it. They spent an hour gazing at, luring, and ultimately catching the monkey in the office before Drew sent us back to police headquarters in a squad car.

I got in back, and as Will climbed in beside me, a brown face popped out of his shirt. "The monkey can't come with us," I said.

"Ma'am, we need to leave."

"We need to take that animal back inside before it bites."

The deputy was as impatient and firm as William was stubborn and fretful. In the end, the cop allowed someone to bring a carrier out of the barn, but I couldn't get the little animal away from William and out of the vehicle.

"No cages, no cages," Will protested.

"Could he ride in the carrier with you, instead of staying here?" the deputy asked.

I started to say no, but Will's face lit up. *"Yes!"* We rode downtown, monkey and all. It was easier to clamp the carrier into William's arms than cope with the meltdown setting up to happen if we took it away altogether. And given the choices between "no cages" and leaving the animal behind, Will opted for the cage.

At the station, I asked the deputy assigned to question me something I should have known in the first place. "Deputy Greene wasn't on duty last night, was he?" My questioner's blank mask evaporated for a moment into a fearful glower. I had my answer. "But he's . . ." When Art was killed, one of the few moments of levity had come courtesy of Deputy Greene, when our spider monkeys stole first his service revolver, then his hat. I could still hear the echoes of Drew cursing him for being a rookie. ". . . so young."

The phone on the deputy's desk rang. After a curt, "Yes sir," he passed it to me.

"Noel!" Drew didn't mask his fury. "Those spider monkeys have two objects I need back *right now*, there's two of the rhesus things hanging on the cage with them, and if they get that ring . . ."

"Ring?"

"Never mind. It doesn't matter what it is. You are *not* coming in here. What do I need to do?"

"We're out of candy and raisins both."

"What?"

"Best bribes in an emergency. We've got crickets in our refrigerator . . . the fridge! The fridge! Look in the fridge, Drew. That's what was wrong. There was a food prep table pushed in front of the refrigerator."

"What are you talking about?"

"I never figured out the first thing I saw wrong this morning. Our walk-in fridge was completely blocked shut with one of our big silver food prep tables. You have to—"

"Right! Chester, help me out here. They may have been locked in the fridge. Drew didn't bother to break the connection when he dropped his phone, so we heard the grunting and dragging, as the table gave way to brute force. "Careful now," said Drew . . . "no, be careful opening . . . Never mind now. Get me those EMTs. Get those off. Carefully! Trussed up like a . . . Noel?" He came back on the line. "You still there?"

"Are they okay?"

"I think so. Can't say for sure. We'll know better when the EMTs check him out."

Across the desk from me, the young man in brown, who was surely no older than Deputy Greene himself, whooped and jumped up. "Mom!" he shouted. "Mom, Aunt Penny, Ms. Needham, Anna, they found him alive."

As news filtered through the department, shouting and cheering made conversation with Drew increasingly difficult. But I finally walked him through tricking the spiders out of their purloined goods. One object was outside the cage and easily retrieved. The other was a ring. It had been pulled inside the cage, making it harder to get back. Eventually, Drew sacrificed an entire container of hibernating crickets in exchange.

When I finally hung up, the beaming young deputy had returned from his short tour around the building. "Eugene's my first cousin. I'm the one that convinced him to do this side job in the first place."

I guessed, correctly, this young man wouldn't be particularly thorough in questioning any of us now that his cousin was safe. I hadn't even considered the family connections in the department. Aside from the fact that he considered us Deputy Greene's saviors, it was nearly impossible for him to hold a conversation with the twins. Tasha and Lance, who had both seen more, were being interviewed by others, but these two and their primate buddy had been left with me. The macaque was a juvenile, and it had only come to us recently. It still hadn't quite learned how to be a monkey, so it stayed perched on William's shoulder when he let it out of the carrier over my opposition.

I could have put it back. In fact, I *should* have put it back. My position on monkeys and apes has always been they aren't people and they aren't pets. They don't belong in diapers, and they shouldn't wear leashes. It isn't cute when they sit on human owners.

Yet here sat William, my son, holding a sanctuary macaque like a pet. I couldn't let this persist. But I also couldn't do anything about it right now. He could not melt. He might have valuable information we wouldn't get out of him if he was stressed, and the monkey was clearly soothing him. I was going to have to flex.

Sara's answers were choppy and long, half-sentences punctuated with commentary about the macaque. Sometimes, she started sentences mid-thought without any context, as if we all had been chatting about a topic for ages. Other times, she gave entirely too much information, most of it irrelevant. She answered the question, "What did you see?" with, "I saw tons. I don't like Mrs. Grim anyway, and I don't want to go back to school ever again."

When I had explained this reply and its reference to the day before, the officer tried, "What did you see this morning?" and received a complete rundown from waking through our arrival at the station. "I saw a dead guy with no head out the back door, and Mr. Lance, he's the guy who isn't my dad quite, because see, I'm in foster care, only he's adopting me, he pushed us all into the office, and I nearly tripped on my laces. Did you know I can't tie my shoes yet?"

As she rattled on, the officer gazed at me for support. I had to wait for her to wind down before I could get a word in edgewise. "Sara, the only part the deputy wants to know about is when we were in the barn this morning. You have good eyes. Tell us everything in order."

"I think I need some paper." The deputy passed a sheet and his pen across. Sara wrote, in an unsteady scrawl, *1th, 2th, 3th, 4th, 5th*. "There," she explained. "I forget those all the time." Then she sat back and looked at the monkey on her brother's shoulder.

"Sara?" I glanced to the deputy for permission. I didn't want to take over his job. He nodded. "Good work telling us the order. But now we need to know what you actually saw at the sanctuary. What did you see first?"

She contemplated. "Firth," she corrected my pronunciation to match her spelling, "I saw William sneeze. The barn is too dusty. You need to clean it up better."

"Okay. What was second?"

"Seconth," Clearly, it was important for us to get these words *right,* and *her* pronunciation was the right one. "I saw Mr. Lance rattle the back door open. It was not locked."

The deputy jerked to attention. "Are you sure the door wasn't locked?" He picked up another pen and jotted in his notebook.

Sara closed her eyes. "Yes. Because Miss Noel had the keys."

"So I do." I patted my pocket, surprised by the realization. "So I do."

"Open door." William's eyes were closed, and his knees were tucked under his chin.

"What?" *Are you echoing, Will, or talking?*

William's voice went tight and robotic as he struggled to speak our language. "It was not locked. It was open," he finally spat out. "Open this much." He opened his eyes and held his hands an inch apart from each other. My guilt about the monkey lessened significantly. *Three sentences in a row.* That primate was in for some serious enrichment activities if we could ever get it back in its enclosure.

Thirth, fourth, and fifth were irrelevant observations, and William's further contributions were so inscrutable neither the deputy nor I could make sense of them. "Brown smells are happy" was easy enough. He had buried his face in the monkey's side, and the monkey was brown. But "Circle dots are bad cars" still made no sense at all. It was something he repeated often under stress, especially around police cars.

It was noon before we were allowed to go feed our primates, and the uproar greeting us proved they felt the neglect. Deputies still scuttled from place to place in the barn dodging the falling scat balls and monkey spit, shouting to each other over the din. I saw at least two hats floating around in the rafters, and I doubted they would be returned in one piece. Trudy and Darnell had arrived long ago, doubtless invited in by Drew, who knew their roles.

I settled the kids and the monkey into the office. "Everyone watch the door. Don't let William get out. William, you have twenty minutes until you have to put the monkey back in its enclosure." *This is* not *the most unethical thing I've ever done in my career. That particular monkey is not, because I say so, going to bite. Nor is it in any way being violated in its temporary therapeutic role. It's going to be fine.* So why was I close to hyperventilating? "Do you hear me? You have twenty minutes until you have to give up the monkey." *Did that sentence actually come out of my mouth?*

"William hears you," he all but purred. Somewhere in the back of my mind, I registered his need for a more appropriate therapy animal. If a monkey could reduce his anxiety, I wagered a dog could do the same.

"Tasha, if you want to help with breakfast, we've been cleared to feed the primates, and we could use your hands."

"What about . . . ?" She tapped her own wrist as if tapping a watch, but her look to William indicated she was asking about his tracking device and whether I didn't think he would wander away.

"Trudy's here. That makes four of us watching him. One of us will always be in the barn, and if we check the office each time we go out, and that door doesn't open in between, we'll know he's safe." *I hope.*

"I want to help." Sara's nose was doing its rabbit twitch, and I knew she was on high alert.

"Honey, it's cold out there. You and William need to stay . . ."

"If you're worried about me getting upset, you can quit. I already saw the headless guy."

Yes. You told us. Did everybody but me notice that? Trudy and Darnell, now fully presenting themselves in their guises of sanctuary volunteers, had been joined by Jen, one of Art's last and best recruits. All of us had a police escort to every enclosure. I didn't have time to stand around arguing with Sara and dealing with the meltdown sure to ensue. "Fine. You can help me with the spiders."

"Spider monkeys, spider monkeys, I'm going to feed the spider monkeys!"

Someone had been decapitated, but all Sara cared about was feeding the spiders. "Come on, then." I waved her out. William was in his own little world, rocking and cooing at the monkey he had captured.

Trudy, falling into her nanny disguise, asked if we needed her to sit with William.

"No, I need you feeding with us. We've got to get these macaques put away, and we aren't going to have time to do multiple head counts before we get turned out." I turned to one of the deputies Drew had assigned to stay with us. "I'm starting in the middle, with the spiders. You carry this and go with Natasha and Trudy to start in the colobus area. Jen, I know you're normally over on the other side, but none of those volunteers are here. Start with those poor chimps, and everybody work inwards toward Sara and me. We'll round up the rhesus macaques last of all." The man took the bucket and bobbed thanks that he could escape the barn and its rhesus-filled rafters. Lance stayed indoors, chopping fruit and monitoring William.

Drew himself came along with Sara and me, carefully walking so her view of the sheet-covered body was obscured. But his actions were needless. Sara's eyes were all for the monkeys.

"What's that?" she asked at the enclosure.

Sara's, what's-that's were legendary. She asked it about foods, about flickering light bulbs, about people's clothing, and about stormy weather. Her questions had become the background music of my days, and I had learned to give perfunctory answers. "It's the enclosure."

"No. *That.*"

"It's . . ." I glanced in the direction of her pointing finger. "What *is* that?" And hadn't Natalie warned me to pay attention for the important questions? Two of the spiders were engaged in a fierce battle over something glinting silver in the early-morning sunlight filtering through the trees.

"Damn, I thought I took everything they had."

Involuntarily, I looked back to the headless man's body, mentally measuring the distance between it and this enclosure. "Impossible. Even *their* tails couldn't reach so far."

"No," said Drew, "but what if someone was standing near it . . . near him . . . say about there?" He pointed to an obvious pile of vomit. "What if our killer is kind of green? What if he's never done this before? He staggers away and throws up over there and passes by the spiders on the way?"

"And then leaves the mess in the grass for the police to find it and get his DNA?"

Drew rolled his eyes. "Don't believe everything you see on television, Noel. It will be weeks before we can get it analyzed, and even then, the possibility of our using it to get an ID on the perpetrator is slim. In court, we might be able to use it as evidence, *after* we nab the guy. We need to get that thing back from those monkeys much more." A third little spider had entered the fray, and they were all squawking madly at one another while each tugged on the prize, a chain of some sort. "Do you want me to throw my hat around?" When the spider monkeys had stolen Deputy Greene's hat back in June, and Lance had needed time to download files behind Drew's back up in the barn, Trudy and I had made a great show of tricking the hat out of the monkeys by borrowing another, Drew's, and playing disc golf with it.

"Uh, no. I think . . . in this case we can probably still bribe them with breakfast." Indeed, a few choice bites offered up by Sara soon diverted the primates' attention enough for me to snag the chain by sticking a broom handle through it and pulling.

"Careful. Try not to touch it, Noel." It was a heart-shaped locket, and either the spiders had opened it or it was perpetually open. I slid it down the broom handle and extended it to Drew, who took it with a small stick, then held it up where we could see it. The front of the locket was engraved *In memoriam* in narrow script.

"She's the same woman," said Drew, "as the one in the picture Hugh supposedly sent his wife. Natasha's mother." This image was different, a simple head shot, but the woman's face was unmistakable.

"Hey, that's mine!" Natasha joined us and peered at the slowly rotating heart.

"There goes *my* theory." Drew pointed the stick for Natasha to take the necklace.

She stepped back and held up her hands. "No, you don't get it. Granddad gave it to me at her funeral, and Terry took it away three hours later for himself. It's mine, but I never got to own it. I never got most of my stuff back from him before he died."

"Who would have it?" Trudy looked to Natasha.

Tash considered the question for some time. "Terry's brother, Charles Dalton, is the only one I can think of who would have had an interest," she finally said. "All the guys . . . um . . . shared the girls. Mom was one of their favorites. Noel, he was furious when Terry died. What if he blames me? What if he's coming after me?" She grabbed my arm. "Don't make me go to school! I'm not safe there."

My answer was automatic. It came from a place beyond thought, where protection of one's children superseded all other concerns. "Honey, nobody's going to school today." I thought she might have the right of things.

William trundled out of the barn holding Lance's hand, the monkey once more perched on his shoulder. They went to a rhesus enclosure, and Lance removed the new padlock, one of the ones we had purchased on our way back from the police department. Rick would be coming out later to make formal repairs.

Chuck was absolutely not responsible for this most recent exodus of monkeys. If he had opened the cages, he wouldn't have done it neatly with bolt cutters. Not that he couldn't have learned to use the tool. He was smart. But those slice lines were human.

They joined us. "William is school timed," said the little boy.

"Say, 'It is time for me to go to school,' " Lance corrected.

"It is time for you to go to school," William said agreeably. Lance pressed a hand to his forehead.

I had told Natasha nobody was going in. On the other hand, because of his wandering nature, William and one other child shared an aide. His IEP had more stipulations than did Sara's. The other child needed academic help. William needed watching and someone who could understand him. His whereabouts were probably better monitored at school than they would be with us. And we had already confused his schedule. Messing with it further was a dangerous invitation to upsetting his emotional apple cart.

"Also," William added, "it is William's turn to ride in the convertible."

When did we start taking turns with that? "Later, Bud. All we've got here is the minivan," I said. "I'll pick you up in the convertible, okay?"

He didn't answer me, but he turned and chugged away toward the barn. I followed him, doing the mental gymnastics required to keep my job interview from my husband in the morning, now Sara was home at a time she would normally not have needed care, and Trudy had an obvious job to do here. It wasn't going to happen. Any way I twisted it, the math didn't work out. I needed to find a few minutes alone with Lance to tell him the truth, and sooner, rather than later.

CHAPTER 21

ATTN: ADVICE

Dear Nora:

I bet these kids have never had attention lavished on them. The best and most precious gift you can give them, and your daughter, is your time. Do special things nobody else can. In other words, be a normal grandmother. That's what you should do.

A Grandma Who Knows

"Honey, I've been meaning to tell you . . . No, too offhanded." I stared at my reflection in the bathroom mirror. She didn't seem to know how to start this discussion any better than I did. But with the rhesus outbreak contained and the police mum about nearly everything, I didn't have any excuses for keeping silent. "Lance, I want you to know . . . No, doesn't leave room for conversation." My reflection and I glared at each other. "Lance, we need to talk."

"Okay, sure, what about?"

"Lance! Where did you come from?"

"I thought you said my name."

"I did, but I wasn't . . . I didn't . . . I was *working up* to actually saying your name to *you.*"

"Ah. The mirror pep talk."

"Yes."

"Do you want me to go away so you can keep working up?"

"No. Yes. No. Let's get out of the bathroom."

"The bathroom's a great place to talk."

"No, it isn't." Lance's bathroom conversations typically turned into bathroom floor conversations. Our thick rugs were testament to our admission we'd gotten too middle-aged to enjoy those floors without some kind of padding.

I led him back to our room and closed the door. Natasha was entertaining the twins downstairs, and she had promised to feed them dessert from the deep freeze down there, which contained a wide array of unhealthy treats. She had never been in favor of my secrecy and was more than happy to play the babysitter tonight. Trudy was due to arrive in a few minutes for backup, vehemently insisting there wasn't something more important needing her attention.

I perched on one corner of the bed, and Lance scooted a rocking chair over so he could prop his legs beside me. We stared at each other without speaking, and I knew he wasn't going to help me any more than my reflection had. I took a sidetrack. "Drew told me Deputy Greene and his partner had mild hypothermia and carbon dioxide poisoning, but they'll be okay in the long run. They were dressed pretty warmly thanks to the season."

"Great. Did you seriously need to work up to that?"

"No, but it was better than any of the introductions I was thinking about. It sets a positive atmosphere, and invites you to be an active participant in the conversation."

"You sound like Natasha's therapist."

"Hey, it was worth a try."

"What are you so nervous about telling me, Noel? Did you catch pregnant?"

"What? No! I applied for Art's job." Lance had begun to laugh at his own joke but stopped short when I finally spat out the truth. "I have an interview tomorrow morning." He stared at me open-mouthed for a few moments, and I launched into my line of justifications. "I know we talked about this! We agreed we didn't want to be tied down to the university, but that was before we cut out my sanctuary salary and moved into this house. And now, with the twins, I doubt we'll ever make it to Ecuador. I was too afraid of having whoever got the job wind up over us and changing Art's vision. I didn't . . . why are you laughing at me, Lance?"

He swung his feet down off the bed. "Honey, I thought you were mad because you'd looked at our savings account."

"What?"

"I spent the Ecuador money on the materials for the new rhesus enclosure." Now I was the one staring at him. "The bidding kept going up, and I knew how badly we needed it. And I didn't know when we'd make it on our honeymoon. I figured we were out the plane money either way. The fee to move the tickets to next summer wasn't so bad, and the sanctuary down there was so accommodating . . . I figured we could save up by then. But it was . . . before the twins. Honey, I'd never have done it now."

"I would still do it. Not the money. But I'd apply for Art's job. And I am. I have. I've got . . ."

". . . an interview tomorrow. You already told me. Honestly? I'm glad. I feel guilty you have to do it. We're field people. Art was supposed to be our university anchor. And if you've looked in the checking account . . ." he shrugged.

"That was what I figured had happened to savings. I would have asked about it, but I've been watching how close we've been walking the line, and I assumed you'd moved the money over to cover all these damned Christmas expenses and these kids having December birthdays."

"No," he said. "We're managing those. Barely. But I've had to use the credit card too much."

"Me, too. If Stan hadn't funded the cars, we'd have been

stretched to get a sedan *or* a minivan."

"I'm scared without the cushion." He took his feet off the bed and rocked forward. "I know we have the money market account your great-aunt left you, but it would only carry us six months or so."

"Yeah. And the state won't continue the twins' stipend once the adoption's final. If I can't get Art's job, I may have to apply in the research department." I shuddered. Field research was one thing. Stale lab work didn't appeal.

"Honey, if you can't get Art's job, we may both have to go work for Groceries to Go."

"I hear they have great benefits."

"What do you think?" Lance stood and struck a pose. "Would I look sexier in a cashier's apron or manager's tie?"

"Absolutely the apron. It would cover up the pudding stains much more evenly than a tie."

He sat beside me on the bed. "We have *got* to get William to quit eating pudding for breakfast."

"You want to scrape bran cereal off the ceiling?"

"Hey," he said, suddenly serious. "Look at me. We're going to be okay."

I turned in his direction and let him pull me into an awkward embrace. "I've missed you."

"How much?" He started untucking my shirt and kicked the rocker back to where it belonged.

"Is the door locked?" We had quickly learned boundaries had no meaning for our twins.

"Mm-hmm." He nuzzled my neck, and I smelled the cologne of cleanliness that followed a messy day at the barn.

"Good, then let me show you."

Our blaring alarm woke us at three a.m. *"Carbon monoxide,"* an artificially calm voice announced. *"Carbon monoxide."* The burglar alarm didn't talk. Its warning simply bleated.

"Christ, get the kids." I stumbled into pants and fumbled my shirt over my head, then staggered out, staying low to the ground. *What the hell's wrong with the furnace?*

William's panicked screaming, *"Eeeeee,"* propelled me down the hall.

"Tasha, you okay?" Lance called, catching up.

"Right behind you."

"Stay low," I told her.

"This isn't a fire, Noel. Holding your breath is more helpful."

I scooped up Sara, and Lance grabbed William. It was hard to run hunkered over, but it seemed logical in my half-asleep state that the carbon monoxide would be up high, since our detectors are near the ceiling, never mind our vents are in the floor. The burglar alarm had also kicked on, but its noise hadn't fully registered.

Only Natasha took the time to grab shoes at the front door, but she threw every pair out onto the frozen lawn as she pelted outside. Ignoring my own discomfort, I immediately got to work on Sara's feet. Footsteps thundered behind us, and I suddenly remembered our federal guest. "Trudy!"

"Go!" she shouted. The minivan keys flew over Natasha's head to land at Lance's feet. "All of you get in my car. Go! Darnell, make them leave." She darted back inside.

"How did you get here?" I asked Darnell, even though I had just seen him jump out of Trudy's car.

Trudy reappeared and pelted around the side of the house. "You're parked at the curb, aren't you? Get out of here!" she called over her shoulder.

"What?" I had pulled on my own tennies, but I couldn't follow her instructions. William was a screaming ball, huddled in Lance's arms.

"What are you all standing there for? Get in. *Leave.*" *Darnell was on stakeout! He was watching the house from Trudy's sedan. But why?* Without putting William down, Lance took off for the van, parked at the curb, but I stayed put.

"Go where? What's going on, Darnell? Do you know where the leak is?" I demanded.

He came close and spoke low. "There's not a leak. Somebody busted out an upper pane in your kitchen window and pushed a hose through up by the detector. Somebody *wants you outside.* Come on. Let's get in your van and get your children out of here."

Natasha didn't need urging. She grabbed Sara from around my neck and dashed to the van. "Noel, come on." Her voice verged on hysterical.

"But where do we go? What about Trudy?"

"Trudy can . . ." Darnell began.

At that moment, Trudy ran back into view and jumped in her own car, barely pausing to grab the keys her partner extended to her.

"They took off in a van," she snapped. "Why are you *still here?*"

Lance deposited William in my arms in place of his sister and urged me toward the road. "In," he said.

"But . . ."

He lifted me in through the side door and bopped the auto-close button. "Going," he said as Darnell swung in the passenger door beside him.

As usual, I had frozen up when I didn't fully comprehend the situation, while Lance took charge. I needed a burglar action plan for the next time this happened. *Wait!* There wouldn't *be* a next time. But I needed an action plan. Just in case.

We drove after Trudy, though at a much more sedate pace, as the first wails of police sirens caught my ear.

I finally had a rational thought. "Can we go to my mother's?"

"Probably safe enough," Lance agreed. After a few moments, Darnell acquiesced as well.

The cruisers passed us going the other direction. In my arms, William moaned. "Circle dot cars are bad; circle dot cars are bad." I couldn't possibly put him down to work on a seatbelt. Tasha buckled Sara in beside her. *Did* police drive circle dot cars? Their lights were circles projecting spinning dots of light.

"Drive slowly," I told my husband. I rode unbuckled, cradling our son.

By dawn, we were on our third pot of Mama's fancy coffee, the kind Lance and I used to use. Nobody had slept. There was no pudding for William to massacre, but Daddy, with a great deal of help from Natasha, had persuaded him to try a waffle. Pancakes had produced a near meltdown, their relationship to circle dots being entirely too close. William hated round things. He couldn't look at the wheels when we put him in the car, and he never looked out the window when we drove. He didn't even want pizza if he saw the whole pie.

However, my parents' waffle-maker produces a square product, and William loves squares almost as much as he hates circles. When Tasha demonstrated her technique of applying perfect butter squares and drizzling syrup everywhere, Will was sold. And he was so busy eating he forgot to fling his leftovers up until the end.

Mama had been waiting for this maneuver, and she seized the plate on its way skyward. "Not in this house, Buster."

William squealed his dismay, but Daddy swooped in with a pair of pruning shears. "Bad idea," I said as he passed them to Will, who was startled into silence. "It's not safe outside, there's nothing he can do with them in December, the novelty is going to wear off, and those are sharp."

"Sshh," Daddy commanded me. "Want to help me in the garden?"

"*Oh yes.*" William bopped along after him and out the door. He had a jacket at Mama and Daddy's, but he refused to put it on, just as he refused to wear a coat for us most of the time. William hated to have his arms covered and only endured long sleeves because he had been forced to do it for at least one winter before he was ours.

Darnell was muttering on his phone in the corner. I appealed to him with my eyes, and he followed Will and Dad outside. The property had been examined and deemed "safe enough for the present," but I felt exposed with my coatless son out there.

"Mama, that could have ended badly. It still may. It's impossible to predict . . ."

"Have a little *faith*, dear," Mama chided. "It's perfectly safe. We bush-hogged at the end of the season. We can see people coming from any direction but the road. The rose garden is the safest place on our property. And your daddy knows what he's doing. If I'm not mistaken, those shears are blunt plastic. It's the pair Poppy and Bryce used before they graduated to the real thing. And there isn't anything to cut anyway right now. They're playing out back."

"Oh."

Trudy arrived, looking as weary as ever I'd seen her. She had her tablet again, and Darnell came in and produced a pen and paper. Before they would tell *us* anything, they had each of us, including William and Sara, relate everything we could remember from the time we left the center until we got here. We had already been through this with Darnell alone, but we repeated it now for Trudy's benefit. Drew arrived looking like he'd had even less sleep than the federal agents, and we went over it all a third time.

Then Darnell said, "Okay, we don't know exactly what happened last night, but we have ideas. There's what we know, and there's what we guess. We *know* two individuals, probably men from what I could tell, broke out a pane of glass in your kitchen and sent car exhaust through the window. We *know* they have studied your house's layout in some depth, because they knew where to break in to be closest to a carbon monoxide detector on the side of the building."

"And," Trudy added, "we know they're not the brightest, because they stood there arguing when you failed to come out the back door. I saw the hose and heard their voices when I started to leave via that door myself. It was why *I* came out front instead."

"Why would we go out back? We only ever use the back door to go in, almost never to go out." Lance jiggled his leg under the table.

"They didn't seem to realize that, which suggests they've been studying the place when you aren't home." Darnell tapped his pen against his pad.

Drew accepted a cup of Mama's coffee. He yawned deeply. "Here's what I figure. Most people around there use the back door for everything because of the way the driveway is situated, and it was your kitchen detector going off. I think they assumed you'd run out back and straight into their arms."

"Yeah," I echoed Lance's position. "But our driveway is full with the convertible and primate-mobile. We park the minivan in the street. If we could figure out how to leave our mud on the stoop, we'd go in *and* out by the front."

Drew let me finish talking, then repeated patiently, "Which is why we think they were checking the place out while you were gone. Acting on that misunderstanding, I think they parked in the alley running between your house and Elm Avenue. You'd have noticed if they were there during the day, and Darnell would have seen them if they'd come by way of the front after dark. They pulled up out back after dark and tried to run you out. When you came out the wrong door, they took off back down the alley. Trudy followed until I caught up, then I chased them almost to the bypass, but they pulled into a box store lot and down a dirt road. I followed the road to the end, but they had turned aside somewhere, and it was too dark for me to do anything else. I've got a team out there this morning trying to follow up."

"It doesn't explain why they were there in the first place." I was watching William and Daddy out the window.

Will had forced Darnell to come outside to interview him, and he'd provided nothing more helpful than, "Circle dots are bad cars." Now, he had on gardening gloves, and he was using his shears to hold up woody hibernating rose stems for Daddy to actually cut. He should have been freezing. Natasha was upstairs with Sara, helping the younger girl play dress-up with Mama's clothes.

"Why did they leave a decapitated body at your sanctuary but hogtie my *living* deputies in your refrigerator?"

"Do you *know* it's the same people at the center and our house?"

"I don't believe in coincidence. Natasha's necklace didn't get into your spider monkey enclosure by magic. Right now, we want to question Charles Dalton about Natasha's necklace, but I doubt he'll be much help. Our force is too small to have surveillance teams everyplace we expect trouble, though, and we figured it was more likely to crop up at the sanctuary, since that's where it came before. Frankly, if Trudy and Darnell hadn't been available to keep an eye on you, last night could have gone a whole lot worse.

"For now, don't go home. Stay here with your folks or go to a motel. It's kind of hard to do in a small town, but try not to take the same route twice in a row going places. Make sure the kids are accompanied to and from the school doors."

"But it's Christmas!" I protested. "We've got presents to

wrap, and our tree is up. We can't . . ."

". . . live like the devil is watching over our shoulders." Lance finished my thought.

"I think he is." Drew rose. "But it's nine o'clock in the morning, I've been awake since *six* o'clock *yesterday* morning, and if I don't get some sleep, I'm going to fall over dead from exhaustion. And that would be no good, because until we find Hugh, I'm the acting senior detective."

"You're . . . wow . . . congratulations," I said. "Wait. What time did you say it is?"

"Nine."

Mama's analog clock confirmed this truth.

"What am I going to do? I have the most important job interview of my life in an hour, I haven't had a shower, I'm still wearing yesterday's cruddy blue jeans, and all my work clothes are at home in my closet!"

CHAPTER 22

ATTN: ADVICE

Dear Nora:

You can read all the advice you want, but nothing will substitute for a long talk with your daughter. Find out what you can do for her. Ask her what she needs most. Build up your bond, because she's going to need you, Grandma!

Your Therapist

"But Trudy, I *need* my clothes."

"You can't go over there. I can bring you what you want and meet you at school."

"No time! I need fifteen minutes to drive to the college, ten to walk to the Bio Science building, another ten to get set up . . . Setup! My slides! Okay, calm down, I have a copy on the hard drive at school. I've only got twenty-five minutes to get showered, dressed, and in the car."

"*Plenty* of time," said Mama.

"What? Even if Trudy leaves when I hop in the tub, she'll be twenty minutes to the house, at a minimum. It will take her *at least* another five to find my stuff, then she'd need fifteen more to get to school, get parked, and I'd be wearing blue jeans in the middle of my presentation before she walked in."

"Why would you have time to get your stuff if I wouldn't?"

"Because . . . because . . ." *I know where it is; I'll speed the whole way; I'll . . .* "I wouldn't. What am I going to do?"

"I may not wear them often, but I do still own dress pants, Noel. We're of a size around the middle, and I have *plenty* of time to hem a pair of slacks while you're in the tub. She knew how I eschewed skirts. I've still got all of your measurements from the wedding."

"Mama, I love you." I appreciated being descended from a professional seamstress now more than I ever had in my life.

Fifteen minutes later, she greeted me at the bathroom door with a muted tan suit. The pants bore inexplicable pale red squares that were almost, but not quite, professional looking. *Beggars can't be choosers.* I buttoned myself in cursing the scratchy, hot wool. I couldn't decide whether to wish Mama's blouse was long sleeved to stave off my itching or to be grateful it was short sleeved to keep down the heat.

Although foot problems had long since driven her out of high heels, Mama had never gotten rid of a single pair. The ones she gave me were maroon, presumably to go with the unappealing un-plaid design on my pants, and they were only half a size too large. A little newspaper in the toes, some borrowed lipstick on my face, and I was ready to roll.

In the kitchen, Lance was waiting to drive me in. He had a 10:30 lab he couldn't cancel any more than I could my interview, even though all three children were home from school for a second morning, thanks to last night's adventure. "Hey, hot stuff," he greeted me.

I tried to look appreciative of the compliment, but grimaced instead of smiling. I reached for one final swig of coffee as I followed him to the door. Right then, William catapulted in from the garden and collided with me from one side, and Sara pelted into me from the other.

"William is timed for *school*!"

"Don't leave me! I want to come with you!"

Coffee sloshed up onto my face, lapel, and white blouse. "I

don't have time to change!"

"I've got an easy fix." Mama scurried out of the room.

"William is timed for *school.*"

"I thought you were pruning?" I plucked a thorny leaf out of his hair. Moments before, I would have sworn it would have been difficult to roust William and Daddy from the rose beds anyway. Never mind that the child wasn't wearing a coat, he had looked settled in for the *day* out there. None of the other grandkids would have humored Daddy for half so long as William already had, especially with everything bloomed out and the work revolving around rose hips and repeating already completed winter preparations.

Darnell was prepared to come with Lance and me. Trudy had work to do in Columbus, but the kids and my parents wouldn't be staying alone. Drew had given them a pair of deputy watchdogs.

It seemed far safer and more logical to leave the kids there. But now, William was rocking, glancing back and forth between Lance and me and the open door. There wasn't a threat there, but I saw the temptation to run etched on his forehead.

Lance did, too. "Okay, I'll have time to take you in after I drop Noel."

"Lance, it's not *safe*. And he's wearing *pajamas!*" Also, no underwear. We hadn't exactly brought any of his undies along, and the pull-up he'd been sleeping in was decidedly soaked by the time we got here.

"He'll be safer there than anywhere else. They've got detectors on the doors, a fence around the playground, and an aide to keep him from running. And they keep an extra set of his clothes in his cubby. He'll be fine. Get in the car, buddy."

I began dabbing my shirt with a wet paper towel in a futile effort to clean it. "Fine." We watched until we were sure he was scrambling into the minivan.

"But what about *me*?" Where she had been querulous at first, demanding and angry, now Sara's voice had taken on a plaintive edge.

"Don't you want to play with me today, Sara?" Natasha tried.

Sara didn't so much as glance away from me. "Don't *leave* me."

"Sara, there'll be nothing for you to do," said Lance. "Noel has to give an important presentation, and I . . . honey, we're dissecting fetal pigs today. You *cannot* come to my lab." Lance hated teaching classes like this. He questioned the ethics of dissection when we had vividly detailed computer programs available.

Sara sat on the floor and howled. "Don't *leave me!*" she sobbed.

"Go on, you guys. We'll be fine." Natasha hunkered down beside her younger sister. Layla might *sound* more like an adult than a child, but Tasha was the one who acted the part. When I first met her, she had seemed like a typical goth teen to me. But I hadn't known about Gary's ongoing abuse then. As the fragments of the deep depression she had lived with for the last four years began to lift, the young woman who emerged wasn't a child at all. There was nothing typical or goth about Natasha.

Mama dashed back with an enormous, flashy brooch. She pinned it below my right shoulder, perfectly hiding the remains of the coffee stains. I leaned down to kiss Sara and tell her she'd be fine, but when I buried my nose in her thick, soft hair, with its faint honey scent, I found myself squatting down and wrapping my arms around her middle. Somehow, when I stood up, I hadn't let go. She slid easily over to my hip, smashing her face against the side of my neck that wasn't now covered with the appalling brooch.

"Please," she sobbed. "Please, please, please. Don't *leave* me." Her whole body shook with tearful tremors. Intellectually,

I knew this was simply a meltdown. It had been due ever since the burglar alarm's first screeches, and it could have been triggered by anything at all, when the real cause was a combination of fear and overexhaustion. William had melted right away and would now, with careful management, likely be fine until the overtiredness caught up with him this evening. Sara had instead, as was her habit, waited until the crisis was over to fall apart.

I remembered the first meeting on our lawn, when she threw herself into Natasha's arms, accepting me only when Tasha had to go to the bathroom. She had howled then with the ferocity of terror at losing her brother. Now, she was afraid of losing him again. The people who broke into our house could easily have been coming to take him from her. And to take *her* from *me*. Sara wasn't the only one having a delayed reaction. I squeezed her back.

And suddenly I realized she had come to me. *They* had come to us. Neither of them had gone to Natasha. Indeed, Sara had rejected Natasha and games in favor of my boring presentation. William hadn't demanded Natty to arbitrate, either today at Mama's house or yesterday at the sanctuary. I couldn't place when the shift had happened, the changeover in loyalties from them to us. But our children had finally come to us. Now, I couldn't put Sara down. I couldn't *possibly* put her down. "Okay. You can come. But you have to quit crying." *Or else I'm going to start.* "And you have to sit in my presentation as quietly as ever you can. Somebody get me some crayons. Tasha, what about you? You staying here or kicking around with us up at school?"

"If I'm not staying here, I'm going wherever Trudy is. Um. If it's okay with you, Trudy."

"It's fine. In fact, it's my preference. I'd rather you *all* stayed where someone could keep an eye on you. I'd rather I didn't have something needing attention elsewhere. But that's neither realistic nor likely to happen. Let's ask if the deputy can get you some clothes from your house. Tasha, you can look at some pictures for me this afternoon." Though Mama was clearly irked to be stuck with the final deputy, Daddy seemed happy enough to chat the man up.

Fifteen minutes later, Lance dropped Sara and me at the Bio Science building. "Knock 'em dead, babe."

"And text us when you get there safe and sound," Darnell added.

We reached the conference room with ten minutes to spare. Only one member of the search committee had arrived before me. "Anything up, Doc?" I greeted him with false casualness. *Should I call him Dr. Chambless? I work with him every day. But he barely knows me. Don't set the wrong tone.*

"Nothing up here, Doc." He returned the ritual department joke, then sat comfortably in a seat to the right of the projector, where he was guaranteed to see almost nothing of my slide-show.

"Ooooh, what *stinks*?" Sara tried to put herself at the head of the table, where I would go, but I transferred her to the seat opposite James Chambless, where she would also miss seeing most of my slides.

The conference room carried its usual reek of long-forgotten lunchmeat and vastly overdue milk, along with a nasty fishy smell. *Didn't Tasha and I clean this out again after it nearly ruined our ice cream? Are they bringing in the rotting food from home after it goes bad?* There was another smell as well, a hard water smell, almost metallic. I couldn't quite place it. For some reason, I associated it with the center. I mouth-breathed and cursed whomever had tanked my presentation before it even started.

Naturally, the chair arrived last, after the rest of us had been seated and making awkward conversation for some time. I had been on job interviews as a graduate student before I realized my work lay here in Ironweed and I wouldn't be leaving the center after graduation. But those had been outside affairs. If I was nervous, it was only for a little while. If I screwed up, it was in front of strangers who would never see me again.

But as the inside candidate, all my actions carried a different weight. The search committee was filled with my colleagues. When they ultimately filled Art's position, I would have to face these people in the halls. I would see them less frequently, of course, when I went back to my part-time schedule, but it would still be embarrassing for all of us.

We had moved beyond the nervous chit-chat about the twins, Natasha, and our adoption process and reached a lull where I was clearly expected to speak, when Dr. Prescott stomped in and all but threw himself into a chair. "All right, get on with it," he snapped. And I commenced.

The first part of the interview involved the usual questions. Qualifications, experience, and, my least favorite question in any interview, why they should hire me. Then I gave a short version of a lecture of the variety I might use in a freshman classroom. Here, my insider knowledge benefitted me because I could safely choose a somewhat edgy topic.

With the exception of Dr. Prescott and the mandatory reviewer from outside the department, I knew everyone's position on genetically modified organisms and their role in our food. GMOs always made for lively discussion, and even among our small group, who largely agreed with one another on the subject, the conversation ranged broadly, and the interview ran well over its allotted hour.

Sara colored quietly for every moment. She didn't say one word, though she did change seats to crawl into my lap when I sat down at the end of the slideshow. Finally, we wrapped up, and I set her down. I was beginning to think the interview had gone off without a hitch in spite of the odor when Mama's brooch snagged on a cabinet handle as I stood. The door flew open and smacked me in the nose. "Ow!"

Two members of the committee screamed, and the chair's face paled. "Oh, no." He staggered back away from his seat.

What the hell? I'm the one with the bloody nose. We're nearly all biologists. We've seen blood before. The brooch wouldn't come loose. *Blood. The metallic smell.* It was iron, it was . . . it was blood. I had smelled it yesterday when the macaques tracked it through the barn. I jerked and pulled, all the while trying to cover my nose with my shirt. *What would smell like blood, though?* The more I wiggled, the more tightly wedged the brooch became. Finally, with one great wrench, I ripped it off the jacket. Something splatted out of the cupboard with a meaty thud.

"Oh, no," the chair repeated. "Oh, no. Oh, no."

"Shut up, Winnie," Dr. Chambless snapped. "You'll scare the kid."

It didn't sound a bit like lemon cleanser hitting the ground this time. *What would have smelled like . . . blood?* "Oh, no." My nose sent another geyser of red down my shirt. I couldn't stop myself from looking, even though the only question I had now was *who* I would see when I peered around the door.

The head was rolled onto one side, saving me from seeing the other, and I was looking at it upside down, from the scalp. Two hands and two feet were collected in a baggie and tied in its hair. It looked like Detective Hugh Marsland would not be returning to claim his badge. No beach bunnies for him. No cozy fireside dinners with his wife, either. My bloody nose seemed suddenly trivial.

"Sara, grab hold of me and make like a choo-choo train, but walk right behind me so you can't see a *thing*."

"What's going on? I don't like to be blind."

Listen for the important questions, and answer them honestly. "Honey, you remember the headless guy yesterday? We found the rest of him."

"I know. I saw."

"I don't want you to look at it again. It's awful. We're heading for the bathroom, little caboose, so I can clean up my face, and then I think we're going to spend another afternoon at the police station." I edged her around the conference table and toward the door.

"Oh, *no*," babbled the chair. "He's going to kill me. I'm *next in line*. Somebody save me." And then he collapsed in the middle of the doorway, completely blocking our exit.

CHAPTER 23

Dear Nora:

How right you were! I should have trusted you more. I do love your attorney. As soon as my divorce is finalized, we'll be announcing our engagement. Instead of a ring, he gave me my own housekeeping company. Please say you'll come to the wedding.

Formerly Worked to the Bone

By the time we got home, it was late afternoon. My Nana had arrived at Mama and Daddy's, as had all of our unwrapped presents and enough clothes to get each of us through several days. I felt increasingly edgy about being here. There wasn't a burglar alarm, and Ironweed was a small town. We wouldn't be hard to track down.

"We ought to go to a hotel. In Columbus."

"Maybe so," Lance agreed.

But Mama wouldn't hear of it. "Honey, you're better off than if you'd joined up with those witness protection people." Drew's people were needed elsewhere tonight, and we were left with the federal agents. Even though there were only two of them, my mother had total faith in Trudy and Darnell.

And then there was Natasha. For the first time since she had joined us, she was wearing makeup, not the heavy, overdone stuff I'd seen her in at our first meeting many moons ago, but bright colors in moderate amounts. And instead of black, the

251

eye shadow and lipstick were paired with a pastel top and flowery shorts, because Mama kept the kitchen unholy hot. "I wish you a Merry Christmas, I'm going home, home, home, home," she sang. "They're springing Granddad from the retread hospital, and I'm going home in a week."

"Retread? What?" We had barely achieved some kind of normalcy in our house with our three children. Now one of them was leaving?

"Retread. It's what he calls rehab. Like fixing the tread on a car, only . . . yeah, you get it," she explained. Then she added, as if maybe I'd missed her point, "He's getting out next Wednesday if everything goes right this coming week."

Sara wrapped her arms around Natasha. "I'm going to miss you!"

"Me, too!" Tasha said at once, as if this portion of the equation hadn't occurred to her. It seemed we had inadvertently dampened her good humor. "But," she knelt beside Sara and beckoned for William. "Remember. We talked about this. Sleepovers, movie nights, and you can come swimming whenever you want to in the summer."

"*You* have a burglar alarm!" The words were out of my mouth before I could stop myself.

Natasha understood at once. "You're brilliant! I could go home *now.*"

"Noel, our house is safe," said Mama.

"No," said Lance. "It isn't."

"And," Mama overrode him, "We have more than enough room for all of you." There, at least, she had us. She and Daddy lived in a vast old mansion that had once been a funeral home. When we got married, they had boarded not only Lance and me, but also Nana, my sister and her husband, their four children, and ultimately Natasha.

"I want it to be," said Lance. "We love it here. But if we

hadn't had an alarm to go with our federal escort, we could still have been in trouble last night. Stan has space *and* an alarm."

Mama ignored him. "Plus, we have a tree up here, *and* all of your presents *and* my presents, *and* your sister is coming down in a couple of days." My mother crossed her arms. "If you're going, I'm coming along, and so is all our stuff. I *guarantee* everyone else will stay where I land."

"Don't be absurd, Mama."

"You can't go without me, Lenore." Daddy sounded outraged. "See?"

"Not you, too, Daddy."

"Now you hold on!" said Nana.

"Finally! Someone with sense."

"You're not leaving me here all by myself." She sounded as plaintive and grouchy as Sara had earlier. "I came over here expressly to get the dibs on your escapades, and you will *not* get away from me until I hear every word of what happened yesterday, last night, and this morning."

"Nana . . . you can't . . . would all of you stop and think! We have no idea how long this is going to drag on, and Stan does not need to come home to a madhouse. Everybody forget it. We're staying here."

"That's better," said Nana. Lance and I exchanged resigned shrugs. Daddy reclaimed William and they returned to the morning's imaginary pruning. Lance went along to supervise. Sara trailed after Mama to go feed the dogs.

Natasha and I were left alone. "Sorry," I said. "Didn't mean to get your hopes up."

"The madhouse would probably be better," she mumbled. "The two of us rattling around up there are going to be mighty lonely."

"What about . . . oh. Gert can't leave yet."

"You mean *won't* leave." Her ebullience had completely disintegrated.

"Sweetheart." I wished I could hug her.

"She *could* come home, Noel. The absolutely worst part is that she's determined to mope and waste in the stupid nursing home. She's not very old, and she's not even very sick anymore. But Granddad said it's like . . . like she's lost the will to live. The doctors are all out of ideas, and even her favorite nurse can't think of anything. Granddad's all out of ideas. She thinks it's all her fault, and I know exactly why she does, because I always think the same thing myself."

"What same thing?"

Natasha looked out at me from her made-up face and didn't say a word.

"I'm sorry, honey, you don't have to answer."

"It's okay. My shrink says I ought to get it out there and make myself believe it isn't true. I'm starting to agree with him. I guess I thought you would know."

"No. I'm sorry, Tash. You and I have been through some similar things, but this is one I can't touch." I had ended the abusive relationship with Lance's younger brother only when Alex nearly beat me to death. Memories of that time in my life could only help me so far in connecting with my foster daughter.

"See, as long as I believe it's my fault, then it can't be Mom's. And then I won't be mad at her."

"Man. I *should* have seen that." I wanted to hug her. I wanted to wrap my arms around Natasha and hold her as close as I had held Sara earlier. But this sister didn't want for holding. My arm around her shoulder at the poetry slam had been a huge step forward. Natasha would come to me if she wanted physical contact. "Does Gert know you're fighting with the same things as her?"

"I don't want to dump on Gran."

"You might be able to give her some perspective. You've always been close to her, haven't you?"

"Even when we hardly ever got to see them, Gran and Granddad were like my sun and moon. It was always peaceful out here in the country. When I was with Mom and Terry, there was . . . I don't know exactly how to explain it . . . an edgy feeling. I thought I liked it when I was a kid. I never knew what was coming next, and life felt like one big adventure after another. And then . . . I guess when I found out how the adventure got funded, things weren't so good anymore. There were six of us girls around the same age, and I wanted to impress the others so much. I acted tough, like I didn't care, or like I thought it was as great as they did. But behind their backs, I was begging to get out. I know those girls hate me now, wherever they are.

"I kept hoping Mom would come around, like I could change her mind, and then she'd save us both. But she never did. And I wonder now, what if I'd argued with her a little harder? What if I hadn't pretended to like it when I was with the other girls? What if . . ."

"What if you could have changed her." It wasn't a question. This, I *did* know. "I used to blame the alcoholism, instead of Alex. I thought if I could change him, he'd stop hurting me. It was always inherent in *me* to make *him* different. It doesn't work that way."

"I know. But it's hard to accept when you're brainwashed . . . or when you've brainwashed yourself."

"Honey, Gary brainwashed you."

"I don't mean me. I think that's what Gran's doing. Brainwashing herself. It's like she's all of a sudden admitting Mom's dead, and everything else is collapsing around her."

"Listen, tomorrow, you've *got* to go to school. You're already going to be buried under makeup work from missing two days. But after school, I want to take you in to the . . . what does

Stan call it? Retread home? And let you visit with Gert."

I could not save Hugh Marsland. And I couldn't erase the look of horror from Drew's eyes when he walked out of the conference room earlier after seeing his old partner's desiccated head. But I could help here. I understood the isolation of depression, and so did Natasha. "Your Gran needs to know she's not alone."

Nana stumped back, impatient for news. "Is Gertrude stuck in the home your mother stuffed me away in when I broke my hip?"

"Yes, Nana."

"They do okay for the body, I guess. I'm back up and running, and it hasn't even been a full year since I got out. But they don't do much for the mind except tell you to stop feeling sorry for yourself. Your granddad needs to get her a better psychiatrist or psychologist than whatever they're giving her in there."

"He does?" Natasha's daze was lifting, returning hope making her straighten her back. "He can make that happen. *I* can make that happen. He can *buy* that."

"Now come on. I want to know what happened to that poor man at your center."

"We're coming." I shook my head at Nana's retreating back. "We aren't going to get your Gran home next week. But we're *not* going to up and leave her in there to fester."

"Thanks, Noel."

"Come on, let's go see if we can convince my mama to order pizza instead of cooking for this crew."

Less than an hour later, I was thoroughly enmeshed in parent mode, and Nana was brooding on the sofa. I had promised her a long talk after the twins were in bed. The pizza delivery car pulled up behind our van in Mama's driveway. Sara, who had been watching from the window, called out, "Pizza for me-e!"

and dashed for the door.

"Not so fast." Lance intercepted her. "Grownups answering the doors, yes?"

"Right." Her face fell. This wasn't merely a reminder she was seven and we were a fair bit older. It was a reminder we would only be sure it was the pizza guy on the other side of the door when he handed Lance a hot square box and departed with a tip.

In the living room, William shouted, "No! No, no, no!" He ran at me, flapping madly, jumping up and down when he reached me. "No, no, no, no, *no!*"

"Easy, easy." I got down on his level to show him I was listening, and I tried to catch the hands. Pointless, as he needed that stimulation to calm himself, but completely automatic on my part.

He pulled them loose and shook them harder. "Circles!" He finally howled. "No circles!"

No circles. "No pizza?" Pizza was round. William hated round. "We're making you a waffle, remember?"

"No, no, no! No circles. No *dots.*"

"Do you see the police car?"

Lance was talking to the delivery guy. "We already paid by credit card."

"Sorry. Should have checked the receipt. I don't usually do deliveries. I'm supposed to be a cook. But we're down a manager and Robby's been filling in for him."

William persisted. "Circle dot cars are *bad cars.*"

"Isn't he a little young?" Lance was making small talk now, when he should have been bringing in the food. But he had a point. Our pizza was almost always brought by the teenage Robby, who was perennially late, but always friendly. And he did seem awfully young to sub for a manager.

"No circle dots!"

"Yeah, but Merle, our manager, had kind of taken him under his wing. And the Gibsons have been out of touch ever since we upgraded the technology. Robby's the only one who knows how to do practically everything."

"I didn't know Merle worked for the Marine."

"You know him? Merle Evans?"

"How many Merles do we have in this town? He volunteers at the sanctuary. What's up with Merle? Sick?"

"No call, no show. I think he's sleeping something off in Columbus."

"Really? He always seemed responsible to me."

"Yeah. When he isn't drinking. But get him on a bender? Different story."

The driver left, and William pounded on my hips. "No! No!" *Circle dot cars.* "That car?" He had been watching at the window with Sara. With some effort, because he struggled, I took him back there and pointed. Abstract concepts like "that" were hard for him. But he was a visual kid. He used a tablet at school and had a specialized chart with images depicting words. The Marine's delivery car backed down the drive, and for a moment, the magnet on its door rolled into view.

"Circle dots," Will shrieked. "Circle dot cars are *bad cars.*" The magnet had the Marine's logo, that scuba diver holding the outsized pepperoni pizza. From the right angle, it looked nothing like a pizza at all but like a wavy, polka-dotted oval. Circle dots. Pizzas were circles. The weird oval might be a circle. Pepperoni might be dots. But so might be police lights. Though Drew's people had gone, a parked cruiser remained on the curb, and it was illuminated in the departing vehicle's headlights.

William was going to start screaming soon, and then he'd be gone for half an hour or more. "William," I said, looking for, and not finding, something to calm him down. I couldn't ask him the obvious question; it was too abstract. *What are circle dot cars? Why are they bad?* I tried to think of familiar vocabulary words. "William . . . was that car," I pointed again to the retreating vehicle. "Did that car see you under the Dumpster?"

He cocked his head. "Cars can't see," he told me, bewilderment momentarily overcoming his hysteria.

Damn. "Was that car . . . did you ride in that car?"

"The day we went to town!"

I didn't know what to make of it. Those were the final words of his favorite book, *We had fun in there and everywhere the day we went to town.* He liked that book. *Loved* it. But he didn't sound happy now. He sounded intense, desperate, and on the verge of a meltdown. The exhaustion was hitting him hard.

"You rode in the circle dot car the day you went to town."

"The day we went to town, I *did not have fun.* Circle dot cars are bad *cars!*" And then he broke and threw himself into my arms, sobbing.

Later, when he was calm on the couch, I made another phone call. "Natalie," I said, "you told me one time you felt like you still owed these kids something."

"Y-e-ess. Noel, we're doing baths . . ."

"This will only take a minute, I swear, and it's the most important thing in the world."

"If . . . yes . . . but . . ."

"Can you remember what you saw driving home from the pizza place the day William was taken?"

"He wasn't taken, Noel. I forgot him. My memory is all screwed up."

"Humor me." *Humor the authorities who don't think you forgot him.* "Assume, for the sake of argument, you do remember clearly. Think about what you saw. Do you remember anything funky in the rearview mirror when you pulled out of the pizza place?"

"Noel, I can't . . . I don't remember anything at *all* about the rearview mirror. All I remember is we were blocking the pizza guy getting out of the Marine, and he zoomed around us as soon as we got out of the parking lot."

"I . . . thanks."

"Did that help? Because I left Adam with two toddlers in the bathtub, and . . ."

"It helped. Thanks. One more thing, and I swear I'll let you go. Did William *always* hate circles, or was it only after he . . . went missing?"

"It started about then, I guess. It's relatively recent."

After we'd hung up, I asked Trudy, "What do you think?"

"Could be," said Trudy. "Or it could be the cruiser, or nothing. He might have seen a pizza car when he got picked up. We interviewed both drivers working at the time. We can go back over them. I'll look into it more tomorrow."

"Can I ask you something?"

"I may not have an answer."

"Why are you and Darnell still here?" I had asked her this before. She had always been evasive. Although a slightly wider circle of people knew their real roles, Trudy and Darnell were still working largely undercover. "If the June bust took care of your job, why are you still hanging around at the center pretending to be a grad student?"

"Not everything fits yet, Noel. This isn't the movies where there's a perfect slot for every tab, and I don't expect to fully understand all of it ever. But there's still too much unaccounted for. I want those bastards we arrested to spend a long time in prison. I don't want a single one of them to get out on a technicality.

"I'll tell you three things. One: Gary's organization apparently had patchy records, at best, even though everything Natasha has said leads me to think her cousin was meticulous. She believes he had a journal, and I can't find it. It's one thing to bust a guy for *owning* child pornography. It's another to catch him for distributing it. I don't think we've sorted out all the distributors from the owners yet, and I think Gary had lists of which were which.

"Two: we don't know *how* the material was distributed, only how it *wasn't*. We know it came on discs, not how those arrived at people's homes. There's no evidence they were mailed. We can't find any traces of him working via the Internet. We can't be sure, but Gary even appears to have stayed off the dark web, where it can be hard for authorities to go. He kept everything in pen and ink and worked by word of mouth. I have to think he planned to give up his clients to plead himself down if he ever got arrested. But we've gone through his apartment and his mother's house, and there's nothing. He tried to plant pictures in Stan's home and your new building, but we can't find anything else. The last places he was affiliated with were the university and the center, and that leaves us acres of unsearched land. His records haven't shown up yet. He *might* have destroyed them, but I won't accept it until I've looked everyplace.

"Three: He'd *made* us, Noel. He told Natasha we were federal agents. Why did he leave us alone to track him after he found out? Was he hoping to lay low and vanish? Did he figure it would be as dangerous to go after us as leave us alone? Or was he confident for some other reason? He was young to be the head of an organization, and there might have been someone above him. *Someone* still knows exactly who we are, and they want to see what we're doing."

"Don't you think they'll stop acting until you go away?"

"The body at your sanctuary suggests not. The bottom line is we're still here because there's still something to find."

"But . . ."

"Noel, I can't tell you anything else, and it's more than you can tell your family. Let Darnell and me manage your Nana."

"Sure. Good luck."

"I have a job for her, if she's up for some holiday fun."

CHAPTER 24

Dear Nora:

My mother won't admit my children need medication to help moderate their behaviors. Please help.

Caught in the Middle

Dear Noel:

All right *already! I've never missed a dose! And for the record, I've watched them often enough that I'm beginning to see your point.*

Love,
Mom

Trudy humored my family with a halftime highlights version of the last two days. She focused on the heroic rescue of the deputies (by the time she was finished, the center's walk-in fridge sounded more like a deep freeze) and the grisly horror of the dead body. She didn't pull any of those details for the children, all of whom had seen at least the headless body. She also confirmed what we already knew, that the head belonged to Hugh Marsland.

It was old enough news for the kids, and both Sara and William were exhausted enough to fall asleep on the sofa, halfeaten plates in their laps, long before she got to the part about the head anyway. I moved Sara's pizza to the floor but carried the remains of William's syrupy waffle back to the kitchen before it could drizzle temptation everywhere for Mama's dogs.

When I returned, Trudy was dodging a question from Nana, who wanted to know how long it would take to solve the case. "It will take some time," said the agent.

"I watch crime shows," Nana continued. "And the head you and Noel described was all dried out. How did *that* happen in only one day?"

I expected a lecture similar to the one Drew had given me about not taking too much from CSI shows. Instead, Trudy said, "Hugh had Type O blood. The body was Type A. We're still missing *that* head. And its extremities. And we don't have Hugh Marsland's body." Then, before Nana could ask anything else astute, Trudy changed the topic. "Now, Ms. Cox, I need a favor from you."

"A favor? From me?" Nana was instantly suspicious. But also interested. Trudy might have found the path to earning Nana's silence tonight.

"Yes. You're an innocent old woman, frail and easily broken, which makes you perfect for what I have in mind."

"*I'll have you know* . . . Wait. What do you have in mind?" Curiosity was winning out over skepticism. Nana put down a piece of pizza she had been preparing to devour. Her tiny frame belied a voracious appetite. Only Lance could out-eat her when it came to the Marine.

"T-Bow Orrice is notoriously protective of his children."

The pizza won out over curiosity *and* skepticism, and Nana answered around a mouthful of sausage. "Mm?"

"*You* are notoriously protective of *your* family."

"I certainly hope he has no idea who I am."

"He's probably looked Noel and Lance over more thoroughly than social services ever tried to do. He may be better connected to the world through his prison cell than I am through a career in federal law enforcement. In the past, my office has asked Stan in to do something like this, especially since he's dealt with Orrice before. Of course, he's in no condition to drive himself two hours to prison and two hours back home again right now."

"And I am?" The pizza was down again.

"I'll drive you most of the way. You'll go the last few miles on your own."

"What do you want?"

"Two things. I want you to go in there deeply concerned about the danger to your new great-grandchildren. Pretend like you think he might be responsible for it. Get under his skin, but then accept whatever he tells you. He's sure to deny it. He may even act like they aren't his kids. He doesn't want them associated with him, but he wants them alive preserving his line. He hasn't interfered in two other adoptions besides Natasha's, and I have to assume his fury with Terry Dalton lay in the deception. As I understand it, even Stan had to push *hard* to get him to say he was Natasha's father, and then *Orrice* was the one pushing *Stan* to adopt.

"He'll want you out of there as fast as possible as soon as you bring the twins up. But I want him off kilter when you ask him if this guy," Trudy produced a picture, "means anything to him."

"Who is he?" It was a profile shot of a middle-aged white man at a party. He was laughing beside a young blonde, whose smile looked camera-frozen.

"Terry's brother. Charles Dalton," Natasha said flatly. "I should have known him straight off, but he stayed away from me at the gala, and I was kind of distracted by Granddad."

"*Our* gala?" I took the picture and scrutinized it more closely. But the shot wasn't from our party. We hadn't been outdoors. The picture had been zoomed, so little besides his face and that flash of his companion showed. He could have been anywhere with trees.

Trudy cleared her throat in a "let me do the talking" sort of way. "You're going to tell him you met him at a friend's daughter's party," she said to Nana, "and now you've seen him twice in Noel and Lance's neighborhood."

Nana ignored the picture. "But who *is* he?" Trudy didn't say anything. "You're not answering my question." Nana had forgotten her pizza. Lance swiped it.

"No, I'm not." Trudy looked around the assembled circle. "I can't."

"How am I supposed to know if he's telling me the truth or not?"

"You won't. Accept whatever he says and leave. Darnell and I are, at this moment, *this* close to losing our jobs."

"They don't believe her that he's Charles Dalton," Natasha snapped. "They don't believe *me*."

Trudy's shoulders slumped. This was clearly something Tasha had *not* been supposed to say. "We have to go about proving you right carefully just now. We could wind up in cells ourselves. If the two of us up and vanish, you leave town and go fast."

"Jesus. It's your *boss!*" Now Lance put down the pizza he had stolen from Nana. She took it back. "You introduced him at the gala."

"My boss is a woman. And yes, I did introduce you to this man. I won't say more." She looked around the room one more time, and her gaze lingered especially long on Natasha.

Lance studied Trudy's face, as if it might hold answers. "What are you hoping to accomplish?"

"To get your kids out of danger, for one thing."

Nana twitched and stretched until she couldn't hold her silence any longer. "Do I get to wear a wire?"

Trudy pressed her fingers to her temples, much in the way Lance was apt to do when William deliberately got something wrong. "We're doing this . . . I believe the term I want is under cover of under cover."

Nana sighed. "No."

"Yes," said Trudy. "No."

Mama and Daddy gave up their bedroom and slept in a guest bed. While plenty of their rooms were spacious enough for two, none were capacious enough for five, and Mama couldn't roust us from the living room unless we were sleeping where we could see each other. Tasha curled up on Daddy's recliner, and Lance and I bedded down in my parents' king-sized bed with the twins between us. William's pull-ups rarely leaked anymore, and I hoped they wouldn't tonight, even after Mama pointed out Marguerite's water had broken on that bed when she was eight and a half months pregnant with Bryce.

"It survived that. It can deal with anything your little boy can dish out," she assured me.

When Natasha was softly snoring, and I was drifting toward sleep, Lance prodded me across the kids. We crept into the hall and shut the door to a crack. "What? We're going to wake up the dogs if we move around much more."

"What the hell is going on with Trudy?" he whispered back.

"Clearly, she thinks she—"

"No, go back. Why are the feds babysitting us? I don't care how grave or immediate the danger, I doubt they have the resources to dispatch someone to play house with us all the time. Darnell's not much better than Trudy, but he's at least not hanging onto us like . . ."

". . . our nanny? Isn't she supposed to be our nanny?"

"I don't buy it. Not anymore. When she introduced that man at our gala, she presented him like he was a superior."

"Are you sure he's the man we met at the gala? Was the picture taken there? We didn't go outdoors."

"I can't tell. All I know, Noel, is something is seriously wrong here. I don't want your Nana going up there alone."

"After everything she's done for us, you can't seriously think Trudy is some kind of threat. I trust her. She's already told us more than she should. We need to let her do her job and try to live our lives right now.

"She's not going to kidnap Nana. If she wanted to take William, she could have done it. If she wanted to take *Natasha,* she could have done it. If we weren't completely safe with her, she'd have killed us all and hidden the bodies. She has your class schedule. She's babysitting us. Would you . . ."

"Noel, somebody's out there." Natasha's hand shot out the bedroom door.

"You had a nightmare. If somebody were out there, Mama's dogs would be . . ." The living room erupted in a fury of yelping.

"You guys woke me up," she explained, "and I heard the wheels on the gravel. I crawled over to see. Look. There's somebody resting his head on his arms on top of a car." She pointed to the window.

"What's going on out there?" Mama called. "Noel, is everything all right?"

"There's somebody out there," Natasha called from the hall. It was all too loud. The twins couldn't possibly sleep much longer.

"Out where?" Mama shouted. "In our *driveway*? Isn't it a little late for . . . ohh."

Daddy shouted, "Should I get the gun, Lenore?"

Lance glanced toward me, and I rolled my eyes and shook my head. Daddy did *not* own a gun. The full moon illuminated the figure at the car, who had not moved since Lance and I first looked out.

"Now you people see here," Daddy bellowed. "I'm seventy-two years old, and I need my sleep. You are seriously interfering with my *lifestyle.*" The front door banged open, and Daddy stormed onto the porch holding something that looked, from my admittedly limited vantage point, like a shotgun.

"I thought you said . . ." Lance glanced back and forth between my father and the still-sleeping twins. I knew what he was thinking. *A gun? How accessible is it? Why could he get it out so fast? How dare he . . . with children in the house! How long has he had it?*

"Now you turn around slowly and put your hands up in the air."

The man, and it was a man, stood slowly, lifting first his head, then his arms. He turned so we could see him clearly. "I'm sorry, Mr. Rue. I didn't know where else to go. I can't . . . I'm not going to hurt anybody, I swear. I knew Lance and Noel were here, and I need to talk to them. Travis is gone, and I can't find him, sir."

"Bryan! Daddy, don't fire." I pelted around the corner into the living room.

"Easy, Noel. I see who it is." Daddy lowered his gun slowly and set it lengthwise inside the door. It was a broom handle. He'd gone out there to bluff a potential killer with the broom handle he used to pop the latch when he needed to open one set of particularly high attic stairs.

"I didn't know where else to go," Bryan repeated. "Can I come in? Your detective friend is looking for him, but I'm scared to death."

Has Drew gotten any *sleep in the last two days?* "In," I told him. "Mama, we need coffee."

"*You* need coffee," Lance corrected me. "I need sleep. Wake me up in four hours and we'll trade."

"Travis called at nine in the morning," Bryan said, "and we set up a lunch date . . ."

"How often do you actually get out on those dates, Bryan?"

"I don't know. Once in a while. Anyway, he never cancelled,

but when I got there at noon, the Bio Science building was crawling with cops, and they wouldn't let me in. He never answered my texts, but then I thought he was caught up in whatever was going on inside. Then he didn't come home for dinner, and his phone stopped ringing altogether, like he'd turned it off or the battery had run down. I expected the police to put me off when I called him in missing . . . I mean, he's an adult man, and the cops have been known to make assumptions. But your detective friend was out at my house in fifteen minutes. And that's got me more scared than Travis going missing in the first place."

Although Bryan was a family friend, I only considered him close in a professional sense. It would have been surprising for him to show up unannounced at my parents' house, except he knew about today's interview from Travis. And thanks to Hugh Marsland's head and the chair's panicked response to it, it seemed like everyone in town knew where Lance and I were staying. Dr. Prescott had all but shrieked every detail of *any* conversation he overheard for the *world* to hear. He wouldn't say why the head distressed him so much more than the rest of us, but, as Drew muttered, the man gave a good impression of someone who'd been threatened. All the more reason for us to move on quickly.

In all the chaos, I hadn't seen whether or not Travis was even at work, which was the real reason Bryan had come here . . . to pick my brain. He had tried several other professors, all at more decent hours, then driven sequentially to places Travis might have gone. We were his last-ditch effort, and we didn't have anything to offer him, though I could, and did, to Trudy's irritation, give a firsthand account of the afternoon.

This he requested repeatedly, as if by searching my interpretation of the event, he could somehow project Travis into the background of the conference room. Lance had taken the smarter route. I wasn't swapping him out for rest in any four hours. I was going now.

"I've been up for twenty-two hours," I finally told Bryan. "I am going to bed." I left him with Mama, who was getting a pair of pajamas my brother-in-law had forgotten here. He creaked up the stairs to a guest room as I crawled in beside my husband, who had a protective arm thrown over both twins.

I woke up exactly three hours later to the sight of my own watch dangling upside down in one eye. "William is school timed," a pleasant voice informed me.

"William, say 'I am school-timed' . . . crap, no, say 'I am ready for' . . . never mind. It's too early. Go back to sleep."

He crammed the watch more urgently against my eyelid. "You are late."

I pushed the watch far enough back to read the numbers. He was right. I was late. I didn't want to take him to school at *all*, given the night we'd had, but, as Lance had pointed out yesterday, he was probably safer there than anyplace we could be. Mrs. Grim or no, I almost wished Sara could go, too.

"Mrs. Grim!" I jumped up and dumped William on the bed. Lance had arranged a meeting with the principal and teacher from hell for us this morning before school. We were supposed to be there in fourteen minutes.

Unlike the job interview, we wouldn't be pulling this one out at the last second. Lance had gotten far more sleep than I had. I jabbed him in the ribs. "*You* call up and reschedule."

"Mmm. What?"

"We're missing our appointment at Sara's school. *You* can call and tell them. William is school timed. *I'm* rolling him out the door."

"*Roll!*" William beamed and matched deed to word, tumbling out of bed and across the floor.

We were leaving the kitchen when Lance stumbled out of the

bedroom. "No, I'm coming," he said. "They're waiting for us. Mrs. Grim's students have art for the first part of the morning. This is her free period today." We did not wait for an escort and received irritated texts from our babysitters as we pulled out of the driveway. I ignored them. Lance waited until *after* we had dropped William to drop the next bomb. "I had to use Chandra Evans's name to make it happen."

She scared me even more than Mrs. Grim. Barely three days after her first surprise visit, she had dropped by again unannounced. Merry should have been making these visits all along, and Chandra was making up for lost time. We hadn't expected her so soon after our first meeting, so she had caught us in a hurried morning, complete with pudding on the ceiling, which she pointedly ignored. The *rest* of the house was gleaming, for once, Stan having sent in a service the next working day after the "I'll be back to check on your housekeeping" trip had ended. In theory, we had passed muster in this regard, as she didn't refer to it again. But I didn't plan to cancel Stan's service until the twins' adoption was final.

Chandra had toured our house, nodding and barely speaking, and I could easily imagine her finding concerns in the future. She wrote a series of notes on the yellow legal pad she carried around like a shield, when we responded to her clipped questions. But then, when she was leaving, she said, "Don't hesitate to use my name to open doors for your children. I have good connections, and we all have these kids' best interests at heart. I have met Sara's teacher before, and I don't like your daughter's situation at all."

The last part, "I don't like your daughter's situation at all," still chilled me. Everything in Chandra's demeanor, from the rigid body language to the clipped sentences, set off my warning bells. Was it only the school situation Chandra Evans disliked?

Apparently, Lance only heard the words. He had used her name.

"Lovely," I grumped. "Why couldn't we reschedule?"

"Because Sara is morose about this. We need it *behind* her, and the next time they could come up with for us to meet was after she's supposed to go back to school."

"You're right. It's better done and over. We need to *tell* Chandra we used her name at some point."

"I already did." Lance piloted the minivan beyond the bus line and its flow of disembarking students. He parked us in the visitor's slots on the school's other side. "I believe that's her pulling in behind us."

CHAPTER 25

Dear Nora:

Please settle a disagreement for me. My husband wants to jab a meat thermometer into the Christmas turkey. He knows there's already one in there. The button pops up when the meat is done! I hate the unsightly presentation of a piece of metal when my perfect bird comes out of the oven!

Vexed

Dear Vexed:

Good Lord! Why don't you serve up some Cream of Botulism Soup and be done with it! You ought to know those plastic thermometers can be unreliable. And it isn't like your guests see the bird straight out of the oven anyway. Use the thermometer. I'm enclosing the number for poison control in case you ignore me.

Nora

"I'm glad you had the sense to involve me," Chandra informed us as we walked toward the building, "even if it was at the last minute." She had spared only a glance for our rumpled jeans. She had yet to meet me with my hair done, and I rarely wore makeup anyway. "So many foster and adopting families forget the importance of a social worker. They view us as the enemy."

How was I supposed to tell her we weren't sure which side of the ally/enemy line she stood on? "I suppose a little more notice

274

would be nice next time," I said instead.

"I'll take what I can get."

Somehow, our tête-à-tête had grown to include the school counselor, Norma Anderssen, as well. It was like we were playing a game of one-upmanship, each side throwing in a new authority to balance out the last. Lance had added me when he learned Mrs. Grim was inviting the principal. Then the principal added the guidance counselor when we dragged in Chandra at the last second. "If anybody calls 'red rover' or 'cheese stands alone,' I'm out of here."

"Hm?" Chandra looked back and cocked an eyebrow.

"Nothing."

In Principal Mark Jacoby's office, Mrs. Grim (I could only think of her in Sara's terms) set forth our daughter's offenses. In addition to the cupcake incident, she had a laundry list of complaints ranging from an unwillingness to sit quietly in her seat to refusing to play with others at recess. "She's so *stubborn*. When she's on the playground, she sits off by herself and makes rock piles."

I had watched Sara organize rocks like William organized his trucks, and it brought her obvious pleasure. "What's wrong with that?"

"She isn't *interacting*. She can hardly expect to have friends if she won't play with anyone." Mrs. Grim's expression and tone suggested this should have been obvious. "And it embarrasses her."

"How?"

"Last year, she filled her jeans so completely with pebbles her pocket ripped out, and she had stones running down her leg all day."

"That was *kindergarten*!" Lance protested.

The principal agreed. "I think it's probably sufficient to discuss the present academic year."

"She still does it! I've told her half a hundred times to stop picking up shiny things, but she won't stop. She'll collect anything from jewelry that's fallen apart to speckled plastic, and she gets as grimy as you can imagine without even playing. If she got so dirty from something reasonable like a game of tag, I might understand, but picking up junk? And then she has to touch *everything,* whether her hands are clean or not."

Sara's most grievous offense, however, was what Ms. Grim called her "smart mouth." "She gives me sass nearly every day. She asked permission to go to the girls' room the other day. She was gone so long I sent Shelly Anne to go find her. Do you know what Sara said when I asked why she hadn't come back?"

"What?" I felt like the straight man being set up for a particularly bad comedy routine. I wanted to take this vituperative woman by the shoulders and shout, "She's autistic! She's barely *seven*!" Instead, I tucked my hands under my thighs so no one could see me clenching my fists.

"She said, 'I didn't know what to do when I got done, because you only gave me permission to go *to* the bathroom, not to come back.' And don't you know three other kids have tried it since then."

"But she probably *meant* it!" My nails dug into upholstery, as if that could root me to the spot.

"She's never needed permission to come back from the bathroom before."

"How does she ask? What does she say? No, I'll tell you, because she raises her hand to ask permission at home instead of following her body's instincts and using the bathroom *without* permission. She says, 'Can I go potty and be right back after I'm done?' She's crafted that sentence, honed it, so she covers everything, the going, the coming, the using of the toilet. I bet the only reason she doesn't ask to flush is because there are big reminder signs in those first-grade stalls!" I had hovered over one of those child-sized squatty potties on the Day of the Cupcake.

"Stop," said Chandra. "This conversation isn't productive."

But Mrs. Grim couldn't stop. "She only gets recess one day in three, and she tells me at least once a week how boring my lessons are."

This time, Lance interrupted her tirade. "Why haven't we been told any of this?" The child we knew at home was only similar to this one. Outspoken and opinionated, yes, but not anything close to what I would call defiant. We knew about Sara's inability to sit still or be quiet. These, along with the running in the halls, were the reasons given when Ms. Grim or the principal called us. I had guessed, but not been told, she struggled to socialize with the other children. But until she called her classmate a "floop-de-dooping dummyhead," we had not known she argued outright.

Before Ms. Grim could either answer or continue, Norma-the-guidance-counselor jumped into the ensuing silence. "Our speech therapist has suggested a social skills group on several occasions."

"Great," I told her. "Where do we sign up?"

"Speech therapy isn't in her IEP," Mrs. Grim complained.

"Yes, it is," I said. Was she missing her time with the speech therapist, then?

"I believe Dr. Rue is correct, but if it isn't, we'll schedule an emergency IEP meeting and amend it," said Chandra. Had she just used my title on purpose?

Norma shook her head. "It's not a service the school offers. Our speech and occupational therapists travel between the three *non-charter* elementary schools in this county all week long. You'd have to arrange to participate in one privately."

"Why does the school have to have a therapist to teach something? Couldn't you bring in a good teacher or someone from the community who knows how to get kids to be nice to each other?" I asked.

"Who? What kind of certifications would this person have? How would we fund the program?" Norma's eyes showed nothing of her emotions, so I couldn't gauge if she was being sincere or sarcastic. "Our resources are strained to capacity already, and I don't hear any qualified volunteers stepping forward."

I thought of Natalie but said nothing. The woman was overwhelmed.

With the atmosphere slightly less venomous, Chandra returned her attention to the real purpose, managing Sara's "unruly," to use Mrs. Grim's term, behavior. "Dr. Rue, Dr. Lakeland," she *was* drawing deliberate attention to the degrees, "I hear you saying you have received inadequate communication from the school regarding your daughter's behavior." It wasn't a question.

"Yes," said Lance.

"Ms. Anderssen, have *you* been informed of Sara's behavior?"

"I . . . well, some. I was aware of the social problems, but this is the first time I've heard . . . some of the more specific concerns about her interaction with her teacher." Norma looked everywhere *but* at Principal Jacoby.

"And what I hear *you* saying, Mrs. Grisby, is you are unable to manage the behavior of a child with special needs."

"No, that's not what I . . ."

Chandra ignored her. "I have taken the time to read Sara's file. Her former foster mother was extremely detailed. She documented some ten efforts on her part to have Sara transferred to another class both during the last school year and before this one began. All of them were either rejected or ignored." She stared an unspoken question at the principal.

"It wouldn't have made a bit of difference. The child is out of control," Mrs. Grim complained.

"If we transferred one child to a different class because some parent disliked the teacher, we'd have to do it for *every* child," the principal snapped.

"Mrs. Forrester's notes point out concerns about classroom management and Mrs. Grisby's experience with special needs children. She specifically remarks about how her concerns have been consistently 'blown off' by your front office. That sounds like a woman trying to get her child an adequate education to me. In my opinion, Sara should be transferred to a different class upon her return from suspension."

The principal opened his mouth to speak again, but Ms. Anderssen said, "A word?" to him. She jerked her thumb toward the door.

Norma and Mr. Jacoby held a hurried conference in the hall, and when they returned, he said. "Very well. When Sara returns, she will be allowed to join Miss Henderson's class, contingent upon Miss Henderson's approval. Should her behavior improve, any academic penalties incurred from the suspension will be expunged from her record."

Mrs. Grisby stalked out to use the remainder of her planning period, and the rest of us only spoke a little while longer before the meeting ended.

A plump woman in a tan coat whose olive skin and soft accent suggested India or Pakistan bustled up to us before we could depart. "Are you Noel Lakeland?" she asked.

"Rue." I plastered on a smile I hoped was polite. Even before we'd gotten married, people assumed Lance and I shared a last name. Occasionally, they turned him into a Rue, but mostly, I was dubbed Lakeland. I had been known to splutter "Rue, Rue, Rue, Rue, Rue!" at mail carriers and acquaintances. I tried to keep my tone light for strangers or others who might have an excuse for not knowing better, but my smile concealed smoldering anger.

"Sorry. I ought to get it right. My husband and I don't have the same last name either, but I still mess it up for everybody else."

Her answer disarmed me, but I remained wary. "Did you need something?"

"I'm Agrima Bhatia, Mrs. Grisby's room mother." *Why does the name sound familiar?* "My daughter, Julie Carver, was the one who helped Sara pass out cupcakes the other day. Can I walk with you?"

"Of course." Wariness dissolved. Reluctant or not, the Carver daughter had been kind to Sara where others had been cold.

"I'm worried for your daughter," she said quickly. "Mrs. Grisby is convinced Sara doesn't want to play with the other children, but I think she does not know how."

"She has Asperger's syndrome, you know."

"That makes sense. And kids can be as bad as the mafia when it comes to loyalties and ostracism."

"I appreciate your daughter's help the other day. It's not easy to be different."

"She's a good daughter. Every day, I am proud of her beyond belief." She stated this in a tone of deep sincerity, not as a braggart might, but as if she had been given an extraordinary and unexpected gift. "She would like very much to hold a playdate. And that is her speaking, not me. I do not control Julie's friendships."

I threw my arms around her shoulders. I couldn't help it. I loved her more with every word. She patted my back and we went on. Once we got outside, she reached her main point. "Here's the thing," she went on. "I've been extremely worried about Sara coming back to face that lot. Mrs. Grisby doesn't see what goes on right under her own nose, and she only pays a certain amount of attention to me. Julie and I haven't heard the children say anything specific, or I'd have put a stop to it, but

I'm sure those kids are plotting some kind of revenge. And where Sara got in trouble for creaming John, bad behavior toward her from the others won't even be noticed."

"She's moving to Miss Henderson's class."

"Excellent news. This is a huge relief. But it still leaves complicated territory. She needs to stick around the recess monitors for a couple of weeks. Julie and her friends said she can sit with them at lunch."

"Thank you. Thank you so much. I . . . honestly, I wouldn't have expected so much generosity from a total stranger."

"Julie's a good daughter. So is Sara. I grew up bullied. I know what it looks like. And Sara, she's like a bully target, you know? I don't want to see her get hurt."

Suddenly, the name clicked. Bhatia. "Wait. I do know you. I thought your first name was Ruby."

"That was a long time ago. My parents tried to Americanize me so I wouldn't stick out so badly. But I couldn't help it. Between my accent, my skin, my clothes, and my culture shock, I might as well have had a target painted on me too."

"You were in my sister Marguerite's class. I'm so sorry! The Ruby Touch! I can't remember . . ." But of course I played the Ruby Touch game. I was lying to myself if I thought otherwise. She would have been in second grade the year the whole school passed around "the Ruby touch" like it was leprosy. It became a game of tag, where the "it" kid tagged a victim and shouted, "You've got the Ruby Touch, pass it on before you're gone!"

"It was a long time ago now," Ruby . . . no . . . Agrima said.

"But it was *horrible!*"

"We cannot change the past, Noel, only learn from it. Do you know, I wanted so badly to fit in that *I* played that silly game? I thought if I made fun of myself, the other children would accept me."

"Where did you go?" I couldn't remember a second year of

the Ruby Touch game. She must not have returned for third grade.

"My father teaches at the university, in the Religious Studies department. We moved to Columbus and he commuted to work for a long time. My parents only moved back here when Kenny and I got married and I came back myself. I think they expected to be sheltering me again, you know. But things are quite a bit better now. Julie doesn't face the kind of prejudice I did. And she's not the only child in the school looking out for bullies. Many of the kids here are quite kind." She smiled warmly. "I should be getting back to class. The students have reading after art, and I help Mrs. Grisby break them into groups once a week so the slower learners have a prayer. Take care now. I'll try to keep an eye on your Sara when she gets back."

She walked away, leaving me rattled. Was her past the future my daughter faced in this school? Or could she help me change Sara's position? I had such good memories of elementary school. I loved school and my friends. But how could Sara love a place where she was nothing but a victim? No wonder she hated to come.

"What happened back there in the principal's office?" Lance asked Chandra.

"I said the magic word."

" 'Doctor'?" he guessed. "I thought the magic word was 'please'." Nobody had been saying "please" or "thank you" in there.

"In education, the magic word is 'adequate.' "

"Adequate?"

"You have to be careful never to ask for an *equal* education for your child. The state is only required to provide her with an *adequate* education. The school system will instantly fall back to the position that you've asked for too much if you want your child's education to be equal."

"Is that what Ms. Anderssen was telling the principal?" I asked.

Chandra laughed, a quiet, humorless sound. "Ms. Anderssen was probably reminding him why I share a nickname with Margaret Thatcher."

"I didn't know . . ."

"I know what the children call me behind my back, Noel. But to be truthful, I'm rather proud of it. Nearly all of us have nicknames from the kids who have been in the system long enough. Some of them can be quite derogatory." *Orangutan Lady. Merry, Merry, Quite Contrary.* "Iron Lady suits me perfectly. Going up against me is like beating your head against an anvil."

"Ah." We had reached the cars. I hoped I would not be going up against her soon.

"I'll tell you another thing. Sara needs to be at William's school. It's much better geared to give her any kind of education at all. She has the grades."

"Too bad she lost the lottery."

"Actually, there's an appeals process for families of multiple children, when one child is accepted but the other isn't, as long as GPA isn't an issue."

"Shit," said Lance.

"Most people don't know about it," she reassured him. "And those who do often choose not to draw attention to their families by applying. But if you're willing to complete the necessary paperwork, I can . . ."

"Noel, don't open your door."

Too late. My hand was already on the handle, and I was listening more closely to Chandra than to my husband. Moreover, I wasn't paying attention to the way the car was jiggling. To make matters worse, I had never adjusted to the ease with which the minivan and convertible opened in contrast to the primate-mobile. I didn't merely open the door, I threw it wide with all my force.

Travis Kendal, in his trademark plaid shirt, spilled into the parking lot, trussed up like a Thanksgiving turkey and thrashing like a caged animal.

CHAPTER 26

Dear Nora:

I'm failing algebra. I do okay on homework, because my prof's computer program tells me the right answer when I plug in the wrong one. I just type in the wrong thing for everything so I can turn in the right answers and get a good grade. But the exams don't tell me whether I'm right or wrong, and the prof grades whatever I submit without giving me a chance to fix the errors. What do I do?

Non-plussed

Dear Non:
Study.

Nora

"I'm a scout mom." Norma Anderssen followed Chandra back outside. "I always have a lighter, a knife, and a corkscrew handy."

While I called for emergency services, Lance grabbed several times at the cloth grocery bag knotted over Travis's head, but Travis wouldn't be still. Lance finally got Travis's attention as Chandra returned from reporting the emergency to the school. "Travis, it's Lance Lakeland. Cool down and let me get this off of you."

Travis said something incomprehensible as the bag ripped free.

"And in case you're wondering," Norma continued, "you can

use a corkscrew for lots of things besides opening wine. *Lots.*"
From her car, she had retrieved a giant pocket knife, the sort of
thing a school would never have allowed indoors. It took a few
yanks for her to pry it open, making me doubt its efficacy in an
emergency, but it served its purpose now. Travis grew still and
let Lance saw away at the ropes binding his body.

"The school guidance counselor . . . uh . . . found something
to cut him free," I reported to the emergency dispatcher. "But
his face is going to be harder. He's got a goose egg on the back
of his head and duct tape wound around his mouth and scalp."

Travis kept trying to talk, urgently grunting the whole time
Lance released his bonds. When he was finally free, he rubbed
his wrists then clawed at the duct tape, and Lance set down the
knife to help him.

After the tape was dislodged and jammed under his chin, he
took two deep breaths. "Noel, I caught you in time," he babbled
in a hoarse voice. "The chair is trying to tank your interview. I
saw him putting rotten fish in the conference room this morning. I wanted to text, but he's suspicious I know, and . . ." Suddenly, he stopped, breathing heavily. He touched the swollen
knot above the duct tape in his hair and flinched away from his
own fingers. "Ow," he said.

"Head between the knees, don't pass out on me, Buddy."
Lance prodded Travis into a semblance of the appropriate
posture.

Travis shook him off. "It's not today anymore, is it? No,
that's stupid. Of course, today is always today, and tomorrow is
. . . never mind. The point I'm after . . . I guess I've forgotten."
He brooded a few seconds, with his chin on his knees. "Lost
track of time, I think. That's what I meant. I haven't been able
to see much. How long ago *was* today? Damn . . . I mean . . ."

"I know what you mean." Lance hunkered beside our col-
league. "Yesterday. Noel's interview was yesterday. You should

try to relax."

"What happened to you?"

Lance shot Chandra a glower that suggested she shouldn't have inquired. The dispatcher and I weren't talking now, but the woman remained on the line, holding my hand across the miles until emergency services arrived.

"I don't know. I smelled something heinous and looked out in the corridor. The chair was carrying a picnic-sized cooler into the conference room. I almost offered to help him with it, but . . . you know how many stupid chores I do for him already. I hid at my desk. But something still stank to high heaven. I followed the smell to the conference room and found that cooler under the table with the lid half off. It was full of dead fish. Raw dead fish. Disgusting. I dumped the whole thing in the trash and put the trash in the hall. I know he saw me do it, because he came along to ask about the odor not a whole minute later. Ha! As if he didn't know where it came from.

"I said I was cleaning out the fridge for Noel's interview. As if he didn't know! But he couldn't exactly call me on it, could he? He told me to take it to the Dumpster. I did, and I was standing down in front of the Dumpster. I had my phone out to text you, but then, nothing. Then, I was tied up and screaming. I don't know."

As soon as the ambulance arrived, I hung up with the dispatcher and texted Bryan. "Travis found. Doing okay. Head bump. Talking. Meet him at Ironweed General." Then Lance and I rode down to see Drew and spent a long time answering questions and signing reports. We finished long past lunchtime, and only after several flurries of texting with Natasha and my mother.

Mama is even more of a texting neophyte than I am. For the first six months of owning a cell phone, she only took pictures. Answering the machine was a catastrophic adventure, and nobody ever knew if she'd pick up or forward the call through mystic means to another relative. Texting required her to use her phone's tiny keyboard, pay attention to its autocorrect, *and* be concise, none of which were easy for her. I could sympathize with the first two, at least.

Lenore Rue: Do you ever forgive this child?

Noel Rue: What? What happened? Do you mean Sara or Nasturtium?

Lenore Rue: Lunch! She acts like she never saw food in her entire life. I found her half a pound of spaghetti noodles, then she still wanted desert!

Natasha Oeschle: She means feed, Noel, not forgive. She's asking because Sara's all the sudden way hungry.

Noel Rue: She's usually picky.

Natasha Oeshchle: I said so, too. But she's eating broccoli so your Mom will make cookies. I think she skipped breakfast to play dress up.

Noel Rue: Broccoli?! You got her to eat bronchitis, Mama?

Lenore Rue: All it needs is cheese.

Lenore Rue: Relax. It's organic. And none of the cookie ingredients concern palm oil. I know how you furl about that. And Tuba is eating some, too.

Natasha Oeschle: Hey, I want the cookies! It's not a bad deal.

Noel Rue: Carry on, then. It sounds like you have everything under control.

Lenore Rue: Well u see hours understudy project.

Noel Rue: What? Mama, I can't make that one out.

Natasha Oeschle: I think it's supposed to be wait until you see our upstairs project. But she's in the cabinets now. Do you want me to ask?

Noel Rue: Don't. If it's upstairs, it's seamstress stuff, and I don't want to find out she has Sara running her Sergei.

Natasha Oeschle: The serger? That's *my* job. Sara's in charge of the sewing machine.

Noel Rue: WHAT?

Natasha Oeschle: j/k

Noel Rue: WHAT?

Natasha Oeschle: Just kidding. Okay, she's got a bunch of stuff out. I think we're on to baking.

"It's like one of those word substitution games," said Lance, reading over my shoulder.

"Only harder to understand." I tucked the phone away, but it buzzed immediately. The conversation I exchanged with Trudy was more concise.

Trudy Jackson: All's well here. Don't leave the police station without Darnell.

Noel Rue: As if he'd let us.

"And to think I'd never even sent a line of text before June," I grumbled, stowing the phone for a second time. Once more, it buzzed. "Seriously?" I ignored it.

Drew was still talking on the phone to Darnell, who was en route. "While we're waiting, I'm going to see if the vending machines have anything edible," Lance said.

"Did you check in on William?"

"He's fine. Nothing unusual at all about his day, unless you count crabbiness."

"That's something." Now the phone didn't buzz, it outright rang. "For pity's sake! What?"

"Noel, is this a bad time?" It was Christian.

"It's as good as any, I guess."

"Did you get my text?"

Did you get my text? I mouthed the words back at him, glad he couldn't see me rolling my eyes. "No, Christian. I didn't. What did you need?"

"Hang up and look at it." He clicked off, precluding me from a reply, because he knew both that I was irked and that I didn't know how to talk and text simultaneously.

"Lance, Lance, look at this!"

My husband was halfway down the hall in his quest for edibles, but he came back at a run. "What's wrong?"

"No, nothing, *look*!"

Someone had rigged up a tablet computer, and Lucy was pressed against the mesh of her enclosure, fingers poking for it, every bit the excited kid.

"Who gave her a computer to pull apart?" I called Christian back after giving Lance the barest of glimpses. He had, after all, been copied on the message.

"The machine never goes all the way in, and it comes out of reach when she's through with it, but it's helped her feel less isolated from the rest of the group. Today's the first time with the baby, but . . ."

"The baby?"

"Didn't you see what she was looking at?"

"I saw the top of her head, the side of her face, and a screen, Christian."

"She's chatting with Sabine about her baby." Sabine was the orangutan who had become caretaker to Lucy's infant, since the hand-reared Lucy had no idea how to parent. "We weren't even sure she knew it existed. But they're talking about the baby!"

"What are they saying?"

"I don't know. There's mostly pointing and waving, but they've both signed 'baby' a couple of times." Until now, Lucy's socialization had been going slowly, much as Chuck's would have been doing if we had been housing him in appropriate social conditions. Without company, he was lonely and bored, probably a large part of the reason he kept getting out. (If, indeed, he *was* getting out. Did the people who tied up the deputies have orangutan boots?) Looking at Lucy with the computer reminded me how much we needed to remedy Chuck's situation.

"I wonder if we could get something like that. Maybe she and Chuck could chat."

Before I could get too caught up in discussion about the center, Drew joined us in the hall. "You two eat yet?"

"Gotta go, Christian. We'll talk later."

"We hadn't had time to peruse your fine wares." Lance waved in the direction he was hoping to find vending machines.

"Not much besides stale candy and weak coffee," said Drew. "Let's grab a bite down at the Marine."

"We're supposed to be waiting for Darnell," said Lance. "He's on his way."

"And I'm feeling squeamish about the Marine right now."

"We're waiting, he won't be long. What's wrong with the Marine, Noel?"

I told him about William's overreaction to the delivery guy's car, my theory that one of the drivers might have been involved in his kidnapping seeming sillier every second. "I told Trudy," I finally concluded. "But I doubt she's had any time to do anything about it."

"Huh," said Drew. "Pepperoni pizzas and circle-dot cars. Sounds pretty far-fetched, but that's the thing I'm getting the hang of with your son."

"That he's far-fetched?" Lance demanded.

"No." Drew sounded surprised. "That he's got a whole lot to say, but we need to learn how to listen. Where do you want lunch, Noel? My treat."

Sara wasn't the only one who skipped her morning meal. "Let's eat at the breakfast chain on the bypass. I haven't had food since last night, and I don't care if it's good for me or the

291

environment, I think I could murder an overly processed cheese omelet right now."

"Here's what we're looking at." We were seated in a booth near a window while waitresses and customers buzzed past. I wouldn't have imagined a breakfast chain could be so popular for the afternoon meal, but we were far from the only tardy lunch diners this afternoon. The moment I sat, my energy drained away. Throughout the meal, I yawned uncontrollably.

Darnell had requested a children's menu and some crayons, and the befuddled hostess had provided them. Now, he had flipped the menu over and drawn a waxy red circle on it. "We've got at least two groups of individuals." He added another circle intersecting the first. "Possibly more."

"How do you know?" I tried to remember the last time I had functioned on so little sleep. It had to have been grad school. Maybe undergrad. Or maybe never. College came with all-night study sessions that concluded with bleary classes and parties that only ended when I had to be at work the next morning. But it was only ever a day or two of exhaustion at a time. I hadn't slept soundly in months, and I felt as if I wouldn't ever truly do so again in my life. Words and ideas were bypassing me without ever connecting to anything concrete to help me recall them later.

Darnell had slept as little as Lance and I had recently. Probably less. Yet he was drawing diagrams and whispering ferociously about things we should not be discussing in the open. "Why are we even talking about this?" I wanted to crawl in a bed, *any* bed, before I simply fell over.

I could tell I had interrupted him. "I'll get there. As I said, the clearest indicator we're dealing with the two groups is the behavior we're seeing. Your head detective disappeared from a conference in DC, his head came back here in one location, and his body is still missing." *Why did you have to say that as the eggs got to the table, Darnell?*

Darnell ignored his food and doodled squares into the places where the two circles overlapped. "Two men have been dismembered. But your deputies were *not*. They were, in fact, hidden in a place where they were all but guaranteed to be found when the sanctuary opened in the morning. The biology department secretary was bound and abandoned in Lance and Noel's van. William was taken but not substantially harmed. All of these people were, in fact, ultimately either released or able to escape.

"Plenty of killers of adults would hesitate to kill a child, and someone who kills once might hesitate to do it again, depending on circumstances. But we have two murders here. Someone delivered that head to the biology department when the secretary was kidnapped. Someone murdered the person on the sanctuary grounds. Someone isn't squeamish at all about murder. Someone else is. Two groups. At least. Working together.

"We have some common denominators. William is probably Natasha's biological brother. Natasha was living with *you* at the time. Someone was killed on the sanctuary grounds. Where *you* work. The head was dumped in the conference room where *you* gave a job presentation, Noel. Your department secretary was abandoned in *your* car. You're sure you don't remember locking it for certain?"

"I don't remember anything for certain." Drew had asked me this a dozen times. My window was not jimmied; my door wasn't scraped. The door was unlocked with a key, if it hadn't been left unlocked. And I was so tired I couldn't remember.

"And we're talking about this in a restaurant because it's the first place you've stood still all day that isn't swarming with your family. They *aren't* cleared to know all this. Trudy and I don't know who we can trust. She's with them right now, because if one of us *isn't* with you, we don't know if you're safe. Your friend Drew here checks out, and unless he killed his own boss and disabled his own men, I think he's worth the risk."

"I'm honored."

Darnell patted my hand, and I flinched away from him as strongly as Natasha ever had from me. "Sorry," he said.

"It's not you." But it *was* him. It was him, and it was Trudy, and Art, and Ace, and even Stan and Gert, who were about as peripherally related as it was possible to be.

"The federal government doesn't send in agents to babysit bystanders, Noel. Trudy and I have been free to help you on our own time while we waited to make progress. When we were left in place here in June, we had vague instructions to investigate for additional suspects. When we didn't find anything in three weeks, we should have been recalled. In July, our boss was doing everything she could do to buy us time at the sanctuary. Before Art was killed, back when we thought we had an animal smuggling ring, the higher-ups didn't want to waste limited resources on a case they considered small scale. And after, they considered the job done and wanted us moved to other cases.

"But our boss has been told to leave us in place, then told the opposite. And now nobody is saying anything. Suddenly, *nobody* wants us moved. We had begun to think there were people above our boss who wanted us relocated because they *knew* what we might find.

"But when she stopped getting heat, we began to question ourselves. Natasha identifying that man as Charles Dalton was the last proof of our original theory. We were sure we had been betrayed by a federal officer, and we could prove it. But when Trudy took the evidence to our boss with Natasha, the woman was furious. She said, 'All the work I've done to let you stay down there, and you're chasing some conspiracy theory?' "

"Stop." I understood his reasoning. Not about the betrayal and such. That floated through my muddled brain in a fog. It was the common denominators. I was studying his overlapping circles and the things in their center.

"Noel, you . . ."

"We're not the *only* people connected to both the sanctuary and the college. Travis said the department chair dumped a bunch of rotten fish in the conference room before my interview. But the *chair* claimed Travis hadn't been in the office yesterday, and nobody else could remember seeing him. So nobody missed him until Bryan started asking questions later."

Drew rubbed a hand along his jaw. "Dr. Prescott still swears he didn't know Travis was there. But you're right, the man's strung like a guitar right now. I doubt he has the physical strength to disable Travis or move him unconscious without help, if that's what you're suggesting."

"He does the weakling routine," said Lance. "But don't get taken in. Check out the picture on his desk. He's holding up a prize marlin on some charter boat. He's got the muscles."

"And he dislikes me and disapproves of Travis. He hates the idea of my being promoted. He's been in the department as long as Art had been, and he loathes the sanctuary. When the detective's head fell out of that cabinet, the chair is the one who went nuts screaming he'd be next. *He* knows something."

"Okay," said Darnell. "We'll talk to him. Maybe he can help us. But listen to me. I wasn't finished. The person we're ultimately looking for is a man posing as a federal agent. The man you met at the gala and the one in the picture Trudy showed you are *not* the same person, though we thought they were. The person you met was Liam Metcalf, but the picture is of Charles Dalton, who has been imitating him for some time."

"Ohhh." Even in my sleepy state, I understood the importance of Charles Dalton's name. This was Terry Dalton's brother. The man Natasha had been afraid of ever since we found her necklace.

"Liam's ID was taken at your gala. He had it replaced without much fanfare, because the monkey stole something from everybody and destroyed much of it. Liam found his wallet at the end of the chase, but his things were scattered and his badge was gone. My boss asked me to check the monkey's cage in the quarantine area to see what it had, whether it might have taken a license or badge, and it looked like it could have done it. I don't think so now."

"The monkey didn't take it?" My head hurt. It ached with the weight of exhaustion. "It had dozens of things. How can you be sure?"

"No, I don't think the monkey took it," said Darnell. "I think the monkey's owner did. That capuchin would have destroyed it, and Charles Dalton wouldn't be imitating Liam in every location where he doesn't think he'll be caught. Liam only remembered that the woman crashed into him when he realized he'd been compromised. She took the badge and gave it to Dalton. Dalton had been fooling people before the gala, but we think the badge gave him access to a federal prison.

"It took our misunderstanding to bring the deception to light. Agent Metcalfe never stopped asking our boss to recall us. But she was confused because he seemed to change his mind every other day. Acting as Metcalfe, Dalton was sending messages that directly contradicted the things the *real* Metcalfe was saying.

"We have enough evidence to arrest Dalton, but we can't find him. He was *counting on* an office full of people who never talk to one another. The man's brazen. He's also missing."

CHAPTER 27

Dear Nora:

My friend talks incessantly during our morning walk. I don't want to be rude, but the very sound of her voice is starting to grate. Please help!

All Nattered Out

Dear Nattered:

It's winter. Wear earmuffs. Or take up knitting and stay inside. I'm sending yarn and a nice beginner's pattern.

Nora

"She and Noel have been friends since *grade* school."

I woke up with a crick in my neck and Lance's upper back filling my window. I had fallen asleep on the way home, and my body was *not* thankful. In front of the van, Hannah and Sara were locked in nearly identical poses, arms crossed, brows lowered. But Hannah's hair was, as always, impeccable, while Sara's was an unkempt wreck. I couldn't decide whether they were glaring at me or at the agents arguing with Lance outside my window. I seriously debated going back to sleep.

No such luck. My open eyes had been seen. "Make her *stop!*" Sara pointed at me and shouted loud enough to be heard through the glass.

"Make *who* stop? Lance, honey, move." I climbed out of the

car in time for the meteorite who was my daughter to crash into my stomach.

"Make Miss Trudy stop. She won't let Hannah-Banana do my *hair.*"

"Trudy, Hannah is fine. Let her twist the child's hair."

"*No.* I want *braids.* I want a million long beautiful braids hanging to my knees *like hers!*"

"Sara, you picked at the twists so much I've barely been able to keep them in! How are braids . . ."

"I want *braids!*"

"Lance, Noel, I don't think you understand the gravity of the situation . . ." Trudy's innocent wide eyes didn't work on me. It was a cozy-up tactic, and I wanted nothing better than to keep my distance.

"We picked up our son under what amounted to an armed *guard* between Drew, his partner, and Darnell," Lance snapped. "Don't tell me we can't fully appreciate . . ."

"You can't distrust everybody." Drew, at least, was trying to be a force of reason. "I can personally vouch for . . ."

"I don't need anybody to *vouch* for me," Hannah snapped. "I don't abandon my friends when they're in trouble. I've got a ton of teeny-tiny rubber bands out in my car and a whole lot of fiber to weave in . . ."

". . . and she probably took the day off work to do this for us, so *lay off.*" I *so* wanted to go to bed.

Their voices erupted around me again into a new babble of arguments, but Hannah was already heading for her car, which was parked in the cul-de-sac. Because the house used to be a funeral home, it's situated at the end of a tree-lined road designed to get mourners in and out of the area without jamming up traffic.

Because it stood so far apart from the other buildings in the small town of Granton during the Great Depression, it didn't burn with the rest of the village. And it now has its own street, and my parents own the land between the house and the state route out front. Periodically, realtors pester my parents about buying the excellent road frontage, which they consider the perfect excuse to build yet another suburb and pull Ironweed a little bit closer to Columbus's urban sprawl.

But Mama and Daddy won't budge. They don't want neighbors, and their position was one of the reasons the previous owner sold it to them when she moved to live with her daughter in Arizona some twenty years ago.

"Where's William?" Mama called, heading out her front door. The question, issued in a conversational tone, stopped the argument as sharply as if she'd screamed it.

"I thought he was with you and Natasha!" Lance pushed through the assembled group.

"He was, dear. Then Natasha took him out back to play hack-up-the-roses, and I haven't seen either one of them since."

Mama had barely finished speaking when Natasha started screaming. "Give him back! What do you think you're doing?"

She wasn't behind the house. She wasn't in the roses. She was nearly at the edge of the field, chasing after a pair of people who were hauling William toward a car stopped at the end of the lane. How long had it been there? A few minutes? A few hours? Had someone hidden it in the scrub on the other side of the road? That was the only direction where hills prevented my parents from having a perfect view of the surrounding area.

Lance hurtled into the field. William thrashed mightily, slowing the pair, but not enough, and certainly not stopping them. I planted myself, my arms wrapped tightly around Sara, preventing her from chasing the chasers and preparing to shield her. Drew and his partner, along with Trudy and Darnell, had drawn guns.

Hannah froze halfway to her car, then broke into a run

herself. All four guns exploded. Sara rocked backward and screamed, hands over her ears. But nobody stopped running. Hannah's white sedan screeched down the lane and reached the road far ahead of any of the runners. She parked in the middle of the state route, partially blocking it. Though the other car could have edged around, doing so would have taken time.

The guns banged again. Sara didn't scream this time, but she huddled against me, whimpering. Then a plume of steam rose from the other vehicle's hood. It seethed to the ground. They weren't shooting at any*body*. They were firing on the car. "Damn," Drew's partner muttered. "Aimed too high." He flicked a finger at the steam. "Got those wheels anyhow."

The man and woman running with William wouldn't be going anywhere except on foot. And . . . they *weren't* a man and woman. It was a pair of kids finally skidding to a halt. The girl looked familiar.

"Layla! You give him back, you give him back, you give him *back*! You *lied* to me!"

Now Trudy, Darnell, and Drew ran, while Drew's partner dropped back to use his radio. They passed Lance easily, even though he's in good shape.

"That's my car!" The male in the pair dropped William and extended his arms helplessly toward his vehicle. "How'm I going to get to work? Kid, let go!" Freed, William now affixed himself to his would-be kidnapper, biting the flesh on the underside of his arm. "Kid, that *hurts*!"

"Let Robby go." Layla pulled on William's middle until Natasha finally caught up and landed a punch on her sister's temple.

"Go Will! Go Tasha!" Sara sprang to life in my arms. I had gone somewhat limp, and she burst free easily and sprinted after everyone else.

Mama and I were left standing beside the van, staring from

each other to the unfolding scene. "Noel, who did you and Lance make *mad*?"

"I don't know. I wish I did. I don't know if this is even related. Tasha, stop it, she's not fighting back!"

"Down! Down on the ground!" Nobody listened to Darnell.

Natasha continued to pound on Layla, even though the younger girl had collapsed to sitting. "What were you doing?" Natasha screamed. "What did you think you were doing? How *could* you?"

Lance arrived and pulled her off, still swinging. "Natasha, you're not doing any good," he said.

"She lied to me. She *lied* to me!" Natasha sobbed. "She said she was moving out of the state and wanted to see them one last time."

"Down on the *ground*!" Darnell repeated.

My mind had stopped giving orders to the rest of my body. I wanted to run after Sara, prevent her from joining the fray, but I was frozen. *I nearly lost him. Again. I nearly lost him again. They nearly took him from me.* I staggered back against the van.

"Noel," Mama asked. "Are you okay?"

I couldn't even shake my head to tell her *no*, I was *not* okay; I was horrible. Hannah backed her car out of the road, then turned around in the lane and drove back down to us.

"When? When did this happen?" Lance still held Natasha tightly against him. "How did she know they'd be here, Natasha?" He was trying for a neutral tone, but he had to shout to be heard. Natasha stopped struggling. "We picked him up early. Why didn't they think he was still in school?"

"And why did I *believe her*?" Natasha wailed. She melted out of Lance's arms. "She said she and her mom were getting out of this stupid little town, and couldn't she see the twins one last time? I didn't know she meant right now, but then they pulled up out front while you guys were all arguing, and she said she'd settle for William if Sara wouldn't come out back. It happened so fast, and it wasn't her mom, it was . . ." Suddenly, she leapt up. This time, instead of attacking her sister, she went after the guy, who was still struggling to free himself from William's teeth. "Him!"

Lance lunged, but missed her, and she connected a series of kicks to the boy's shins as she tackled him to the ground.

"Noel? *Noel?*" Mama shook me, but I still couldn't move.

I nearly lost him. We brought him home to be safe, and someone nearly took him from home. It's true. I can't trust anybody.

"Hannah, help me with her!" Mama's voice was urgent and distant. Though I felt the pressure of her hands on my shoulder, it didn't carry the sensation of real touch.

"Noel!" Hannah got in front of me, blocking my view.

Move, I tried to tell her. *Don't get between me and my babies.* But my jaw and vocal cords weren't working either, and the words stayed locked in.

"Ed! Edgar! Noel's having a spell!"

A spell. That's what they called it. After I barely escaped alive from my abusive relationship with Alex, flashbacks would claim me without warning, trapping me away from friends and family and throwing me straight back into his world. It took years of therapy, along with self-defense and tae kwon do training, to overcome those horrible flashbacks. Though I wasn't flashing *back* anywhere right now, I might as well have been.

Hannah seized the shoulder Mama wasn't shaking. "Get her, Lenore. She's going down." Hannah braced me on one side and Mama on the other as my knees buckled and my legs gave way. They lowered me gently. "Head between the knees, Noel." Hannah, who had nursed me through many such incidents, still remembered the drill. Together, she and Mama propped my knees up and pushed my head forward and down. "Breathe, honey," said Hannah. "Don't think about any of it. Breathe.

Come on. I forget your word . . ."

"Peace," Mama supplied. "Peace, Noel. Think peace."

Peace. I was supposed to shut out my memories by repeating a specific idea or word until nothing else could get in around it. I had chosen "peace." But they didn't understand I wasn't stuck in memory right now, and I couldn't stop hearing the fighting at the road's edge.

"What did you expect me to tell you?" Layla was shouting at Natasha now. "Hey, you and your stupid friends aren't doing much good protecting our twins, why don't you let somebody with a clue take a shot? Would you have brought him out to see me, then?"

"I thought I was doing you a *favor.* I was trying to give you a fair shake. *I felt sorry for you.*"

"Here's a news flash, Natasha *Oeschle.* I don't *need* your pity party. Robby and I have it all figured out. We're getting married next week, and we're gonna adopt . . ."

"Shut up!" bellowed the boy, Robby.

"*Married?* You nitwit, you're fourteen years old!"

"My dad's going to sign the papers when we visit him tomorrow."

"He doesn't even have custody . . . how are you going to get to see him . . . you're so *stupid.*"

A loud whistle interrupted them. "Quiet!" Trudy roared.

Blessed silence descended. Silence. Peace. *Peace. Peace.* Finally, I could push out the other ideas crowding me to a standstill. I don't know how long it took, but by the time I came back to myself and persuaded my head it needed to lift, Natasha was once more screaming at Layla, whose confidence was shaken.

"You said we were getting *married,*" Layla wailed.

"You're not only *stupid,* Layla, you're *naive,*" Tasha shouted. "When did he start being your boyfriend, huh? Bet he started coming around after William got away from him last time."

"Shows what you know! Robby picked Will up *wandering* that day and brought him home. He left Will in the garage and went for help. I had already practically moved in by then, you know. I got home and didn't know Will was there. I accidentally let him out. He freaked in a strange house and bolted. Robby and Merle and I searched for *hours.*"

"You *believed* he just found the kid then left him in a *garage*? And why not call the cops after he took off, huh?"

"Cops." Layla clearly disliked the police.

Robby broke in. "We were *going* to if he hadn't shown up by morning. But he *did* show up, and it would have looked suspicious."

"That's the dumbest, worst lie I've ever *heard*!" Natasha screeched.

"William didn't understand," Layla insisted.

"William *hates* the circle-dot man!" Will yelled.

"Robby's one of the good guys. He wanted to *help.*"

"That's not what William says!"

"Who *knows* what William says. Nobody understands him."

"William *hates* the circle-dot man," Natasha shouted. "How do you not get that?"

It made perfect sense to me. Lance held William doubled over in his arms. Sara stood at Lance's elbow on one side, and Natasha sat at the other. The police couldn't get around them to arrest Layla and Robby. They needed me. But I couldn't move.

"Natasha, get out of my way," Trudy finally snapped, and Lance suddenly cleared the children aside to make room for law enforcement.

I rolled to my knees, then stood.

"Easy," said Hannah.

"I'm good." I wasn't. I started across to my family anyway.

Hannah caught my arm on the first lurch. "Let's take it slow." She held onto me all the way across the field.

"Hey, William." I tried to catch my son's attention, but he wasn't listening. I sat, collapsed really, and motioned Lance to hand him to me.

He cocked an eyebrow as if to ask, *you sure?* He had doubtless seen the episode beside the van.

I nodded. As I enfolded William in my embrace, needing to feel the aliveness of his struggling little body, Sara sniffled loudly. "Do I still get my braids?" she asked Hannah.

"I think there's going to be a delay." Hannah stroked Sara's messy hair. "But I'll get you braided, baby doll. We may have to start today and finish up next week, but we'll get you there."

"And I'll have a million?"

"About."

"All the way to my knees?"

"Honey, mine only go halfway down my back. I'll make yours as long as mine. I promise."

Sara studied her a minute. "Okay," she said. Then she burst into loud, hiccupping tears.

"Hey, hey, hey now." Lance picked her up. "It's over. It's over." Only it wasn't. Not even nearly. Darnell said there were at least two groups. We had one. The wrong one. A pair of kids, and while they might be capable of grabbing a child or cutting into the monkey enclosures, I doubted either of them had the physical strength to decapitate someone or take down a deputy.

Natasha and Layla continued to hurl insults at one another as Layla was crammed into the cruiser. "Tasha, be quiet. I'll never get him calm with you yelling across the lawn." In another moment, Layla was inside and out of shouting range anyway.

Robby kicked up some kind of a scuffle at the car, and I finally captured my son's attention. "William. William." I pointed at the boy beside the police car. "Do you hate him? Is he the circle-dot man?"

Sometimes, even when I asked William a question needing a specific answer, he wouldn't give me a reply I comprehended. But not this time. Now, he suddenly quieted and followed the line of my pointing finger, then imitated it with his own. "Yes. Yes, yes, yes," he howled. "William hates the circle-dot man!"

"Is *that* the circle-dot car?" William didn't follow my finger as I pointed to the much closer, all too close, pizza car. Will remained fixed on Robby, who was now finally being stuffed into the cruiser beside Layla. But he said, "Yes. William *hates* that circle-dot car. I do, I do, I do."

I rocked him and cuddled him. "Me too, baby. Mom hates the circle-dot car, too."

CHAPTER 28

Dear Nora:

I may have been wrong about my neighbor. All this time, and I never knew what a sweetheart he could be. The very day after your column ran, he came over to apologize about my dog. He said he couldn't do much about his cat's behavior, but he hoped I'd understand. He was so nice! *He even brought me a pan of brownies. How did he* know *those are my favorites? I've been parceling them out over the last few days.*

They've been wonderful for my constitution, if you don't mind my saying so. Who knew sweets could help you in "that" way? I'm going to make him my mother's famous figgy pudding by way of thanks.

Pooped

Dear Pooped:

I'm glad to know everything worked out in the end.

Nora

I fell asleep having already lost recollection of most of the previous day's events. The weekend passed in a haze. I held onto the most intense images, but the police department blurred into nightmares of Drew towering over me asking me about the circle-dot man. Sleep was elusive, and Lance and I found ourselves awake and holding onto our babies, jumping at every tiny noise in the house. At some point Sunday night, my body overrode my psyche, and I drifted into a deep sleep for the first time in days. When I finally woke up Monday morning, I was alone in Mama and Daddy's bed.

"You have to sit *still* for your braids." Hannah had finished Sara's hair Saturday afternoon before she took off on an adventure. When William saw the finished product, he had immediately started pestering Hannah to do the same thing with his. But Hannah was leaving from our house that day for an estate auction somewhere in Pennsylvania on Sunday. Besides finding vintage clothes for Hannah's Rags, she was travelling with another local business owner who sold antiques. They would be gone Saturday and Sunday night. If she was back, I had either slept in mightily, or she had showed up with the chickens.

"How are *you* this morning, Natasha?" My grandmother's voice answered my question before I had properly formed it. If *she* was here, I *had* slept in. Franny Cox might go to bed late and wake up early, but she was never on the road before nine or ten. She didn't trust her eyes until the third cup of coffee, and she didn't trust her bladder for long after. At eighty, we all wondered how much longer she'd be driving herself, and at what point she'd start accepting our offers of a familial taxi service for more than the highway rides.

"Sara, come try this on," said Mama.

"My *princess gown!*" Mama had been busy this weekend making play clothes for both children. Now, William was home because "not school-timed until he haved braidy hair now" had become Sunday's refrain. It was odds on he was still wearing the ring-bearer suit from our wedding that he had worn all weekend. But the suit was working wonders. We had let him sleep in it, and he discovered bladder control he couldn't have imagined, leaping out of bed twice a night to go to the bathroom, sleeping lightly for fear of wetting it.

"I guess I'm okay. I feel so *stupid* . . ." Natasha began.

"No, don't think that way." Nana was practical. She didn't tolerate much moping and might be the perfect antidote to the blues that had enveloped Tasha since Layla and Robby nearly stole William. We had an emergency therapy appointment scheduled for her this afternoon.

"But I *hate* her. I *know* not to trust her. I shouldn't have even answered the *phone* . . ."

"Natasha, you're fifteen. You're human. You made a mistake. Nobody is angry with you but yourself," said Mama in her and-that's-final voice. Lance and I had both told her the same thing, our memories of our own monumental mistakes keeping us vocalizing sympathy instead of criticism.

"But the worst thing is I *still* feel bad for her!"

"I know," said Nana. "It's hard."

I rolled out of bed and fumbled for my clothing in the suitcase Lance and I were living out of. The first thing I found was my cell phone. It had a sticky note affixed to the top. "Took some video. Push play. No worries. XOXO."

I fumbled with the screen and considered asking Tasha for help. But the handwriting was Lance's, and if he was leaving me messages via cell phone, there was a good chance he wasn't sharing with anybody but me. Indeed, when I finally got the video going, the first words he spoke were, "Hope you figured this out without help. If not, Tasha, off you go." Then he waited, presumably for Natasha to leave. In the silence, he aimed the phone all around the bathroom he was speaking from. "It's me here. No bad guys." No, no bad guys. I heard my own voice shouting something in the background, confirming my suspicion he had recorded himself at some point during a period when I had been unable to find my phone.

"I want to check something out," he continued. "And I'm sick of our police escort. I'm going out early to run errands and set up the lab for my class. I'm telling everyone else that. And I'm *not* letting Trudy, Darnell, and Drew come with me. And when I'm gone, I'm parking my car in Natalie Forrester's street and walking the whole way back to the Marine. I don't care what Robby the Wreck says; he didn't pick William up on a misguided rescue mission last time, and he didn't do it for Layla on Friday."

Didn't Lance and I have this conversation already? I thought so. When Robby and Layla's story had spun out, we saw holes in the portions we heard. Law enforcement agreed with us. Possibly Robby was playing Layla. But possibly someone was playing both of them. From what little we knew of him, which was admittedly limited to accepting pizza deliveries and watching him try to abscond with our son, we thought Robby was too stupid to have acted alone in developing either kidnapping plot. Last I heard, Drew was petitioning the court to have both Robby *and* Layla removed from parental custody.

"Come on, Lance. Tell me something new," I muttered to the phone.

"I'm not going to school at all today. I'm cancelling my class. Robby was too upset on Friday that he'd be missing delivery day Monday . . . well, today by the time you get this I'll be at the Marine. I want to see what goes on in the blind spot on the other side of that truck out back.

"We all know William went in the kitchen when he got away from Natalie in the restaurant that day. I think he saw something back there in the first place. And I don't think anybody has taken the time to learn what it might have been. Don't worry about me. I'll be freezing in the honeysuckle bushes behind the Dumpster at the Marine all day. My phone will be *off*.

"If I'm not home by seven or so, tell our Drew what I've gone and done. But buy me time until then, because he's the only one we can fully trust. Trudy and Darnell have their own agenda, Noel, and I don't care what they claim, I don't think our safety is anywhere near its heart. You can play them the next video if you need a time-waster." He blew a kiss at the camera and the video ended. I groaned, briefly played myself the second video, then finished dressing.

Darnell seized upon me before I got as far as the kitchen. "*What* is Lance doing?" he demanded.

"You tell me."

"Noel, we can hardly assure your . . ."

Buy me time. I wanted to play the first video. But I *needed* to trust my husband. I had more faith in our federal friends than Lance, but I also agreed with him the Marine was unexplored territory and a great deal could have happened on the other side of the security cameras.

"Coffee." I refused to talk to Darnell until I'd poured myself a cup of Mama's exotic finest. *Then* I played him the second video.

Lance repeated the routine with "no bad guys" and then launched into a detailed and completely falsified version of the activities he was planning. "I should be home by seven this evening. If I'm not, *then* I guess I did something idiotic. See you later. Love you." He blew the kiss again.

Darnell and Trudy launched a plan to find him. They figured out Natalie Forrester's within five minutes. They would have worked out the Marine in ten. "Quit," I said. "I think he was pretty specific this morning about not wanting company. You've already got today mapped out, and I don't think your plans should change."

That started another argument, one centering on my ability to make wise decisions under the current circumstances. But Nana saved me. "Come on, Trudy. If you're driving me down to prison, you'd better hurry up. You're already going to be making pit stops every ten miles."

"All right." Trudy surrendered. The information Trudy wanted to know from T-Bow Orrice had become more, rather than less, urgent once she started getting support from Columbus.

"I need to know if he can tell the difference between Liam and Charles," she confided. "That's not something he's going to tell an agent, but I need a fast, direct answer. He knew Dalton on the inside, and he's worked with Metcalfe extensively on the inside. If *he* can't tell the difference, there's a good chance I'm right about Dalton getting into the prison posing as Metcalfe. If Dalton came up with a good enough story, Orrice might have given him access to significant resources."

"Why the deception? Orrice worked with Gary and the Dalton brothers. Why not ask as Charles Dalton? I'd think T-Bow Orrice might be as worried as Dalton about what Gary might have in a journal."

"This isn't about a journal. Or not wholly. We have every reason to believe Dalton is hunting Natasha. And Orrice wouldn't give Charles a thing. He shut down Terry Dalton, perhaps had him killed, for a deception. And he has learned how Natasha was exploited. No, if Dalton wants access to Orrice, he would have to get in by lying. And what would Dalton find sweeter than to use T-Bow's network to kill T-Bow's kid?"

"That's . . ." I fumbled for a concept and ultimately chose Darnell's. "Brazen."

"Yes. And if he did it, but Orrice caught on, that may have been Dalton's body at your center."

She left Darnell to babysit us for the day. I heard him calling Drew at least once. Darnell needed a distraction.

"I'm supposed to be at the center this morning," I informed him. "And I'm taking everybody but Mama and Daddy with me." I had all three children, Sara because of the suspension, Natasha because she was so depressed and scared that it was hard to get her to leave my sight, and William because Hannah had to go to work *long* before finishing his braids. "I presume you're my personal escort, and I could use your help out there. We're short of hands these days. Would you rather babysit the old folks or the youngsters?"

He tried to cajole Mama and Daddy to come with us, but neither had any interest in being rousted from their daily routines. They may simply have wanted a break from their chronic houseguests. They enjoyed company, but they were quite fond of their solitary lifestyle, and Mama had Christmas gifts to get ready. Plus, there was the squad car parked at the end of the cul-de-sac. They insisted watchfulness and caution would ensure their safety.

In the end, Darnell accompanied us, grumbling about people who didn't have regard for their own safety or respect for the people trying to protect them. Truly, I wasn't merely getting the agent out for an airing. I needed to get Tasha to the center. I had research of my own needing completion, and it held absolutely no life-threatening potential whatsoever and every potential to distract her out of her blues until her therapy appointment.

"What have you figured out?" I asked Ace when we reached the orangutan enclosure.

Our resident keeper was instantly on the alert. "Chuck been roaming again?"

"Not that I know of," I told him. "But we still don't know enough about what he was doing when he *was* on the loose. *If* he was on the loose."

"He's getting out, all right, but I don't know much more than that."

"Fair enough. We *do* know he's bored, so I've got a new toy." Our chimps are bright. They've got smarts most people wouldn't believe. But we've had chimpanzees at our facility since early in my tenure here. Orangutans, on the other hand, are completely new to us. Ours is only the second sanctuary in the United States to house the orange apes, and Chuck, our pleasantly grouchy single resident, was about to have his mind blown.

The program Lucy had been using to communicate with her baby and the surrogate wasn't unique. As soon as I looked into it, I realized there was an entire electronic enrichment program available to our bored friend, assuming he didn't simply poke his fingers through the mesh and chuck down one of the two tablets that had been waiting in my department mailbox when Lance and I stopped by the university yesterday. I hadn't expected a twenty-four-hour or weekend delivery after I placed the order in a stupor Friday night, but Natasha wouldn't answer me when I asked her if she knew anything about our mailbox's Sunday surprise. Where Lance was interested in gallivanting off to save the world, I didn't care much. Not today.

As I got out the tablets and brought up the series of apps available to Chuck, Ace came back to the subject of the roaming. "I put a stop to it easy enough. He was using a stick to jab the security camera in the lens until it pointed off in the wrong direction. I took away the stick, and I've been careful he doesn't get another one in there. But I'm darned if I know what he did *after* he moved the camera. I'd love to find out."

"You and me both. And *I* want to know how he let the monkeys out up there without tearing anything apart."

"Check this out." Tasha, who had been greeting Chuck, now brought me a key.

"Where'd you get that?" I turned it over in my hand.

"I saw Chuck hiding something shiny and got him to trade."

"What's *he* doing with a key?" asked Ace.

She shrugged.

"It's too little for his enclosure," I mused, "day *or* night. This is more the size of . . ." I turned to Ace, an unspoken question on my face.

"Nawww," he said. "No way."

"It doesn't explain how he got out," I went on. "But . . . listen . . . if you have a minute later, would you humor me and test this on the old door from the enclosure we got from the Michigan zoo? I think Rick brought all the junk down here after he fixed us up."

"Yeah, he did. It's in the new admin building," said Ace. He accepted the key. "I'll tell you something," he finally admitted. "They used to have the worst trouble keeping a couple of the exhibits locked up there."

"Did they? I wish I knew more about his life up there."

"I was *with* him, and I wish that."

"And I wish he wasn't so canny about the cameras." Security footage either cut off before any useful filming began, or else the cameras were spun, apparently from behind.

"Either way, I'll try to see if he's got other keys besides this one."

With the exception of Natasha, only Ace had a strong relationship with Chuck. For months, the primate waited patiently for Ace to shear off his fecally encrusted dreadlocks and clean him through the mesh. If anybody could coax additional purloined goods out of him, it would be Ace.

"Okay, but I need to show you this!" Natasha pulled out the tablets and, being far more electronically savvy than I, took over Ace's training. It was mental enrichment of a kind we had never before been able to offer any of our apes.

Soon, we would give the chimps a shot at the program. For now, though, they were occupied, and we had to replenish our supply of volunteers and learn how to use the tablet before they got a turn. Chuck's situation was disturbing, and I wanted to alleviate his loneliness. Tasha went over the basics and left Ace and Chuck with one of the tablets while she kept the other.

Now, I *knew* she had been responsible for the speedy delivery. I did recall that she was the one who made me place the order on Friday in spite of everything that had already happened. I didn't care. My plan to shake her ennui was working.

I left Ace holding one tablet within Chuck's reach while the big ape tapped the screen and chuffed joy at the various pictures and sounds he could generate. Natasha tethered the other tablet to her phone, and she climbed into the van waiting for Chuck to find the vid-chat program.

"Don't wait too hard, Tasha. He may get obsessed with something else today. This may take a while." Now I could see the naked hope on her face. She wanted more regular access to Chuck. She looked so fragile. "I think it will work," I told her. "But you've got to be patient." *And I'd better order a third tablet. I'm sure I'll find I didn't pay for the first two in any case.*

We arrived at the larger portion of our facility at feeding time, where all our hands were needed. William was clearly regretting his choice to skip school now. It was one thing to miss school when Hannah was braiding and quite another when he was bored. I had a distraction ready for him, too. We would still likely face a meltdown later, but being given his own small bucket to follow with me from enclosure to enclosure was a pretty good substitute in the short term.

Ohio's new laws defining "sanctuaries" as areas free of children under sixteen would soon pose us problems in this area. Natasha would turn sixteen in time and wouldn't be affected. But the twins soon wouldn't be able to accompany us to work unless we chose to skirt the law or abandon our sanctuary to become part of the Ohio Zoo.

Our dwindling budget made the second possibility feel all too real. Short of a major grant coming in, we were going to have to ask Stan for help soon. Since he had so recently paid for the orangutan enclosure, Lance and I were both hesitant to take this step. Purely aside from the fact that he had already given us too much personally, we didn't want to abuse the man's generosity.

There was real argument for merging with the Ohio Zoo. Although affiliated with Ironweed University, Midwest Primates wasn't a formal arm. The university *might* remain a major funder if we became an educational zoo and guaranteed we would only accept primates already in captivity while we continued to offer research opportunities for those studying their behaviors. Lance, Art, and I had volleyed this idea around many times over the years.

Ultimately, we had always come down against it, even though Christian and his employers at the Ohio Zoo were more than open to increasing *that* source of funding to add an exhibit with major tourist appeal to the primate collection. But now? How much would the university continue to provide without Art up there advocating for us?

I couldn't realistically expect to get his job, not when the department chair resented me so much that he was trying to influence a job committee by scheduling my teaching demonstration in a room polluted with a bucket of dead fish. Not to mention the severed head. He swore he knew nothing about that, but he also refused to explain why he thought his own life was in danger when he saw it.

It might be time to ask our board to reconsider the zoo's offer, even though it would mean making drastic changes to Art's vision. Besides, even though I had previously been opposed to having children on our grounds, it was now hard to imagine the center without Sara and William on site.

"Noel!"

How long had I been ruminating? Judging by the number of crickets hopping around the bottom of the spider monkeys' enclosure and the giggles from the children I'd been allowing to help me place them, quite some time.

"Noel, would you come here?" Jen, standing over by the rhesus macaque enclosure, looked less than impressed by my lack of focus.

"Sorry. Come on, kids. That's enough enrichment to keep these guys from stealing anything for at least a week." Sara and William only offered token protests when I prodded them forward, further confirming my suspicions. I'd been mentally absent for some time. "I don't know what we'd do without you holding the reins here, Jen. What did you need?" I swore to myself to give her a more formal thanks in the near future. She was, after all, not even on our paid roster, but a complete volunteer.

She waved me off. "I think we have a problem?" She sounded a bit like Sara or William making a statement-question.

"What's up?"

"I should have said something sooner, but you've been overwhelmed, and I kind of thought I was losing my mind. How many rhesus macaques do we have?"

"I can't say off the top of my head. I'd have to look at the sheet. Why?"

"Fewer than two hundred twenty, right?"

"Many fewer. We don't have capacity for more than one hundred fifty, and that, in and of itself, is a huge number."

"The sheet says a hundred thirty-eight."

"Sounds right."

"Noel, I've counted multiple times since Wednesday. I thought it was because I'm doing too much, and maybe we didn't get them back in the right enclosures. I thought I was maybe double-counting. But I had my husband come in and count with me. We have two hundred twenty monkeys in those enclosures. We've got major bloodshed. I'm refilling bowls as two or three monkeys fight to share it. We didn't have this many before that poor man got killed here. We had a hundred thirty-eight. One monkey to a bowl, and nobody ever missed a meal. I should have said something right away, but it seemed outrageous to have so many monkeys."

"How did it happen? Why didn't we notice Wednesday?"

"We barely got to do a head count Wednesday. All we did was put away as many as we thought we had. There were so many of us working, we probably *all* counted to a hundred thirty-eight and thought we had it. Who would think we'd have *extras*? And it's been pandemonium in these enclosures ever since.

"This is Merle's area," she went on, "and he hasn't called back to even say he won't be returning. I thought maybe I misunderstood something and rhesus macaques were different from the other kinds of monkeys. Like maybe you had to count some other time or you'd get confused. It's not like I've got some kind of degree to be an expert." Jen felt self-conscious because she didn't have any affiliation with the college. She was just a member of the community with a fascination and desire to help.

And she was right. Normally, feeding time is also head count time, because the monkeys all come down for chow. We can verify we don't have anybody missing because each individual comes to its bowl. Monkeys are territorial little critters, so there isn't much danger of bowl hopping causing an accidental oversight.

"Jen, thank you for telling me about this. The rhesus macaques *aren't* any different from the others. And as for expertise, you don't need a degree. The person with the expertise is the one on the ground. Most sanctuaries aren't attached to colleges. They aren't normally overflowing with overeducated people like me. In fact, it's ironic that this one *is*, since part of Art's mission, part of *our* mission, is to validate the experiences of keepers, many of whom get discredited because they haven't got credentials or haven't conducted a properly scientific study. You've been here long enough to know when something is wrong. Trust yourself. I know I do."

Her whole face brightened when I said I trusted her, and I realized I had given her more than any medal or award. She hadn't known until then she had been given the gift of my respect long before today. "What do we do?" she asked. "Somebody besides us is putting monkeys into our enclosures."

She was right. We never would have accepted more monkeys than we could house. The wizened little macaques in this one enclosure were crowded together in far greater quantities, and a cursory count revealed far too many of them.

"We need more houses if we're going to make room." My mind spun backward over the last few days. Although I wasn't completely sleep-fogged, I still felt jet-lagged and slow. I had an idea in there if I could clear things out long enough to think of it, I felt certain. "In the meantime, let's start moving the extras to our quarantine areas. We've got all the most recent newcomers placed, and that gives us a little room to spread these guys out using those right now. That isn't acceptable for the long term, but it will allow us to establish a healthier environment in the present tense."

"Something wrong?" Darnell had been over by the colobus enclosure, but he joined us now.

"Merle?" I said to Jen. "Did you say Merle was in charge of this area?"

She nodded.

Merle is in charge of this enclosure. Merle is a no-call no-show at the pizza parlor. Merle was with Robby and Layla when Will vanished. "What's Merle's blood type?" I asked of nobody. There were, of course, no answers. I had a nasty feeling it was Type A.

Darnell looked a question and I opened my mouth, then closed it again. What to say? *Lance thinks William saw something at the Marine. Something serious enough Robby was told to pick him*

*up. And pick him up again. We have too many monkeys. Merle works
at the Marine. Merle is in charge of the now vastly overpopulated
rhesus macaque area.* "Something?" I answered. "I'd say lots of
things."

"Something *new*, I meant."

"Count the macaques," Jen said.

"One, two," Sara and William complied immediately.

"Not you," I told them. But I was only half listening, and
they went on counting, both of them saying "five-teen" instead
of "fifteen." *The first time he came here, William melted down about
the rhesus enclosures. He didn't like the cages. He didn't like circle-
dot cars. Circle-dot cars might not be police vehicles.*

"Too many," Darnell said after a minute. "But I thought
Chuck was the one breaking in before last week."

What was I missing? "I think it happened last week," I said.

"Who breaks in to dump animals *into* an enclosure?" Jen
sounded completely lost. "Why not donate or surrender them
the normal way?"

Her question crystallized the idea I had been trying to get in
focus. "Because those aren't somebody's unwanted pets." *That*
was it. *That* was what I had been missing. "Those animals are
being smuggled, and somebody is using our sanctuary as a
clearinghouse." I nearly said more, barely remembering in time
Jen didn't know Darnell in his agent role.

I held the rest of my theory in until I was alone with Darnell
and the kids in the van. "You and Trudy were tracking a smuggling ring." It wasn't a question. "And you thought Gary was at
its heart."

"But he was doing something else entirely," Darnell pointed
out.

"No, he wasn't. He was doing something else *additionally.*
Let's say your smugglers needed a holding zone between dropping their animals and moving them to a final destination, a pet

store or someone's home. They received the animals asynchronously and made their activity harder to track by disappearing them in between arrival and delivery. Where better to hide a bunch of monkeys than a primate sanctuary?

"I checked our files briefly before we left. Because the number of macaques kept going up, I assumed our volunteers were taking in more of those than others, but at a glance, I saw no more rhesus macaques than any other monkeys on the list, even though the sheet totals increased. Merle told us we had more. We never thought to see if he logged them formally. I think we've been getting extra macaques for a long time, and the real problem is Gary and Merle aren't there any longer to siphon them off.

"*And*," I wound up, "We need to be looking at the Michigan Zoo's former employees."

"Like Ace?"

Did Darnell have to sound so hopeful? "Maybe. Whoever is bringing the animals in may know Chuck. But Chuck wouldn't have to bust loose to see Ace, and I'd wager he's breaking out to visit a friend. He follows along, watches the human messing with the macaque cage, and after the person goes, he tries his own hand at it. With the key that Ace stopped everything to test when I called him."

Darnell had a major hole to poke in my theory. "Why doesn't this person show up on the security footage?"

"Remember? The cameras were turned off or moved."

"Not the cameras back here. The cameras on the road didn't pick up anything."

Natasha had been eavesdropping. She poked her head forward. "Bet they took the service road. It goes right by Chuck's enclosure, there are no cameras, and it's not much of a hike up the back way from his place to main if you know what you're doing."

This was true. It was one of the few periphery areas on the property without at least one camera, and so few people knew about the entrance we had never stationed a deputy there until after last Wednesday. We had plenty of places to take video, but our cameras only showed some of our enclosures fully, and there were enough gaps in our coverage that Chuck had been able to let himself out and ramble up to the main area, moving those cameras that might have caught him. That he knew where to find the cameras so he could move them bespoke a human connection, too. It took a muddy Sasquatch footprint to give him away.

"We need to look at their cars, too," Darnell said. "Or are orangutans so good at discerning sounds they could figure out some unusual knock a human ear couldn't pick up?"

"I don't think so. As far as I know, it would have to be something distinct enough you or I would hear it."

Natasha stuck an arm between us and turned the stereo up to blaring.

"Hey!" I turned it back down. "Put your seatbelt back on and sit back!"

"Bet the whole neighborhood heard that," she said.

"Yes, I'm sure they . . . oh. You're saying it could be a loud radio." The deputies wouldn't have heard even a blasting machine over the sound of monkey chatter, if the primates were keyed up.

"He comes to music."

"Next time, say so instead of giving William and Sara the screaming meemies."

"Sorry. My point was it could be anybody who listened to rap and was dumb enough to blast it when they drove in during the night."

Darnell followed her where I did not. "It's the kind of thing a teenager would do."

"Don't look at me! I can't drive! But Layla can. I don't care if she is only fourteen."

"Or Robby."

Darnell wasn't completely on board yet. "But where would those two get a bunch of monkeys?"

"Bet Merle knows," I said. "Too bad nobody can find him." As I said those words, a sinking feeling took over my gut. I hated to give my husband away, but if our volunteer who worked at the Marine had now gone missing, Lance was in more danger than he thought. Plus, if he was looking *behind* the truck, he was searching the wrong gap anyway. "Now would be a good time to ask Mr. Gibson what exactly arrives in his Monday delivery truck. I don't think it's necessarily flour and pizza sauce."

Chapter 29

ATTN: ADVICE
Dear Nora:

You're a seamstress! Make those kids some fun togs. That's what I say.

Well Dressed in Muscogen

"Why didn't you tell me where Lance was in the first place?" Darnell jabbed buttons on his phone while I sped home. He had dispatched Drew to the Marine as soon as I admitted my husband was holding his own personal stakeout. Now he was trying to dial Trudy.

"Because I hadn't figured the thing about Merle or realized what was in the truck."

"What makes you so sure . . . hang on . . . Trudy! Why didn't you answer the first three times? Oh . . ."

"It's the only thing that makes sense."

He waved me off. "She what? Noel, your grandmother got flummoxed and told T-Bow Orrice everything."

"What did you expect?" And I doubted she'd gotten flustered in the least. Franny Cox told the truth, and she did it bluntly. "What did he say about the picture?"

I heard Trudy's answer through Darnell's phone. "He said, 'I never should have trusted that crook.' "

"And which one of them had she shown him at that point?" Darnell went on.

"Both. He thought they were the same guy. That's what threw her off so badly. He didn't explain what he never should have trusted the 'crook' about, though. He wasn't handing out news bulletins, and I'm not sure he really thinks she came alone. But Darnell . . . Noel, can you hear me?" I could, but Darnell put the call on his speaker anyway. "He told her to 'get those babies out of sight.' We need you out of your parents' house by tonight, no matter *what* your mother says." I tended to agree.

"Sorry, Tasha." I turned up the video playing on the overhead DVD player to drown out our conversation. Though I was trying to keep the twins from overhearing, she took two inhaler puffs, and I thought she didn't need to hear this either.

Darnell flipped off the speaker. "Are you coming back now, Trudy? Good. I'll see you in an hour." After he hung up, Darnell explained.

"Besides the badge he stole at your fundraiser, which he used to access Orrice, Dalton had already hacked some passwords. I told you how he sent emails to our boss that made it look like Liam was changing his mind about what to think of our investigation.

"*Charles* was the one who was so adamant Trudy and I needed to stay here. We think he felt sure the feds would have *someone* involved, and he preferred for it to be people he'd already made. Trudy wanted you to invite Liam to your gala so he could see how large of a territory we really had to search."

"They *were* there in their official capacity."

"Yes. He wanted us recalled. He has influence, and we wanted to show him we were still needed here. That woman showing up with the capuchin convinced him for a little while, but he was on our boss again after about a month. And then he wasn't. And then he was. It was the waffling all over again."

"Ironic the crazy capuchin lady would cause you guys to think something was up."

"Seemed pretty obvious to us."

"Darnell, we get people like her all the time. They don't usually show up in the middle of fundraisers, but they all think they're donating something valuable to us and want legal acknowledgment. And they run the gamut from naive parents with heartbroken kids to . . . well, her. You've seen them."

"Noel, she was a work of art. She used the monkey as a distraction to steal Liam's wallet and badge."

"How could she have known he'd be there?"

"Like I said, hacked computer passwords. But you didn't hear me say that. Those were more damaging by far than the badge was to us. He could never have used the badge to enter one of our offices."

"Ouch."

"Not long after, Trudy started seeing Liam around town, but he walked away every time she tried to approach him. She was suspicious there was something he didn't want us to find in the city. We figured that was why he suddenly wanted us here half the time. When Natasha identified the man in the picture as Charles Dalton, we thought we had it. We thought, just like Orrice did, that Dalton *was* Metcalfe, which would have meant serious high-level corruption. But when Trudy took the picture to our boss, our boss took the pictures straight to Liam, because *she* saw the differences quickly enough. She interacts with Liam more regularly and wasn't as easily taken in. It's a good imitation, but not perfect. The two of them figured out Dalton's deception and how long it's been going on."

"Okay, I'm following . . ."

"I want to come back to you and Lance. Why do you think the Marine's supply truck is what's being used to smuggle animals? And what does your husband think he's doing?"

"I have no *idea* what my husband is thinking. And I think the Marine has become a monkey-house because my sanctuary has too many macaques."

"I'm not seeing the connection."

I thumped the steering wheel, and the horn blatted. "You weren't *there* the first day we brought William with us. He recognized those guys, and he didn't like them. He wasn't upset about the chimp enclosure. He was completely fascinated by the spiders. It was the rhesus macaques bugging him. He'd seen *all* of those things at the zoo before, and there was no reason for him to be especially upset by this one species. He *saw* something upsetting about the macaques. We thought it had to do with the monkeys themselves and didn't pay enough attention. He kept saying, 'no cages.' I think he saw them in cages in that delivery truck. I think he was afraid of what we would do to them, and by extension, him, since the *last* time he saw rhesus macaques, he wound up locked in somebody's garage."

"But maybe it's because the macaques looked so human."

"Come off it. Rhesus macaques look like little old men. Capuchins and chimps have more humanesque features. He *saw* something at the pizza parlor, and somebody is either afraid he's going to tell us or thinks he already has."

Darnell didn't argue with me further for the rest of the drive home, though he clearly remained unpersuaded. I could see why Lance had chosen a solitary stakeout. Darnell's skepticism was wholly misplaced. My husband was going to be furious with me. But I had already decided I preferred him alive and angry. Darnell, and probably Trudy, wanted to waste too much time being sure when the truth was warbling around in my macaque enclosure risking the little animals' sanitary conditions and all of our lives. Once I saw all those monkeys, I knew we had reached the point of needing Stan's help, and we'd gotten there even sooner than I'd anticipated. We needed a new enclosure. Maybe two.

Firth (*firth? Were my ordinals devolving into lemon-nanners?*), we needed to re-catalog *all* our monkeys. Was it only rhesus macaques? What if we had extras everywhere? What if *all* our head counts were off? Seconth (*yes, lemon-nanners and cheese-lights*) we needed to stop the inflow before things got worse.

Nana went to have what she called a lie-down as soon as she and Trudy arrived. Since she hardly ever napped at Mama's house, I knew this morning had taken a toll on her. "Noel, come help me get settled," she ordered.

I followed. It saved me Trudy and Darnell's demands and Lance's towering silence. Drew had cleared him out before going inside to confront the Gibsons, and we hadn't heard from Drew since.

"You were right," I hissed at my husband in passing. "And you couldn't have done anything else but get hurt by staying back there." We didn't have confirmation, and it was always possible this particular truck had held no monkeys. But I was sure. The monkeys were coming through the Marine.

As soon as I returned to the kitchen, Natasha called, "Here she is. Sit down, Noel. Close your eyes."

"What . . . ?"

"Sit." Once I was arranged, she went on. "I now present to you their majesties Sara and William, crown princess and prince of the Rue-Lakeland household." When I didn't do anything, she added, "Uh, you can open your eyes now."

Sara's princess gown was finished. It was elegant and pink, with drapes of fabric fitting for any royalty, but a practical hemline ending above its owner's ankles. "Nobody has *ever* made me a dress before for my own," she proclaimed. I doubted most kids her age had custom dresses. But it clearly meant more to this one than the other children my mama had sewn for in the past. Margie and I took her for granted growing up, yearning for department store clothes so we could be more like our friends. My nieces had lost their love of her creations several years ago. And my nephew never did have much interest to begin with.

"It comes with the territory of having a seamstress for a grandmother," I told Sara, thinking suddenly of the stream of similar dresses my mother had produced from this exact pattern. All three of my nieces had princess outfits, and I wasn't sure, but I thought it resembled the one Marguerite and I used to fight over as children. I wondered if it was too late to ask Mama to sew my clothes again.

Far more amusing was William. Mama had retrieved and washed the suit with powder blue lapels Will had worn all weekend. She had already altered it for my son, and the fit was perfect. It was the way he wore it, rocking even as he strutted, flapping his arms and spinning as he moved, that made him so delightfully funny. The suit and dress clashed majestically, and I had to hold back laughter. The twins carried themselves tall, both beaming lopsided joy. "Your highnesses," I told them, "you look wonderful."

They paraded out. Lance followed them, still pointedly ignoring me. He returned quickly enough when Trudy sat down and started talking, though. "You have to understand, T-Bow Orrice isn't your average gang-banger," she began. "He's an empire-builder. He's probably got thirteen kids, and he's intensely protective of them, even though, except for his oldest son and Layla, he pretends they don't exist. He'd rather not claim Layla, but he had custody of her for too long to deny it. His son is running his empire right now, not that anybody can prove it, and Layla's running wild. He'd go to great lengths to ensure their safety, *if* he thought it would work.

"I have it on good authority Layla's life has been threatened more than once in the last several weeks. I think Orrice believes he has been working with Liam Metcalf to ensure her protection. In all reality . . . I already told you what I think Dalton intends." She shot a glance toward the hall, where Tasha had the twins modeling on an imaginary catwalk. He was probably the person pulling Gary's strings last June. I just wish Orrice didn't know so much. Assuming Dalton *is* alive, I'd like the man to live long enough for me to arrest him."

Maybe Nana *had* been flummoxed. She certainly sounded worn-out upstairs, and like she didn't want the man to know any more than she had to reveal. "Don't get mad at somebody whose last act of subterfuge was pretending to be married to Mama's daddy to keep from getting ostracized in the 1950s. She can't lie smoothly."

"Point taken. And Dalton surely would love to find that journal. Natasha has said before that he was one of the group's distributors. We knew his name, but we had no formal evidence connecting him to the group. Since he has not been arrested, he must know we don't have all the evidence yet. He may think Tasha knows but has kept the journal from us to use for herself."

"I would never!" Natasha called from the hall.

"I didn't say *we* think it," Trudy assured her. "We need to go over all the places Gary spent time in this county again."

Not long after, Drew arrived. If Lance wasn't speaking to me at this point, he was at least standing close to me again. "You will not be surprised to learn," Drew said, "the Gibsons didn't invite me in back or volunteer to hand over the monkeys you think they're harboring."

Lance shot me a look. *See?* I returned his glower with my best Intractable Professor Rue face.

Drew sat down, and Trudy brought him up to date. "Now what?" Drew asked, when she had finished. "Anybody got a magic lamp or psychic to show us to that journal?"

"Can I ask a stupid question?" Natasha returned from playing with the twins. "Relax, the front, parlor, and patio doors are locked," she said as Lance and I turned her way. "William can't get out except through *this* door."

Of course he could. But the kitchen door was open, I could see him parading, and quite honestly, this conversation needed Natasha more than me. I moved to a position where I could monitor the twins and smiled, hoping my expression was light and relieved, not heavy with worry. "Thanks, hon. Ask away."

"You guys have searched the old records room with the film equipment, right?"

"The what?" said Lance.

"The old records room at the sanctuary."

"We've been through our office a dozen times." Lance caught my hand on the way by and held it, so that, although I could still keep an eye on the twins, I couldn't leave the kitchen.

"Not your office. The old records room."

"Tasha, what are you talking about? We keep the outdated records in our old barn office, up at the school, or in the basement at home."

Natasha stared open-mouthed between Lance and me, then sank into the chair I'd just vacated, her head in her hands. "I guess I should have asked sooner," she muttered. Then, quickly, defensively, she added, "I only even remembered last Friday, okay?" This explained some of her despondency. Whether the information was relevant or not, her flashbacks *always* came with guilt.

"What room do you mean?" asked Trudy.

"I should have said something on Friday, but I kind of assumed you already knew. It's right on the edge of the sanctuary. I assumed you'd have tripped over it six months ago."

"Don't you think we'd have asked you about it, if we had?"

Tasha shrugged and looked back at the table.

"Natasha, help me." It was yet another moment when I wanted to mother her but instead had to respect her space.

Everything about her body language said she didn't want to be touched. I kept my hands to myself. "I know all the sanctuary buildings. There is no 'old records room'."

When she finally replied, Natasha's voice was flat, almost emotionless, as if she'd had to cut herself out of the discussion to hold it at all. Everything, *all* of this, was supposed to be between her and a therapist. It should have been private. "When we . . . when we filmed with the monkeys," she said, "we always used the old records room. It's the . . . it's over on the other side of the creek behind the sanctuary. It looks like you're going into a fruit cellar or something, but it's the size of a basement. You get there from the employee road behind the mall site, but you break off before you get to the new enclosure."

"Can you take us there?"

"She's got therapy in less than two hours, Drew," I told him.

"This won't take long." Trudy clearly shared Drew's perspective.

"It's okay," Natasha insisted. Then she turned away from us. She was talking to Drew, Darnell, and Trudy. Lance and I weren't even there as far as she was concerned. Maybe she needed us to be elsewhere so she could come back to herself later. "You knew so many names and stuff, I figured you'd found the place already."

Trudy shook her head.

Natasha shrugged. "Let's go," she said. "I want to do something first, though."

"What?" We all wanted to know.

"Can I talk to Layla?"

"Why do you want to?" Lance demanded.

"Because as dumb as I feel about Friday, I feel worse for her. She's stupid and naive, and . . . maybe I can help her. I don't know."

"I'll have to ask her guardian ad litem," said Drew.

"They did take her from her mom?" Tasha asked. We were all entirely too familiar with Drew's legalese. A guardian ad litem was a court-appointed individual who was supposed to act in place of a parent and ensure the best interests of a child were being met.

"For the moment. Let me make a call. Why don't we take care of all this after your therapy appointment? It's not like two more hours' delay . . ."

"No. I want to deal with all of it *now*. I've *got* to be in school tomorrow. We're getting ready for midterms, and I'm barely keeping up. *Barely*. I have a C average, and I know they regret letting me jump ahead a grade. I need to be in class. I need to be in bed and *calm* tonight. And right now, I'm worried sick."

"Let me see if I can get an answer," said Drew. "You have to promise you won't assault her."

"Yeah, I know. I was majorly freaked out on Friday."

He walked outside to place the call.

"It sounds like I'll take Natasha down to the station," said Trudy. "Then she can show the deputy where this extra room is. I'll bring her to her therapy appointment and home, and you can all . . ."

"No," Lance and I said at once. Whatever personal differences we might have, we were still on exactly the same parenting page.

"You aren't taking her anywhere without me," I added.

"Us," Lance corrected me. He gently squeezed my shoulders.

I gripped his hands with my own. "Us. Natasha needs us right now. The twins will be fine with Mama and Daddy for a couple of hours. Drew's got people back out here. Mama, don't forget to wake Nana up to pee."

Trudy and Darnell didn't like it, but they ultimately split up again, Darnell staying with the twins largely because William had trapped him into a game of trucks, and his departure would have caused a meltdown.

When she saw who the guardian ad litem was, Natasha started walking backward away from her. Lance stepped gently to one side, so she backed straight into him.

"Hello, Chandra," I said.

"Hello, Noel." She turned to Natasha. "If this conversation becomes unproductive at any time, I will bring it to an end. Clear?"

After her initial retreat, Natasha seemed to have recollected her resolve. "Completely."

"And," Chandra said, "before we begin, I want to know what you hope to accomplish."

"I need to know she's as naive as she seems. I need to believe I wasn't completely screwed up to think she, at least, seriously didn't mean any harm on Friday. I want to help her. I mean . . . she's my sister. I don't want to hate her guts forever."

"I won't allow her to incriminate herself," Chandra warned us. "I'm no lawyer, and anything she says cannot specifically reference Friday's events."

"I don't want to talk *about* Friday. We'll accomplish a big argument if we talk about *that*. She'll be all '*Robby-my-true-love*,' and I'll have to puke and leave. *I* want to know about *Layla*. I want to know she's not a . . . not already a player."

"Come on, then." We all started to follow, but Chandra stopped us with a glance. "Only the two of us," she said. "This isn't a party."

I might have protested, but Natasha agreed quickly. "Good."

Left suddenly at loose ends, we trailed along with the detective back to his office. "I think you're right," he told us. "If they don't have monkeys back there, the Gibsons sure seem to have something. Tony was downright agitated about my questions, and he had no intentions of letting me into the back room. And now he's wise to me. I don't have anything concrete a judge could use to grant me a warrant to look around before all the evidence drives off, but what you're saying makes sense. I wish those two kids weren't mixed up in it."

He didn't mean my children. "Why are you sympathetic to Layla and Robby?" Natasha's life was in danger. William was the one who nearly got stolen. I tried not to sound indignant.

Drew held out his hands in a placating gesture. "They're being used by some powerful people, Noel. *You* know what those people can be like."

"They tried to take—"

"Robby convinced Layla she was playing hero. Now they've been caught, he's ready to throw her to the wolves, but she won't say a word against him. But he's not telling me everything useful about *himself,* either. We all agree there's a good chance he's the one who took William in the first place. But he's terrified. Somebody has him convinced it's better to go to jail for kidnapping than sell out. He'd love to be rid of Layla, but he won't give up the people who *are* responsible.

"They're both getting used. And they're kids. If they can't make some good choices in the near future, they're likely to wind up in detention until they turn twenty-one."

"Good."

Drew looked to Lance in supplication, but my husband said, "I'm with Noel."

Drew gave up. "Tell me about your monkeys."

We were still talking when Chandra and Natasha returned, too soon.

"She won't talk to me." Natasha looked weepy and shaken.

"She demanded her aunt again," Chandra confirmed, "and then she turned away and refused to say a word to either one of us."

"And I . . . I . . . I need to sit and breathe. She looked like . . . she made me think of . . . the angle of her face when she

. . . it made me think of when Mom died."

Drew had her seated before she finished speaking. I stood ready with her inhaler, but she slowly mastered her emotions.

"I appreciate your effort," Chandra said. She turned to go.

"Listen, I don't know if I can help her, or if I even want to," said Natasha, "but I feel sorry for her. Here's what I think is going on." Chandra turned back, and after that, Natasha seemed to only be speaking to the social worker.

"She's in deep with Robby. He goes to school with me, but he's flunking out this year. The scuttlebutt is she practically lives with him. Her mom works in Columbus and travels with her job. She thinks she's leaving Layla with one friend when she goes out of town, but Layla convinces *that* friend another one has her. The other one thinks she's with the first. Her mom only ever calls Layla's cell. She never really checks up."

"Wait," said Lance. "You know she's doing this?"

"It's only gossip. But come on . . . she thought the guy was going to marry her. Plus, she brags as bad as her mom. Robby's been giving her driving lessons, and if he was smuggling monkeys into the sanctuary, I bet Layla was helping him out the whole time."

"You think so?" Layla's mother had arrived, and she was furious.

CHAPTER 30

Dear Nora:

I never get places on time. Even when I leave fifteen minutes early, I arrive late. What can I do?

Missed the Bus

Dear Missed:

Identify "Tardy" as your new lifestyle choice and hope to be invited places anyway.

Nora

"How *dare* you," Shannon Dearborn demanded of Drew, "prevent me from seeing my own daughter? She is a minor."

"Excuse me," said Chandra. "I am Layla's guardian ad litem . . ."

"Hello." Shannon's greeting didn't suggest she was happy to see Chandra Evans at all.

"Sorry." Deputy Greene looked in. "She kind of bulled through."

Drew rolled his eyes. I clearly heard the words "damned rookie" in his mutter.

"Let me tell you something," Shannon said to Chandra. "Every word these people have been telling you is a lie."

Shannon Dearborn was my own height, barely five feet tall, and the rare acquaintance who didn't tower over me. This made it unfortunately simple for her to glare past Drew and right into my eyes.

"I'm trying to *help* her," Drew insisted. "Right now, she's got at least six credible witnesses who saw her attempting to kidnap *their* son." He jerked a thumb toward Lance and me for illustration.

"We'll see. I know how cops work. You lie to get a person to speak . . ."

"She hasn't said a word," said Chandra. "And you, ma'am . . ."

"I saw her." I hadn't meant to say anything. Shannon was already furious enough, and Chandra was more than capable of handling her. But here I stood at the police station with my husband while my foster daughter's life was in danger and my son, the child who had nearly been kidnapped, cooled his heels with my parents, an FBI agent, a made-over ring-bearer suit, some toy trucks, and a pair of fake gardening shears. How could this woman think her daughter had done nothing? Still, keeping in mind what Chandra had said to Natasha about productivity, I tried for a reasonable tone. "I think . . . I hope her intentions were better than they seemed, but she had one arm, her boyfriend had the other, and they were dragging him toward the boyfriend's car." In spite of my efforts, I ended on a snarl.

"Layla doesn't have a boyfriend, and that's hardly how she puts it." But the look Shannon threw at Drew suggested I had confirmed his story, and now the eyes she narrowed in my direction were wary, but less hostile. "She said she was sitting at home when *he* showed up with handcuffs."

"She was in my mother's front yard. I absolutely saw her . . ."

"How would you know who you saw? How can you be sure it wasn't some other biracial child. Don't they all look alike to you?"

Now I didn't snarl. I shouted. "My *son* is biracial. *Both* my children are biracial, and they are *both* Layla's biological siblings." Probably. Probably they were her siblings. I tried to think about that, not my own rising anger. I forcibly lowered my voice. "No, 'they' do not look alike to me any more than you look like *me* because we're both five feet tall and white with brown hair. I'm hardly going to forget the kid who was distributing sex tapes of Natasha this year."

"Excuse me? What did you accuse my daughter of doing?"

"We spoke on the phone about this before I met with your sister to get them *back.*"

"I never spoke to you before in my life. I . . . wait. You met with my *sister?*" She whipped her head around to Drew. "*When* was Ivy here? I specifically barred her from visitation."

"You don't have a say," said Chandra.

I tried to break in. "It was before Layla went back to school in the fall."

Shannon plowed on without listening, planting herself directly in front of Drew so he had to bend down to maintain eye contact. "I have a longstanding restraining order against her. She is not permitted to be near me or Layla, either one . . . wait . . . what?" She turned back to me.

"I said it was back before school started."

Shannon licked her lips. "How long before school started?" She didn't give me time to answer. "I was at a conference the week before school started. Layla was with my *brother* in Cheboygan. She was fishing on the *lake.*" Her fury drained for an instant, only to be replaced with frantic energy. "No. He wouldn't. He *couldn't.*" She grabbed her phone out of her pocket as she spoke. When her brother answered the call, she demanded, "Did Ivy con you into letting her see Layla this summer?"

The hostile glowers Shannon was directing at Natasha slowly

dwindled to sorrowful glances. When she hung up, Shannon was an entirely different person. She slumped into a folding chair. "All right," she said. "I'm ready to listen."

"It seems like you may need to talk," Drew suggested.

"I'm not talking to *anybody*."

"Shannon, I cannot break the law to help Layla. As her guardian will tell you, I've already stretched it as far as it goes. But I was a stupid teenager in my day. If a sergeant in Columbus hadn't lost some evidence and taken a serious rap, there's the possibility I'd have been in jail when I was fifteen. If I was lucky. And from there, I'd . . . let's say I'd probably be serving time instead of serving the law."

"Your colorful history is fascinating, but I think the rest of us . . ." Chandra began, but Drew cut her off, still speaking to Shannon, utterly ignoring Layla's guardian.

"This cop lived in my neighborhood. He knew my family. Knew my situation. I don't know if he did what he did on purpose. Maybe he *was* an idiot who couldn't maintain a chain of evidence. But it was the first time I'd seen my dad might be wrong about the boys in blue being out to get us. And this cop, he was a black man, like me.

"That man saved my life. And I'm not going to forget it. I'll do what I *can* to help your daughter, but you've got to help me help her. Chandra has been appointed by the court to make sure Layla's best interests are met here. We aren't the enemy."

"I don't know if I have anything to say," Shannon said. "I don't think I know anything anymore. But I'm beginning to think Layla was *not* on the lake this summer. What if my con artist, crazy-ass sister cried crocodile tears to my *stupid, fluff-brained* brother and got ahold of Layla, then came back here instead? Let's *entertain* the possibility Layla is lying to me about how she spent her summer vacation and what she did yesterday. *If* those things are the case, what are we talking about here?"

We all rushed in to update Shannon about her daughter's behavior, but Natasha drowned us out. "I'm going to tell you everything I possibly can," she said, "but you're going to answer one question for me when I'm done." She turned swiftly to Chandra and added, "I swear the question's got nothing to do with Layla," before returning her attention to Shannon.

Shannon studied Tasha for a long time, and then nodded assent. Chandra did, too, but Natasha wasn't watching her.

Natasha didn't only summarize the summer. She took the conversation back to the time even before she and Layla had been at Nelly Penobscott's together, when Shannon was in Gary's pornography company, before it consisted entirely of illegal activities. She built her relationship with her sister one word at a time for Shannon, until the woman sitting in front of us was staring with wide eyes and a loose jaw.

"Lies!" Shannon finally said. "It's all been one lie after another." I thought she was referring to Natasha, and I got ready to defend my foster daughter, but then Shannon said, "I wonder if she even catches the bus half the time! She's had truancy issues this year, and I always believed her when she swore she missed the bus and had no way to get to school. But if Ivy convinced *you* she was *me* on the phone . . . and Layla . . . She lies so *much*. And she sounds like an adult. She's exactly like Ivy. Exactly like her. I was a wild kid, but I've grown up, do you understand? This is bad."

"I said I had a question." Natasha had long since assumed the dispassionate tone she had used back at Mama and Daddy's when she was telling us about the records room we didn't know existed.

"You did. You did say that." Shannon sounded half hysterical now, and I wasn't sure what kind of answer she would give.

Natasha said, "I never thought I'd met Ivy before August. When I saw her at your place, she looked a little familiar, but I

342

couldn't place her. I figured I'd seen her around or something. It's a pretty small town, you know. I never knew she was in with Gary and his people. She must not have acted?"

Shannon shook her head. "Ivy was above that," she said.

"But now I'm scared," Natasha went on. "I think I *have* seen her before. When I saw Layla a minute ago, she turned her head away at an angle, and I was looking, for a second, at the EMT who first responded when Mom . . . when she died. And I want to know if Ivy ever poses as a nurse or doctor or anything like that. Does she ever go around pretending she's a medical professional?"

"She doesn't have to pretend," said Shannon. "She was a paramedic for a few years, and last I heard she had her RN."

"That's worse." Now Natasha was the one heading for hysteria, and I found myself fumbling through my purse for the inhaler I had only recently put away. She wheezed out those words, and I knew if I didn't hurry, we'd be needing a paramedic for *her.*

Tasha took the inhaler, but she waved me off when I said she should move from the chair to the floor. She took several shaky breaths and asked Shannon, "Do you know if Ivy uses purple syringes almost exclusively?"

What kind of a question was *that?* My desire to know wrestled with my pride in Natasha for mastering her panic long enough to continue the conversation. Tasha had demons. Bad ones. But she also had victories, and this one was enormous. Still, the question made no sense.

Shannon cocked her head to one side. "Yeah," she said. "When she can get away with it. If she's the one placing the order. See, she came to Christmas right after she got her paramedic license, flashing those things around the house. Needles. Around a kid. Around *my* kid. I knew she wasn't using those things at work. Those were for personal use, if you follow me. She wanted me to shoot up, when I'd only gotten clean a year before. As much dope as I did, Layla was always clean. That was when I cut Ivy off. And she did so many things after that I was forced to get the restraining order. She . . ."

We didn't get to find out what other things Ivy had done to Shannon, because Natasha crumpled sideways off her chair.

"Tasha!" I thought she'd passed out.

But she looked up at me and reached out like Sara or William might. "Noel?" she wailed.

"I'm right here, honey." I sat beside her. "Lance, get her therapist on the phone."

"Noel?" she repeated, as if she hadn't heard me.

"I'm right here." I gently took her arms, trying to simultaneously respect her need for space and affirm my presence.

She seized me and folded herself around me, heaving and shaking. "I think she killed my mother!" And that was the last coherent thing we heard for some time. This wasn't a panic attack. It wasn't accompanied by the gasping for air and complaints of chest pains that came along with those. This was grief. This was a hysteria born from years of holding in pain. Natasha clung to me sobbing, and eventually let me worm around to hold onto her instead, until she was reduced to hiccupping whimpers on the floor.

When I could pay attention to anything else again, Shannon was describing her sister to Drew and Trudy, and I felt a rush of gratitude for law enforcement officers who were willing to take the word of a fifteen-year-old girl who'd once had a sketchy relationship with the truth.

Lance had joined us on the floor. "I'm glad you got me out of the pizza place," he said. "Look at the family fun I might have missed otherwise. Dr. Hanson says you can take some more of your anti-anxiety medication, Tasha. We're missing your appointment right now, but he'll wait for us."

"I'm fine." She was still anything but.

As if she'd been waiting for that moment precisely, Trudy shifted her attention from Shannon and Drew and down to Natasha. "Honey, can you talk?"

Lance stiffened. I wasn't impressed with the demands being placed upon Natasha either, and I started to voice my concerns. But, as she had been doing all afternoon, Natasha overrode me. "Listen, I don't *know* anything. And I don't know how you'd prove any of it. And . . ."

"You tell us what you *believe,* and we'll work on finding proof." Trudy had her tablet out.

I rose and helped Tasha to her feet. An artist was working with Shannon to draw Ivy. The woman emerging only looked slightly like the one I had met when we retrieved the DVD. This woman bore far more resemblance to the one who surrendered her capuchin in June. Her name hadn't been Ivy, but a false ID was easy to get. Darnell was right about the real reason for her to crash our party.

"No." Natasha wouldn't let Trudy start recording. "It's not only Mom. I don't think Granddad and Gran are safe. I think she maybe works at the nursing home. I think she's maybe Gran's favorite nurse. Granddad doesn't *have* until next Wednesday. Trudy, there's *got* to be somebody you can trust to get them *out* of there. *Both* of them."

Tasha was starting to squeak again. "Take your pill," I advised.

She complied. "I'll try to slow down," she promised. "But, please, Trudy. There's a nurse there who always seems to be around when I visit Gran. Gran says it's her favorite. I've never gotten a decent look at the woman's face because she sees me and goes, even if she's in the middle of a procedure, and sends someone else down to finish whatever she was doing. What if Gran isn't depressed? What if she *can't* walk? What if Layla's aunt is sitting around down there playing with both of them and going to . . . to . . ."

"Give me five minutes," Trudy said. "A word, Noel?"

I stepped into the hall with her, but left the door open so I could still see Natasha. Trudy didn't waste time getting to the point. "I can get Stan and Gert moved. It's you I'm worried about. You need to get home, get your kids, get your parents, and *go*. You need to hide until we sort this out."

"So you're putting us in a protection program."

"For a few days. We'll take care of Natasha. I think once she shows us this room, we'll have enough information to make another round of arrests. You should be home by Christmas."

I barely heard the second half of her sentence and fastened instead on the first words she'd said. "I am *not* leaving Natasha."

"We'll reunite her with her grandparents . . ."

A hand on my shoulder told me Lance was behind me. "Noel's right," he said. "Not a chance in hell. The next place we're going is to therapy with Natasha, then back to our children. We'll *all* go wherever it is you suggest together. Stan and Gert Oeschle can come to us. We are *not* leaving Natasha right now."

Chapter 31

Dear Nora:
Night after night, the guy in the apartment next door wakes me snoring! I'm sure the whole floor hears it, but we're all too nice to say anything. What can I do?

Sleepless in Ironweed

Dear Sleepless:
Either get a little rude or move.

Nora

"Noel, Lance, use a little common sense . . ."

"We *are* using common sense," I snapped. "We're getting Natasha's grandparents to safety, and then we're getting Natasha to her therapist. Then we'll all go someplace fun together. Stan likes to give us things? Tell him to make it somewhere tropical."

"And I want to know where the hell this records room came from that it seems like even Art didn't know about," Lance said. "He *never* told us. I'm calling Rick. Maybe he can show us instead of Natasha."

Trudy gave up.

I explained our plans to Natasha. "I better call Granddad," she said. "If he doesn't know who's coming, he's likely to be uncooperative right now. And I'm *going* to show them the room. I want that behind me."

On the way to Natasha's therapist, I asked what Lance had

learned from Rick. "Some," he said. "The first contractor the university hired to build the center was one Merle Evans."

"I had no *idea* Merle used to be a builder."

"We had no idea he worked at the Marine, either. He kept to himself all the time. Anyway, he's related to a certain Winfred Prescott. In addition to going bankrupt and backing out of a couple of different university building programs, he chose a floodplain for the center's original site, and the whole place had to be moved after it was half completed. The original site was abandoned. Rick thought any actual structures had been demolished or filled in, but I guess one got missed."

"You think this old records room was part of the original site?"

"I think maybe Merle saved it for himself and joined up with Gary when Gary moved his operations out here."

"It would explain why Dr. Prescott thought his head was next on the chopping block," I mused. "If he thought the people who killed Hugh Marsland were looking for the old site and he might know where it was because his relative built it, then he would have been pretty scared. But why would he have known they wanted to know that?"

"What if they'd already asked him? What if he'd already been threatened? What if Hugh's head wasn't supposed to intimidate you, but *him*."

"Or both of us."

"It doesn't matter. He probably blames the university for the problems with Merle's company. But Rick says our Merle has a rather well-known drinking problem. His company went bankrupt because he couldn't keep customers."

We had reached the therapist's office. I hoped Natasha didn't take long. I wanted my babies back. I wanted them safe. I would feel better when I could touch them.

Apparently, they felt the same. I had told Mama where we

were heading, and she arrived unannounced. "Here," she said. "I'm exhausted, and I have no idea which one of these things is the 'afternoon' meds." The pills were all laid out in a seven-day minder, clearly marked, so I didn't know what she meant.

I quickly found out. The kids were arguing with her about which ones they were supposed to take. We had recently changed a blue pill out for a green one, and both of them were convinced they should still be taking the old medicine. They didn't want to take the new one. "It makes me tired," Sara complained.

"That should wear off in a week or two," I coaxed.

"Look, if you take the meds, I'll get you ice cream," Mama promised, reviving now that she knew what was going on.

I groaned. We tried not to buy the twins' cooperation. But it was a better solution than fighting with them in the middle of the therapist's waiting room. And it meant Mama was trusting us about the need for the meds, a victory of its own.

Lance and Mama went back outside with Trudy and Darnell. They sat in the van, comparing notes, and in their lieu, I was left with the newly returned to duty Deputy Greene. Drew had sent him and his partner with us as an easy job that couldn't possibly get him into trouble, especially since Trudy was along.

He was obviously uncomfortable in the therapist's waiting room, and he shifted in his chair and tried to hide behind ancient reading material. "That's a kids' magazine," I told him.

"I always liked those better than the adult ones." He had missed my teasing tone.

I abandoned it. "How are you doing?"

"Whole lot warmer. I started trying to convince my wife to move to Florida. If I'm never cold again, it'll be too soon." Then he changed the subject. "We searched your grounds pretty thoroughly back in June, you know."

"I know." They had retraced the days Gary spent in hiding to the point of finding his car buried in underbrush near the new enclosure. They thought he had been sleeping in it.

"This records room Natasha is talking about has got to be hidden."

"But *where*? I keep trying to think who else would know the center's history. Maybe Stan does. I'll have to ask him. But I'd like to talk to somebody *now* and he's . . . preoccupied." I didn't want to advertise Stan and Gert's move until it was over. "There's been so much turnover in bio science in the last ten years, we don't have many holdovers."

"What about your secretary? Do you think he's got any files?"

"Not a bad idea. But he's . . ."

"Yeah. Got a concussion."

"Among other things." Travis's hospital stay hadn't been a long one, and he was home recuperating. But he wasn't due to return to work for another day, and I had no intentions of bothering him to go in sooner. His kidnapping had brought his and Bryan's parenthood crisis to a head. They were getting ready to start all over with social services and adopt from foster care. "I wonder if I can raise the old secretary."

However, I was denied this opportunity as Sara swiped the deputy's magazine. Deputy Greene grabbed it back. "Hey!"

Trudy and Darnell returned. "We've reached a compromise of sorts," Trudy said. "We're all going to stay in the hotel on the bypass tonight. Natasha stays with us, we stay with you, and we all join the Oeschles day after tomorrow."

"Your dad and grandma went out already," Darnell said.

"And we're going to go swimming at the pool! They have an inside pool for me to use!" Sara announced in a sing-song voice. She threw herself at Deputy Greene and ripped the magazine out of his hand once more. "Read me this, cop guy," she commanded. "I've got a cop guy who's a friend of mine, but he's a black guy like me. And he doesn't read. Also he has a hat."

"He does so read! I do too have a hat!"

"Nuh-uh. I don't see it."

"It's rude to wear a hat indoors. I left it in my cruiser."

"Oooh, can we play with your lights? Our cop guy lets William and me play with the lights when he comes to change Will's batteries."

Deputy Greene cast me a look that plainly begged, *Help!*

"The batteries in his tracer bracelet."

"I know which batteries. But I'm not sure . . ."

"Sara, now isn't a good time to play with the lights."

"But I love the lights. I don't like the siren so good, because it's noisy, and I hate loud."

"Loud. Yuck." As always, Will was chugging trucks around the floor. Then the outside door creaked open, and he lunged across the room. "William hates the old guy circle-dot man," he bellowed. Tony Gibson staggered as William arrived with a crash. Before I could stop him, William had fastened onto Mr. Gibson's ankles. Fury, guilt, and fear warred in my chest, leaving me paralyzed. Deputy Greene moved to block the door between Mr. Gibson and the therapy area even as Darnell blocked the newcomer inside.

"Easy there, bud. That hurts." Mr. Gibson's tone was almost conversational. "I can see why you don't like me. I guess I scared the bejeepers out of you, and then you getting . . . well . . . made off with." He looked around the room at us. I wanted to peel Will off him, but I couldn't move. "I should have said something about it sooner, but I felt awful about how I'd behaved, and it only would have made me look bad. Nothing I can do to help looking bad now, though, I guess. Anyway, I thought I saw your van outside, and I wanted to apologize before I go turn myself in or whatever."

"Turn yourself in?" Lance sat on the floor beside the man and worked Will's fingers loose. My body finally released me, and I joined him.

"I should have retired a long time ago," Mr. Gibson muttered. "I found what your boss was looking for," he said to the deputy. "I thought I'd hired trustworthy people! They never stole from me! They . . ."

Suddenly, the old man toppled over as William made a renewed effort, attaching himself to Mr. Gibson's knees now instead of his ankles. "Will, let go." I finally recovered myself enough to speak.

"No." I felt torn between delight that my son had responded to me directly and concisely, and frustration because he was offering up defiance. "William." I reached for him.

"The old guy circle-dot man yelled at me!"

"You startled me, kiddo. That kitchen's not safe for a kid."

Mr. Gibson only moved to pull himself loose when Lance and I began prying Will off, and he was careful not to hurt the child, even though William continued to thrash and kick. Free, Mr. Gibson did not stand up, but remained seated, looking between Lance and me. "On the day he was taken, he'd walked in back, and he was heading for the ovens. I shouted at him. Hell, I didn't know he was autistic. I thought he was some goof about to get burned and land me with a lawsuit. I chewed him right out! He bolted for the back door, and one of my people caught him running up the ramp onto the truck. He squirmed loose, but then he went back up front.

"When I saw he was with Natalie, I thought I had the long and short of it. Everybody knows the Forresters are overwhelmed with all those kids. I didn't want to dump more on her head telling her about him making trouble in back. But I guess . . . I think the employee who grabbed him on the truck was Robby. And then poof, the kid went missing not long after. I watched him go outside, and I would swear to you he left my door in Natalie's group.

"But I . . . I . . ." his voice faltered as he turned to Deputy

Greene. "I'm not so sure now. It must seem hard to believe, but it's been years since I got on my own trucks, and now I'm not sure at all. I've got arthritis, and the truck ramp is steep. I've had one of the kids unload for me for a couple of years now. But after the detective was asking so many questions this afternoon, I went out there myself. I guess I need animal control. I've got a truck full of monkeys, and I don't know what I'm going to do with them. I can't even imagine what the health department's going to say. I don't think the animals ever came inside the restaurant . . . surely I'd have seen that! But . . . you're not going to believe me. I own the place. How could I have not known . . . and for how *long*?"

I caught this speech in fragments, as I wrestled Will into a gentle restraint. Deputy Greene said, "Uh, if you've got things under control here, I guess I'd better take him down to the station with me. Sir, what makes you think the truck hasn't driven off?"

"Because I have the keys right here, and I locked the driver in back."

"You *what*? Do you know how *hot* . . ." Deputy Greene wavered. Finally, he said, "It's December. It's forty degrees. They won't boil. I think you're probably under arrest and have a lot of rights that need reading. But we're going to settle this outside." And taking Mr. Gibson by the arm, he left. I hoped his partner in the cruiser had a less befuddled response to the whole situation. If not, I didn't have any trouble at all seeing how the pair had wound up sitting in my refrigerator with knots on their heads.

In my arms, William relaxed only when Tony Gibson was out of sight. Natasha emerged from the therapist's back room looking exhausted. To my surprise, she sat down on the floor beside me and curled in for a hug. I had expected her to pull back after her previous need for contact. It was what she'd done in the past. After a while, she said, "I want to show you that records room now, and then I don't want to talk about it again for a long time."

The path was overgrown, and we had to park at the top of the hill, near the non-mall, and make our way on foot. When she realized she would be leading, Natasha reluctantly handed me the tablet she had been toting all day. Now, she had a battery pack attached in place of a power cord, and she still intended to carry it through the underbrush. I had long since forgotten it. "When we get done, we'll check in and see if Chuck wants to take a run at the chat program," I promised her.

"Okay. But you have to put it in your purse in case he does something while we're down here. I don't want to miss a chance."

"Natasha, Ace has moved on to other things by now. He and Chuck aren't down there staring . . ."

"Please?"

"All right." The tablet went in my purse, which I slung over my shoulder.

"Your mom's a saint," said Lance. The officers from the house were to accompany her to the hotel by way of the ice cream parlor. Trudy and Darnell were *both* with us this time. We had stopped at the barn to pick up flashlights and make sure we hadn't grown any more monkeys while we were away. Jen was there with yet another deputy serving as a security guard. Our emergency was seriously depleting Muscogen County's police force.

Trying to distract myself from crisis and danger, I looked for other topics. "What are we going to do with that mall?" I asked Lance as Natasha led us into the underbrush.

"Three months ago, I'd have said we should donate it to the center and make it something useful." The property was ours, an inheritance from Art. Technically, the orangutan enclosure had been ours, too, but we had hurried to donate it, not wanting either the insurance nightmares or the semblance of maintaining anything but a sanctuary.

"You think we should do something else now?" Blackberry thorns, always prevalent around here, snagged in my jeans, and I cursed as I pulled them free. "How far is this place, Natasha?"

"Not far," she said. "Not by car, anyway. We never walked in. I didn't know the woods took over so fast." Even though there wasn't any greenery showing in winter, the woody underbrush was hard to navigate. An axe or saw would have helped. But ours had been stolen. The saw had probably been the tool used . . . I decided to stop thinking about axes and saws.

Lance mistook my shudder for a shiver and wrapped a warming arm around me. He said, "I think we can make it generate funds."

"Are you thinking of turning it over to the zoo or something?" I didn't want to tell him I'd been thinking along these exact lines.

"Nope. The sanctuary needs to have a youth fundraiser."

"A what?"

"Let's host birthday parties."

"You're not serious."

"See, we've already got webcams, right? And now we've got the enrichment program for Chuck. We'd put in a couple of bounce houses and charge for kids to bring in a dozen friends and watch the webcams and wave back and forth with Chuck and the chimps. They can even watch the monkeys if they want. Maybe they'll figure out how fascinating they are."

"It might work," I said. We had already held one birthday party. In order to capture Lucy, I had been forced to borrow a radio from a little kid. In return, I'd invited him and several of his friends to tour the sanctuary. His mother, who drove our fruit delivery truck, asked if she could turn it into his birthday party. We had agreed with reluctance and been amazed by how smoothly everything went. Of course, it helped we hadn't had the twins yet, and we *had* been housing Natasha, who had been willing to run kid interference.

We had never advertised the event, and it wasn't something we could ever do again if we wanted to maintain our sanctuary status. Still, birthday parties and other educational events had been one of the things on my mind when I had been contemplating joining up with the Ohio Zoo. If we moved the parties away from the sanctuary proper, to a facility off the actual grounds, and if we used cameras to connect the kids to our animals instead of allowing them to tour, it seemed possible we could alleviate some of our financial woes without violating either our role as a sanctuary *or* Art's vision for our research work. Of course, all of this assumed we could drum up the money to finish building the mall and change it from "mall" to "youth fundraiser facility" in the first place.

"Okay, we're here."

Lance and I had been so engrossed in our conversation that we had lost track of the brambles and holes. While we were talking, we had been tramping down the hill from the little-used employee entrance, but toward the creek, instead of toward Chuck's enclosure. At first, I didn't see anything. But then I realized there was a concrete edifice poking up above the ground, almost completely obscured by undergrowth. It was a matter of looking at it from the right angle. From three sides, it looked like disorganized brush. But from the front, the rectangular structure was plainly visible.

"This is the front door. There's another entrance closer to the creek. That's where it's more likely to flood, but it opened easier, so we used it more often." Natasha pointed to another structure, equally hidden in the brambles.

"Did Gary stumble over this or what?" I asked. I wondered if Merle *had* shown it to him. Perhaps Merle had been part of the smuggling ring but not the pornography ring. I wondered if Merle was dead. "Surely he had people to film down here."

"I think they're all in jail. He's been using it for ages, though. I never knew where it was until I moved out here. And then . . . it's hard to explain the forgetting. When I was coming in from the city, I was always lost by the time we reached this point. I didn't know about the center or where he was getting the animals until then. It looks different during the day."

Lance and Darnell braced themselves and lifted a metal bar from across a door, then pulled the handle. The door was practically frozen shut, but slowly it ground open, revealing a set of stairs. "I'm not going down there," Natasha said.

"I'll stay up here with you," Lance and I volunteered together. That pit oozed claustrophobia.

"Stand out of sight inside the door," Darnell coaxed. "Let Trudy and I go down and look around. Once we see what we have here, we'll all leave. The two of us can come back later with the police."

"Who's going to see us?" I protested. Nonetheless, we crowded into the entryway and turned on our flashlights. We could have *had* some police if not for Natasha's insistence on getting this over with now. If we could have waited for either Deputy Greene and his partner or the pair currently sitting at the ice cream parlor with Mama and the twins, Darnell and Trudy wouldn't have needed two trips. But Deputy Greene was already going to have his hands full until he deposited Tony Gibson with Drew, and Drew himself had inherited a busy afternoon. And, in spite of all appearances to the contrary, the Muscogen County police department *did* have problems other than ours to solve today. If their senior detective hadn't been one of the victims of this crime, we never would have merited as much attention as we were already getting.

Lance and I shone our lights as Trudy and Darnell descended through cobwebs. Natasha turned away and looked outside.

The place stank of mildew. "It's cleaner downstairs," said Natasha. "Or it was. But not much." She called down to Trudy and Darnell, "He used to have a bunch of filing cabinets behind the props along the back wall, but don't get caught up in those. There's one wall that isn't concrete in there, and he's got a hidey hole in it a little like the one where Will was stuck back at Lance and Noel's house. Try there."

In the distance, the sanctuary was audible, a constant accompaniment of warbles and hoots, and my purse had started chuffing and grunting. It seemed Chuck was ready to chat today after all. That might be the *perfect* distraction for Tasha right now. Distracted by this, I initially failed to realize the basement sprang to life with racket when Darnell and Trudy descended.

Darnell whistled. "Lance, Noel, you've got monkey problems," he called.

"What?"

A creaking crash, then, "Found the hole, but it's empty. I said you have monkey problems."

Natasha held up a hand for silence. "Do you hear that?" she whispered.

"The basement or my purse?"

Tasha shook her head. "Out there," she whispered.

Then I did hear it. Somebody was crashing through the forest toward us. "Trudy, Darnell, help! Who's there?" I had a glimpse of someone large, and then a human shape blotted out the light.

"Noel!" Ace nearly knocked me down the stairs.

"It's okay! It's Ace." For a moment, my gut unclenched.

Now, the noise from my purse was unmistakable. "Chuck!" Tasha took the purse and rooted out the tablet. "But you

shouldn't leave him alone with his end, Ace! He'll toss it, and
. . ."

My muscles tightened again. Ace hadn't run all this way to
tell us Chuck found the chat program. "What are you doing
here?"

Drew was a solid man, tall, square, and muscular. But his
brother Ace was enormous. There wasn't room for him and us
in that tiny space. "You didn't answer your phone," he gasped.
"Somebody followed you down here."

"Yeah, you!" Natasha still hadn't figured out Ace wasn't here
about Chuck's new enrichment program.

"No. It's nice enough for Chuck to be outside this afternoon,
and I thought we'd try again with that computer. Then another
car pulled up and stopped beside your van, and a couple of
folks got out. They didn't pay me any mind when I hollered. I
don't know where they went, though. Thought I'd have found
them—"

The door slammed behind Ace. Forced forward, he pushed
us all down the first two steps.

"Hey!" For a big man, he could move fast. He spun around
and shoved, even as the bar crashed down on the other side.

Natasha gasped.

"Tasha, hang in there with me. I'll get your inhaler." I started
fumbling through my purse.

"They were looking for this," she babbled. "Ivy, and Charles.
I bet they've been following us every time we're even nearby in
case we show them. I bet it's why your chair guy got so bent
out of shape. I bet *he* knows where it is, or they think he does,
or . . . or . . . he thinks they think he does . . ."

Or else he slammed the door himself. That fear sent prickles
down my neck.

"Down. Get down here," bellowed Darnell. "Let Trudy and
me up to the top."

I didn't think Natasha would follow, but then she led the way. "Back door! Come on. It doesn't lock."

"No, you stay put down there," Darnell ordered. "For all we know, the person who slammed the door at our end is waiting at the other."

But Natasha was speeding down. "Wait, Tasha."

"I can't *stay* down here."

I had the impression of more concrete, dank and unfinished, as she pulled me through. And the noise of monkeys down here made conversation almost impossible. At a fast glance, I saw a dozen carriers jammed against the wall. How long had those animals been here? When had they eaten? Been watered?

There was a bed shoved up into one corner. While I was distracted with the monkeys, Tasha had run to it. "Help me!" She handed me the tablet, where one huge orangutan eye gazed at me.

"Tasha, wait."

"Noel, I can't!"

Keying off of our emotions, the monkeys in the cages screamed. Ace grabbed the bed. He yanked it free with one meaty fist and went to work on a wooden door behind the bed. The layer of dust seemed thinner here, the cobwebs fewer. "This end of the room's been used, guys. And if there isn't a third exit, Darnell's right. Somebody could be at the other end of the passage waiting."

"Back up," Ace said, and he started kicking. Three hard blows, and the door came down. This wasn't any show of martial arts. It was adrenaline and strength. He was as panicked as Natasha.

"We need to—"

My voice died in my throat.

Ivy Dearborn stood in a tunnel, just clear of the fallen door. My flashlight illuminated an axe in her hands. Most likely *our* axe. I couldn't be certain, but I thought I saw dried blood on the head. "Trudy!"

Could Trudy hear me over the monkeys?

Ace could have jumped her. He was big enough, and he'd just driven down a huge piece of wood. Instead, he threw his hands over his head without being asked. "Don't!" he squeaked.

Behind us, Trudy and Darnell were shouting, but their words were lost. Ivy called, "Throw your weapons down the stairs and join us. *Now.*" She took a swing at Ace with the axe, and we all jumped backward.

Trudy shouted down, but I couldn't hear her.

"Axe," Lance yelled. Ivy swung again. This time, when we retreated, Ace shoved Natasha and me behind him, and he and Lance formed a protective shield. Chivalrous, but stupid, because we were being backed against the bed, and I was the only one with any kind of hand-to-hand training.

"Noel, I *can't stay here.*" Natasha gasped and wheezed. The monkeys nearly drowned her out.

"Hang with me," I said. Then, inspired, I added, "Hang with Chuck." Ivy had not seen the tablet. Or if she had, she hadn't considered its importance. In my hand, an enlarged orangutan nostril floated into view. Too far away to pick up on the panic, Chuck chuffed amusement.

When I was in eighth grade, a classmate got his hands on a musical flip-top lighter. Our school was slow to fund buildings and furniture, so we still had wooden seats that had been out of date a decade before. One day, when we had a particularly odious substitute teacher, my classmate flipped open the lighter so it would play, slid it under his leg, and let the sub prowl the room trying to figure out who had the radio. When I later asked why she couldn't pinpoint him, he said, "The wood disperses the sound."

He flashed into my mind when I realized Ivy didn't know

what I was holding. *Wood disperses the sound.* The bed had a wooden headboard. I shoved the tablet into Natasha's hands and moved them behind her back. I pushed her, up onto the bed, with the tablet jammed between her body and the bedframe. "Breathe slow," I told her. Her hands trembled, but she nodded. "Breathe and talk to the orangutan." Nearly at once, Chuck chuffed again softly. Damn, I'd forgotten to turn up the volume.

"What the hell was that?" I demanded when Ivy failed to notice.

"Don't try to distract me." Had she seen us messing with the tablet behind Ace? I didn't think so. What little illumination we had came from our dropped flashlights, scattered around our ankles, and every few seconds, Ivy jerked her head from side to side, trying to locate the screeching monkeys. Chuck made another noise, this one louder, and I mentally thanked Natasha both for calming down and for being agile enough to turn up the volume without seeing what she was doing.

"It's the orangutan!" I didn't have to feign hysteria. "He's out again! Ace! I thought you had it fixed."

"What?" Ace was not following my game. "No! I don't know what he's doing once he moves that camera, Noel. But he's never gotten out in the day before. I swear nothing—"

"Chuck!" called Natasha. "Chuck, it's me! Help me, Chuck, because I'm losing it down here."

I eased out from behind the men and gently twisted Lance's arm when he tried to hold me back. Ivy couldn't see any better than we could. If she was shadowy to us, then so were we to her.

"Shut up, all of you! And call off your monkey." Ivy shifted slightly, her arm wavering.

"You don't call off a great ape!" shouted Trudy from almost behind her in the semi-dark. Ivy whipped around to see who had spoken, and Trudy enflamed us with her flashlight.

Ivy ran at Trudy as a rhesus macaque skittered into view in front of the flashlights on the floor. Ivy screamed and swung wildly, missing its tail. It had been coming to inspect our flashlights, but now it turned and ran up her leg.

Ivy shrieked and dropped the axe. She flung out her arms in an effort to throw the monkey, but it only clung harder, and, panicked, it bit her. "It'll give me rabies!"

I kicked her in the knees. This wasn't tae kwon do. It was from a women's self-defense class. As soon as she fell, Lance dove onto her legs, immobilizing her with his own weight. Ace kicked the axe away. The monkey bit her ear, and, not satisfied with that result, screeched like a banshee.

Trudy stood over Ivy with the gun. "Don't move," she said. "You're under arrest."

I spared a glance behind me. Natasha, who I had expected to see collapsed and struggling to breathe, instead hunched over the tablet in her lap, tapping the screen with each finger of one outspread palm. She was smiling. One, two, three, four, five. It was an old game she and Chuck had played often face to face. She tickled his palms by tapping them with her fingers. Watching her do it was, apparently, as funny as having her do it in person. The orangutan's chuffing laughter increased in intensity until he was downright cackling.

Natasha held up the tablet close. "Hey," she told the ape, "good to see you."

"What's going on down there?" shouted Darnell.

"It's okay, come down!" Lance called.

"No, I've got problems up here. Trudy, can you—? No. Hang on . . ."

The door grated open, and Drew bellowed into the entrance, "Ironweed police! Drop your—you don't look like Ivy Dearborn in the least."

"It's us," shouted Darnell. "How do you know who's down here?"

They descended, their voices rising to be heard over the monkey chatter. "We've apprehended a man we believe to be Charles Dalton, but you'll have to tell us for sure. He looks *nothing* like those photos. Ace said there were two, a man and a woman, so I was expecting Ivy."

"Ivy's here," I called. "And I doubt she's leaving under her own steam."

"Ace, you down there?" Drew shouted.

"I'm here."

"Good. I'm glad you're all right. I'd have had some serious explaining to do to Mom and Dad if you got hurt."

"Thanks for coming so fast, man."

"Thanks for calling."

"You called Drew?" I was frankly shocked. It wasn't that I thought Ace would lack the presence of mind to phone the cops if things got bad. It was more that I thought the brothers' personal enmity would have prevented him from doing it.

"Yeah, if he's going to be the local law, I better make him do *something* to earn his pay."

Chapter 32

Dear Nora:

Thank you for giving my daughter the courage to fight her worthless ex in court, but now she's getting remarried, and I have a problem. The groom's mother has chosen the same outfit as I have for the wedding. I don't want to cause friction, but all the books say I get first choice. The wedding's in a month. What do I do?

MOTB

Dear MO

Whatever the dress is, take it back! Short of the gown itself, the hurt feelings aren't worth the victory! Besides, I don't care if the wedding's tomorrow. I can whip up something that will drop that woman's jaw. Think about your budget and meet me at the Free Press *Thursday morning. Be sure to bring your daughter's colors!*

Nora

"Santa's outside!"

No, Santa finished stuffing your stocking at two o'clock this morning. "I'm coming, Sara. Let me find a robe. Lance, get out of bed."

"Come see, come see!"

William joined his sister, "Santa's Claus! Santa's Claus!"

As I shuffled into the hall, William was followed by the

365

middle-aged rescue dog we had gotten him for an early Christmas gift. It slept in Will's bed now, in place of his sister. Sara had moved to her own room, where her pillow was occupied by a somewhat snobbish cat that barely tolerated the rest of our ministrations but came immediately to our daughter's purring call.

I stumbled to the front room, our front room, in our own home, behind the boy and dog. But I felt a pang of sympathy for whichever of our neighbors was celebrating Christmas with a trip to the hospital when I saw what the kids were hollering about. "Honey, I don't think Santa drives an ambulance." Then the driver turned off the lights and swung down, revealing a full Santa suit. Understanding dawned. "I guess he does sometimes. But I think this is a delivery for your big sister. Wake her up quietly."

In spite of the fact that Gert and Stan had been sprung from rehab, they simply weren't ready to have Natasha home yet. Her grandparents tired quickly, and Gert especially still needed a slow, quiet pace of life. Tasha tried to pretend it was okay she had to come home to our place, not to her own home, every day, but except for daily visits with Chuck, she had been dejected ever since we escaped Charles and Ivy.

"All that, and the journal was in his apartment the whole time, if I'd remembered it," she moaned.

"They found *plenty* of other things to wrap up their investigation in that basement," I reminded her. "And if not for *that,* you'd never have remembered him asking Merle to cut a hidey hole in his apartment wall."

"Yeah. I guess that's what matters. They got it in the end." The apartment had long since been rented again, and nobody would have thought to search it so thoroughly again. And the journal was every bit the goldmine authorities had hoped for. Among other things, it contained the first solid leads on the other children in the organization. Natasha should have felt only pride.

Instead, her hysterical nightmares had returned, and it was hard for her to even talk to her therapist about the flashbacks that were surfacing. If Ivy Dearborn and her friend had not been safely under lock and key, they might have been in serious danger from Lance's and my fury at the progress they had unraveled.

Perhaps the red-suited gentleman walking up to the front door might turn her around. "Tasha, Tasha! Santa camed here for you!" Sara wasn't quiet in the least as she bounded past me down the hall. "He camed! He did! He's here right now!"

"All the way from the Northpoleland!" The dog chased Will, barking at his heels.

"Lance, honey, hurry up. I'm going to pull the cars out. We've got a couple of wheelchairs to get inside through the kitchen."

Later, I told Stan, "We were going to bring her to you."

"I know, but then she'd have missed out on your family's celebration this afternoon, and she's been looking forward to that, too. This way, she won't have to choose, and we got to watch them all open their stockings. We forgot we were old and infirm for a morning, *and* I finally found someone capable of signing my cast." I wasn't sure whether he actually wanted that last or if he was being polite because Sara hadn't offered him a choice in the matter. "Noel, she needs to be around you kids a while longer. It's been good for her. Gert and I won't give her up forever, but as much as she's impatient for it, she needs to come home slowly as much as we need her to."

We pretended not to notice Gert had dozed in her wheelchair for a good portion of the morning. She was improving daily as the effects of Ivy's poison wore off, but she had several doctors who would have preferred she return to the nursing home for care. They only consented to Stan's insistence she go home because he could practically re-create a medical ward in her bedroom.

They were lucky. The nursing home was a huge facility, and Stan and Gert had been in different wings. Trying to be inconspicuous, Ivy had no justification to visit Stan's room, even if she was Gert's favorite nurse. As long as Stan was alive, Gert was potentially valuable to use against him. If she had managed to kill Stan, Ivy surely would have done the same to his wife. She still did plenty of damage.

The morning had been suspiciously devoid of Stan forcing gifts upon Lance and me. We were grateful. But our radar was turned down by the time we left the twins with Mama and Daddy to go shut down at the center for the evening, Jen having let the other volunteers in that morning. We met a whistling Rick in the parking lot of the new enclosure and found surveyors' stakes in the space adjoining Chuck's outdoor home.

"What's that?" I asked him. "What are you doing here on Christmas?" I spun in time to catch a glimpse of Natasha fleeing toward Chuck's enclosure, doubtless to text her grandfather the picture she'd just taken. She was giggling, the first happy sounds I'd heard from her in weeks.

Rick ignored the second question to concentrate on the first. "Come spring," he said, "it's going to be your rhesus macaque house."

"It's enormous."

"I hear you've got the state involved to hold onto those extras for you. Nobody else is liable to want them, right? He said you've got ideas about your mall, too. Let me know so we can start working with the architect to get some plans together." Rick did not have to say who *he* was. We would be writing a *lot* of thank-yous to Stan Oeschle.

"When can you fill in that basement?" Lance wanted to know.

"It will have to wait until spring, and I guess the authorities will have to clear it. I know you want it gone, but I think we're all going to have to be patient while they finish sorting all this out."

There wasn't much left to sort. We had all guessed a little bit of the puzzle. Ivy and Charles hadn't known precisely where Gary recorded when he filmed with the animals, but they *had* known it was on the sanctuary grounds. And they knew he had a journal, and, having searched for it everywhere else, they narrowed in on here.

They had apprehended Hugh Marsland, thinking he would know where the filming room was because of the police's thorough search of the area back in June. When he proved useless, they killed him. He had been dead for some time, his head most likely stored in lye before it was placed in the university's cupboard. Then they started looking for the man they believed built the sanctuary, Merle Evans. They didn't have to search hard.

Gary had kept his monkey smuggling activities largely separate from his filming. Though, as the journal revealed, he delivered his films disguised as pizza deliveries, he did not tell this to the employees at the Marine who helped him smuggle the animals. Robby and the Marine's delivery truck driver, Justin, along with Merle, were all in on the macaque smuggling. Merle was the one who had shown Gary the "old records room," which he had built to brew drugs years before when he had been forced to take down the beginnings of the original sanctuary. Now that he knew it was a floodplain, he also knew nobody else would want to build there, making it ideal to hide his own activities. But Merle was, it seemed, as bad at drug manufacture and distribution as everything else, and he hadn't used it for years before he introduced Gary to it.

After that, Merle had only ever known it as a holding space

for the rhesus macaques they were moving in and out. Gary never explained the other equipment stored there, and nobody ever asked. Because Gary and Merle took care of the rhesus macaque area at the sanctuary, they were able to juggle the headcount sheets to look right as animals flowed into the center, arriving once a month on the pizza truck's weekly delivery.

It was difficult to say, but at a best guess, the monkeys had started piling up because the chain broke at some point after Gary died. Not immediately, because Justin, who was all too willing to talk to possibly avoid jail, said he was still getting paid through July. But when the money dried up, Merle didn't stop accepting monkeys. He kept storing them in that dank basement, siphoning off our food to care for them, since there were more than he could sneak into an enclosure.

Merle, his driver, and his sixteen-year-old protégé were left with an increasing number of rhesus macaques to hide in our facility. Justin didn't know who brought the monkeys. He was in charge of collecting them from a barn, where he led us to thirty more of the little animals caged. He claimed he and Robby had fed them until the Friday when Robby was caught, but I doubted this.

Robby, when he finally broke, insisted that when Merle was about ready to give in and start bringing the animals in again, even if he couldn't once more move them back out, Chuck started opening the enclosures and Lance took over the head count.

Merle planned a return to Michigan to attempt to set the old distribution system back up. Trudy said she thought it was more likely Merle was getting ready to skip town. When Lance finally gave the care of the rhesus macaque area back, Merle immediately began moving animals in. It was on one such journey that Ivy and Charles accosted him, tipped off by Justin.

Justin said he was accosted at the Marine several times by

Charles and Ivy, who scared him. He was increasingly out of pocket to Merle and, like Trudy, he felt the man was about to skip town. Finally, he claimed to Charles that he and Robby didn't know where the records room was located but that Merle might. Thinking Charles was another disaffected member of the smuggling ring with a plan to get the money from Merle, he told Charles when to find Merle alone at the sanctuary.

The day William ran up the delivery truck ramp was also a monkey delivery day, and Charles, having already tried Robby and Merle for information, had been harassing Justin on the opposite side of the truck when the child appeared. Besides seeing rhesus macaques in cages inside the truck, William probably also saw the two men talking nearby. Ironically, it was Will's appearance that delayed Charles's discovery of the monkey smuggling, since he left quickly once he thought the child had seen him.

According to Robby, Merle dispatched him to capture Will, and Justin backed Merle's authority. Neither he nor Merle recognized the significance of the conversation Justin had been holding at the same time. None of them had met Charles until then, and it wasn't until Charles killed Merle that Justin realized Charles had only learned about the monkeys at all by talking to the three of them.

Merle simply wanted to intimidate the child into silence about the monkeys. But when Robby brought William home, it quickly became clear that he couldn't explain what he had seen. Unsure what to do with him until Merle's shift was over, he locked Will in his garage. That was where Layla found and accidentally freed him. Panicked, and completely believing Robby's story, Layla got Ivy involved. Layla revealed little, but it was clear from what she *did* say that Ivy had learned how attached Natasha was to the twins from the whole affair and filed it away for future use.

After they killed Merle, Charles and Ivy decided Natasha was the only one left who could tell them about the records room. They sent Robby and Justin one of Merle's fingers and an anonymous threat to their own lives if they didn't catch the little boy for them. Justin convinced Robby to use Layla to steal Will. Ivy meant to use him to get Natasha.

Of course, Charles and Ivy denied all of this and all responsibility for Hugh Marsland's death. Authorities believed the deputies nearly caught Merle transferring monkeys into the enclosures. He instead disabled them and hid their cruiser out of sight well before Ivy and Charles arrived. When *they* found him, perhaps Merle refused to tell them what they wanted to know even when threatened. Perhaps he didn't have time to answer them. Ivy seemed the impulsive type.

Nobody was admitting what happened after, but it was clear Merle never left the sanctuary. His head, hands, and feet remained missing. But the ring Drew recovered from the spider monkeys had belonged to him, and he did indeed have A-negative blood.

"None of that goes to tell us who gave you that knot on the head," said Mama. She and I were lunching with Bryan and Travis, whose duties had lightened considerably. Mama and Bryan were working up one-liner responses for "What's Next, Nora?" I was mostly along for the ride, having developed a new appreciation for my mother, now that I had children myself.

Travis rolled his eyes. He disliked talking about this. "Knots," he said. "And it was Winnie. Can't prove it. I barely remember anything except waking up in the dark a couple of times. The closest they have to a picture of my assailant is when he roars up and dumps me in Lance and Noel's car. He was driving a common vehicle without license plates, and it's impossible to say who it is.

"Have I ever told you how grateful I am you forgot to lock

your van, Noel? Lenore, you can see in the video that I was already struggling by the time he threw me in there. God only knows what he'd have done if I'd had time to really come around again."

"You think he did that over a cooler of fish?" Mama demanded.

"See, we know he'd been intimidated." Dr. Prescott had received a finger, just like Robby and Justin. Like them, he had thrown it away in a field, where it was never found. "I think it sent him off the deep end. By the time that detective's head fell out of the cupboard, he'd already conked me out. But when he saw it, I think he figured out poor old Merle was dead."

Dr. Prescott admitted all of these things except taking Travis. He even said he located the original plans for the sanctuary in Merle's old records and delivered them to an empty field. Unless those plans were different from the ones Rick had, the records room wasn't on them, which was why Charles and Ivy had begun to focus so heavily on Natasha.

"Well, I'm glad he's leaving you alone now," said Mama. "Letting you have lunch once in a while."

I snorted. "He's retiring in May. The fish cooler incident was egregious enough that tenure was not enough protection. Ironic that the thing that *really* tanked my interview was the one intended to intimidate *him*."

"You're such a pessimist," said Travis.

T-Bow Orrice seemed to be biding his time. I thought Robby ought to watch his back whether he got out of jail or, as was far more likely, was prosecuted more deeply into the system. William was safe from Robby. But Robby wasn't safe at all from William's biological father, especially if Layla ever turned on him.

That Will *was* safe now, we felt certain. Or anyway, as safe as he could be with a murderer for a parent. I wasn't sure how

Lance and I could move out from under that shadow, but the threat felt more distant, more like it would be to us, not our child if it came at all. T-Bow Orrice knew too much about us, but we couldn't live our lives in hiding from him, and we seemed, at the moment at least, to be out of his scope of interest.

Jen dragged in her husband and his sister to replace Trudy and Darnell in our volunteer roster. The husband was good-humored about having been wrangled, though it was clear his passions didn't lie in monkey dung and lunch buckets. His sister, on the other hand, already seemed as passionate as Jen herself. As for Trudy and Darnell, they left us for Columbus nearly immediately after they had collected all the information they could from Gary's storehouse. Liam Metcalf had always wanted them back in town, and he convinced their boss to recall them quickly.

While he was working with Chuck and his tablet one day, Ace saw a flash of gold in the big ape's mouth. Through a great deal of bribery, he traded for the item, which proved to be a key identical to the one Natasha had retrieved.

"I think I figured it out," he told me. "Chuck poked the camera with that stick, then used the stick to grab my keys off the hook. It took me so long to figure that part out, because he put the danged keys *back*. Not quite on their hook, but on the ground underneath, so I thought they'd just fallen."

At the very least, he hadn't gotten out since Ace took his stick, and his new electronic enrichment was improving his mood dramatically. "It's too bad he *couldn't* get out when those people killed that fellow up at main. I'm no fan of the boys in blue, but what happened there was plain wrong."

Back home, Sara couldn't start Miss Henderson's class until after the holidays, because she came down with a nasty case of the flu the day her suspension ended, having caught it from Julie Carver on their one playdate. The playdate was successful, so getting the flu was worth it. I expected it to hit Will next, but in fact, it took down Lance and me. Will was the only one who stayed healthy. The illness lasted until Christmas break began. Christmas with the Oeschles was the first time I allowed any of us but Natasha near anyone elderly, and I hadn't planned to do that. Nana didn't catch it from us, and neither did Margie's children, but I kept us mostly quarantined until school went back in session.

When she did go back, if she didn't flourish in her new classroom, at least she seemed to suffer less, and I only had to deal with one call from the teacher, early on.

It came less than a week after the new year. "Mrs. Rue," explained Miss Henderson, "You need to discuss appropriateness and context with Sara."

"What do you mean?"

"The short version is she grossed everyone out at lunch."

I could hear Sara sobbing hysterically in the background. "Let me talk to her."

"I only told them what *you said*," Sara bawled.

"What did *I* say?"

Suddenly, the tears dried up, and she began a recitation. "Do you know what's in the chicken you're eating? Have you considered what genetically modified organisms are doing to our foods?" *The GMO lecture. I knock down a dead man's head, and she remembers my classroom spiel word for word instead.*

"Honey," I interrupted her, "I think I see what went wrong. You should never talk about GMOs at the actual lunch table. The point is to educate, not to make people vomit." She put the teacher back on, and I promised it wouldn't happen again.

A few weeks after that, in the middle of February, Travis called while we were getting the kids dressed. "I am not on the phone and you are not talking to me," he practically sang.

"Congratulations! Social services approved you that fast?"

"No, no, no. Nothing to do with that. Like I said, this call isn't happening."

"Okay," I interrupted him. "I'm assuming the job search has been put on hold."

"Not exactly, no."

"Well, I had assumed since Dr. Prescott is retiring at the end of the year . . ."

"They don't want two empty seats to fill, Noel."

"But I thought he left the search committee."

"He tried to."

"Mmm."

"So act *surprised* when he calls you."

"Wait. The search hasn't been put on hold. The APES meeting was back in January. And you're not calling me to say somebody else got hired. Are you?"

"Nope! You can tell Lance he's now a trailing spouse. But maybe he'll put in for Dr. Prescott's slot."

I hung up and stared at my husband, who was wrestling William into a sweater, an attempt to make him presentable for court. Chandra had reassured us at every meeting that things were going well. While I wouldn't fully believe it until the judge shook all of our hands later this morning, I was beginning to think at least some of her words might be true. "Honey," I said, "I think we might be able to afford this after all."

"Well, that's good." The sweater popped over Will's head and immediately shot off again. "Because it's a little late to do anything about it."

Yes, it was. More than a little. But that was fine with me. Indeed, it was wonderful. "Lance, don't fight the sweater," I advised. "We'll take it along. Come on, kids, let's go! We've still got to drop off Tasha at school on the way in."

We headed out the door, a motley little parade. Lance kissed my cheek in passing, then locked the door behind us as the kids piled into the van. He still hadn't figured out I'd gotten hired. Well, he'd know soon enough. I kissed him back, not on the cheek, but on the lips, full on and hard. "You're going to be an awesome daddy. No. Check that. You already are."

ABOUT THE AUTHOR

Jessie Bishop Powell grew up in rural Ohio. She now lives in Montgomery, Alabama, with her husband and their two children. She has master's degrees in English and Library Science from the University of Kentucky.

Her children have Asperger's syndrome, though their issues differ drastically from those of William and Sara. The first book in this series, *The Marriage at the Rue Morgue,* was published by Five Star in 2014. You can find out more about the author and her works on her blog Jester Queen, at http://jesterqueen.com.